Freya North gave up a PhD to write her first novel, *Sally*, in 1991. For four years she turned deaf ears to parents and friends who pleaded with her to 'get a proper job'. She went on the dole and did a succession of free-lance and temping jobs to support her writing days. In 1995, throwing caution to the wind, Freya sent three chapters and a page of completely fabricated reviews to a top literary agent, and met with success: five publishers entered a bidding war for her books. In 1996 *Sally* was published to great acclaim and Freya was heralded as a fresh voice in fiction. Her next books, *Chloë*, *Polly*, *Cat*, *Fen* and *Pip*, are all bestsellers. She lives in London with her family.

For more information on Freya North, visit her website at www.freyanorth.co.uk

For automatic updates on Freya North visit HarperCollins.co.uk and register for AuthorTracker.

PRAISE FOR *LOVE RULES*:

'Freya North has matured to produce an emotive novel that deals with the darker side of love – these are real women, with real feelings.'   *She*

'Tantrums, tarts, tears and text-sex . . . what's not to love about this cautionary tale for true romantics?'   *Heat*

By the same author:

FREYA NORTH

Love Rules

HarperCollins*Publishers*

HarperCollins*Publishers*
77–85 Fulham Palace Road,
Hammersmith, London W6 8JB

www.harpercollins.co.uk

This paperback edition published by HarperCollins*Publishers* 2005
1 3 5 7 9 8 6 4 2

A catalogue record for this book
is available from the British Library

'Something's Gotten Hold of My Heart'
Words & Music by Roger Cook & Roger Greenaway
© Copyright 1967 Maribus Music Limited & Cookaway Music Limited.
Universal/Dick James Music Limited.
Used by permission of Music Sales Limited.
All Rights Reserved. International Copyright Secured.

'Summer Breeze'
Words & Music by James Seals & Darrell Crofts
© Copyright 1971 Dawnbreaker Music Company/Trousdale Music
Publishers Incorporated, USA.
The International Music Network Limited (87.5%)/Universal/
MCA Music Limited (12.5%).
Used by permission of Music Sales Limited.
All Rights Reserved. International Copyright Secured.

'He Wishes for the Cloths of Heaven'
By W.B. Yeats
Reproduced by permission of A.P. Watt on behalf of Michael B. Yeats.

ISBN 0 00 721355 7

Set in Sabon by Palimpsest Book Production Ltd, Polmont, Stirlingshire

Printed and bound in Great Britain by
Clays Ltd, St Ives plc

For Lucy Smouha, Kirsty Johnson and Clare Grogan
My glory is I have such friends.

Something's gotten hold of my heart
Keeping my soul and my senses apart

Greenaway/Cook

Mark and Saul and Alice and Thea

Mark Sinclair liked to think that there was an inevitability to happy-ever-afters. He believed that they were granted to those who were good in life, to people whose thoughts were honourable, who had worthy goals, whose deeds and dealings were principled. However, at the age of thirty, Mark Sinclair understood that he would need to modify his belief, revise his dream and compromise. He intended to do this without turning into a cynic or allowing his ethics to suffer. He'd just have to let his dream of twenty years fade. It wasn't going to be easy. But there again, the dream wasn't going to come true, no matter how virtuous he was.

Mark Sinclair's dream was Alice Heggarty. But she had gone and fallen in love with someone who wasn't him. Again. Just as she had at the age of twenty-five. And at twenty-three. And before that, annually at university. And before that, with the captain of the first XV at his school. The girl Mark had loved for so long had gone and fallen in love again but this time Alice was nearly twenty-nine. Mark knew she'd have made a calculated decision that this love ought to take her into her thirties and onwards, into matrimony and children and a house in NWsomewhere. The time was right for her own happy-ever-after. 'So dream on,' Mark told himself sternly, 'dream on.'

In the two decades he'd known Alice, Mark had always had hope because he'd always had the dream because, being a man of patience and principles, he'd taken a philosophical view on waiting. He theorized that Alice had never broken his dream because he'd never brought it out into the open. Besides, she'd been so busy, permanently falling madly in love and despairingly out of love with all those other men. At the time, Mark felt this to be a positive thing and he did not regret keeping his own feelings secret. After all, it meant that Alice had never made a decision against him, she'd never turned him down, never ditched him in favour of another, never suggested they revert to being 'just good friends'.

As lovers charged in and stormed out of her life, and as girlfriends breezed into his and left quietly, their friendship had remained unscathed. Alice was never possessive of Mark and Mark accepted her periodic disappearance into the fast eddies of new love-lust. Indeed, Mark had always found it encouraging that Alice went for a type – and that the type she went for was the antithesis of him. It meant she'd never fallen for someone like Mark; she'd always gone for men who were diametrically opposed to all that he was. Tall, loud, movie-blond beefy blokes with heartbreaker reputations or ice-beautiful arrogance Alice was convinced she could conquer and melt. Consequently, Mark could not feel jealous of the men in Alice's life though he envied them Alice. Rather, he was irked that they were delaying his personal happy-ever-after.

Very very privately, he was also relieved that invariably it was they who left her. Looking after Alice with her heart all hurt was actually even more rewarding than being in her company when she was hyper-effervescent with the distractions of love. Though it scorched Mark's soul to see her distraught, he knew he could make her feel better. It was a job he could do brilliantly. And it augmented his hope. Because when his dream came true, he'd never leave her. Of that she could be as sure as he was.

Whereas Alice rushed headlong into love affairs, Mark merely dabbled in what he believed to be just an interim after all. Now, with Alice in love once more, yet again not with Mark, and given their respective ages, he acknowledged, sensibly, that an interim was a period between two points and that there really was no point in holding out for Alice. Because he loved her, and because he'd been privy to her teenage turmoil and twenties torment, he wanted only peace and fulfilment for her in her thirties and beyond. Even if her joy and contentment meant he'd never have her cry on his shoulder again.

Mark was happy for Alice, but he was not so altruistic not to be sad for himself. He had believed, mistakenly, that if he lived well and worked hard, if he was honourable in his thoughts and actions, his reward would be all he had dreamt of. Reluctantly, he had to accept that good behaviour and a belief in the potential of one's wishes ultimately might not win the prize. Neither Alice, nor the Man Who Will Marry Her, were at fault or to blame. And, just because he now no longer believed in happy-ever-after didn't mean the future need be misery-for-evermore.

He was going to moderate his desire without seeing compromise as a tragedy. He'd have to stop letting down gently all those lovely girls after the fourth or fifth date. He'd need to see the wider picture and take a view. There had been two or three he had liked enormously. Previously, when he'd reached the stage of thinking of them fondly, planning holidays, masturbating in their honour, browsing Liberty for trinkets of his affection, an image of Alice glancing at her watch had always sprung to mind. As if she was waiting for

3

him. And though the lovely girls were let down gently, all wished to remain friends. Mark, as Alice once told a girl-friend who was single, was one of life's great good guys.

Mark was a good person because for twenty years he had always believed that if you are a good boy, all your dreams come true.

* * *

Saul Mundy stumbled on his Road to Damascus at roughly the same time that Mark Sinclair stepped resignedly onto his. Saul had been with Emma for three years when he met a pretty and friendly blonde in a bar. They chatted and smiled and flirted lightly. Saul had no true desire for her, no inten-tion of asking for her number or grabbing a furtive snog. Until that night, he had quite enjoyed the occasional, harm-less, forgettable flirt because his affection for Emma and monogamy had remained unsullied. That night, however, it wasn't that he wanted the blonde, it was that he didn't want Emma.

He blanked the blonde, made hasty excuses to his friends and stumbled out in a daze onto Tottenham Court Road. The sudden clarity of the situation was ugly but he knew he mustn't look away. If he did, complacency would wheedle in soon enough and honesty would be replaced by betrayal. Saul wouldn't let that happen. He believed in doing the right thing and he was going home directly to do so. He had to, he was committed. It would be far easier to stay than split, far easier to act fine than confess, to hide than confide, but Saul's belief in his relationship had gone and the only hon-ourable thing he could do was go too. Waiting for a taxi, he shivered and sheltered in a shop doorway, gazing at the rain-sluiced pavement. It looked polished to perfection, like a meticulously varnished floor. Actually, it was just grey concrete that was wet and grimy. The truth was it was dull, no matter what tried to cover it. Surface details were worthless if the integrity of structure was lacking. Saul couldn't believe that the last three years of his life amounted to a comparison with London pavement.

That morning, he had left the house to go to work. Now he was returning only to leave home. Had he kissed Emma that morning? He couldn't remember. Would the offer of just good friendship be a possibility or a cowardly digression? Would she believe him when he said that he was so sorry, that he did love her and felt wretched for hurting her? That it wasn't her, it was him? Would she believe him that he truly felt she deserved more than he could give? That he didn't mean to sound exactly like all those articles in the women's mags she pored over in her long bubble baths and that he browsed through when he'd forgotten to buy an *Evening Standard*? He doubted it.

He had the taxi drop him off on Upper Street and he walked, reluctant but resigned, towards the house, to Emma blissfully unaware, sitting beside the home-fire she'd kept burning.

'I don't burn for you any more,' Saul whispered, eyes closed, forehead resting against the door frame, 'and I should. It's a prerequisite. I can't compromise.' He couldn't even summon a spark of it from the deepest recess of his soul. His heart might be warm for her, and would continue to be, but he was absolutely sure that it wasn't enough. He wished there was a kinder way of being so seemingly cruel. But to use a cool head to decipher his heart would give the cleanest cut, though he knew that all Emma would read written all over his face was Heartless. Saul put his key in the front door for the last time.

*　　*　　*

A decade before Mark and Saul had their epiphanies, Thea Luckmore had hers when Joshua Brown ditched her at Alice Heggarty's eighteenth birthday party. It was irrelevant that he proceeded to snog Rachel Hutton in the kitchen. It didn't matter that Alice, incensed, had poured Woodpecker cider over his head and told him he was a wanker who should fucking fuck off. It wasn't even that Joshua no longer wanted her, it was that Thea was still in love with him. She didn't ask Alice how she could win him back, instead she asked her what she should do with all the feelings of love.

Alice suggested getting off with Joshua's mate to piss him off.

'But I don't feel anything for him,' Thea had qualified.

'Exactly, it'll be easy,' Alice had encouraged.

'Alice,' Thea balked, 'I can't kiss someone I don't feel something for.'

Though Joshua Brown's friend would have done anything for a snog off Thea, Thea decided then and there that unless she experienced a shudder of desire for someone, unless she could detect potential, unless her heart swelled approvingly, she'd be keeping her kisses. Warmth or revenge were not enough. She realized that it was the love she had for Joshua that was the point. Despite the fact that he was a cad. She'd read enough Austen to know that love was a good thing and, whether it made one feel wonderful or wretched, it was her ultimate requirement for a fulfilled life.

It was the dyed-dark drama student who captured Thea's heart during her second year at Manchester University. Though she was never quite sure whether he was proclaiming his innermost feelings or reciting his lines, she adored him and was glad to lavish love on him. They smoked dope. They had his-and-hers unkempt pony-tails. They made vast vats of ratatouille. They found deep and meaningful tenets in Joy Division. They rejoiced in the intensity of their world of Us.

They went InterRailing together during the summer vacation and slept on beaches, watched sunsets and professed to truly understand e. e. cummings. He fell out of love with Thea just before her finals a year later, citing that love was life's torment and proclaiming the wring of his feelings was a headfuck.

'Did he actually say "headfuck", Thea?' Alice asked, not sure whether it was interference on the Cambridge–Manchester phone line or Thea's sobbing.

'Yes,' Thea said, 'but he also said that his love for me was so all consuming—'

'– that it threatened to devour him?' Alice interrupted. 'Life is love's torment or vice versa?'

'Yes!' Thea gasped, comforted that Alice had obviously been in such a situation herself, no doubt with that third year from Trinity with the double-barrelled surname.

'Did he say something about only the winds of time could determine where his seed would fall and take root?' Alice asked.

Thea paused. 'Yes,' she said, hesitant.

Alice continued gently. 'Do you remember that God-awful theatre-thing, that art-performance-bollocks you dragged me to when I visited just before Christmas?'

'Yes,' Thea wavered.

'He was performing his friend's prose poem?' Thea didn't reply. 'You were gazing at him too adoringly to actually hear any of it, weren't you?'

Thea's broken heart clanked heavily against a sudden twist of mortification in her stomach. She was speechless.

'Thea,' Alice continued quietly but firmly, 'I promise you, you'll find love again. And I promise you one day you'll laugh about this one. We both will. We'll laugh until we pee our pants. Trust me.'

Alice always kept her promises and she was the one person Thea always trusted. Alice, it turned out, was quite right.

Memories of Headfuck Boy continue to provide them with much mirth and they can still quote his friend's prose poem verbatim. Headfuck Boy did not cause Thea any lasting damage, nor did he in any way alter her belief in the virtue and value of falling head over heels in love. Thea Luckmore was not one to compromise.

* * *

Alice had her epiphany over a bowl of soup, ten years later – just a few months after Mark and Saul had theirs. She left her office near Tower Bridge, grabbing new issues of magazines just arrived from the printers. Though she'd never intended to take public transport anyway, the whip of November chill that accosted her outside further justified the taxi.

'Chiltern Street, please,' she told the cabbie, 'the Paddington Street end. You know, off Baker Street.'

'And do you tell your granny how to suck eggs?' the cabbie teased her. Alice looked confused. 'It's my job, love,' he continued jovially, 'the Knowledge? Short cuts? Crafty backdoubles? Bus lanes? I do know Chiltern Street – amazingly enough.'

'Sorry,' Alice said meekly, 'I didn't mean to.'

She thought how Bill absolutely detested her habit of giving directions if she wasn't driving. In their early days, he had gently teased her, even indulged her. A year on, it now irritated him supremely. 'Which way do you want to go then?' he'd give a henpecked sigh before they'd set off. And if Alice's route proved circuitous, or with a proliferation of speed bumps, or beset by roadworks or vengeful traffic lights, he'd let his stony silence yell his disapproval and annoyance.

'I'm not a control freak,' Alice said out loud, not intentionally to the cab driver but not out of context either. 'It's not an obsession, it's just a trait of my character.' She gazed out of the window, about to ask him why he was going along the Embankment rather than via Farringdon at this time of day. But she bit her lip. Was it a loathsome quirk of her personality? Should it be something she should resolve to change? She could feel her tears smarting and prickling. She'd kept them in check all morning and her throat ached from the effort. 'Here!' she unintentionally barked at the taxi driver who swerved and shunted to a standstill in response.

'Can you tell Thea I'm here,' she said to the receptionist in Thea's building.

Thea's 'there there' was precisely what Alice had come halfway across London in her lunch hour to hear. The sound of it triggered the tears. 'There there,' said Thea again, and Alice cried all the more. 'Let's get some soup in you,' Thea soothed, guiding Alice to Marylebone High Street.

Alice sipped obediently. 'I'm going to sound like Headfuck Boy,' she admitted, after a few spoonfuls, 'but if I don't end it now, it's going to consume me. And I'll end up all spat out. Again. I'm just so tired.' Though Thea knew her friend's face by rote, objectively she noted a sallowness to the complexion, a flatness to the eyes, cheekbones now too sharp to be handsome, a thinness attributable to stress rather than vanity. 'I'm nearly thirty,' Alice concluded in a forlorn whisper. 'When am I going to learn?'

'You're not fretting about *that*, are you?' Thea asked, due to turn thirty a month before Alice.

'Look at this,' Alice said, showing Thea the new copy of *Lush* magazine. 'It's the "Alice Heggarty This is Your Life" issue.'

Thea read the cover lines out loud. '*More Shoes Than Selfridges*.' She looked at Alice. 'But I've never known you to buy a pair and not wear them out. '*A Chef in the Kitchen, A Whore in the Bedroom*.' Thea patted the cover of the magazine: 'Why, that's a skill others envy you.'

'Look!' Alice declared. '*Falling For Mr Wrong*.' She jabbed her finger at the magazine. '*Passion Drove Me Insane*,' she proclaimed, '*Lovelorn or Lustaholic*. For fuck's sake, I'm meant to be the publisher – not the inspiration for every sodding article.' She sighed and continued in a quieter voice, '*Lush* is directed at the early-twenties market, Thea. I'm basically thirty and *still* slave to all these insecurities and issues.'

'Bill,' Thea said darkly, buttering a doorstep of bread and dunking it, watching the satisfying ooze of butter slither off the bread and dissolve into the soup.

Alice covered her face with her hands. 'If I say it out loud, it has to be real,' she said, 'if I look you in the eye, I can't hide from the truth.' She laid her hands in her lap and regarded Thea. 'He's Mr Wrong,' she whispered, 'it's as simple as that. I'm exhausted. I'm a lovelorn lustaholic and passion is driving me insane.'

'Gentle sympathy or hard advice?' Thea asked.

'You're my best friend, I need you to tell me what I need to know,' Alice said, 'even if it's not what I want to hear.'

Thea regarded Alice levelly. She tipped her head to one side. 'You're right,' she shrugged, 'Bill is Mr Wrong.' Momentarily, Alice felt like springing to Bill's defence only Thea jumped in first. 'In Bill's defence,' she said, 'he's a gorgeous and charming man. With a great car. Physically, you make a beautiful couple. But your relationship is ugly.' She'd witnessed enough blazing rows, spiked sarcasm, hostile silences and relentless bickering to speak with authority.

'It's been such hard work,' said Alice, stirring her soup as though it was a cup of well-sugared tea, 'constantly trying to safeguard his love and lust for me. Even though, sometimes when I get it, I don't actually want it,' Alice confided. 'I hate feeling so pathetically insecure, when actually I don't think I really like him anyway.'

10

'He is what he is,' said Thea fairly, 'gorgeous and aloof and rich and a sod.'

'It seems we're always playing some horrid power game – either I'm the one who's pissed him off or else I'm in a manipulative sulk with him.' Alice paused. 'We just ricochet from his stony silences to my flouncy strops. It's exhausting.'

'The renowned playboy,' Thea told her, 'he was captivated by your feistiness but to be honest, he'd be better suited with a bimbo or a mousy-wifey.'

'Could change?' Alice said meekly and with some ambiguity.

'You or him?' Thea asked pointedly. 'Don't you dare go compromising. And what would you change *him* into? And don't say a frog.'

But Alice was off on a tangent, gazing into the middle distance, reinventing Bill. Or, rather, creating an entirely different man simply clad in Bill's likeness. 'Someone calm. Someone who adores me and I'll never doubt it. Someone who won't mind the way I'm a back-seat driver. Someone who makes me feel safe, someone who won't cause me panic when I find their mobile phone is switched off. Someone who won't play games. Or play around. Someone who won't flirt in front of me. Or when I'm not around.'

Or with your friends, Thea thought to herself remembering more than one occasion when Bill had paid her a little too much attention. They scraped their soup bowls with their spoons and then used the last of the bread to swab them dry.

'I would have finished it months ago,' Alice said, dropping her voice to a whisper, 'but in some ways it was easy to become addicted to the fabulous passionate making-up sex which always concludes our rows. But you know what? We rarely have sex unless it's concluding an argument. And we've never, ever, made love.'

Thea snorted. 'I haven't had sex, made love, shagged, fornicated, humped or mated for eleven months!'

11

'You and your daft standards.' Alice laughed a little. 'I'm surprised you don't just take yourself to a nunnery and be done with it.'

'Christ,' said Thea, who was actually an atheist, 'I love sex. I'm dying for a fuck. I'm just not so desperate as to lower my standards.'

'Do they actually have to proclaim their romantic intentions, their degree of wholesome love before you'll permit entry?' Alice teased.

'Piss off!' Thea joshed. 'You've missed my point. *They* can feel all they like, they can compose poems and do the bended-knee routine. But if *I* don't burn for them, if *I* don't feel that spark – no chance.'

They ordered tea for two and cake to share.

'You're in love with love,' Alice said, dividing the gateau with her fork and offering Thea the choice of portions, 'while I lust for lust.'

'Sounds like a magazine article, if ever there was one,' Thea said, choosing the end of the wedge, rather than the point.

Alice glanced down at the cover of *Lush* and gave a little snort. '*From Heartbreak to Happy-Ever-After – 7 Steps to Take You There*.' She paused. 'Perhaps I ought to practise what I publish.'

The girls skimmed through the relevant article. Neither of them thought that Number 1 *Time for a New You – Go for a Funky New Hairdo!!* was the answer. Nor was Number 2 *Flirt with Your Best Mate's Brother!!* a remotely feasible idea. Thea's older brother was a densely bearded academic who rather unnerved both girls. Numbers 3 and 4 dealt predictably with *Take Time and Make Time for Me Time!!!!* and *Rebound Repercussions – A Quick Shag is Not a Long-Term Fix!!!*

'Number 5 is interesting, though,' Thea remarked, '*It's Not Who You Love It's How You Love!!!*'

12

'I detest exclamation marks,' Alice said. 'I'll have to have a word with editorial.'

'*Change What's on Your Wish List!!!*' Thea read out Number 6. 'Perhaps there is some sense in rejigging your requirements, Alice?'

'What about you?' Alice retorted. 'Why do I have to do all this personality-dissection, inner-feeling workshopping?'

'Because I'm happy being celibate while true love eludes me.'

'You must have the Rolls Royce of vibrators,' Alice murmured.

'Well, you'd know,' Thea countered brightly, 'you bought it me.'

'Got it free,' Alice stuck her tongue out.

'Should've kept it for yourself then,' Thea gurned back.

'Number 7,' Alice returned to the article, '*Blink!!! He Might be Standing There, Staring You in the Face!!!!*'

'The postman!' Thea gasped with mock eagerness.

'That guy from the ad agency we use,' said Alice, with genuine enthusiasm. Thea regarded Alice sternly, but Alice licked her lips and winked. And then, like a mist descending, anxiety dulled her eyes and turned her mouth downwards. It was just a magazine article anyway, with too many exclamation marks and a target market half a decade younger than them. 'I'll finish it with Bill tonight,' Alice said, quietly but decisively, 'I bet he won't even care.'

'I think he does care about you,' Thea said, 'but I think you're doing the right thing. I'd better go, I have a client in five minutes and I mustn't have cold hands.'

'Will you be around later?' Alice said, her face fragile and her voice wavering. 'In case I need you?'

'Of course,' Thea shrugged, as if it was the daftest question to even think of asking your closest friend.

* * *

So it turned out that Mark Sinclair was right. He was so right that, for some time, he would quietly wonder if something must be wrong. Alice Heggarty *was* to be married, just as he predicted, by the time she was thirty. Actually, she would turn thirty-one on honeymoon because her meticulous attention to detail and aversion to compromise meant the wedding was shunted to accommodate seamstress, florist, venue and cake-maker. Though, normally, she liked to have her birthday planned to perfection too, she didn't actually know where she would be when she turned thirty-one. That was up to the groom and she had relinquished some responsibility to him in return for assurances of untold luxury. After all, she was not so secretly dreaming of the Caribbean.

All that Mark had wrong was her choice of groom. Alice wasn't going to marry Bill. In all other respects, though, Mark had been absolutely right. It turned out that if you are good, you can indeed earn yourself a happy-ever-after. Obviously, Mark Sinclair must have been very very good. Because Alice Heggarty was going to marry him.

Thea Luckmore

Thea Luckmore's twelve-o'clock client, a fit man in his mid-thirties, groaned under her. She kept the pressure steady and insistent until she could feel him yield, sense the tautness of his body ebb away, the grimace on his face ease into an expression of relief. She rolled his flesh between her fingers. Under her hands, he now felt as soft as his appreciative sigh. She lightened her touch and changed rhythm and direction as a wind-down. Finally, she placed both palms on his bare back, between his shoulder blades, and inhaled deeply. She closed her eyes, feeling warmth interchange between them. She exhaled quietly but deeply and opened her eyes.

'OK,' she said softly, lifting her hands away very slowly, 'there you go.' She wondered if he had fallen asleep.

'Can't move,' he muffled, his face buried in the bed, 'amazing.'

'I'll leave you to rest and get dressed,' said Thea as she closed the door quietly behind her and went to wash her hands. She ran her damp fingers through her hair, giving her short, gamine crop what her mother termed 'an Audrey Hepburn nonchalance, darling – if Audrey had been mouse-brown'. Thea hadn't had hair long enough for a pony-tail since Headfuck Boy of her student days.

'God, that was good,' her client grinned, handing over £50 though he would gladly have doubled it. 'Can I have you again next week?'

The session had drained Thea; her bones felt soft and her joints felt stiff. Often, the clients for whom her treatment had the most extreme results were those whose negative energy she absorbed in the process. Which is why they felt so energized and she felt so sapped. She flicked her hands as if trying to fling something away, shook her arms and legs and splashed cold water on her face. She could climb on the bed and sleep for an hour, which was tempting, or she could pull herself together and step out into a gorgeous spring day. Thea Luckmore always tried to do what she felt was right, even if it wasn't quite what she felt like. So she opened the sash window to air the room and went out for a brisk walk. With an extravagantly stuffed sandwich from Pret a Manger, she strolled to Paddington Street Gardens and had an impromptu picnic with a copy of *Heat* magazine for company and light relief.

Her phone showed two missed calls from Giles. And a voicemail message. Thea felt burdened. Giles was nice enough. 'But not nice *enough*,' Thea explained to a pigeon who was bobbing at a respectful distance within pecking reach of any crumb she might dispense. 'I've tried telling him that I value our friendship too much to jeopardize it by taking it further, but he saw that as a challenge rather than a gentle let-down.' Filling from her sandwich dropped to the ground. The pigeon, it seemed, didn't care for avocado. Patiently, it continued to bob and coo. 'I like him but I don't fizz for him. No spark – no point.' A slice of tomato was tried and rejected so Thea gave the pigeon more bread. 'I'm just going to have to be blunt with him. Tell him he's simply not my type. Not that I really have a type.' She watched the pigeon wrestle with her chewy granary crust, fending off the pestering of other birds. 'Just a feeling.'

Thea wasn't expecting her six o'clock to come early – she'd expected him to be at least ten minutes late. She'd developed a theory, based on ample evidence over the years, that her clients tended to be early in the winter months, when inclement weather and darkness by teatime saw them jump in cabs to arrive early yet apologetic, as if sitting quietly in the waiting room, thawing out, was somehow taking a liberty. Come the spring, her clients would stroll to her, or jump off the bus a couple of stops early. They were simply not in so much of a rush to be indoors from outside. With this March being one of the warmest on record, Thea's clients were not turning up on time. Apart from this one. It was unexpected. But not half as unexpected as seeing Alice in reception too. Alice and the client were standing side by side awkwardly, both fixing her with a beseeching gaze like puppies in a pet shop competing for her attention. Thea mouthed 'one minute' to her client and with a tilt of her head, she beckoned Alice through to the kitchenette. Maintaining the mime, she raised one eyebrow to invite an explanation from Alice who thought, just then, that her best friend would make a very good headmistress. Indeed, Alice suddenly felt a little bashful, turning up and surprising Thea while her six o'clock loitered. She proffered a clutch of magazines. 'Here,' she said in a contrived, sheepish voice and a don't-beat-me look on her face, 'these are for your waiting room.'

'Are you all right?' Thea enquired in a discreet whisper.

'Fine,' Alice tried to whisper back but found that her smile of prodigious proportions caused her voice to squeak. 'I have something to tell you.'

'I'll be an hour,' Thea told her, glancing at the clock and

seeing it was now six, 'perhaps quicker. He may not need the full session today.'

Alice waited in the kitchenette while Thea led her client upstairs, small talk accompanying their footsteps. Then she returned to the waiting room and removed magazines by any rival publisher, arranging her copies of *BoyRacer*, *HotSpots*, *GoodGolfing*, *FilmNow*, *YachtUK*, and *Vitesse*. Something to cater for all of Thea's clients, she hoped. She sat and waited, fidgeting with her hair, twisting her pony-tail up into a chignon, then French plaiting it, letting it fall in billows around her shoulders. She smiled, remembering how, when they were young and horse mad, Thea would marvel that Alice's flaxen hair really was like a pony's tail.

'It's so thick and amazing!' Thea would say.

'It's a bother,' Alice would rue, 'I'd prefer your soft silky hair.' Thea would brush Alice's hair smooth, utilizing a technique they'd been taught at the riding school – holding the bunch in one hand whilst softly, gradually, rhythmically, sweeping strands away. Finally, she'd take the bunch in one hand and spin it before letting it fall, wafting down into a tangle-free fan.

'If we were ponies, you'd be a palomino and I'd just be a boring old roan,' Thea had said, without rancour.

'Then pull out any dark hairs!' Alice exclaimed. 'Apparently, palominos can't have more than twelve dark hairs in their tail.'

Even now, Thea automatically searched Alice's hair. Though, if there were any rogue dark hairs to pluck, Alice gave her West End colourist an earful. She was still flaxen, but the glint and shine of her pre-teen hair now required strips of tinfoil and banter with the colourist about holidays and soap operas, for two hours and a small fortune every two months.

Thea's six o'clock all but floated down the stairs at ten

to seven and paid cash for the Cloud Nine privilege. Alice waited behind a copy of *BoyRacer* until Thea came to her.

'Ready?' she asked.

'Nearly,' Thea replied, 'I just have to tidy my room.'

'Shall I come?' Alice suggested. 'Help?'

'If you want!' Thea laughed.

Thea's room, at the top of the building, though small in terms of square footage, appeared airy and more spacious because of the oddly angled walls and Velux windows. It was also painted a very matt white which appeared to obscure the precise surface of the walls and gave the small room a sense of space. Underfoot was a pale beech laminate floor. A simple white small melamine desk with two plain chairs in white frosted plastic were positioned under an eave. The bed was in the centre of the room. Shelves had been built in the alcove and they were piled with white towels. Three baskets, lined in calico, were placed on the bottom shelf and filled with potions and lotions in gorgeous dark blue glass bottles.

'It's lovely since it's been redone,' Alice said. 'Did all the rooms get the same makeover?'

Thea nodded. 'New beds too. It's a great space to work in – our client base has soared.'

Alice pressed down onto the bed as if testing it. Then she looked beseechingly at Thea. 'Go on, then,' Thea sighed, raising her eyebrows in mock exasperation, 'just a quickie.'

'Is that what you say to your clients?' Alice retorted. 'Seriously,' she whispered, 'do they *never* get the wrong idea?'

'What?' Thea balked. 'And ask for "extras"?'

'Most of your clients seem to be gorgeous sporty blokes,' Alice commented.

'Fuck off!' Thea objected. 'I'm a masseuse, I specialize in sports injuries, I barely notice what clients look like – all I'm interested in is the body under my hands and how I can help to put it right. Anyway, sporty beefy isn't my type.'

'Yes, yes – you don't have a type,' Alice said, 'just a feeling.' She and Thea caught eyes and laughed. 'Well, I tell you, I wouldn't mind copping a feel of some of your clients.'

'Well, you're a filthy cow,' Thea said, 'and I'm a professional with standards.'

'Have you let Giles into your pants yet?' Alice asked, taking off her top.

'No way,' said Thea, 'not my type.'

'You'll be a virgin again soon,' Alice remarked as she silently slipped her shoes off and unzipped her skirt. She eased herself onto the bed, lying on her stomach. She placed her face into the hole of the padded doughnut-ring at the head end.

'OK,' Thea said softly, 'let's have a feel of you.' She placed her hands lightly on Alice and then began to work. Within moments, it felt to Alice as though a troupe of fairies was travelling all over her back, lifting her shoulder blades and dusting underneath, doing synchronized roly-polys down her spine, breathing relief in between her vertebrae, unfurling the muscles around her neck, marching over her biceps, soothing her scapulae, giving her hip-joints a good spring clean. She hadn't had a massage from Thea in ages. Guiltily, she recalled how dismissive she had been when Thea had announced years ago that despite her first-class geography degree, she was going to train as a masseuse.

'Pilates has had a really positive effect on your back,' Thea declared, bringing Alice back to the present, 'but you should check the ergonomics of your desk, chair and screen at work.'

Slowly, Alice sat up. Her face was flushed and her eyes were gently glazed with relaxation. 'You're a genius,' she declared woozily, 'you have healing hands.'

Thea, however, snorted almost derisively. 'Don't be daft,' she said, 'they're just "helpful hands" – if you want truly healing hands, you want to have Reiki with Maria. Or Souki's acupuncture. Or have Lars tutor you in the basics of Feldenkrais. My massage is more a satisfying after-dinner mint to the main course served by the other practitioners.'

'Would you just give yourself some bloody credit, girl,' Alice said, almost angrily. 'You didn't see the look on your last client's face. Blissed-out is an understatement.'

'I didn't need to,' Thea shrugged, 'I felt his back say thank you all by itself.'

'Can I make one tiny suggestion?' Alice asked. 'Ditch the plinky-plinky rainforest music in reception. It made me want to yell and wee simultaneously.'

Later that night, Thea sat up in bed, flicked on the bedside light and looked at the clock. It was in fact the early hours of the next day. She couldn't sleep and she knew the worst place to be was her bed. She pulled on her fleece dressing gown and padded out of the room. The brutal change from soft carpet to cold floor tiles still unnerved her though she'd lived with it for four years. By the time she reached her small kitchen – a matter of only a few steps – her feet had acclimatized to the tiles. She made a cup of tea and went through to the sitting room and the comfort of carpet once more. Her mother liked to say that the flat was placed around a sixpence and it made her quite dizzy. The perpetually cold central hallway, small indeed and basically circular, was the hub off which the other rooms radiated. The bedroom, the kitchen, the sitting room, the bathroom. Standing in the hallway with all the other doors shut and surrounding you was a slightly disorientating experience. But Thea loved it. 'It's my little slice of Lewis Carroll Living,' she'd proclaimed to her mother when begging her for a loan for her deposit. Viewed from the pavement, the side of the building where Thea's flat was located was a turreted, cylindrical add-on to an otherwise unremarkable Victorian exterior.

'A satisfying expression of Gothick-with-a-k,' Thea's usually serious and conservative older brother had declared with surprising approval, 'don't you think so, Alice?'

'I reckon your sister just wants her Rapunzel moment!' Alice had said.

Thea scrunched her toes into her shaggy rug and sat down, hugging her knees. She didn't drink the tea – the ritual of making it and cupping her hands around it had been the thing. She saw her mobile phone on the sofa and reached for it. It was on and a text message was unopened.

`u r happy 4 me?!! Say u r!! xxx`

`course I am!!!` Thea replied. `brill news - u deserve hap-ev-aft! Xxx`

Though Alice's news was undoubtedly brilliant, Thea was still somewhat overwhelmed by the shock of it. She thought back to Alice linking arms with her and hauling her off to Blandford Street for sushi.

Guess what!

What?

You'll never guess!

What?

Guess!

What? Don't tell me! Don't tell me! That bloke from your ad agency?

I'm getting married!

That bloke from your ad agency?

No, silly. No! Mark Sinclair!

Mark Sinclair?

Yes!

Mark Sinclair?

Yes! *Yes*!

Mark Sinclair?

22

Yes, Thea, Mark Sinclair!
Does he know?

Alice hadn't met someone. She'd found someone. Those had been her words and she was effervescing with excitement, exclamation marks now peppering her speech.

'I found someone! I'm getting married. Fucking hell! Can you believe it! I've *found* someone!'

Initially Thea was gobsmacked into jaw-dropped silence but Alice's animation was infectious. Though baffled by the simple facts that Alice was now engaged, that Mark Sinclair was fiancé, and though stunned by the speed of it all, Thea soon spun into Alice's excitement. She sketched wedding-dress possibilities on serviettes while Alice, flushed and gesticulating, re-enacted the entire proposal before launching into list-making.

'You know what? I can't believe I didn't think of him earlier. I mean, I've known him for ever! I've always loved him. Because he's always *always* been there for me.'

Thea agreed. Mark Sinclair had always always been there. She knew him, of course, without really knowing him at all. The lovely guy who always made Alice feel better, who had always been there for her when some cad or other had done her wrong. With hindsight, Thea recalled the gaze he'd bestowed on Alice now and then over the years which, at the time, she'd interpreted as brotherly affection. After all, it was Mark who had shared with Thea the job of looking after Alice when some Lothario had broken her heart again. Mark who had gladly taken Alice out to lovely restaurants or opening nights at the theatre when she was without a date and down in the doldrums. Mark who'd been at the other end of the phone as Alice's late-night insecurity guard. Mark who assured Alice that not all men were bastards, that there were fish in the sea aplenty and she was the prize catch. Thea had been grateful to him for this. Without ever really having had the forum to tell him so. Well, she could now. Here was one man she'd never have to take to one side to threaten that if he hurt her friend she'd kill him. He was the absolute antithesis of Alice's previous pick. That's why it was such a shock. Such a revelation.

And yet it made sense. Since breaking up with Bill, Alice had indeed had a quiet, sometimes pensive few months. Maybe she had made a conscientious decision to practise what she published. Perhaps it really was as easy as reassessing her wish list. Blinking and seeing that the man to marry was standing right in front of her. Learning it's not who you love, it's how.

'But how long have you been seeing him? I mean, how come I didn't know you've even been seeing him?'

'Two weeks. Don't shout at me, Thea!'

'Two *weeks*? And now you're *engaged*?'

'Be happy for me – or you can't be bridesmaid.'

'Of course I'm happy for you, idiot. Ecstatic. I'm just shocked. Two weeks?'

'He's perfect. What was the point of waiting? Kind, considerate, calm – there are no safer hands in the world for handling me.'

'Are you madly in love with him? With Mark Sinclair?'

Alice looked at Thea. 'You do know that feeling of "madly in love" is merely phenylethylamine, Thea?' Alice said with a sigh. 'It's just a natural amphetamine – which is why it's addictive. It's the same hormone that's released during high-risk sports and eating chocolate.'

'Whatever,' said Thea, 'but you need to be in love with someone to actually marry them.'

'So fiction and films would have us believe,' Alice said. 'There's more to marriage than being head over heels. In fact, my feet are firmly rooted and my head is now out of the clouds and firmly on my shoulders – that's why I know it's going to work. I'm ready for this.'

'And you do love him,' Thea said.

'Everyone loves Mark,' Alice smiled, 'he's one of life's good guys.'

'And you love him,' said Thea.

'I'm the love of his life. And he's my love for life. That's why we're marrying. What more could I ask for?'

Now, contemplating quietly in the conducive early hours, Thea likened it to Alice having a good tidy-up and coming across something she'd forgotten all about. Like something never worn, bought on impulse, never even tried on, pushed to the back of a cupboard, then rediscovered. A perfect fit, it transpired. A delightful surprise. What disconcerted Thea was that she hadn't ever thought that when Alice did her tidy-up, she'd find Mark. What unnerved her most – and she could now admit it in the silence and privacy of her space – was that she was actually slightly taken aback. Alice had brought Thea the best news in the world. But for the first time in their friendship, she'd done so without the need to ask Thea's advice or seek her opinion first.

Mark Sinclair

Mark Sinclair had an aptitude for diplomacy and an instinct for manners. They hadn't been drilled into him at home, he hadn't learnt them at school or been trained in them after university. They were simply part of his personality and throughout his thirty-two years they had won him friends and influence. These qualities, combined with a head for figures and a heart with a strong work ethic, saw his rapid promotion through the hierarchies at ADS Internationale for whom he worked as an investment analyst. He was invaluable to them. He could speak languages, keep calm under the pressure of City finance, didn't get drunk over business lunches, never fell out with colleagues or associates, travelled uncomplainingly and trained his immediate team into an efficient, likeable unit. The company had no need to incentivize him and every reason to reward him which they did, handsomely.

Whoever met Mark, wished to befriend him. It helped that he was fluent in Spanish and French, passable in German and Italian, and that his work took him abroad frequently. A full Filofax and a packed Palm Pilot kept track of his worldwide friendships. He was a terrific host when people came to London. He'd stock the fridge for them, tailor a list of sights to see, and provide his membership cards for a variety of museums. He'd meet them after work, having secured great seats at theatres or enviable tables in top restaurants. Mark was also a wonderful guest – as comfortable sleeping on the bottom bunk of his godson's bed in Didsbury as he was staying in palatial grandeur in a suite at the Peninsula, Hong Kong. He loved hiking hard in Skye with his old friends the McLeods and he enjoyed putting the world to rights in French with his new friend at the Paris office, Pierre. He went on safari by himself in Kenya and made Jeep-loads of new friends there. He was a Friend of the Royal Academy of Arts and soon made friends at the Royal Academy. He had friends who'd invite him to Glyndebourne and others he'd accompany to Glastonbury. Mark Sinclair was open-minded, kind-hearted and plain good company. He hated confrontations and far preferred to bite his tongue than fall out with anyone he cared for. An even keel was what he aimed for. Which is why he had so many friends but not actually one best one.

Alice looked at Mark expectantly. She smoothed her white shirt, flicked her hair back, cocked her head and regarded him again.

'Are you ready?' he asked, while patting his pockets to double-check on keys, wallet, mobile phone. 'Shall we go?'

'But how do I *look*?' Alice said, standing her ground a little petulantly. 'Will they approve? Do you think I should wear a skirt instead?'

'You look gorgeous,' Mark assured her, congratulating himself on the earrings he'd bought her. 'You look – brown?'

'Thea did my fake tan,' Alice said, with no embarrassment. 'I felt a bit pale and peaky from my cold last week – I don't want your mum to think you're not looking after me. Do you think your parents will approve? Do you think they'll

27

like me? I hope your mum is a good cook – I'm *starving*.'

'Of course they will,' said Mark, 'who wouldn't. Come on. Mum's Sunday Roast is legendary – but don't touch the white wine. They only do Liebfraumilch.'

Gail Sinclair busied off to the kitchen to prepare the dessert, turning down Alice's keen offer to help. Gail was delighted. Better still, she was charmed.

'Charmed, absolutely charmed,' she practised quietly to herself in the kitchen whilst decanting Marks & Spencer custard into a jug and carefully transferring their cherry Bakewell onto her best cake dish. *Charmed*, she continued in a whisper, *Alice is delightful, Hazel. Absolutely winning to look at. A magazine person. She brought us copies – a real variety, Mary. She dotes on Mark, Carole – absolutely dotes on him. Chris and I couldn't be more happy.*

'She's a cracker,' Chris Sinclair, who'd never mastered the art of the whisper, told his son; while Alice sat to his right and tried to look as though she wasn't eavesdropping. Gail heard, even though she was at a clatter changing their everyday crockery for the best china. *Chris thinks she's a cracker, Joyce, and I know you'll agree once you've met her.*

Alice reckoned Chris to be in his mid-sixties, dapper despite the patterned sweater and corduroy slippers. Thinning silvery hair cut neatly, bright eyes, elegant hands and a healthy complexion due to his love of golf and gardening. She reckoned Gail to be five years younger, her hair cut into a short, neat style appropriate for her age, any grey expensively masked by an overall coppery sheen. While Mark talked to his father about PELS and Gail poured Marks & Spencer's coulis into another jug, Alice thought how best to describe Mark's parents and his childhood home to Thea. 'Refreshingly nice,' she would probably say, 'just normal, nice people.' She stifled giggles into her serviette, predicting how she and Thea would then analyse the mothers of boyfriends past. Callum's mother who wore the same Whistles jeans as her own but a size smaller, Finlay's mother who'd insisted Alice call her Mrs Jones despite allowing them to sleep together. Tom's mother who was insanely jealous of his affection for Alice and would thus drape herself over him quite alarmingly for the duration of their visits. But Mark's parents seemed to be simply nice, ordinary people.

'You look like your dad,' Alice suddenly announced though it momentarily halted conversation and fixed Gail's cake slice mid-air. Alice was happy to predict that in thirty years or so, the man seated opposite her, whom she was soon to marry, would look a little like the gentleman currently seated to her left.

Charmed, Gail thought to herself again, *charmed*.

Chris and Mark browsed the Sunday papers while Gail poured coffee and Alice effervesced over the beauty of their garden.

'God, I completely love your verbena.'

'Viburnum,' Gail corrected lightly. 'Have you a garden?'

'Well, at the moment, I'm restricted to what the lifestyle mags call *patio living*,' Alice said. 'It's basically a small, glorified back yard covered with cream gravel and pots with plants that die on me on an annual basis. And twisty wire furniture that looks amazing, cost a bloody fortune and is bloody uncomfortable.'

Gail looked at Alice without expression at much the same time that Alice thought to herself shit! Is 'bloody' swearing? And Mark jerked up from the *Sunday Times* thinking oh shit, she bloody swore.

'Perhaps once you're married, you'll find a house with a garden,' Gail said diplomatically. 'Herbaceous borders pretty much look after themselves and perennials do just what they're meant to do.' She took a thoughtful sip of coffee.

'They needn't be expensive either.' See, no need for 'bloody'.

'Lovely idea,' said Alice warmly, helping herself to another chocolate because she noted that Gail was on her third.

'Now, I want to hear all about the proposal,' Gail said expectantly, 'all the romantic details.'

'Mum –' Mark remonstrated, raising his eyebrow at his father for sympathy and assistance.

'Did he get down on bended knee?' Gail asked. 'Did he take you to a restaurant and have the *maître d'* present you with a diamond ring?' Mark groaned but Alice giggled. She thought Gail probably had the makings of a rather good mother-in-law. 'Perhaps he whisked you off to Venice for the weekend and popped the question aboard a gondola?'

'Last week,' Alice grinned over to Mark who was attempting to disappear behind the *Sunday Times*, 'at Mark's flat. He was cooking that amazing chorizo and butterbean casserole thing with the six cloves of garlic. We had a glass of Rioja. I was eating a carrot.'

Gail had never been a fan of garlic, let alone Spanish peasant fare, but she tried to look enthusiastic.

'It struck me, it simply struck me that it was the best idea ever,' Alice said dreamily.

'Yes, but how was the question itself *popped*?' Gail persisted. 'Mark's father whisked *me* to Paris expressly to propose.'

Alice grinned. 'It was quite matter of fact, actually,' she said, 'I had to turn down the radio to be heard. It all made such perfect sense. Even though I had a mouth full of carrot, I just looked at Mark and said "Marry me, Mark, marry me." He looked at me as if he was having difficulty understanding my language. So I swallowed the carrot, repeated the question and added "please". Still he stared. And then he said yes.'

Gail stared at Alice as if she had difficulty understanding

her language. Chris just stared. 'What's that on your shirt?' Gail exclaimed, looking horrified. 'On the collar and cuffs? It's brown.'

'What?' Alice looked at her collar and cuffs. 'Oh bugger!' she declared. 'It's fake tan. I'll bloody kill Thea.'

'Do you think they liked me?' Alice asked Mark as they drove away.

'Of course,' Mark assured her, concentrating on the road, biting his tongue on being cut up by a man with a sharp haircut driving a car that was obviously meant to look like a Porsche but was glaringly not. Alice gazed out of the car. She pressed her cheek against the passenger window. She needn't have had the fake tan – the wine at lunchtime, the effort of being on best behaviour had made her feel quite warm. She looked at the trees, some bursting into leaf, others in full blossom. She'd learn the names of lots of plants by the time she next met Mark's parents. And she'd try not to swear.

Saul Mundy

Saul Mundy had assumed he'd buy a sensible two-bedroom house in a popular postcode, take out a mortgage with Emma and have a leg-up onto the London property ladder. He had been thinking about Brondesbury or Tufnell Park or Ealing as safe bets. But then he hadn't been thinking about breaking up with Emma. Twelve hours after the relationship ended, Saul signed a short let on a top-floor space in central London, a location he'd previously never considered as residential. It was uncompromisingly open plan, and he reckoned the landlord had probably marketed it variously as office space, storage space, apartment or studio according to the potential tenant's requirements. Saul chanced upon it en route to a meeting in Baker Street and rented it because it was available that afternoon and had a view he knew he'd never tire of, a privileged panorama of the city from a vantage point available to few. He need never elbow his way onto a crowded Tube again. And with upmarket delicatessens such as Villandry on his doorstep, he need never resort to frozen meals again.

When the short let expired six months later, Saul bought the place, having unexpectedly fallen for the charms of city-centre living and having learnt to cook at an evening course run by Divertimenti a stroll away. Twelve months on, Saul has become a dab hand at property improvement and is quite the house-proud DIY-er. He partitioned the expansive area with a curved wall of opalescent glass blocks, dividing the space by a sinuous line into attractive and practical zones. Privacy in an arc for sleeping; an ample and quirkily curved section in which to relax and a clever paisley-shaped bud concealing his home office. He'd mosaiced the bathroom, laid funky rubber flooring in the kitchen, and given great thought to lighting. He loved it.

And he loved the location. He hadn't stepped on the Northern Line for eighteen months. He swiftly attained an enviable knowledge of the capital's hidden secrets and the added advantage of living so centrally was that soon enough he was known and warmly welcomed at them all. Consequently, he was never ripped off at a convenience store. He had no need for a car and therefore never had parking fines or the Congestion Charge hanging over him. Marco, who owned the sandwich shop and deli, let Saul park his scooter under cover for free. He was always guaranteed a table for breakfast at Bernard's Café, usually with the day's papers presented to him too. At lunchtime, Marco always over-filled Saul's sandwich and if it was Maria serving, she'd slip in a chocolate brownie for free. He never suffered a lousy curry. Or a dodgy Thai. Or disappointing sushi. Even if he was out of change, Dave on the corner would still have Saul's *Evening Standard* for him, ready folded. He was able to secure just what he wanted, at the best possible price, during the sales, before crowd-swamping made shopping unbearable. He never had to resort to an All Bar One. He'd never been in a Pitcher & Piano. He didn't have to fight his way through bars thronging with over-excited and over-made-up office girls, or over-indulged and over-the-limit City smart arses. He could have the liveliest and latest of nights out without ever being ripped off by a minicab, he could just stroll home. So, when Saul's friend Ian Ashford called and suggested a night out, Saul was able to say that he knew a great little place to meet.

The Swallow, nestled between a printing shop and an ironmonger's along one of the little streets forming the tight clasp east of Great Portland Street, was an old-fashioned hostelry. It appeared unprepossessing enough from the outside to safeguard against clientele other than locals and regulars. The drab paint, the windows seemingly in need of a basic wash to say nothing of new frames, were a shrewd exterior to protect an interior that was actually bright, cosy and spruce. The place was not big and resembled an elongated sitting room; the bar itself was confined to one corner and cramped enough for the staff to be unable to serve side by side necessitating an intricate but effective *pas de deux*. Whilst one pulled a pint or reached for a whisky glass or discussed the runners at Kempton Park, the other would look over his shoulder to take the next order. And then they'd change position with a courteous glide. A coal fire murmured away constantly from November until March. From May until September, the back door was permanently open to a small patio complete with its own grapevine, increasing the pub's interior capacity of twenty-eight seated and six standing to a further twelve standing. On Tuesdays, Wednesdays and Thursdays, sausages and mash were available. At other times, peanuts and crisps were complimentary.

At the Swallow, though no one actually knew what anyone actually did or where they lived, the atmosphere was congenial and every now and then, a sense of community emerged. Arthur gave everyone a great tip for shares to be bought in a new Internet start-up. Lynton offered Marlboro cigarettes for less than half the shop price. When Barry's flat

34

was broken into, his home was restocked courtesy of the staff and clients at the Swallow. Eddie's cousin owned a locksmith's concession and sorted out new security. Anne ran up two new pairs of curtains for Barry because the burglars had ripped down his to use as sacks. Lynton knew someone who did CD players on the cheap and as they owed him a favour, he secured one for Barry for free. But Saul earned himself complimentary pints for a month. Not that free drinks were Saul's motivation to provide Barry with more CDs than he'd owned in the first place, an electric shaver, an electric toothbrush that retailed at twice the price of the shaver, a digital camera, an Alessi teapot and a lava lamp.

'Blimey, mate,' Keith the landlord had marvelled, pulling Saul a Guinness on the house, 'is all that kosher?'

'You got a little shop or something?' asked Barry, hugely grateful but also quietly wondering what else Saul had. 'Or you got the back of a lorry?'

'Knock-off?' Lynton quizzed, defensive but interested.

Saul had laughed. 'It's kosher, Lynton, your patch is safe, mate! I'm a writer,' he shrugged, knowing he'd told them before at some point. 'I'm sent stuff all the time to test and review. Mostly, they don't ask for it back. I've had a 42-inch plasma since the summer.' Barry glanced up hopefully from behind the ziggurat of CDs. 'They've only just asked for it back,' Saul continued, 'they're talking about installing a home cinema for me to test next.' Saul was called everything from lucky geezer to jammy bastard and the wish-lists of the staff and clients at the Swallow were discreetly presented to him.

So, when Ian Ashford phoned Saul, Saul suggested the Swallow as perfect for a mid-November, mid-week drink, with perhaps sausages and mash if they fancied.

'Jesus, it's been a while.' Ian shook Saul's hand warmly, nodded and grinned. 'What'll you drink?' he asked, glancing around the Swallow and nodding approvingly.

'I'll have a Stella, thanks,' Saul replied, reciprocating Ian's amiable nodding with a friendly punch to the bicep. 'Good to see you,' Saul said warmly, 'it's been bloody ages. Where've you been?'

'Otherwise engaged,' said Ian. He watched Saul take a long drink. 'Literally,' he added. He winked, sighed and took a swig of beer. 'Engaged.'

'Work been a bitch, then?' Saul enquired.

'Work?' Ian said. 'I'm *engaged*.' Again he winked and raised his eyebrows along with his glass when he saw the penny drop for Saul.

'Christ!' Saul exclaimed. 'Bloody hell,' he raised his glass and drank urgently before chinking Ian's, 'bloody hell – and there was I thinking you've been up to your eyes in some crucial trial at the Old Bailey when all the while you were waltzing up the road to eternal love and heading down the aisle to domesticity!'

'You sound just like your column,' Ian protested, 'don't you go featuring me.'

'Here's to you and Liz. Congratulations,' Saul said, with genuine affection.

'Er, I'm engaged to Karen,' said Ian. 'Lizzie and I broke up.'

'Bloody hell,' Saul said. Though he hadn't expected Ian to be engaged, he certainly hadn't reckoned on it being to anyone other than Liz.

'I left Liz for her,' Ian said lightly.

'Bloody hell,' Saul said darkly.

'I know,' said Ian guiltily, 'I know.' He sipped at his beer and looked into the middle distance. 'I always thought it would be Lizzie. Then I met Karen and there was no contest. No conscience, even. It's what you'd call a "no-brainer" – I had to be with her. Simple.'

'Bloody hell,' Saul said, his vocabulary sorely limited by

the shock of Ian's news. He downed his drink thirstily. 'Another pint?' He went to the bar, ordering sausages and mash at the same time. 'How's work?' Saul asked Ian on his return, a packet of crisps between his teeth.

'Oh fine,' said Ian, 'manic. Karen's a lawyer too so she totally understands the stress and long hours issue. She works in Litigation. At Tate Scot Wade.'

'Right,' said Saul, 'right.' He didn't want to dislike Karen before he'd even met her, he didn't want his affection for Liz to colour his acceptance of her. But he couldn't help but resent Ian's surprise fiancée for dominating the conversation thus far and for having monopolized his friend in recent months.

'How about you?' Ian asked. 'What's happening?'

'More work than I can do – but I can't turn any of it down,' Saul laughed. 'I love it. Mostly.'

'Karen's a fan of your column,' Ian said, 'we both are.'

'Which one?' Saul asked, genuinely flattered.

'*ES* magazine – it's so much more than a consumer low-down. It's like a little slice of your life – very self-effacing and engaging. Well written, too.' Ian chinked his glass. 'I chuckle but you have Karen in stitches.'

'Cheers, mate,' Saul said, 'cheers.'

'And you still have your regular slots in the men's mags?'

'Yes,' said Saul, '*GQ* have expanded my section. I do the gadgets pages for that new mag, *Edition*, my columns for the weeklies and the odd bit of roving reporter here and there, some editorial consultancy for launches on the side.'

'Don't suppose you've any iPods knocking around?' said Ian, who could easily afford one but loved the idea of a freebie. 'Any cool press trips? Golf in the Algarve? Scuba anywhere?'

'Just the one iPod,' Saul said, 'and as for press trips, there was Bermuda for sailing and Sweden for sledding. By husky.

And a lost weekend in Prague with Sonja from the Tourist Office.'

'You jammy bastard,' Ian laughed.

'Three thousand words, though I had to censor most of it, thanks to Sonja,' Saul said, as if it was an occupational hazard.

'And how about *you*?' Ian asked again, with a concern Karen had taught him how to access. Saul tucked into his sausages, nodded and shrugged. He'd rather have his mouth full than talk. 'Are you seeing anyone?' Ian asked, partly because Karen had told him to.

Saul chewed thoughtfully. He shook his head. 'Not at the moment,' he said, wishing for more mash.

'Anyone on the horizon?'

'Why?' Saul laughed. 'Has Karen a queue of luscious friends?'

'Actually,' said Ian, 'yes.'

Saul shrugged. 'Cool,' he said, 'why not. There hasn't been anyone since Emma. I'm not sure if I count the tryst with Sonja.'

'Blimey,' Ian said, 'we're talking a good eighteen months, mate. Sounds like celibacy to me.'

Saul shrugged again. 'You know me,' he said quietly, 'I can be quite choosy.'

'Mind you,' Ian theorized, 'your social life is pretty lively and there are always relatively funky work do's on. I bet you don't even notice the absence of a girlfriend.'

Saul considered Ian's overview. 'Actually, it's not so much that,' he said thoughtfully. 'I'm quite into the idea of a steady partner – even the concept of commitment. However, I just can't be bothered with doing the singles-circuit-dating games. It's too contrived.'

'Too time consuming,' Ian agreed, 'and expensive.' God, he thanked his luck for Karen. 'Mind you, celibacy must be a bit bloody frustrating.' He raised an eyebrow.

'I do what a lot of other blokes do,' shrugged Saul.

Ian shrugged back. He also made a mental note to provide Karen with a current description of Saul to circulate amongst her friends. He'd heard Karen refer admiringly to similar hairstyles as 'bed hair' and no doubt she'd declare the colour of Saul's to be like caramel or something. He noted his friend still had a thing about trendy footwear and approved his Oris watch as an indication that Saul's career was going very well indeed. Armani soft black jeans. And a shirt he'd tell Karen was Paul Smith. They were already compiling their guest list for the wedding. It would be cosy if by then Saul attended with a girlfriend who happened to be a friend of Karen's. Ian glanced at his watch. 'I'd better be going, mate. Does this place not have last orders?'

'It's when the last person orders,' Saul informed him.

'It's good to see you,' Ian said, 'let's not make it so long, next time. Come over to ours. Karen is a great cook. You'll love her. I'll call you.'

Saul sat on alone in the Swallow with another pint. Lynton sat by himself too. And Barry was on his own tonight as well. They all nodded amiably at each other but were quietly content to sit separately. That was what Saul loved about the Swallow, its concept of relaxed companionship, that it wasn't necessary to cramp around the same table to be in warm company. Saul looked over to Eleni, snuggled against her boyfriend. He reckoned he was their age or thereabouts. When Anne, the wife of the landlord, had brought over the two plates of sausage and mash, she'd ruffled Saul's hair maternally. He reckoned she was close to his mother in age.

Saul walked around the corner back to his flat. He scanned through the draft of the article he'd be writing the next day and then logged off his laptop, content. There was nothing watchable on television. He thought he ought to run a bath – he'd been sent products by Clarins For Men to test. All that talk of women and wives and girlfriends and his own barren situation had left him quite hollow and horny. So he decided to do what a lot of other blokes do. He'd lie in a bath later. He grabbed his jacket and went back out into the night.

Alice Heggarty

I keep singing the corniest of songs. 'I'm Getting Married in the Morning!' In the daftest of voices. 'Going to the Chapel and We're Going to Get Ma-ha-ha-rid.' The daftest of songs in the silliest of accents. I even sang 'Nights in White Satin' in the cab today. It struck me, for the first time, that it was actually 'nights' and not 'knights'. And then I was absorbed for at least an hour wondering why it had never previously crossed my mind that a knight got up in white satin would be pretty odd in a heterosexual love song.

Anyway, I am going to be married in the morning. Thanks in no small part to the girls on Dream Weddings *magazine and Mark indulging me, it's going to be a fairy-tale wedding. I'm feeling deliriously excited – but a bit stressed too. I'm even feeling a bit pissed off – like I want everyone to continually pat me on the back and acknowledge how much hard work I've put into it all. We only got engaged in March, after all. Eight months later, and I've researched and secured the flowers, the dresses, the venue, held auditions for the band, even written the vows. I want it to be the best day of my life. And Mark's too. And I want it to go down in the annals of the guests as the best wedding they've ever been to.*

I must pack for honeymoon. Initially I wanted the destination to be a surprise, but I pointed out to Mark that I'd be a stroppy cow if I packed salopettes and we arrived in Bermuda. Actually, I just pressed and pestered him because I really did need to know. It's not that I'm a control freak, though I suppose I am, it's just that I know myself well enough to admit that I'm a nightmare if I'm disappointed. So, if I was going to be disappointed, at least I could've had the chance to get over it in advance. Shit, OK, if I have to admit it, I might have subtly persuaded Mark to change the plans if need be! Anyway, bless him, Mark must have picked up on all my not-so-subtle hints and he is whisking me away to St Lucia. A helicopter to the Jalousie Plantation between those two iconic Piton mountains you see in the films, in the brochures. They know we're honeymooning so hopefully they'll lay on all sorts of little extras. I am going to be princess for a fortnight. And why not – because when we get home, I'll be just boring old Mrs Sinclair!

They gave me a great send-off at work. They must have had quite some whip-round as they've gone for the Gaggia coffee machine from the wedding list. Anyway, all my mags will be fine – they can spare me for a fortnight but if they need me, I've told them they can phone the Jalousie.

I'm getting married in the morning. Bloody bloody hell. Ding dong. I really really am. I'll be thirty years old. And fifty-one weeks. I, Alice Rose Heggarty, am going to marry Mark Oliver Sinclair in approximately twenty-three hours' time. How do I feel? Still a touch peaky from my hen-night! I feel ready, actually. Everything is going according to plan. All I need to do is turn up and say 'I do' and look ravishing. I want Mark to feel that he's the luckiest bloke alive. I feel good. There really is no better man for me to marry. Lovely dearest Mark. He'll look after me and cherish me and keep me safe. None of those other wankers ever did. It's so lovely not to worry.

It's a novelty for me. It's so wonderful to be loved so unequivocally. Unconditionally. No one could possibly love me more – so what more could I possibly ask for? Tomorrow I'm going to be the bride of his dreams. I'll make sure I cry a little when I say 'I do' because I know he'll love that.

I'm so happy Thea is staying over with me tonight. I can't wait to snuggle up with her and have hot chocolate with marshmallows and reminisce about our olden days. My best, beautiful friend. My bridesmaid. My only bridesmaid. Me being me, I'm glad out of the two of us I'm the first to wed. Just recently, though, I've been hoping that perhaps she'll not be too long behind. Whereas I'm now the first to admit I used to fall in love with a type – and the wrong one – I've seen that my path to happiness necessitated me walking off course. And in doing so, I came across my kind, gentle Mark. Who'd have thought it? Who'd have thought!

I think, at our age, after the highs and lows experienced through our twenties, the time comes to alter your focus, a shift in perspective. I decided to turn my back on a view which actually gave me little joy. I want Thea to take a leaf out of my book – we're similar and yet so different. I hated ever being single – I used to wait until a replacement was a dead cert before breaking off an already failed relationship. Thea, though, would rather be all on her tod than dally with someone she doesn't experience her elusive spark for. It's actually infuriating – I've introduced her to a couple of Mark's friends who are really nice, successful, balanced blokes. But in each instance Thea has said 'He's really nice – but he doesn't do it for me.' I know she's hardly on the shelf, but still I don't think she should be so choosy. I wish for her all that I'm headed for. Though, if I'm honest, as nice and successful and gentlemanly as Mark's friends are, I concede they are just the tiniest bit dull. Just the tiniest. Well, I'm not marrying them, I'm marrying Mark Oliver Sinclair.

I've just thought – when Thea marries, I won't be called her 'bridesmaid'. What is the term? Something like Lady of Honour? No no – that can't be right – that sounds like an eighteenth-century hooker attempting to turn her life around. Lady in Waiting? No no – that's what royalty have and although I'm princess for a day tomorrow, my delusions of grandeur are not on that scale! Matron of Honour? Damn and bugger. That's it, that's what married women in bridesmaid capacities are called. Bloody Matron. God, it sounds horrendously frumpy. But there again, by the time Thea gets her act together, I'll be the definitive boring old housewife! Maybe we can fix her up with Mark's American cousin tomorrow.

Thea will so fixate on the notion of a dashing hero – it's her yardstick and she resolutely refuses to alter the scale. I've tried to tell her that in my experience – and especially my discovery through Mark – it doesn't really work like that. But she won't believe me. She doesn't want to think that growing up is about understanding that love's no longer about falling in love. I say to her ah, but look where it's got me – getting married in the morning and deliriously happy about it. She'll figure it out, I guess, like I did.

* * *

Jesus, it's here. It's the day of my wedding. I have exactly seven hours to go. How on earth am I going to make time pass? I only need to have my hair done and put my make-up on and then my dress. Not even I can make that last seven hours. I slept pretty well, actually. Thea's the best bedpartner a girl can have because she doesn't snore, she doesn't toss and turn and she always recounts the funniest dreams. Last night she dreamt that the groom was Bill but that I didn't notice and she couldn't make her voice heard because

*my veil was 30 feet long and wafted all around her like cheap
bubble bath and tasted like marshmallow.*

*We tried for ages to find some deep significance to her
dream but we concluded she ought to keep away from sugary
snacks and that Bill wants to be where Mark will be but will
die a lonely old bachelor. Thea brought me breakfast in bed;
a tray laden with pain au chocolat, orange juice, tea and a
blush-coloured rose. She keeps calling me Miss Almost
Sinclair and Nearly Mrs. I told her I wished I could take her
on honeymoon – and I do! I want to be able to run around
the bathroom with Thea getting over-excited about all the
gorgeous toiletries and sumptuous thick towels.*

*People keep phoning and asking if I have last-minute doubts,
or if I'm a bag of nerves. Actually, I feel pretty level-headed
about everything. I'm excited. About my dress. About seeing
all the people. OK, yes – about being the centre of attention.
Bring it on, I say – all is planned to perfection so bring it on.
Yes, I'm full of butterflies but they're fluttering in excitement
and anticipation, not swarming with trepidation or nerves.
This isn't just my big day, it's huge. I'm going to a wedding
in four hours' time and it's my own and I can't wait.*

*I'm meant to be having a lie-down – that's what Thea
suggested. She's just in the bath – she was happy to have my
bath water. I do love my flat but it does make sense for Mark
and me to sell our flats and buy a marital home. One with
a hot water tank big enough for more than just one bathful.
A house with a ready-matured herbaceous border in the
garden. Tell me there isn't a catch. That life can be this
blessed. I need to double-check the cab to take us to the
hairdresser's.*

*I love my hair! Manuel is amazing. Thea's looks gorgeous
too. She actually had hers trimmed today – I just had the*

blow-dry of my life. Her hair is gleaming, slightly shorter than usual, cut into the nape of her neck and tucked behind her ears. I hate the way she says it's boring and mousy. Anyway, she looks like a fusion of Audrey Hepburn and Isabella Rossellini. I've had this beautiful grip made for her – a single orchid. I can't wait to see her in her frock. We chose A-line in crushed velvet the colour of buttermilk; slightly empire under the bust, a low, square-cut neck and wide straps just off the shoulder. I seriously almost wept when I saw her in it. She looks divine. My mum just phoned in some unnecessary flap or other. I spoke to Dad and diplomatically asked him to intervene on any further calls she might be tempted to make. I'm glad the car will take just Dad and me. And I know Thea will cope fine with Mum. I wonder how Mark is. We spoke when Thea was in the bath. I was meant to be having a little lie-down but I couldn't keep my mind still enough for my body to relax. He sounded fine. He said yes to every single thing on my Double-Triple-Check And Check Again List. He was laughing. He loves my quirks. I hope he likes my hair all heaped up like this. In fact, I wonder whether to warn him in advance that if he touches it, it's grounds for an immediate annulment. Whoever thought that hair could feel so heavy! Maybe it's the little pearls that they've pinned into it. Fake. Not that you'd know. In fact, I'm getting a stiff neck from admiring the back view in the mirror.

Thea came to say it's time to get dressed. She's a glorious vision in the pretty panties and bra we bought from Fenwicks for her. We bought my undies from Agent Provocateur. Mark will blush. I love it that Mark blushes at my sexiness. If he wore glasses, he'd be the type they'd steam up on. Thea and I have set the dress out on my bed and we have twice gone through the precise order that things must go on, be stepped

into, have laced up and smoothed down. So I'm stepping in.
And slipping my arms through the sleeves. And Thea is lacing
me up. And smoothing me down. We've gone quiet. We're
listening to some play on Radio 4 but I couldn't tell you
what it's about. I don't know how to describe the feeling of
my dress. I don't want to use clichés. It's duchesse satin,
blush coloured – the colour you'd imagine a child's kiss would
equate to. The sensation on my body is like a loved one
gently, adoringly, whispering to my skin. I almost daren't
look in the mirror. Thea's finished the lacing and smoothing
and her eyes are welling up. She's just nodding at me.
Nodding. And biting her lip. And nodding some more. With
her eyes all watery and her nose now red. I'll have a look.
In a minute. I'll turn around. I'll have a look now. I'll have
a little look at Alice Heggarty in her wedding dress.

Hullo, Daddy. Hullo, hullo. Oh my God – the car is amazing!
Let's tell the driver to drive round the block a couple of times.
I ought to be five minutes late. Ten, preferably. And we must
remember not to stride up the aisle. Mum will kill us. And
please please don't say anything to me that'll make me cry.
Don't call me your little girl. I am your little girl but if I hear
it from you today, I'll cry and want to run all the way home.

I can't hear. I can't hear a thing. I'm watching lips move
over the vows I helped pen. I know it all off by heart. But
I can't hear. I'm ever so warm. Actually I feel a bit hot. Mark
is saying things. Pardon? It's my turn. I have to say some-
thing. Something for everyone to hear. I know this bit. I
know what to say. Please don't let my voice croak.

'I DO.'

Thea and Saul

Thea Luckmore had a remarkable constitution when it came to alcohol. Guts of iron, Alice called it. For some, this would be their downfall. For Thea, it was no big deal. She didn't regard it as a skill, or a gift; nor as a demon to keep at bay, or an affliction to be wary of. She could simply drink as much as she liked, become talkative and effervescent until the small hours yet maintain the presence of mind not to snog indiscriminately, to remember where she lived, to take off her mascara before she went to sleep and to awaken with energy, a clear head and a fresh complexion. Just occasionally, however, a hangover befell her which reminded her that alcohol could be rather a bore. A hangover for Thea bore no relevance to the amount drunk the night before, it was attributable solely to champagne. And at Mark and Alice's wedding, Veuve Clicquot flowed as if it were lemonade.

So, while Alice was trying to procure an upgrade from Club to First on her first morning as a married woman, Thea was creaking open an eyelid, groaning and praying for numb sleep. When Alice and Mark left Heathrow, First Class, two hours later, Thea managed to creep carefully to her bathroom, take two Nurofen and tolerate an invigoratingly cool

48

shower. Although it felt as if the inside of her skull and the rims of her eye-sockets were being maliciously rubbed with industrial sandpaper, that sawdust had stuck her tongue to her tonsils and that her stomach would never absorb any kind of food again, Thea was staggered to see from the mirror that she looked as if she'd had eight hours' sleep, a macrobiotic supper the night before and a challenging Pilates session.

She gave herself a stern look and vowed never to drink champagne again. She let the telephone ring and listened to Alice leave a message.

'Thea? I'm on the plane! I am 38,000 feet high! We're in First Class. Which isn't the reason I'm calling – well, it is. But also, would you mind popping into mine while I'm away – twitch the curtains and all the etceteras? Thanks, babes. Oh! By the way, one of Mark's cousins from America thought you were "hot". And I've given him your email address – apparently, he's over in Britain on business quite often.'

'I can't remember him,' said Thea, wondering if a warmer shower might be good for the cold sweat now gripping her.

'And if you can't remember him, he was the one you danced with on Top Table to "Lady's Night".'

'I was dancing on Top Table? Oh my God.' Thea groaned.

'You also danced with Jeff, one of my features editors. But despite his passion for mascara and glossy lippy, I don't think you were aware that he is in fact gay. And shorter than you. Anyway, must fly – oh, I already am! There's in-flight massage! Bye, darling, bye.'

A purpose was a very good idea. Thea had a purpose to the day. And after she checked on Alice's flat, she walked sedately to the top of Primrose Hill. The air was cold and cut through the fog in her head. The wind sliced across her face and elicited tears which refreshed her eyes. She was under-dressed for the weather but every time she shivered, she found that her nausea quelled. So she stood on the top of Primrose Hill, tears coursing down her face, shuddering violently at irregular intervals. And that was when Saul Mundy first saw Thea Luckmore, all silent tears and harsh, spasmodic shuddering. She was staring in the vague direction of St Paul's Cathedral but to Saul it seemed she was gazing deep into the nub of whatever it was that irked her so. It immediately struck him as peculiar that a seemingly unhinged person he'd never met was in fact capturing his attention. Even more bizarre was his instinct to take off his jacket and place it around her shoulders. He wanted to buy her soup. To sit her down. Though disconcerted, he felt compelled to linger. She seemed oblivious to her surroundings yet at the mercy of the elements. Trembling. Tears. Pale.

'Hullo,' said Saul, whether it was a good idea or not, 'chilly, isn't it.' He couldn't believe he'd chosen the weather as his opening gambit, but he was not in the habit of striking up conversation with a complete stranger, albeit an attractive woman who appeared intriguingly sorrowful. The only other thing he thought of saying was 'nice view', but he managed to resist.

Thea didn't dare turn her head for fear of upsetting the fragile balance she'd achieved. Even glancing down the hill, five minutes before, had made her feel dizzy.

'Look, excuse me for asking,' Saul continued, 'but are you all right?' *Fuck, now I sound like a bloody Samaritan.*

'Thanks,' Thea mumbled, 'I'm fine.'

'I don't mean to pry,' Saul said, though it would appear he was doing just that. She said nothing. She didn't look at him. This was so not his style and yet on he rabbited, grimacing at himself for sounding like an insipid do-gooder. 'I just don't like to see people crying and shivering and alone on a cold November afternoon.'

Oh for fuck's sake, thought Thea, *can't I just have my hangover in peace?*

'I'm fine, OK?' she grumbled. 'I have a sodding hangover. That's all. Go and rescue souls somewhere else, please. The devil's had mine and I'm a lost cause.'

Saul tipped his head back and laughed. 'I take back all my sympathy then,' he joshed. 'I was going to offer you my jacket. But hey, it's Armani. And anyway, your suffering is self-inflicted, enjoy!'

Carefully, Thea turned to regard the sartorial Samaritan. And she caught her breath. She had just discovered another component for Luckmore's Elixir for the Over-Indulged. Fresh air. Nurofen. Primrose Hill altitude. And a rather handsome guardian angel. 'Who are you? Some zealot Methodist?' she sparred back.

Again the man laughed. 'I'm Saul,' he answered, extending his hand which, to his surprise, she took, 'and Jesus Christ do you have the coldest hands. I can't lead you to the Lord because I don't know the way myself. Just take my damn jacket, would you?'

'I'm Thea and if it's all right with you, I will just have a quick go of your jacket.' Saul placed his jacket around Thea's shoulders. She thanked him with a slight smile that obviously caused her a little discomfort but was rewarding for him. 'It was my best friend's wedding yesterday. Champagne,' she said by way of an explanation and shrugged.

'And today you are resolving never to drink again,' Saul said, knowingly.

'Did you know they have telephones on planes,' Thea marvelled. 'Alice phoned me from 38,000 feet.'

'Technology, hey!' teased Saul, who'd made a few calls from even higher altitudes in his time.

'Amazing,' said Thea, earnestly.

'Sit down,' Saul said lightly, as if the park bench was his

own for the offering. 'You'll find some Opal Fruits in my jacket pocket. They've changed the name to something else so if you're decades younger than me you won't know what an Opal Fruit is.'

'I'm thirty-one,' Thea said, sitting down gratefully, 'and I only like the red or yellow ones.'

The sugar rush from the sweets worked wonders. She must patent this cure. Fresh air, Nurofen, Primrose Hill altitude, a handsome guardian angel bearing Opal Fruits. It worked – Thea found she could turn her head with ease. Saul sat beside her. She gladly zipped up his jacket and settled into it. It was soft brown leather, lined with something warm. 'Gorgeous jacket,' she said gratefully.

'Don't you run off with it,' Saul cautioned, eyeing it as if regretting his generosity.

'Yes yes, it's Armani,' said Thea. 'Well, one thing's for sure – I am not capable of running anywhere today.'

'Are there any sweeties left?' Saul asked and Thea delighted in his childish terminology.

'Two greens and a red,' said Thea.

'Well, I'll be having the greens then,' Saul said with exaggerated selflessness.

Thea sucked the red Opal Fruit and hummed. '*Starburst*,' she said, 'that's what they're called now. What a rubbish name for them.'

'*Opal Fruits*,' Saul sang the advert of old.

'*Made to make your mouth water*,' Thea sang back.

'Er, would you like to go for a drink?' Saul suggested.

Thea looked as if she might cry. 'I shall never touch alcohol again,' she declared, 'even the term "hair of the dog" makes me feel nauseous.'

'Why do Americans call it "norshus"?' Saul pondered, unsure whether Thea had turned him down outright.

'I don't know,' Thea mused, 'norshus nauseous.'

'But there again, why do they say "math" and "sports" and we say "maths" and "sport"?' Saul digressed. 'Anyway, how about I buy you some carbohydrates and protein cooked in a pan over a flame?'

'Pardon?'

'I was worried the term *fry-up* might make you nauseous or even norshus,' Saul said, 'but I can recommend a nice greasy sausage, two eggs slightly runny, a mound of chips, a squirt of brown sauce and a blob of red as an excellent cure for the common hangover.' Thea groaned and paled visibly. Saul was amused but also disappointed. He quite fancied a cooked breakfast. Even at almost teatime.

'Perhaps more sweeties?' Thea suggested.

Saul regarded her and she regarded him straight back. She was accepting his advance. He'd struck lucky on Primrose Hill. Good God. 'You'd like me to buy you some sweets?' he verified. He looked at her. *Those eyes aren't watering, they're sparkling, the minx.* 'Opal Fruits?'

'Do you know what I'd really like? Refreshers! Do you remember them? They come in a roll, little fizzy things. Like compacted sherbet. If you chew a few at once, they fizz up and fill your mouth and bubble through your lips.' And Thea settled further into his jacket, dipping her face so that the collar came over her nose. *I can't believe I'm being chatted up on Primrose Hill.* 'Anyway, that's what I'd like: Refreshers.'

'Can I trust you to sit still and not bugger off in my jacket?' Saul asked. 'It's Armani.'

'So you keep saying,' said Thea. 'Are you sure it's not knock-off?' and she scrutinized the cuffs suspiciously.

'Fuck off,' said Saul because he knew she'd stay. He headed off down the hill, thanking God for hangovers and for friends' flats and for phones at 38,000 feet. As he walked back up Primrose Hill, a roll of Refreshers in his back pocket, her smile floated down to him.

'Refreshers, milady,' he announced, proffering them to her.

'I only like the yellow and pink ones,' she said.

'Suck or crunch?'

'Crunch.'

'Me too.'

They crunched and hummed and stifled the burps that scoffing the entire packet in a matter of minutes created.

'I'm thawing out now,' Thea said, 'and I ought to go home, I'm exhausted.'

'Thea,' Saul said, 'take my jacket. Seriously. Every man should have one Sir Walter Ralegh moment in his life. Please allow me mine. My mum would be so proud.'

Thea giggled at the thought of this man rushing home: *Mum! Mum! I was a gentleman today, I lent my jacket to a chilly waif. Do I get more pocket money? Can I stay up late?* 'But I'm fine,' she continued gratefully, 'my car is just over there.'

Saul shrugged and nodded. 'Yeah, but if I lend you my jacket, you'll have to return it,' he concluded with a hopeful trump card. Thea glanced at him and knew she blushed. 'Perhaps same place, same time, a week from now?' he suggested, unfolding and folding the foil from the sweets.

'OK,' said Thea, thinking to herself how Alice's mags would tell her to decline and play hard to get, or to suppress her grin for demure procrastination at the very least. But sod Alice's magazines. 'Same time, same place, next Sunday then,' she said.

'Good,' said Saul, smiling openly. He slid his hand into the jacket pocket, felt over and under Thea's fingers and retrieved his keys. Then he pulled the zip down halfway and slipped his hand into the inner breast pocket, taking his mobile phone. He could feel Thea's breath on his wrist as he pulled the zip up. He looked at her and thought he might suddenly find himself kissing her. But he shook hands with her formally instead.

'Until next week, then,' said Saul, standing.

'Next week,' Thea confirmed, making to move off.

'By the way, where do you live?' he asked.

'Crouch End,' she replied, walking off a step or two. 'You?'

'The West End, actually,' he said, heading down the hill. 'And what do you do?'

'I'm a masseuse,' she said, over her shoulder. 'You?'

'I write.'

Saul spent Monday against a deadline for an article on the new generation iPods whilst trying not to be interrupted by engaging images of Thea. On Tuesday with no deadlines looming, Saul searched 'massage north london' on Google but was led to questionable sites he didn't dare enter for fear of jinxing his PC with a sexually transmitted computer virus. By Wednesday, Saul thought sod it, it's only a jacket and it was a freebie anyway. Thursday came and he strolled to Armani to check prices on leather jackets. Jesus, that Thea better show up with it. He filed his column for the *Observer* and accepted a commission from the *Express* magazine. Saul spent Friday daytime avoiding thinking about jackets and Thea and Primrose Hill, and wrote all day. He went out in the evening with friends and confided to one that he'd met a girl in a park who looked cold and sad and said she had a hangover so he'd lent her his Armani jacket.

'The brown leather one?'

'Yeah.'

'You twat!'

On Saturday night, Ian Ashford invited Saul to meet Karen. And Karen had invited her friend Jo to meet Ian's friend Saul. And Ian and Karen had also invited Angus and Anna so that Saul and Jo wouldn't feel it was all a bit of a set-up. And dinner had been fun and Saul reckoned that if Fate was Friend not Foe, Thea would fit in well with his circle. And

Jo was smitten and hoped Saul would phone her within the next few days.

Thea felt somewhat at a loss without Alice. Sally Stonehill was a close friend but Thea longed for Alice's take on the situation, for the dozen scenarios good, bad and downright fanciful she'd hatch. Thea was appalled at herself for daring to quietly resent Alice – or Mark rather – for their inconveniently timed honeymoon. However, Sally delighted in Thea's challenge and told her to return to Primrose Hill as arranged, but to hide behind a tree early and double-check Saul was worth handing back the gorgeous jacket. 'But if he's wearing black leather gloves – run,' said Sally seriously. 'Psycho.'

Sally's husband Richard thought Saul sounded shady, with or without black leather gloves, and told Thea not to go. Richard reckoned Thea should give the jacket to him instead and put a lonely-hearts in *Time Out* if she was that desperate.

'Or my mate Josh,' Richard suggested, 'he's still single.'

'I'm not that desperate,' Thea declined, while Sally made throwing-up faces behind Richard.

On the Tuesday, Mark's American cousin emailed Thea politely suggesting dinner when he was next over on business. Thea was still unable to conjure a memory of him but replied accidentally-on-purpose forgetting to give her phone number as requested. The next day, she went to Prospero's Books in Crouch End on the off chance that a book by a bloke called Saul might catch her eye. There appeared to be none on the shelves.

'Sally,' said Thea, 'have you heard of a writer called Saul someone?'

'Bellow?' Sally said. 'But your Saul may have a nom de plume, of course.'

'Say he's an axe-wielding homicidal maniac,' said Thea,

'and the police find bits of me all over Primrose Hill on Monday morning?'

'Well, as I said, steer clear of black leather gloves.'

'Maybe I won't go,' Thea said gloomily.

'Say he's not a book writer,' Sally mooted, because she liked the sound of Saul and his sweets, 'perhaps he's a journalist.'

'Maybe I'll go,' Thea said, non-committally.

On Thursday, Thea phoned her mother in Chippenham and suggested lunch on Sunday.

'Darling, I'm going to the Craig-Stewarts' for lunch this Sunday,' her mother said, a little baffled that her daughter was willing to drive down just for the day when Christmas was only six weeks away. Feeling slightly demoralized and in need of unequivocal advice, Thea wondered what Alice would say. She reckoned Alice herself would hide behind another tree on Primrose Hill and keep watch. If she wasn't otherwise engaged. More than engaged – fundamentally married and lying on the white sands of St Bloody Lucia.

'You're still all right to babysit Molly tomorrow?' Lynne phoned Saul on Saturday evening as he was leaving for Ian's. 'We can't take her to the Clarksons' wedding.'

Saul had forgotten. But actually, babysitting Molly was a very good idea. It was a cunning Plan B. He'd be on Primrose Hill whether or not Thea decided to turn up. 'No problem,' he told Lynne.

'We'll drop her round at yours first thing,' said Lynne gratefully.

* * *

Nothing conspired against Saul and Thea planning their trips to Primrose Hill a week to the day that they'd first met.

Neither had nightmares the night before. Both had slept well and awoken feeling fine. The weather was glorious, a degree or two warmer than the previous week and sunny too. An autumn day in winter, as precious as an Indian summer in autumn. Thea decided she'd check on Alice's flat en route to further justify her trip. At Alice's flat, she took the liberty of borrowing her friend's cashmere jumper the shade of blue-bells, leaving her own boring navy lambswool polo neck in return. She also helped herself to a spritz of Alice's Chanel perfume in case her own had faded by now. Thea checked her reflection and gave herself an approving grin. She had an inkling that this might be fun; a long-held belief in serendipity said it might be a good idea. She zipped up her jacket and folded Saul's over her arm. She held it to her face and inhaled. Then she stiffly told herself not to be so daft.

*   *   *

'Come on, Molly,' said Saul, 'best behaviour, now.'

*   *   *

Thea didn't have time to hide behind a tree. As she approached the crest of Primrose Hill, she could see Saul was already there, jacketless and grinning. She picked up her pace and walked towards him, quickly congratulating herself on how handsome he was, axe-wielding homicidal maniac or not. She saw he was gloveless and at that point she smiled and waved. However, when he waved back, it appeared he was carrying a belt in his hand. She was just about to read great tomes into this, wondering what definition Sally would give belt-brandishing, when Molly appeared. Hurtling. Yapping. Running tight rings around Thea. Thea screamed.

'Molly!' Saul half-laughed, half-shouted, loping down the

hill towards them. 'Get down, your paws are all muddy and Thea – And Thea. And Thea – is crying.'

'Get the dog away!' she sobbed. 'Get it *away*.'

Saul was not used to being torn between the needs of two women. But there was no way that, just then, on Primrose Hill, he could relinquish either. All he could do was call out both their names, imploring Molly to come and Thea to stay. He wanted Molly to be still and Thea not to bolt. What would Barbara Woodhouse have said? Heel? Down? Crazy hound? Paul bloody McKenna would be better.

'Molly!' Saul hollered. 'Heel! Come! Down! Stay! Sit, you crazy hound!' To Molly this was double Dutch, to the bona-fide dog owners within earshot, this was comedy. Molly was now careering around at speed, zipping through people's legs, barking joyously and returning to yap and skittle and leap at Thea who stood stock still, her fists squeezed together and clasped under her chin.

'She's not mine,' Saul shouted as if that made the situation better. Molly was now transfixed by the backside of a King Charles Spaniel some way off and Saul crept over to capture her.

By the time Molly was safely on her lead, Saul could but watch Thea hurry out of the park. Beyond earshot. With his jacket.

'That'll teach me to talk to strangers,' Saul told Molly. 'I should know to steer clear of hysterical types who drink.' He decided to think of her no more. Nice jacket, though. That was a shame.

Barefaced Bloke and the Girl with the Scar

Thea went to Alice's flat to prepare it for the newly-weds' imminent return from their fortnight in Caribbean paradise. She took flowers, fresh milk and bread, opened windows, bleached the toilet, changed the linen and stacked the mail. Then she lit a scented candle and sat down with the *Observer* and a Starbucks cappuccino. It was nice to have a Sunday when she felt healthy and clear-headed, with no plans and no need of Primrose Hill. And it was comforting to think of Alice winging her way back. There was something relaxing about reading the papers in someone else's home, no distractions of chores that ought to be done or calls that should be made or fridges that needed restocking or tax returns lurking on the table.

The *Observer* on a Sunday was an institution; familiar, entertaining, non-taxing and sometimes vaguely irritating, like an old friend with whom Thea conversed once a week. She read it in a very particular order; main paper first, 'Review' second, then 'Escape'. 'Sport', 'Business' and 'Cash' were never read but not wasted, kept instead under the kitchen sink to absorb the slow drip from the washing-machine hose. This week, an interview with David Bowie in the bonus 'Music Monthly' magazine was particularly absorbing, rekindling memories of the shrine she and Alice had built in honour of Mr Bowie during their teenage years. Thea pulled out the article and placed it on top of Alice's post. The 'OM' magazine was Thea's favourite component, savoured last. The voices within the pages were as familiar to her as those on Radio 4. A restaurant close to where she worked was reviewed favourably so she tore that page out and folded it into her Filofax. The cartoon made her laugh out loud, so she ripped that out too and stuck it to Alice's fridge. Sage advice from Barefoot Doctor made her think. Mariella Frostrup made her murmur in agreement. But Barefaced Bloke's opening line made her swear out loud.

It was meant to be my Sir Walter Ralegh moment.

'Oh good God!'

Instead, it turned into a Dog Day Afternoon.

Barefaced Bloke was Saul. Saul Mundy. It said so in black and white. And a black-and-white photo confirmed it.

This week I give you the sorry tale of the Barefaced Bloke, the Gorgeous Thief, a Terrorizing Terrier and My Armani Jacket.

'He thinks I'm a thief!'

Well, you are, Thea. But he also says you're gorgeous.

I'm through with good deeds. I'm done with dog-sitting. I'll bet Sir Walter's jacket wasn't Armani.

'Sally,' Thea whispered down the phone, having speed-read the article, 'look at the *Observer* mag – and tell Richard I need that jacket back.'

At the time of writing, I can't tell you which way the tide will turn. Will Barefaced Bloke turn into Soft Git and clamber up Primrose Hill for the third Sunday running, hopeful but chilly? Or has Barefaced Bloke turned into Sod It Saul and stayed warm indoors with his X Box not giving a 4X?

'Saul Mundy is a *spunk*!' Sally declared. 'I *love* his column

– and he doesn't look half bad either. Saul Bloody Mundy – can you believe it? Aren't you the lucky one!'

'I don't know whether to feel flattered or used,' Thea said sanctimoniously, 'and I'm not sure what to do.'

'Tell her I'm keeping the bloody jacket,' Thea could hear Richard in the background.

'Oh shut up!' Sally derided to both Thea and her husband.

Thea was actually fizzing with excitement but it seemed both arrogant and fate-tempting to admit it to herself, let alone Sally Stonehill, so she maintained her contrived ambivalence.

'Yes, but—' Thea attempted.

'Gracious Good Lord, girl, you're being flirted with through the pages of a national newspaper. It's possibly the most romantic thing I've ever heard of!' Sally said impatiently. 'Away with you to Primrose Hill! It seems to me his balls are in your court.'

Thea paced Alice's flat, then she sat down and reread the article.

I hope she likes the jacket. She looked far better in it than I ever did anyway.

Was he making a pass or taking the piss? Should she read between the lines or disbelieve what she read? Alice hurry home!

Ultimately, what could the Gorgeous Thief do but tramp up Primrose Hill for the third Sunday in a row?

He wasn't there.

What could she have been thinking?

Of course he wasn't there.

'I made good copy, that's all,' Thea said with reluctant resignation, having loitered for half an hour. Overhead, a scruff of crows littered the sky, like flits of charcoal coughed up by a bonfire. Thea found herself wondering if the crows were somehow goading the birds caged in the London Zoo aviary, just down the hill and over the road. Perhaps she'd take herself off to the zoo right now. She hadn't been for years. And it wouldn't make her afternoon seem so wasted. Did people go to the zoo alone? she wondered. Were you let in if you didn't have a child in tow?

'Where's my sodding jacket, you gorgeous thief?' a voice behind her halted her meanderings.

Thea did not turn to face him. 'My friend's husband has now nicked it,' she replied, her eyes tracing the rise and fall of the aviary.

'Sod my Sir Walter Ralegh Moment,' said Saul, now pressing up close, enfolding his arms around her waist, 'and sod my image – I'm going for full-blown Mills & Boon.' And with that Saul turned Thea to face him, cupped her head in his hands and kissed her.

* * *

'Champagne, madam?' the stewardess asked Alice who was pressing all the buttons on her vast First Class seat whilst rummaging in its capacious pockets too.

'Absolutely!' said Alice. 'And can you pop my name down for the massage?'

'Certainly – would you like a massage too, sir?'

'No, thanks very much, but no,' Mark declined.

'Champagne?' he was offered.

'Thanks – but no.'

'Paper?'

'Yes,' said Mark, '*Sunday Telegraph*, please.'

'Madam?'

'*Observer*, thanks,' said Alice. '*Tory-graph*!' she teased Mark.

'Limp lefty!' he sparred back. Without having to be asked, he handed over his luxury complimentary travel pack for his wife to rifle through. By the time Alice had reached Saul's article, laughing aloud a couple of times, 38,000 feet below, the author of it was scrutinizing her best friend's scars.

* * *

'Fifty-four stitches,' Thea told him, 'from a weedy little terrier. The bizarre thing is, at the time, I was far more distressed that the dog was destroyed.'

Thea Luckmore had never before jumped into bed on a first date, let alone slept with a relative stranger. Moreover, she had hitherto guarded her scars as fiercely as her perceived chastity. Yet here she was, naked and post-coitally languid above the covers on Saul Mundy's bed, feeling more than fine while he traced the snaking line of scar that scored her waist and the top of her right thigh. He found the site and sight of her injury disturbing but intriguing. The scar was like a single line of pale pink silk braid laid in a particular route. It was obvious where the dog's jaws had clamped, where the teeth had punctured her, where her flesh had been ripped away and the flap carefully sewn back down. It was almost a cartoon scar, so perfect was the impression of the bite.

'I was twelve years old,' Thea continued, 'and it was Alice's dog. Tiddler. I've been petrified of terriers ever since.'

Saul rolled over and dipped his face down to her stomach. 'I'm not surprised,' he murmured, dipping his nose into her navel.

'I'm not too bad with Rottweilers, oddly enough,' Thea added while Saul let his lips touch her lightly, so gently that when she closed her eyes she couldn't tell if he was kissing scar or skin. 'Big dogs tend to lollop, little terriers just go berserk.'

'Your scar suits you,' he said. 'It tells a story – vulnerability behind the feistiness. If that doesn't sound too corny.'

'Corny?' Thea smiled. 'Anyone would think you were trying to get into my knickers. Again.'

'Horny,' Saul confessed, 'again. And anyway, where *are* your knickers?' he asked, glancing up at her from stroking her bush before returning his gaze and snuffling his nose down.

'I think you flung them off somewhere in your living room,' Thea giggled, but Saul was now too preoccupied to reply. He needed his tongue and his lips to explore Thea's sex. And Thea was now rendered speechless by the pleasure of it all. Their easy chatter gave way to gasps and moans and the seductive sound of her own wetness against Saul's mouth. She ran her fingers through Saul's hair, bending her knees up, shifting her hips and tilting her pelvis, rocking and undulating herself against his face. Instinctively, he let her dictate the pace and he didn't change what he was doing. His lips brushed her, his nose nudged her, his tongue flicked over and inside her. She looked down at him and he looked up at her briefly before closing his eyes to focus better. From previous experience, Thea had presumed cunnilingus merely to be a man's way to expedite lubrication and permit swifter entry. But Saul seemed to be enjoying himself very much if his appreciative hums were anything to go by. Thea eased his head away from her crotch to kiss and suck his face. They rolled and romped over his bed, his straining cock pressing hopefully, pressingly, against her. She pushed him onto his back, slithered on top of him, her sex just tantalizingly beyond the reach of his penis, her nipples a few inches away from his desperate mouth. She licked her own lips, then darted her tongue along his.

'For Christ's sake, fuck me,' Saul whispered.

'Condom,' Thea whispered, hoping he had another.

It occurred to both of them that it wasn't even yet evening. It was Sunday teatime. How decadent. It meant they could do this all night. Quietly, it occurred to both Saul and Thea that, actually, they could indeed do this as long as they liked. They had no commitments, after all. Not that evening. Nor the next. Not to anyone – nor had either for some time. It was all above board, with no complications. Out of the blue, from a chance daft meeting on Primrose Hill, the saga of a lent leather jacket, the fiasco with a lent harmless terrier, Saul Mundy and Thea Luckmore found each other.

Mr and Mrs Sinclair

'Bye-bye, Mr Sinclair,' said Alice over a cup of strong coffee, struggling to counteract the light-headed nausea that a night of jet-lagged semi-sleep had caused, 'hurry home to me, won't you?'

'Of course, darling,' said Mark, kissing the top of her head, grabbing a slice of toast, his jacket and his briefcase. 'I'm horrendously late, I really must go.'

'Don't!' Alice implored plaintively. 'Please bunk off! Go on, I dare you. Phone in sick or something. Please stay. I don't want you to go. You could work from home! I've had you all to myself for a fortnight – I don't want to be alone.'

Mark smiled at his wife, gazing at him all wide-eyed and winsome despite the bags around her eyes and her hair all mussed up. 'Why don't you go in yourself?' he asked.

'Because I don't have to!' Alice remonstrated. 'I'm not due in until tomorrow. Anyway, John Lewis are coming with all our wedding-list goodies.'

'Give Thea a call,' Mark suggested.

'Already have – it's her day off but she doesn't seem to be at home,' Alice said with contrived petulance.

'Why not go and register with some estate agents?' Mark

kissed the top of her head again. 'I must go.'

'Will you phone me?' Alice pleaded. 'Don't you miss me already?'

'Alice,' said Mark, happily exasperated, 'have a shower, get dressed, go to Sainsbury's, track down Thea, sign your flat up for sale with Benham and Reeves and put our wish-list out to all agents covering NW3 and N6. Three bed-rooms, garden, no galley kitchens or PVC windows.' He blew her a kiss and left. He floated down the escalator at Belsize Park and grinned intermittently while the Northern Line took him and a packed carriage of scowling commuters to Moorgate. How nice to have a wife, a beautiful wife, who clung to his shirt-tails begging him to play hooky from work to stay with her. Alice Heggarty had married him, was sending him to work with a kiss and would be waiting for him to come home later – could life be much sweeter? Mark arrived at the office, answered his PA's misty-eyed questions about his wedding and honeymoon, checked his diary, noted there were 288 emails in his in-box, rescheduled the lunch that was booked, set up two meetings for before lunch and three for the afternoon and called his team to the board-room for an update. His PA made a note to buy him sand-wiches because she knew he'd be too busy to remember to eat otherwise.

Alice did as she was told. She had a shower, dressed, went to the supermarket and phoned estate agents. She also con-tinued to call Thea but her mobile phone was off and there was still no answer at her home. It had been warm and wel-coming to return to a sweetly scented apartment, fresh linen and neat piles of post, a fridge stocked with necessities, and Alice now longed to see Thea, to thank her at the very least. She was also tiring of her own company. Alice had never been a disciple of the cult of Me-Time though the magazines she published frequently extolled it as a necessary indulgence. Alice functioned best in company, an audience even. Peace, quiet and solitude were overrated, in Alice's book. If one had time on one's hands, why not spend it wisely in company – the return was far greater than silent navel-gazing home alone. If Thea still wasn't in, maybe she would go into work for the afternoon. She dialled Thea's mobile again.

'Hullo?'

'Thea! Where the fuck have you been – I've been trying you for ages! I'm back!'

'Alice! Alice! Oh my God, how *are* you? How's Mark? I've missed you! Did you get upgraded again?'

'First Class – but I'm still jet lagged which I think is outrageous. Wait till you see my tan. Amazing place – you must go. God, I have so much to tell you – shall I come over right now?'

'Um.'

'Thea?'

'I'm – a bit, busy.'

'When, then?'

'Um.'

'Hang on – doing *what*? Busy doing what? You usually chill out on your day off – you and your me-time. Well, have your me-time with me! It feels like ages since I saw you – I'm an old married woman! Wait till you hear about First Class!'

'Er . . .'

'Is it your tax return? Fuck it – it can wait! I can't!'

'Alice—'

'What's that?'

'What?'

'*That*! In the background. I can hear someone – is there someone there? There *is* someone there. I can hear a *bloke*?'

'Er . . .'

'Thea! Thea! Tell me, you cow! Why am I whispering? I can hear a man! Can I? Can I hear a man in your flat?'

'I'm not in my flat.'

'Where are you? Are you in a bloke's flat? Thea!'

'Yes. Yes, I am.'

'Who, tell me, *who*!'

'Saul.'

'Who the hell is Saul! Oh my God, who the *fuck* is Saul!'

'My boyfriend.'

'Your *boy*friend? You don't *have* a boyfriend! Who the hell is Saul? You're meant to be seeing Mark's American cousin. You're going to marry him and then we can be related sort of. I've been planning so all honeymoon. You don't *have* a boyfriend. Thea! Since when?'

'Since yesterday.'

'Stop giggling! What are you talking about, woman? I don't understand. What do you mean *since yesterday*? A boyfriend called Saul? I *have* to see you!'

'I'll come to you later, Alice. In a couple of hours, say.'

'A couple of *hours*? I can't wait that long!'

'You'll have to. I haven't even got out of bed, let alone showered.'

'Thea, for Christ's sake! Promise you'll be here in a couple of hours then? No more than three, tops. I can't wait. I can't wait! Saul? I don't know a Saul! And up until my wedding, neither did *you*.'

Alice had wisely anticipated that returning home from honeymoon would be a comedown, that jet lag would drag her down lower, that her wedding day would seem a dream ago. However, apart from the January magazines already replacing the Christmas issues though it was still December, she hadn't expected any other changes. In fact, sitting with a cup of tea, waiting for Thea to help her unpack the wedding gifts towering in John Lewis boxes around her, Alice admitted that she had been depending on everything being exactly as she'd left it a fortnight before. She had wanted her world to wait and to long for her return, to crave photos and Technicolor detail of her interlude in St Lucia. She hadn't expected the world to stop turning but she had hoped it might revolve around her for a little while longer. She was, after all, still the blushing bride, the newly-wed, just married, just home from honeymoon; she had hoped to enjoy the status for at least a few more days yet.

Alice couldn't work out how Thea had gone off and found a boyfriend when she hadn't even been looking for one in the first place. How could this have happened when she hadn't been around to advise her? Thea Luckmore had never been one for the thrill of strangers. So who on earth was this Saul person?

'How did she manage to do it without me?' Alice wondered aloud and then listened to how awful that sounded. 'Not that I'm her chaperone,' she murmured quickly, unpacking some boxes from John Lewis and wondering if it would be all right to do thank-you notes on the computer, 'it's just I've always known everything about her. I've known when she's feeling lonely, lovelorn, playful, horny or shy. And I've always been aware of names and dates. Because she always, *always* consults me for a plan of action.' Alice unwrapped a bulky item and then cursed friends of her parents for deviating from the wedding list in favour of an unnecessarily patterned soup tureen of staggering dimensions. 'My generation don't do soup tureens – our soup comes fresh in a carton from Marks & Sparks.' She knew she sounded spoilt and ungrateful so she blamed jet lag and post-honeymoon blues and wrote a gushing thank-you note straight away proclaiming soup making to be one of Mark's favourite pastimes.

'Thea's always methodically talked through potential

entanglements with me first. That was half the fun – analysing it all and digging for signs and significance,' Alice muttered whilst wondering why she had chosen cream Egyptian cotton towels when between Mark and herself, they already owned more than a full complement of towels and linen. She felt just a little like a fraud, as if she was playing at being a grown-up, dressing up in her mother's lifestyle. Soup tureens and Royal Doulton crockery. Why had she ordered 'best china' when she and Mark tended to turn to Marks & Spencer ready-meals during the week? She felt a little embarrassed, she worried that she sounded horribly materialistic even to herself. There's more to marriage than wedding gifts. Where would all this stuff go? She made a mental note that ample storage should be a prerequisite on their house-hunting wish-list. 'I do love my flat,' Alice sighed, 'but Mark is right, it is time for us both to move and set up a new home together. How weird that quality plumbing and storage space should suddenly be my priority. But then, I'm not a single girl in my twenties gadding about any more.' She laughed out loud at how ludicrous she sounded. 'What am I like – I've only been married for two weeks and I've been thirty-one for just ten days!'

Alice hung on Thea's every word. They sat together on the floor, drinking tea, eating double-chocolate muffins, admiring the gifts and fidgeting with the polystyrene packing nuggets. Alice lapped up all the details Thea gave. They marvelled that there was no need for Thea to embellish the facts, to take liberties with details or overdo adjectives.

'It's like a film!' Alice declared. 'I can practically hear a Morcheeba and Jimi Hendrix soundtrack. Someone like Anna Friel playing you.'

'I swear to God,' Thea shrugged, 'it is exactly as I'm telling you.'

'And he *licked* your scar?' Alice whispered. 'You actually *let* him?'

Thea nodded. 'It even turned me on.'

'Jesus, I must meet him. Saul Mundy,' said Alice, 'his name *does* ring a bell – in the industry. And of course I know his column from the *Observer*. But tell me again about the sex – that thing with his tongue and finger.'

'Thumb,' Thea corrected.

'I think I might drop a hint or two to Mark,' Alice planned.

'Is married sex a bore and chore already?' Thea teased. 'Is it all "Mr Sinclair, prithee do attend to my heaving bosom"? Is it missionary with lights out? And "That was most satisfactory, dear husband but now please away to your own chamber"? Conjugal obligations?'

Alice laughed. 'For your information, married sex is lovely,' she declared a little defensively, 'it's warm and considerate and we synchronize our climax. Mark's a very attentive lover. True, it's without that element of wild abandon you're describing.'

'Yes, but I'm in the throes of the first flush, remember,' Thea defined wisely.

'I know,' Alice replied softly, 'but Mark and I go back so long that there's never been a first flush. No fireworks, just a gorgeous glow. It's different with Mark,' Alice said with a contented shrug, 'it's what I want – passion was a health hazard for me. I prefer it this way – sex with Mark makes me feel cosy, rather than racked with insecurity.'

'Yet here's me,' Thea said, 'a stickler for old-fashioned romance and the sanctity of monogamy – now jumping into and onto and half-on half-off the bed on a first date and shagging in all manner of contortions for twenty-four hours non-stop.'

'Good for you!' Alice laughed. 'I can't wait to meet him. I mean – you really think this'll be a goer? More than a fling?'

'Alice Heggarty,' Thea chastised, 'when have I *ever* had a fling – let alone a one-night stand? When have I ever even snogged – never mind slept with – a man who I haven't felt an emotional pull towards?'

'You're right in that respect,' said Alice, 'but wrong in another – it's Alice *Sinclair*, remember.'

'*Mrs* Sinclair,' Thea practised.

'Miss Luckmore,' Alice cautioned, 'you must admit it does all seem pretty fast. And with a perfect stranger.'

'There's the rub,' said Thea, 'he *was* a stranger – but already he has the potential to be perfect. He's not strange in the slightest. The real beauty of it is that it all appears to be so uncomplicated. We're both single, we're a similar age, our worlds appear to be complementary – I'm surprised our paths haven't crossed before. We just happened to meet in the open air unexpectedly.'

'So it's headlong into the whole boyfriend–girlfriend thing? You don't fancy an exploratory period of *I-won't-call-him-for-four-days*? You're not going to phone me to fret about bollocks like your bum looking big in this or that? You don't feel the need for us to *workshop* a long list of what-ifs and what-do-you-thinks?'

'Nope,' said Thea, 'as Saul said to me this morning, "I could do that thing of not calling you for a few days to keep you keen, but then I'd be denying myself the pleasure of you in the interim and where's the sense in that?" So, he's asked me to go to his place straight after work tomorrow and I'll be there. Funny how you can feel you know someone off by heart before I've even committed his mobile phone number to memory.'

'Thea *Mundy*,' Alice mused, 'it has a certain ring to it!'

'Fuck off!' Thea laughed, giving her friend a gentle shove. They chuckled and sighed and contemplated the ugly soup tureen. 'Do you remember how we'd do that?' Thea said.

'Tag a boy's surname to our names before we'd even managed to kiss them?'

'*You* did,' Alice corrected, 'you always did a lot of thinking and planning prior to kissing. In fact, sometimes you'd conclude against kissing altogether. If the surname didn't scan satisfactorily. I just went for the snog and then despaired afterwards at the ghastly phonetics of Alice Sissons or Alice Hillace.'

'Jesus,' Thea covered her face with her hands, 'Ben Sissons – he was the one with the bleached quiff!'

'He used his mum's Jolene facial bleach to achieve it,' Alice said, 'rather enterprising, really. Until the hairs started snapping off.'

'And Richard Hillace,' Thea reminisced, 'I quite fancied him myself, actually.'

'I know you did,' said Alice, 'and you could have had him later, but you were so irritatingly principled about my offer of hand-me-downs.'

'Funny to think out of all of them, Good Old Mark Sinclair was the one to ultimately land you,' said Thea, trying to fathom the use of a peculiar-looking kitchen tool.

'*Land* me,' mused Alice, taking the utensil from Thea. 'It's a mandolin – Mark chose it, he knows how it works. *Land me* – yes, I do feel grounded at last.'

'I like to think of hearts breaking amongst all those ex-beaux of yours,' Thea smiled, stroking the towel pile. '*Mark Sinclair*? they are probably weeping, *lucky lucky bastard*.'

'Oh, Thea,' Alice said, throwing a handful of polystyrene squiggles into the air, 'let's promise that marriage and Mark, passion and Saul won't come between us!'

'You daft cow,' said Thea, throwing up the packaging as if it was confetti, 'how could anything, ever, come between *us*?'

'Christ help us,' Alice murmured, having just unwrapped

an odd-shaped item, 'it's a gravy boat and it matches the soup tureen.'

Under duress from his fiancée, Ian Ashford phoned Saul for the umpteenth time that day. Finally, the mobile phone had been switched on.

'Saul! Ian.'

'Ian! How's it going?'

'Er, listen mate, Karen's been on to me suggesting we all go out one evening.'

'Cool. Love to. When?'

'This week perhaps? Friday maybe?'

'Yes, looks fine to me.'

'And Jo. We'll bring Jo, shall we? She loved meeting you.'

'The thing is – I mean, please tell Karen I thought Jo was a great girl – hot too – but I actually have a girlfriend now. Thea.'

'Sorry?'

'Jo – great girl. But Thea – greatest yet.'

'You have a *girl*friend? Since when?'

'Since Sunday.'

'It's Monday.'

'And you can see for yourself on Friday then. You'll love her.'

'Hullo, Mrs Sinclair,' Mark phoned Alice.

'Hullo, husband,' Alice replied, glancing at the clock and marvelling how writing thank-yous could make the time fly, 'where are you?'

'Office,' Mark apologized. 'I'm almost finished – I promise. Another hour. Home by nine. I'm knackered.'

Alice quickly advised herself to be neither disappointed nor pissed off. Remember the jet lag. Remember post-wedding blues. 'Soup for supper?' Alice suggested, half wondering whether to decant a carton into the tureen.

Alice felt a little flat. Her place was a mess and the piles of presents suddenly irritated her. She longed for St Lucia. She tried to phone Thea but the line was busy. Alice didn't doubt that she was talking to Saul. They'd probably been chatting for ages and she reckoned they would be for some time yet. Telling each other about their lives, loves and quirks. They'd be laughing and marvelling and nattering nineteen to the dozen. Ah, the joys and the intricacy of the human mating dance. The thought made Alice feel warm. And just a little lonely.

Mundy, Luckmore & Co.

Saul soon gained everyone's seal of approval. Sally Stonehill considered various adjectives before deciding on 'dashing' to best describe him. Richard Stonehill liked him enough to return the Armani jacket and Saul liked Richard enough to consider telling him to keep it. Instead, he bought him a pint over which they discovered they both played squash. They arranged a game and their standards were so level that it soon became a weekly fixture with the obligatory post-match praise and pints which they enjoyed just as much as time on court.

Mark Sinclair didn't play squash but he was happy to guide Saul on playing the stock market. Mark was more than flattered when Saul asked to interview him for *GQ* magazine, an article entitled 'Barrow Boys and Bowler Hats: Who Stocks the Stock Market' and they had a jocular but productive lunch on expenses. The other therapists Thea worked alongside at the Being Well welcomed Saul's impromptu visits. He usually came bearing gifts: fresh juice and brownies, a poinsettia for reception, magazines for the waiting room, a smile to Thea's face. He also made it his business to recommend the clinic to friends and colleagues moaning about bad backs, tiredness and stress.

Alice had rehearsed an acerbic soliloquy starting 'Let me tell you about Thea' and ending 'so, hurt her and I'll kill you'. However, she was actually pleasantly surprised that she took to Saul, though it meant her soliloquy remained unperformed. She decided not to be suspicious of his good looks and she detected no cockiness in the fact that he was naturally outgoing. She respected him for sparring back when she tried to provoke him. She liked it that they could talk about their industry. Most importantly, he appeared very taken with Thea. How fortunate that her best friend's boyfriend had the potential to become a friend in his own right too.

Thea was instantly liked by all to whom Saul introduced her. Karen Soon-to-be-Ashford had to concede to Jo that Thea was great and would fit right into one of their girls' nights out. Even Lynne took to her, despite having to keep Molly shut in the downstairs toilet for the duration of her visit. Lynne's husband was so impressed with a five-minute speed treatment Thea gave his interminably stiff shoulder that he booked an appointment, then another and also gladly took Thea's advice to see Souki the acupuncturist. Staff and patrons at the Swallow gave her a warm nod of acceptance. Marco from the Deli slipped her a complimentary muffin and slid Saul a knowing wink underscored by appreciative insinuations in throaty Italian. Dave the paper man soon called out to her by name whether or not she was buying an *Evening Standard*. None of them resented Saul taking his custom to Crouch End for half the week. It evened out anyway, because Thea invariably accompanied him when he returned home.

Thea surprised herself at holding her own amongst Saul's editors and fellow writers at dos down in Soho, even calling the bluff of one cocky columnist who asked her if she gave 'extras' with her massage. 'Of course I do. But I don't *give* them,' said Thea most levelly, 'they cost.' He was just about to lick his lips and ask for a price list when those standing near roared with laughter and called him a dickhead. Alice was at that party. Neither married life for her, nor new relationship fervour for Thea, had imposed any constriction on their friendship. Alice decided it was serendipitous that Thea had met someone whose path crossed naturally with her own. And with Mark travelling so regularly it seemed daft not to attend events when Thea and Saul would be there too. What would she do otherwise? Work late? Sit at home showing people around her flat? Simultaneously, Alice's world became smaller and Thea's broadened.

* * *

'Saul,' Alice phoned Saul out of the blue, 'can I tickle your fancy?'

'That's a rather tempting offer on a grim February morning,' Saul laughed.

'Let me buy you lunch and whet your appetite,' Alice continued, her desk diary open, red pen to hand, prepared to rearrange anything already booked.

'Wednesday?' Saul suggested.

'Perfect,' said Alice.

'It's a date,' said Saul, tapping the details into a Palm Pilot.

'Top secret,' said Alice.

'You can trust me,' said Saul.

Quentin

'No one knows about Quentin,' Alice told Saul over a covert sushi lunch near Liverpool Street. She lit a cigarette and replenished her green tea, aware that puffing one and sipping the other was vaguely contradictory.

'I thought you only ever smoked at parties,' Saul remarked.

'And over clandestine lunches about top-secret things,' Alice said, her eyes glinting. 'Don't tell Mark. He hates cigarettes.'

Saul pulled an imaginary zip across his lips. 'OK, Mrs Sinclair,' he said, 'tell me about Quentin and where I come in?'

'Heggarty today,' said Alice, 'I've kept Heggarty for half my life. And Quentin, well, Quentin is my baby.'

Saul popped slippery edamame beans out of their salty pods. 'Quentin,' he mused.

'Code-name: Project Quentin,' she whispered, adding hastily, 'you know – after Tarantino, rather than Crisp.'

'So, we're talking a men's mag, hetero rather than homo,' Saul surmised. He split his wooden chopsticks and rubbed the one against the other to smooth any shards.

'Yes,' said Alice, 'we all know the market for men's mags

is huge. We're not going for anything ground breaking. The main focus is absolutely no compromise on quality. From clothes to cars, columnists to celebrities – quality.'

'Quality?' Saul remarked. 'Sounds pretty ground breaking to me when you think of the tat that makes up most lads' mags. Talking of tat, where do you stand on tits?'

'Again,' shrugged Alice, 'quality breasts. But not on the cover. We're pitching at a slightly older market – ABC1 men, thirty to fifty. Not too blokey, but not too staid, of course. Men like you. The covers will be icons, not babes. Someone has practically guaranteed us Clint Eastwood for the first issue if we get the go-ahead.'

Saul raised an eyebrow. 'Pierce Brosnan had acupuncture with Souki at the Being Well when he was in town.'

Alice raised her green tea. 'Pierce can have issue two, then.'

'And David Bowie's mum and my mum were at school together,' Saul said.

'David Bowie?' Alice had to swallow a squeal. 'Has Thea told you how complete our teenage love was for David darling Bowie?'

'Yes,' Saul confirmed with an overly compassionate expression and a tone of utter pity, 'I know all about sending red roses to his dressing room at Wembley; that you both promptly fainted when the show began and spent the entire concert sipping tea with the St John's Ambulance crew.'

'And the mural,' Alice laughed, 'did Thea not tell you about our mural?'

'No,' Saul said patiently, 'though she told me you both saved all your pocket money to buy one pair of blue contact lenses to share between you so you could both have Bowie eyes.' He poked the tip of his chopstick into the lurid green wasabe. The horseradish shot tears into his eyes and fizzed heat through the bridge of his nose. Fantastic.

'We did this incredible mural on my bedroom wall – based

82

on the "Scary Monsters" LP cover,' Alice reminisced. 'My mum went berserk. Mind you, we hadn't even been able to smuggle in the paint pots past Thea's mum at her house. Anyway, if we had Bowie as cover for issue three, I'd be happy to sweep floors for the rest of my career. But I digress. Project Quentin is our big secret – and potentially the company's biggest launch to date.'

'What's the timescale?' Saul asked.

Alice cleared her throat. 'Dummy in six weeks, then into research, and if we get the green light, first issue will be June out May.'

Saul calculated dates and weeks in his head. 'Who else knows?' he asked. 'Nat Mags? IPC? Because I know that EMAP are developing too, at the moment.'

'Will you tell me?' Alice asked with a coquettish pout and a beguiling wriggle in her chair. 'Tell me about silly old EMAP? I promise I won't tell a soul. I swear on David Bowie's life. Trust me?'

'Absolutely not!' Saul laughed, inadvertently shaking a piece of sashimi at her. 'Like I said – if I'm given a secret, I keep it. No matter how absolute your love for Bowie is. Suffice it to say, I'm not involved.'

Alice contrived to look sulky and offended but her enthusiasm for her project soon overtook. 'Initially, I was hoping you'd work on the dummy with us, Saul,' she said, still in a whisper, 'basically oversee editorial – it would mean committing three days a week for the next month or so. Take the dummy into research, then head up the launch issue if we get the go-ahead. With, of course, absolutely no guarantee of a staff position at the end.'

Saul laughed. 'I know the score,' he said, 'and I'd love to be involved.'

'Fan-bloody-tastic,' Alice beamed.

'Alice, you haven't eaten a thing,' Saul observed.

'I can't eat when I'm excited,' Alice declared. 'Great for weight loss, though.'

Saul thought aren't girls silly sometimes.

Apart from Thea, of course. Saul didn't think her silly at all. Her fear of dogs was understandable, her propensity for weeping during *ER* or re-runs of *Cold Feet* he found quite endearing, her belief in drinking only juice until noon each day he thought eccentric. But he didn't think her silly.

'She's not a calorie-counting, chardonnay-swilling, Mui-Mui obsessive,' he quantified to Ian Ashford over a pile of poppadams and a mound of chutney, 'but then neither is she a drink-your-own-pee, salute-the-sun and wear-hessian-to-Pilates type either.'

'Does she do Pilates?' Ian asked.

'Yes, with her mates Sally and Alice,' said Saul, 'and she has a gorgeous figure because of it. But my point is she may drink only juice until lunchtime but she's also partial to a Marlboro Light with her vodka-tonics after dark. She makes soup with organic produce – but her preferred lunch is Pret a Manger egg mayo sandwiches and a Coca-Cola.'

'What's with the juice-till-noon thing?' Ian asked, wondering whether it might be a good regime for his acid and thinking that the madras he ordered probably wasn't.

'She simply doesn't have an appetite until then,' Saul explained. 'I bought her a juicer for Christmas because she was spending a fortune on smoothies.'

'What you're talking about is balance,' Ian said, spooning pilau rice onto his plate.

'I am,' said Saul, 'a girl who balances M&S socks and a top she's had for ever with an Anya Hindmarsh handbag. Do you know how much those bags cost? But balance, yes – she connects with the yin and yang and whole shebang of meridians and energy flow and shiatsu stuff – but her

84

CD collection is more the White Stripes than whale music.'

'She's at ease with herself,' Ian defined, passing the dhal to Saul.

'It's one of the most attractive things about her,' Saul nodded, passing the Bombay aloo to Ian.

'Does she keep *Men are from Mars and Women are from Venus* under her bed?' Ian asked suspiciously.

'No,' Saul laughed, '*Heat* magazine.'

'So what's she like in the sack?' Ian posed, working his fork dexterously through the curry and rice like a bricklayer trowelling cement.

'She's great,' said Saul evenly, 'for all the same reasons – sometimes it's deep and meaningful lovemaking. Other times it's fast and furious shagging. She doesn't pester me to whisper sweet nothings but she writhes when I talk dirty. She doesn't sulk to the other end of the bed if all I want to do post-coitally is roll over and snore, and I'm just as likely to wake up to a blow-job as to Radio 4.'

'Sounds like you've hit the jackpot, mate,' said Ian. 'I'd suggest you snap her up and put your name on her, quick.'

'You know how with some women you end up playing along with them just for peace and quiet,' Saul mused, 'and you find yourself apologizing for the bits that make us blokes?' Ian nodded with the weight of someone most familiar with such a syndrome. 'You know how some women fulfil one part of our criteria but are so sorely lacking in other aspects?' Saul continued. 'Beautiful but boring? Interesting but just not sexy? Horny as hell but dumb as fuck? Well, it seems incredibly simple, but I like all of her a lot.'

'To Thea,' said Ian, raising his bottle of Kingfisher beer and telling himself he really did not need that last rip of nan bread. He'd do juice until noon the next day, he decided.

'I wasn't looking,' Saul mused wistfully, 'I was just on Primrose Hill and she came into view.'

'Good luck,' said Ian, presuming the evening to be subliminal payback for the time he'd droned on about Karen.

'It is,' Saul agreed, 'it is very good luck.'

'So that's it then?' Ian said slyly. 'Temptation can lead you by the balls and you'll resist?'

'Thea inspires fidelity.' Saul paused. 'In my heart and mind, at least!'

Ian and Saul looked at each other for a moment and then chuckled into the last of their curry.

'Not on a full stomach – surely not!' Ian said.

* * *

'Your wife's footing the tab,' Saul laughed, taking Mark to a restaurant that still believed in starched linen at lunchtime. 'How was Hong Kong?'

'Knackering,' Mark said quietly, 'but essential. Hong Kong is crazy – but the business is a dream for us at the moment. Tokyo next week.'

'I guess the bonus will be your bonus?' Saul said.

Mark tipped his head and chinked glasses with Saul. 'I need to keep my wife in Jimmy Shoes.'

Saul wasn't sure whether to correct Mark. He let it go. 'You get what you pay for!' he said lightly instead.

'Actually, Alice is brilliant at blagging,' Mark confessed. 'I always offer to buy stuff but she always declines and says she can call in favours at work. I think she gets more of a thrill from getting a bargain or freebie than from the item itself. Have you seen those monstrous rocks in her ears?'

'The diamonds?' Saul said. 'You can't really fail to notice them.'

'Three carats?' Mark suggested. Saul shrugged. He had never bought a diamond. 'QVC,' Mark said triumphantly.

'Is that the sparkle factor or the colour clarity?' Saul asked, trying to sound like someone who'd bought diamonds.

Mark roared with laughter. 'QVC – the shopping channel! Alice is forever buying stuff from QVC. Those earrings were £29.95 – and she got a hideous suedette presentation box for being one of the first hundred callers.'

'Are the Jimmy *Choos* fake too?' Saul said subtly.

'Unfortunately not,' Mark groaned, 'they're bona-fide Jimmy Shoes shoes.'

'I suppose it evens out,' Saul said lightly. 'Think how much you'd pay at Tiffany for gems that size.'

'Hey, I'm not complaining,' said Mark, 'Christ no. I have the most beautiful wife – I was about to say "I could ever dream of" but in fact she *is* the beautiful wife I always dreamt of.'

'You've known each other ages,' Saul recalled.

'Since school days,' Mark said, 'friends for years. Confidants. And then one day, Alice says to me, "If you ask me, I'll say yes." I hadn't a clue what she was on about. I mean, I hadn't even kissed the girl, let alone taken her to bed. I just stared at her gormlessly. She proposed. It wasn't a leap year. I hadn't bought diamonds from Tiffany or QVC. I was washing up and, calm as you like, she turns to me and asks me to marry her.'

'And you still can't believe your luck?' Saul laughed.

'That's just it,' said Mark, 'it's not about luck. To me, the more you love someone, the more you deserve them – and I'd loved her for a long, long time. Albeit from afar. I hadn't resented the fuckwits she dated though I hated them when they hurt her. I hadn't found anyone special and was happy to see women in a non-committal way. And then Alice decided she'd like to marry me.'

'So, you have this gorgeous woman, successful in her career, who buys her own diamonds, no matter how fake they are, and simply stings you for a pair of Jimmy *Choos* every now and then,' Saul quantified. 'Can life get much better?'

'Well, I'm looking forward to the bonus,' Mark laughed, 'which will hopefully coincide with the next Jimmy Shoes sale!' He glanced at his watch. 'Anyway, are we here about Quentin?' he murmured covertly, with a wink and a surreptitious tap of his nose.

'We are,' Saul nodded, privately bemused that such an expensive restaurant hadn't bothered to fillet his monkfish. 'Now, because we're pitching at a slightly older market – not so much aspirational, as can afford it anyway – I was thinking of a City section. You know, investments, portfolios, gift horse and traps; lively overviews on finance and our times, a note of light relief from the *Financial Times*.'

Mark nodded. 'Interesting,' he said, 'how can I help?' He glanced at his watch again. 'I'll need to make tracks in half an hour, Saul. But I'm back from Tokyo at the weekend.'

* * *

'You bastard,' Richard Stonehill panted, hands on his knees, his squash racket between his feet, 'you bastard. You're just a jammy bastard.'

'And you're a bad loser,' Saul laughed, wiping sweat from his brow onto his T-shirt. 'My game, my match – your round.'

'Let's make it the best out of seven then,' Richard said, slashing a ball against the court.

'Fuck off,' Saul laughed, returning the shot perfectly. 'What would your wife say when I call her to say you've thrown yourself into Highgate Ponds with concrete in your pockets because you lost five–two?'

'Yeah, yeah,' Richard said, 'you're younger than me. Anyway, I have a cold coming. But next week I'm going to roast you, mate, *roast* you. Annihilation.'

'I look forward to it,' Saul said, slicing the ball and intentionally missing Richard by a hair's breadth.

'You won't even *make* it to Highgate Ponds,' Richard said, returning Saul's ball impressively, 'you'll do the hara-kiri thing right here on court.'

'And on that note,' Saul said, 'let's go for a drink.'

For a moment or two, both men just gazed at the pints of pale, chilled lager with unreserved affection before raising the glasses to their lips and taking a long, well-earned drink. They said 'cheers' to each other, chinked glasses and then downed what was left. 'My round,' said Richard, going to the bar at the Swallow and ordering sausages and mash for them both. 'How's Thea?' he asked, on returning.

'I had a set of my keys cut for her just today,' Saul grinned. 'And Sally?'

'It's our wedding anniversary this weekend,' Richard said, 'five years.'

'Cheers!' said Saul, with admiration.

'Who'd have thought a crazy fling would lead to marriage,' Richard marvelled wistfully.

'Are you whisking her off to Paris?' Saul enquired.

Richard laughed but shook his head.

'Venice?' Saul tried. 'Barcelona? Babington House? No? Well. I assume you've been to Tiffany's.'

'No,' Richard groaned, 'not yet.'

'Mark Sinclair was telling me Alice buys her own jewels,' Saul said.

'Really?' Richard responded, 'but on his credit card probably. She has some fuck-off diamonds, that girl.'

'No, she buys them herself,' Saul revealed. 'They're *fake*,' he said, 'fake! How cool is that?' He really was more impressed than he would have been had they been genuine. 'She buys them for small change from the shopping channel.'

Richard laughed. 'Seriously? Bloody hell. She certainly wears them well. Perhaps I'll ask her to order double – I'm sure I could pop them into a Tiffany box.'

'Talking of Alice,' Saul said, dropping his voice, 'I'm working on a project with her – top secret. But I have an idea for a property section. I'm not talking estate agents' advertorials. I'm not talking Laurence Llewelyn-Bowen makeovers. I was thinking of a section that is part DIY, part property improvements, part investment savvy. You know, kitchen extensions or loft conversions or knocking through – a how to, how much, how long.'

'Sounds good,' Richard nodded.

'You're an architect,' Saul shrugged, 'can I pick your brains?'

'Cool,' Richard nodded, 'sure. What's it called?'

'Top secret,' said Saul.

'That's a bit naff,' said Richard.

'The *title* is top secret,' Saul said very slowly. 'I'm not telling you the title because I can't. I'm sworn to secrecy.'

'Code-name?' Richard asked.

'Quentin,' Saul revealed rather reluctantly.

'Gay?'

'No – as in *Tarantino*,' Saul explained. And he and Richard proceeded to quote salient lines from *Pulp Fiction* until their sausages arrived.

Beth and Hope

When Beth Godwin and Hope Johnson set up their Pilates studio in Crouch End, Sally Stonehill joined on a whim because there was an introductory offer on. Thea signed up on the recommendation of Lars, the Feldenkrais practitioner at the Being Well. Alice joined on account of the effect of Pilates on the physique of Elizabeth Hurley. Mostly, the three of them synchronized their sessions. It hardly mattered, though. They were so busy concentrating on engaging their pelvic floor and pursuing core stability that they barely said a word to each other apart from 'great Pikes, Thea' or 'your reverse-monkey looked good, Alice' or 'I'm finished with the Reformer, Sally'.

Invariably, if they'd been training together, they'd go for a meal afterwards, determined to consolidate the merits of Pilates with healthy salads or bowls of hearty soup and glasses of mineral water. Usually, though, there was some reason for a glass of wine too – from it being good for the blood, to it being necessary to toast one of the girls for something or other. However even the one glass of wine, when mixed with the endorphins of exercise, led to the inevitable ordering of chips. To share, of course. Just to pick at. And mayonnaise too, please. Who's for ketchup? Anyone for HP Sauce?

'A large bottle of sparkling mineral water,' Alice ordered.

'It's my wedding anniversary this weekend,' Sally remarked, with intent.

'Is it? Right then,' Alice responded, 'a bottle of Sauvignon too, please.'

'I'll have the avocado and mung bean salad,' Thea told the waitress with scant enthusiasm.

'Grilled trout for me, please,' ordered Alice, 'no butter.'

'I think I'll go for the stir-fried veg,' Sally muttered.

'Anything else?' the waitress asked casually.

'Oh, one portion of chips,' Thea added as an afterthought.

'Actually, make that two,' Alice said, 'to share between the three of us.'

'And some mayo, please,' Sally called after the waitress.

'Cheers!' said Alice, raising her glass. 'Here's to you and Richard and to marriage in general.'

'I'll drink to that,' said Sally, 'here's to my husband and five lovely years.'

'Cheers,' said Thea, 'here's to – chips.'

'You'll be next,' Alice nudged Thea and winked at Sally.

'I hardly see the boy,' Thea remonstrated, tapping the prongs of her fork against the pad of her thumb before pointing her cutlery at Alice. 'You have him working all bloody hours on your hush-hush project.'

'How's that going?' Sally asked Alice. 'Richard likes to think of himself as Editor of Architecture and Interiors or something. The prat.'

'We're launching next month,' Alice said triumphantly.

'Will there be a glamorous party?' Sally asked hopefully.

'Of course,' Alice said.

'And may lowly primary school teachers attend?' Sally asked.

'You may,' Alice confirmed graciously.

'And will there be room on the guest list for a sports masseuse?' Thea asked.

'God no,' Alice laughed in mock shock, 'but I might turn a blind eye to the girlfriend of the editorial consultant sneaking in.'

'Cow,' Thea stuck her tongue out at Alice.

'How are things with Alice's Editorial Consultant?' Sally asked Thea. 'Richard has spent a small fortune on a new squash racquet. Bad workmen, tools and blame, springs to mind.'

'Lovely,' Thea grinned, 'it's fun. It's cosy. It's sexy. It's everything I want. And everything I need.'

'You mean it's love,' Sally deduced.

'Yes,' Thea confirmed, 'yes, it is.'

'Six months after I started seeing Richard, we were already engaged,' Sally recalled. 'Mind you, six months after *you* started seeing Mark you were practically married, Ms Heggarty.'

'Mrs Sinclair to you,' Alice retorted. 'Actually, the craziest thing about it all was that I didn't even start seeing Mark *until* we were engaged. Chaste is an understatement.'

'Chaste is overrated,' Sally said with a wink, confessing she'd bought Richard, for their anniversary, some peculiar-looking love beads which apparently he was to use on her – if they could figure out how and where.

'Did you go into a sex shop on your own?' Alice asked, slightly unnerved by an image of petite Sally unchaperoned amongst stacks of gadgets and racks of hardcore.

'Mail order,' Sally giggled.

'Of course, Saul and I have absolutely no need for gizmos on account of his stupendous natural equipment and our exceptionally resourceful technique,' Thea began primly. 'But actually,' she added in a sly whisper, 'we have a particularly well-stocked toy chest as well.'

'Dirty girl,' Alice marvelled.

'That was one kinky shopping trip,' Thea reminisced. 'I happened to make just a passing remark I'd never been in a sex shop. A week or so later, we were heading back to Saul's from a restaurant in Soho when he suddenly bundled me through a doorway. Slap bang into this den of iniquity and plastic things.'

'You never told me!' Alice objected.

'Well, it was hardly Joseph or Whistles,' Thea reasoned. 'Actually, it was a peculiar experience. Down a really seedy side street yet inside it was all bright lights and the most normal-looking customers imaginable. Though I seem to recall the sales assistant being quite alarmingly tattooed.'

'Did you giggle like mad?' Sally asked.

'At first,' Thea admitted, 'but actually, everyone was browsing the wares so casually that I soon found myself assessing the merits of one dildo against another as I would ready-meals at Tesco. Saul spent a fortune. We couldn't wait to get back to his to try things in.'

'On,' the editor in Alice corrected automatically.

'No,' Thea laughed, 'I really do mean *in*!'

'Do you have any of these bead things?' Sally asked, now regarding Thea as the doyenne of kinky paraphernalia.

Thea went through a lengthy, though obviously mostly fabricated, inventory. 'No,' she apologized at length, 'no beads. My advice would be, if it fits, wear it out.'

'Mark doesn't know I have a vibrator,' Alice confessed, half wondering whether he ought, yet unable to predict how he'd react. 'In fact, I can't imagine using toys with him. The thing is, our sex is admittedly pretty straightforward but actually all the more satisfying for it. I had boyfriends who couldn't get it up unless they could get something battery-operated up first. God, sometimes I used to crave simple, quick missionary in the dark.'

'I guess I bought these plastic things to sustain the spice,' Sally said, 'not because our sex life is lacking or uninspired. I like surprising Richie – though nowadays I sometimes have to remind myself to – because I know he loves it. The day I can't be bothered is the day to worry.'

'Keeping the marriage alive?' Thea asked.

'No, it's not that,' Sally declared, 'no need to – all is dreamy. I just like to envisage Richard thinking to himself that he's a lucky boy. I like to think of him all distracted and hot under the collar at work by knowing what's under my pillow.'

'It's funny,' Alice mused, 'how you and I have actually contrived our relationships. You ensure that you maintain the allure of a vamp all these years into your marriage. I eschew my previous incarnation as feisty temptress to secure the stability and fidelity that defines Mark. I guess you could say I'm in an arranged marriage which I arranged.'

'Richard proposed out of the blue, when we were still at the height of our heady falling-in-love phase,' Sally reminisced. 'Me being ludicrously dramatic, I ran away from him to hide in the wilds of Scotland, broke my bloody leg and he then turned up and wrote "will you?" on my plaster cast.'

'It's such a great story,' Thea laughed.

'God, my proposal is mundane in comparison,' Alice admitted. 'I asked Mark to marry me with a carrot in my mouth.'

'I bet it wasn't mundane to him,' Sally said.

'Funnily enough, it's the mundanity that I love now,' Alice defined. 'Christ, when I think of all that passion I used to put myself through.' She paused to privately recall it. 'It was so damned draining; replete with suspicions. Now I am loved unconditionally. I can just be myself and I'm adored for it. It's such a relief that my worries are now confined solely to work or to trivial things like whether we made a mistake using Cath Kidston florals in the bedroom with the rest of the house so minimalist.'

'How is your new house?' Sally asked Alice.

'Gorgeous,' Thea enthused on Alice's behalf, 'it's so grown-up!'

'It really is gorgeous,' Alice agreed. 'I'm very lucky.'

'I love being married,' Sally enthused with no smugness. 'Richard is my best friend, my best shag, my confidant.'

'I love it that to the outside world there's this normal bloke called Saul – but in my eyes I see this knight in shining armour,' Thea said proudly, 'a man I burn for. I lavish my love and lust on him and it's reciprocated. That's the best thing – finally with Saul it's this gorgeous two-way rally. Like a ball caught between flingers in a pinball machine – affection, lust, empathy, friendship, love ricocheting between the two of us.'

'You're a hopeless romantic,' Alice said fondly, 'the first person to compare love to a pinball machine, that's for sure. And how many times do I have to tell you there's no magic or mystique in your feeling of "burning" for a man – it's just sudden surges of adrenalin and dopamine released in your brain.'

'Oh shut up, Alice,' Thea laughed.

'Let the girl enjoy her chemical reaction!' Sally said.

The food arrived and they picked at the salad and polished off the chips. Alice raised her glass and lowered her voice. 'Look at that gaggle over there at that table.' Thea and Sally glanced surreptitiously to a table of three women much like themselves. 'Short of actually eavesdropping or lip-reading, I'll bet you anything they're bemoaning all men are sods and stuff. They look miserable. Down in the doldrums, drowning their discontent.' Alice replenished their glasses and raised hers, chinking it against Sally's and Thea's.

'We're bloody lucky, us three. We each have what we want and life ticks along happily because we're blessed with precisely what makes us tick.'

Girls and Boys

Alice sat up in bed; coddled by cloud-plump pillows and finest goose down, bedecked tastefully with Cath Kidston roses, in a waft around her. Her hair tumbled in a breeze-soft fan over her shoulders, glints of spun gold splaying over the creaminess of her skin. She looked like something out of a Merchant Ivory film, Mark thought to himself. Actually, Alice felt playful and horny and was surreptitiously fingering herself lightly as she watched Mark undress. She smiled at how particular his routine was. The order in which he took off his clothes, checked the pockets of his suit jacket before hanging it on a broad wooden hanger, rolled his belt up and put it in his drawer of rolled-up belts and took his dirty laundry through to the basket in their ensuite bathroom. Alice noted her skirt draped over the back of the chair, over jeans she'd worn at the weekend, her jumper strewn on the seat, her knickers scrunched on the floor. She wondered whether she was slovenly or if Mark was particularly fastidious. She wondered if her disregard for end-of-the-day neatness and order irked him.

'Mark,' she asked quietly, 'do you despair of me being a mucky pup?'

'Mucky pup?' Mark frowned, slipping cedar shoe horns into his shoes. Alice gestured to her discarded clothes. 'Don't be daft,' he smiled, selecting tomorrow's shirt. 'When I wake up, whichever way I'm facing, I see Alice rumpled. I like that.' He picked up her jumper. 'But this is cashmere and you really should fold it.' He did it for her. 'Which drawer?'

Alice looked over to the chest of drawers. 'Middle one,' she said, suddenly remembering her vibrator was in the drawer beneath. And then she wondered whether perhaps tonight was as good a time as any to introduce Mark to her bright pink, battery-operated friend. 'Not the middle drawer,' she announced, 'I mean the one below.' Find it! Don't find it!

Mark didn't find it. Alice didn't know whether she was disappointed or relieved. He continued his bedtime routine, inching the curtains back and looking down to the street, up to the sky. 'Clear night,' he assessed. It had been cloudy yesterday. Blustery the day before. He flicked his bedside light on, went back to the doorway and switched the main light off, hung his robe on the back of the door, rolled his head to either side while he walked over to the bed. He plumped his pillow, took off his watch and wound it up, checked the alarm clock though he never changed the setting. Though he always awoke moments in advance of the bell, he'd never not set it. He liked the physical act of silencing it just before it trilled so as not to disturb Alice. He reached for his Ian Rankin and skim-read the last paragraph from the night before, settling himself further into his pillow to read a chapter tonight.

He sighed. 'Long day,' he said, smiling apologetically at Alice, 'long day.'

Alice put her novel down. She reached for him, ran her fingertips along his forearm, stroked her hand up to his biceps, rested her touch tenderly on his shoulder. She nestled against him. He stretched out his arm and draped it round her shoulders though this made page-turning a little awkward. He kissed the top of her head. She kissed his chest in reply. Kissed it again, optimistically. Put her mouth over his nipple and changed her kiss to a suck. She looked up at Mark, he looked down from his book. He looked tired.

'Are you tired?' she whispered, her fingers tantalizingly tiptoeing a path down his chest and over his stomach.

'I am a little,' he admitted, 'work is a bit of a bitch at the moment. I'm carrying all David's while he's convalescing.'

'When he's back, why don't we take a week off?' Alice suggested, her hand resting lightly on his stomach while the conversation remained prosaic.

'Hopefully,' said Mark, deciding not to tell her about the imminence of trips to Singapore, Australia and Japan.

Alice decided distraction was good action. She traversed his torso with the palm of her hand. His nipples sprung to attention. 'Mark,' she murmured, licking her lips lasciviously, eyes asparkle, 'are you *tired* tired? Or just tired tired?'

He laughed through his nose. 'Are you laying claim to your conjugal rights, Mrs Sinclair?'

'I most certainly am,' Alice winked and kissed him on the chin, his mouth, nibbling his lower lip, 'if you're up to it.'

'I'm tired, but *he*'s certainly up to it,' Mark said as he led Alice's hand down his body, underneath the duvet to his hardening cock. Alice closed her eyes, closed her hand around him, felt him grow and stiffen and felt herself start to melt and moisten.

Mark held her head in his hands and kissed her softly all over her face. Alice rated him a very good kisser but actually, just then, she didn't want lips romantic and gentle, she wanted him to thrust his tongue into her mouth and gorge. Gently and evenly, he fondled each breast in turn before sliding his hand down her stomach, over the undulations of waist and hips, lightly over her bush and as far down her thigh as he could reach without breaking off from kissing her. She hungered for his mouth to feast on her breasts, she wanted his teeth to rasp against her nipples, she wanted his hands to knead her buttocks, she craved his fingers to delve greedily inside her. She pulled her face away and tried to guide his head down and his hand up. But he buried his face in her neck and nuzzled her there instead, cupped his hand over her sex without exploring further, stroking and stroking the length of her body. Desire for what he wasn't doing was heightening her arousal far more than what he was doing to her. It was as if her body was screaming and he couldn't hear it, so engrossed was he in his slow, tender lovemaking. The deafer he became, the more desperate her longing. It was strangely fantastic and frustrating.

Mark brought his face level with hers and gazed deep into Alice's eyes. 'You're so beautiful,' he told her. Gently, he parted her legs with his knee and, without taking his eyes off her, he carefully pushed his way inside her. He was pleasingly hard and Alice could sense her sex wanting to suck him in deeply. Her body tried to buck and grind against him but he had her securely enfolded in his arms and was setting a dignified, rhythmic pace. He moved inside her, gyrating subtly, moved and gyrated intoxicatingly slowly. She wanted to yell out fuck me you bastard but her mouth was plugged with his. She wanted him to thrust into her as if he had no self-control but he maintained his quiet, measured rhythm. He rolled her on top of him, sweeping her long hair from his face, scooping it up behind her head, holding her gaze. 'You feel so good,' he murmured. She sat up, the change in angle making her gasp. He stroked the fronts of her thighs whilst marvelling at the sight of her; the dip of her waist, the toned run of her stomach, the soft weight of her breasts, the eagerness of her nipples, the grace of her neck, the beauty of her face. 'I love you,' he whispered, 'God, I love you.' She was starting to pick up her pace, rotating and pumping as she straddled him. Mark pulled her down, rolled her over and kissed her and kissed her as he came. Deftly, Alice moved against him, the sudden rush of stickiness within her facilitating her own orgasm.

'That'll put me to sleep with a smile on my face,' he grinned at her. She smiled back. She could see how sleepy the orgasm had left him yet it had energized her.

'Did you know that the national average for sex amongst cohabiting couples is less than twice a week?' Alice announced, the jollity of her voice, as much as her topic, causing Mark's eyes to spring open.

He had a head for figures. 'Well, darling, we're above average, then.'

'Did you know that 50 per cent of women own vibrators?' Alice said, glancing at her chest of drawers, her heartbeat picking up a little.

'They must be the ones who are restricted to the national average,' Mark deduced.

Alice wasn't very good with figures and presumed Mark to have calculated some statistic, so she changed her tack. 'Have you ever used a vibrator on a woman?' she asked carefully.

He looked at her with a quick frown. 'Why?'

She gave him a sly smile. 'Just wondered.' Again, he frowned. 'You have!' she exclaimed, triumphantly. 'You have! Who? Tell me who!'

'No,' he said quite sternly, 'I assure you I haven't.' Because Alice believed him, she suddenly wasn't sure how to progress the conversation.

'Anyway,' Mark said, 'aren't vibrators used in lieu of the real thing?' Alice was about to suggest they needn't be restricted to such times and would you like me to show you mine; but she sensed that Mark was mid-sentence. 'Or ridiculous props in dodgy vids,' he remarked.

'Have you ever filmed yourself?' Alice probed with a mischievous glint to her voice and eye.

'Christ, Alice!' Mark exclaimed, looking at her as if she was suffering sudden manic insanity.

'Might be fun?' Alice prompted coyly.

'Vibrators?' Mark said. 'Camcorders? Do I not satisfy you?' He regarded her with a flicker of suspicion to his gaze. Actually, he looked hurt and it shocked her. 'Do you find our sex life lacking?' he asked.

'No!' she protested. 'Not at all.'

'Am I travelling too much? Is that what's brought on this talk of vibrators? Were you faking your orgasm just now?'

'No,' Alice said, 'no. I was just— For an article. I was just editing out loud. Thinking.'

'I can't see how a shuddering lump of rubber could possibly better what's great as it is,' Mark said defensively. 'Wouldn't it detract from the intensity and meaning of our lovemaking – cheapen it?'

Alice felt badly. She hadn't anticipated Mark's hurt. She'd thought, at most, he'd be endearingly embarrassed and grateful for her dominance and initiative. Or else regard her as harmlessly kinky without taking offence. 'I was just editing an article,' she lied again, 'that's why I brought it up. That's all.'

He nodded. Full of surprises, his wife. He kissed her. 'Goodnight, Alice,' he said, 'I love you.'

* * *

'If you peel onions under a running tap, your eyes don't water.'

Saul watched Thea peeling onions under a running tap. 'How do you want the aubergine?' he asked. 'Sliced or diced?'

'Sliced, please.'

'Under running water?'

'No need. But spread them out then sprinkle salt over them to take away any bitterness.'

Saul sliced the aubergine. He reached up to take the salt from the cupboard. Thea sensed the closeness of his body just behind her. His shirtsleeves were rolled to the elbow. Just a glance at his forearm, the soft hairs spattering down to his wrist, the delineation of muscle, shot desire through to her stomach. She could smell him and the pleasure of it flickered her eyes shut. Saul brushed his hand fleetingly between her shoulder blades and then set about salting his sliced aubergine. Pass the butter, please. Fingertips touched and electrical impulses charged. Eye contact. Adrenalin. You have flour on your cheek. I'll just brush it away for you. Thank you – here, let me feed you a fingerful of home-made mayonnaise. I need to reach up for that casserole dish. Yes, and when you do, I get to see your stomach lengthen and tauten and when you bring your arms down, your breasts swell.

'Saul, can you pass me that tea towel? Thanks.'

'Glass of wine? Red? Budge over – the corkscrew is in that drawer.'

Saul gently moved Thea to one side, his hands either side of her hips. She leant back lightly against his body and the proximity of his bulk sent a shiver of anticipatory pleasure through her. Suddenly Saul forgot about corkscrews. It seemed his reason for being there, behind Thea, was expressly to have his hands on her hips, his lips at the ultra-sensitive kiss of skin behind her ear. She pressed back against his chest and turned her cheek quickly; his lips leaving her neck and travelling over her jaw line to her mouth, her lips parted and her tongue tip was eager to dance with his. Behind her, rocking against her, her neck twisted round to reach his face, Saul gorged on her mouth. Something clanged down to the floor but they only half heard it. Thea whipped herself around

104

so that she was facing him, her arms now thrown around his neck, her fingers enmeshed in his hair, urging his face against hers. He had a hand in the small of her back, his other clasping her right buttock. He pressed against her and she pulled herself up at him. The seam of her jeans was catching the swell of her sex and she parted her legs to find Saul's thigh for further friction. He backed her up against the fridge, his leg wedged between both of hers, his hands now in her hair, over her breasts, pulling and grabbing; the smattering of his evening bristles rasping against her cheeks, her chin, her neck.

Thea tried to unbutton Saul's shirt but it was taking too long so he pulled it over his head, undid his belt and ripped down his trousers to his knees. At the same time, Thea wriggled from her T-shirt and Saul pulled her bra straps down over her arms, not bothering with the clasp, not minding that it remained on, just as long as her tits were exposed for him to feel, to see and to suck. Thea's hand worked energetically over and under his boxer shorts, at last liberating his straining, leaping cock. They crumpled themselves down onto the rubber floor, romping and humping and snogging and sucking. Saul tugged Thea's jeans down, freeing her right leg. He moved her knickers to one side and took his mouth down to her. He could have spent hours feasting on her juice but tasting the rush of her moistness gave an urgency to the moment. With his trousers around his ankles, eyes closed, breathing fast and audible, Saul thrust into Thea and she ground against him. They humped and bucked and grunted and fucked, coming simultaneously; eyes scrunched shut, voices loud, faces racked into near-grimaces with the intensity of it all while their bodies spurted and sponged. And then they rolled apart, lay on the rubber floor, sticky and slippery and sweaty and satisfied, unable to speak while they let their heartbeats settle down.

'Jesus Christ,' Saul exclaimed on rolling towards Thea, his eyes slightly bloodshot. Just a few centimetres to the right of her face, a Sabatier knife lay glinting.

'Christ,' Thea agreed, her face flushed, a rash to one corner of her mouth. She reached her hand to Saul's face and gently flicked chopped parsley from his hair.

* * *

'Ouch!'

'Sorry, babe.'

'I don't think the beads go *there*, Richard.'

'I'm sure I saw it on some porn vid once. All right, how about here?'

'Well, they fit – but I can't say my world is shuddering. Porn vid? What porn vid?'

'How about if I try this with them? Hang on.'

'Do what with them where?'

'This! I'm doing it!'

'Are you? Oh.'

'Hang on, what about—'

'Don't you dare!'

'We're kind of running out of orifices, Sal.'

'Do you think it's orifices or orificii?'

'Wait a sec, let's try – this. Move that leg a bit. A bit more. There.'

'Ouch. Give them here. *You* roll over.'

'You must be bloody joking!'

'Look, shall we just bin the beads and have a good old shag?'

'Now you're talking.'

'Happy anniversary, big boy.'

Adam

Seven months after Alice and Mark were married, after Saul and Thea had formed a couple, Adam came into the world. Until then, Alice had hailed her wedding as marking the zenith of her creative and organizational talent. But Adam surpassed all of that. Adam was Alice's baby. Her true love. Her life's work. Her future ambition. Her past achievement, her present success. Her key to larger offices two floors above.

Just before her first wedding anniversary, Alice won Launch of the Year for *Adam* at a prestigious industry awards ceremony. The trophy, a rather dramatic slash of perspex in a gravity-defying swoop into a lump of softwood, shared pride of shelf-space in her executive office two floors up, alongside a framed first issue of *Adam* – the one with Clint Eastwood on the cover.

'Our project name was Quentin,' Alice told a packed Grosvenor House ballroom at that awards night, 'but as we kept having to stress "as in Tarantino, not Crisp" we needed something synonymous with Alpha Male. So our magazine became *Adam*. Biblical connotations end with the title – as we all know, publishing is no Garden of Eden, it's a men's mag jungle out there. However, with our spectacular circulation figures – and now with this major award – *Adam* reigns supreme.'

As she returned to her table, carried on a cushion of generous applause, the trophy pleasingly heavy, a reassuring ache in her arches from her Jimmy Choos, Alice believed the moment to mark the apotheosis of her career. Unfortunately, there was no Mark to the moment – he was in Hong Kong and she couldn't even phone him because of the time difference. With no husband to cuddle up to, Alice intended to get justifiably drunk on the company credit card and stay out ridiculously late.

'Mr Mundy,' she said whilst leaning around their round table topping up her team's glasses, 'Mr Mundy, you are a dickhead.'

'Thank you, Miss Heggarty,' Saul acquiesced, chinking glasses and sharing a raised eyebrow with the fashion editor and advertising manager.

'I mean,' Alice qualified, 'if you'd only come off your freelance high horse and join the mag as staff, you'd be up there awarded Editor of the Year.' The fashion editor and ad manager nodded earnestly.

'That's kind of you,' Saul said, pausing to applaud a woman on stage receiving her jag of perspex for being Specialist Editor of the Year, 'but I've told you, I don't want to trade my freedom – my access to variety – for commuting, office politics and a lump of plastic.'

'It's perspex!' Alice retorted. 'It's sculpture!'

'Sure,' said Saul, 'but if I did *Adam* full-time I'd have to relinquish all my other work. And I'm a loyal bastard.' He clapped with everyone though he had no idea of the award just won.

'But me pay top dollar,' Alice said in a peculiar Japanese accent.

'Your dollars can't buy my desire for diversity, Alice,' Saul said, tonguing the words theatrically. 'I spend more time on *Adam* than on any of my other commitments. But I like my tutti-frutti life. I like dipping my finger in a fair few pies. *ES* mag versus the *Observer*, *T3* versus *GQ*. *MotorMonth* versus *Get Gadget*. I *need* variety.'

Another award was won, this time by a former colleague of Alice's so she wolf-whistled through her fingers – a raucous skill amusingly at odds with her sartorial grace and sleek deportment. 'Desire for diversity?' she balked, turning again to Saul. 'finger-dipping?' Alice wagged her finger at him. 'Your need for variety better not go beyond your professional life, Mr Mundy.'

Saul laughed. 'I may flirt my working way around publishing circles – but at play I'm working on being all Thea's. In my mind, in my heart,' he said, 'I'm all hers.'

'Promiscuous by pen is fine, promiscuous by penis – not!' Alice declared, rather pleased with that and wondering if she could regurgitate it in print. Not for *Adam*, obviously. *Lush*, perhaps.

'Has it escaped you that your first wedding anniversary also marks my first year with Thea?' Saul said defensively.

They chinked glasses.

'To Thea,' Saul drank, 'I couldn't love her more.'

'I love my husband, I love my job, I love my posh house, I love the plants I can't pronounce in my garden,' Alice proclaimed with regular sips, 'I love *Adam*. I love Thea. I love you!'

'This isn't the Oscars,' Saul laughed.

'It's the champagne,' Alice rued, 'it makes me emotional.'

'Switch to water,' Saul suggested.

'Bugger off!' Alice retorted, topping up everyone's glasses.

Mark flew back from the Far East and was immensely proud of Alice's Launch of the Year award, so much so that he persuaded her to bring it back home from the office at weekends. Until one weekend when he was abroad on business and Alice didn't bother. His excessive travelling and deal-mongering paid dividends in the form of a large and timely bonus. He whisked Alice off to Prague for their first anniversary and replaced Alice's shopping-channel paste earrings with genuine diamonds. Only larger. And set in platinum. She'd bought him a papier mâché globe because the girls on *Dream Weddings* reminded her that the first anniversary is paper. Alice was overwhelmed by Mark's gift. In fact, she was a little taken aback.

'I feel too young for such fuck-off rocks,' she confided to Thea, 'like I've sneaked my mum's for dressing up. Only my mum doesn't have diamonds even half this size. I have to keep them in a safe when I'm not wearing them or else they're not insured.'

'They're *stunning*,' Thea marvelled, privately thinking that, despite their dazzle, they were almost too big to be attractive or actually look real.

'They're serious,' Alice assessed. 'The fun of the fakes was that they were cheap tat. A joke where I had the last laugh. Do you want them?'

'Sure!' Thea said. 'Which ones?' she added.

'Where can I take you?' Saul asked Thea, a few days before their first anniversary. 'Cartier? TopShop?'

'Memory Lane,' Thea answered decisively.

'Is that some spa in Barbados?' Saul half joked.

'Primrose Hill,' Thea laughed. 'I want to retrace our steps.'

'Christ, you're soppy,' Saul said.

'I just want to walk hand in hand on Primrose Hill!' Thea protested.

'And if it's raining?'

'We'll get wet.'

'Can't I whisk you off to Babington House or somewhere, in a top-of-the-range Jag?' Saul all but pleaded.

'You don't have a car,' Thea reminded him patiently, 'you have a scooter.'

'Actually, that's where you're wrong. I've been given said Jag for the weekend – to take for a spin and assess for *MotorMonth*.'

'What colour is it?' Thea asked, slightly tempted.

'Racing green,' Saul shrugged, 'cream leather.'

'But I *want* to go to Primrose Hill to *our* bench,' Thea said with a petulant pout Saul couldn't resist.

So they compromised. They drove the mile or so to Primrose Hill and paid-and-displayed for two hours at great expense. At the top of the hill, Saul pulled out a roll of Refreshers and a family-size pack of Opal Fruits though it said Starburst on the packet. For Thea, the gesture was far more romantic than a country hideaway accessed by sports car. As an expression of her gratitude, she took off her jumper, and with no bra beneath her T-shirt, her nipples stood to Saul's attention, reminding him instantly of a year ago, when she was up there, all cold and hungover. He stroked her arms, giving her far stronger goose bumps than the November air.

Thea gazed at him, marvelling to herself that she hadn't noticed the slate-grey flecks to his irises. 'I love you, Saul Mundy,' she said.

'Happy First Whatever,' he grinned, 'Happy Us.'

* * *

When did you stop qualifying your age with *and a quarter*, or *and a half*, or *and three-quarters*? Thea continued until she hit her teens. In her mid-twenties, Alice was still in the habit of saying 'next year I'll be . . .' which, according to the time of year, enabled her to add up to two years onto her current age. However, the precise notch in the scale of their thirties soon seemed of little concern to others, it was the age of their relationships which generated interest now. Though both Alice and Thea had loved their first year with Mark and Saul, they were impatient for their first anniversaries to give their relationships status. As soon as Alice had passed the six-months mark, she took to saying she'd been married 'almost a year'. Thea spoke in terms of seasons rather than months. She'd say she and Saul had been together 'since last autumn' – which, by the following summer, seemed a distant time indeed. Thea did theorize to herself that November probably qualified as winter, but last November – *their* November – really had been mild. On average. According to meteorologists. According to high-street retailers. Hadn't ornithologists been concerned that certain birds hadn't yet flown south?

By the close of their first year, Thea was deeply in love with Saul and Alice loved being married very much. Alice rejoiced in believing that she knew everything there was to know about Mark. That there were no surprises was a blessing. She didn't envy Thea always learning something new about Saul, be it grey flecks to his eyes, or his expulsion at fifteen from boarding school, or his threesome with two Danish girls in his twenties on his first press trip. No, Alice was happy to embrace predictability at the expense of thrills. Thrills, her experience had taught her, were far too costly. If her head was now not for turning, it followed that her heart could not be for breaking.

Mark continued to be all she'd had a feeling he'd be – that hunch on the back of which she had proposed in his kitchen through a mouthful of carrot. He was a husband perfect for her. Loving, straight and responsible. And, now that she'd managed subtly to supervise his entire wardrobe, dapper too. Nice even brown eyes, unblemished education and career history, no deviations from the sexual norm. They didn't argue, there was nothing to fall out about. Tolerance was a key quality of Mark's and it sat well with his belief in the attraction of opposites. He never reacted when Alice over-reacted, he gladly sprang to his duty to calm and cool her down. Anyway, such times usually transpired only when work interfered. And it flattered and touched Mark that Alice should care so much and need him so. Best of all, he loved the baby-voiced, doleful-eyed ways she had of pleading with him not to stay late at work, not to fly to Hong Bloody Kong again.

Though Alice herself adored her job and was as ambitious and committed to her career as Mark, it seemed the pressures of Mark's job were actually more challenging to Alice than to him. No matter how demanding his day, how fraught the financial world, how difficult the deal, he always came home with an easy smile, eager and energized by his role as husband. The frequent travel he undertook was strenuous for him, yet it appeared to be far tougher on Alice. He just had jet lag to contend with, the vagaries of business etiquette around the world, the precarious threads that deals hung by, the tedium of chain hotels no matter how luxurious; his timetable was so full there was rarely an opportunity to think, let alone relax. Alice, however, was left with only half her home; all the trimmings of marriage but with no husband. It wasn't that she actually moped for Mark, nor that she felt forsaken. It simply wasn't much fun playing home alone.

Their house in Hampstead, with all its gadgets and gorgeousness, was meant to be their Wonderland. However, Alice didn't feel in Wonderland when she was on her own; she felt she shrank in the house, as though she had downed some Carrollian Drink-Me potion. Her luxury kitchen suddenly seemed stage-set oversized with its echoey French limestone floor, cavernous American fridge, catering-standard range cooker and abundant bespoke units. Had she not sourced the designer bath precisely on account of its curves and capaciousness being calibrated for two, not one? The surround-sound system connected to the vast plasma screen in the sitting room was too technical for her. Their bed was so enormous it seemed downright daft to sleep in it alone when Mark was away, so Alice would take to her old double bed, now in the smaller of their two other bedrooms. Consequently, she usually ate heartily at lunchtime on the days when Mark wouldn't be home, having just a packet of crisps or a KitKat or two in the evening, curling up on his lounger watching a DVD on the Mac in his study until she was too sleepy to take a bath which would have taken too long to run anyway.

Alice did not like it when Mark travelled. She didn't like it when he travelled because she didn't like living alone. She also didn't like it when he travelled because she didn't like it when he returned. She didn't like it when he travelled because she didn't like it when he returned because she couldn't prevent herself from being snappish and ungracious. She didn't like it when he returned because, though he was the one justified in being scuppered by jet lag and drained by the pressure of transatlantic deals done or lost, he was always calm and delighted to see her. She was the one who was inexcusably ratty. She'd sullenly turn down dinner, in or out, claiming no appetite. She'd yawn that she was too tired to talk on any of his thoughtfully chosen topics. She'd go to bed early and pretend to be asleep; feign headaches and exhaustion when he deserved a soothing back rub or craved an affirming blow-job. She'd pretend to be too deeply asleep even to acknowledge, never mind reciprocate, his affectionate kiss goodnight.

Mark always brought her something – from fabulous Hong

Kong kitsch (a luminous limited-edition Hello Kitty digital watch) to trinkets from Barney's, New York; from gorgeous toiletries brazenly swiped from the housekeeping trolley at Hotel Costes in Paris, to the catalogue from a Paul Klee exhibition just opened in Chicago. Invariably, Alice initially accepted the gifts with a startling lack of grace, ignoring her conscience until the next day when she'd phone or email or text Mark to say she loved him and that she was wishing away the hours on her Hello Kitty watch until home time. And then she'd prepare a gorgeous supper and have Mark in stitches with anecdotes from work. She'd run a bath for two with Costes bath foam and have candles lit in the bedroom. She'd lavish attention on his body, faking her own orgasm if necessary, ensuring Mark went to sleep with an exhausted smile on his face.

One of the mags Alice published ran an article defining Reverse Punishment Syndrome – *'he's trying to be nice but you're just nasty'*. Perhaps that's me, she thought. But the piece went to repetitive lengths (she'd scold the features editor) to tell her not to bollock her bloke for having a few beers down the pub with the boys, not to punish her fella for playing footie with the lads every single Sunday, not to hassle her man for inviting his mates round for Xbox marathons. Mark, however, didn't play football, didn't own an Xbox, pubs weren't his thing and he preferred a good burgundy to beer. She could never accuse him of choosing over her. She never had cause to doubt that she was absolutely the love of his life, the axis around which his world revolved.

'Is it that you don't like being on your own? Do you resent his job? Because you often work long hours too. Or is it that you simply miss him when he's not around? They're interlinked, undoubtedly, but fundamentally separate issues,' Thea asked, whilst wrestling with the home-cinema system one night when Mark was in Chicago.

'You actually *choose* to have nights off from Saul, don't you?' Alice digressed. 'You choose to spend time apart.'

'I like my flat. I saved for ages. I like to escape into my own little slice of Lewis Carroll Living,' Thea qualified, 'and you've avoided a direct answer. Look, do you really no longer have anything as dependable and old-fashioned as a video?'

'Not any more,' said Alice.

'Jesus, how many remote controls does a girl need?' Thea despaired, fiddling with another one.

'You'd think just the one,' said Alice.

Thea had been in love previously, but prior to Saul, love had lacked balance. It was only now, through the equilibrium and reciprocation achieved between the two of them, that she could see this. In the past, she had invested far more affection and trust, loyalty and generosity, than was ever returned to her. She'd attributed virtues and qualities not present to past boyfriends, in the deluded hope that if she believed they were faithful, loyal and as in love with her as she was with them, then perhaps they would be. Her dogged veneration of the concept of Romantic Love saw her turn a blind eye even when transgressions had leered back at her directly. Though her heart had been hurt, she had never let the pain harden her; she never questioned her belief that true love makes the world go round, she'd never lost hope that love could conquer all.

Before she met Saul, Thea had believed that the deeper the love the more wrought with complexity it ought to be. However, she also thought that great art was only born of angst until Saul took her to a Matisse exhibition at Tate Modern. And so it was with Saul that Thea discovered to her amazement that love could be the simplest thing in one's life. Being in love with Saul introduced her to the balance necessary for longevity. With this heaped magnificently on one side of the scale, Thea found all the other elements and concerns of life were invested with correct weight and proportions on the other. She was in love with Saul and he was just as in love with her and the plain fact was enough to keep a steady equilibrium in her life. All the love she gave him, he gave right back to her.

She loved Saul's spontaneous visits to the Being Well armed with orange juice or the new issue of *Heat*; how he'd pop in for a kiss en route to a meeting, drop off a raisin-and-biscuit Yorkie on his way back from an editorial brainstorming session. She loved how he would occasionally materialize behind her in the lunchtime queue at Pret a Manger, murmuring 'they say that banana cake is an aphrodisiac' or 'gissa bite of your baguette, love'. His text messages arrived at all hours and she never knew whether they'd be chatty, romantic or downright dirty. Sometimes he'd make love to her with great tenderness, taking time to stroke her, absorbed in just looking at her, watching the effect that altering the angle or a subtle variation in pace could have on the flush to her cheeks or the dilation of her pupils. And sometimes he'd fuck her most carnally, his eyes screwed shut as he screwed her, clenching his teeth as he grabbed her buttocks and bucked forcefully into her until he came. Sometimes, he was as sated purely through cunnilingus as she was; though she'd sleepily offer to return the favour, he'd hush her with a goodnight kiss, turn out the light and spoon tenderly against her. Thea didn't mind that he was grumpy when he woke up, that his farts were noxious and that he could snore for Britain. It didn't bother her that his timekeeping was lousy, that he'd snap at her if she talked during films, that their taste in music had few overlaps, that sometimes he bolted his food. She was glad to love him enough to allow him his personality. She had no higher ideal to project onto him. 'Rounded with rough edges,' she defined to Alice, 'he's not perfect and so he's ideal.' At last, Thea had fallen in love with someone she had no inclination, no need, to deify. Alice's wish for Thea had only ever been that someone would find her who deserved the depth of the love she had to give.

Thea and Saul could have frantic late nights gallivanting around the bars of Soho, or they could plunder Villandry and go home for extravagant carpet picnics. They could be the loved-up couple at dinners hosted by friends, or they could arrive together at parties but socialize separately, with the occasional grin or wink over to each other. They'd have backgammon tournaments which became quite tense, Scrabble sessions that were downright serious or raucous evenings watching DVDs of Spinal Tap or the Blues Brothers, aided by shots of home-made Mars Bar vodka. Then there were the evenings when they were so engrossed in their own thing that they hardly knew the other was there; the Saturdays when Thea ironed for most of the day and Saul tapped away at his laptop in her bedroom; the Sundays spent in affable silence over the newspapers. There were also Saul's evenings at the Swallow with Ian or Richard that Thea had no intention of gatecrashing. And evenings when Saul smiled at the thought of Thea all by herself, unplugging her phone so she could watch *ER* uninterrupted.

Thea read everything Saul wrote, but only once it was in print.

'Shall I start putting you in my columns?' Saul mused.

'What – Michael Winner style?' Thea looked up from the *Sunday Times*. 'Christ!'

Saul laughed. 'I was thinking more *à la* A. A. Gill, hon.'

But he didn't. Barefaced Bloke's readers had heard no more about the Gorgeous Thief since that article published the day they first kissed. Saul Mundy had a public voice and a private side. And when he finished writing an article with laddish overtones for one mag, or a column infused with sarcasm for another, or a review so cleverly barbed it was downright spiky, what he found most satisfying was to log off, look up and see Thea. Engrossed in a book, or quietly sipping a cup of tea, or embroiled in a text-messaging marathon with Alice, or simply daydreaming.

'She's my mate,' Saul qualified one evening to Ian, 'in every sense of the word. Soulmate, best mate, bed mate.'

'Flatmate?' Ian posed.

Saul sipped thoughtfully at his pint. 'Not yet,' he said cautiously, 'but there again, we've only been together a year.'

A Year Between the Sheets

ADAM

January, Issue 8

Jack Nicholson cover

- Is this the coolest man in the world?
- The year in preview – wear it, see it, hear it, buy it
- Health & fitness: six weeks to a six-pack
- Motors – penis extension or life support?
- Sex – do it
- Money – make it
- Property – live it
- Win! Gadgets and gear up for grabs

ADAM

February, Issue 9

Nicole Kidman cover

- Nicole, we love you, marry us
- Hot property – buy abroad, get a tan, make a profit
- Fitness: back your back
- Hand-made shoes and bespoke suits, every wardrobe
  should have them
- Sex – it's good for you, fact

- Tool kits and WD40: every woman loves a handyman
- Plus! Reviews – we've seen 'em, read 'em, heard 'em, tasted 'em and played 'em
- Win! Sail into the sunset: two weeks on a luxury yacht

ADAM
March, Issue 10
Sean Connery cover
- Connery – the real McCoy
- There's something about Mary, Isla and Jen – supermodels with brains *and* bod
- Prison – it's a step closer than you'd think
- Double your money in half a year
- Bachelor pad or disaster area: architects, designers, cleaners show us how
- Love handles? Man boobs? Stop it with the names and get rid of them in 4 weeks
- Sex – come together or drift apart
- Win! Top seats at Top 10 sporting fixtures

'Thea, I've blocked out your eleven-o'clock slot,' Souki put her hand over the telephone receiver and told Thea, who was arranging magazines for the waiting room and flowers for the reception. 'New client – sounds desperate.'

'Sure,' said Thea.

'That's fine,' Souki told the caller. 'May I take your name? Mr Sewell. Lovely, we'll see you in a couple of hours. Yes, Baker Street Tube. That's right. Goodbye.' Souki filled in the appointments diary and turned to Thea. 'Cup of tea?'

'I was half hoping Saul might pop by with lattes all round,' Thea remarked.

'Two days on the trot might be wishful thinking,' Souki said. 'Do you think we could offer Saul free fortnightly massage in return for daily lattes?'

'I'll put it to him,' Thea said, 'though he claims to hate massage. Says it makes him feel uncomfortable and exposed.'

'Just wait till he puts his back out through squash or something – he'll be begging for it,' Souki declared. 'Earl Grey or Red Bush?'

'RB, please. So who's the eleven o'clock?'

'A Mr Sewell – said he's done his back in,' Souki informed Thea, 'but as Brent and Dan are fully booked, I reckoned yours were the second-safest hands.'

Mr Sewell arrived ten minutes early. He was far younger than Thea had expected. In fact, he looked like Peter O'Toole in his Lawrence of Arabia period, which was a very pleasant surprise. Though dressed smartly, the pain from his back caused his suit to hang oddly, as if he'd forgotten to remove the hanger. Likewise, his face had an exaggerated angularity caused by teeth clenching; what appeared to be extraordinary blue eyes were dulled.

'Usually, clients who refer to themselves as Mr or Mrs Such-and-Such are older,' Thea remarked by way of small talk as she led the way to her room at the top. He didn't say his name was Gabriel until Thea took his details and asked for it outright. She noted him shift gingerly in the seat, a greyness flood his face as he did so. If pain was this visible, the poor man must be in torment, she thought. In her experience, men in pain either exaggerated its intensity or downplayed it entirely.

'Tell me about the pain,' Thea said, pen poised.

'Oh, it's nothing,' Mr Sewell lied.

From Mr Sewell's personal details, Thea considered his lifestyle and its possible ramifications on his current predicament. Gabriel Sewell was thirty-eight years old with a home in Clapham and an office in Mayfair. He was an actuary by profession – Thea didn't know what this entailed but ascertained it was sedentary and high-powered. He appeared to be relatively fit, playing five-a-side once a week, plus regular golf and occasional cycling. It seemed he was fairly healthy, good diet, good weight, just a social smoker and a regular but not heavy drinker.

'So,' Thea said, 'tell me about your back.'

'I'm sure it's nothing,' Mr Sewell began.

But it wasn't nothing. It transpired that leaving his wife over the weekend and hauling suitcases out of the loft and personal possessions out of the marital home had conspired to cause Mr Sewell's spasm.

'OK,' Thea said after working on him for an hour, 'I'll leave you for a moment. Take your time.'

She hovered outside her room, listening to silence followed by a sigh and the sound of Mr Sewell dressing. She knocked and after a moment, entered. He was sitting in the chair, gazing out over rooftops. His expression was unreadable but to Thea's trained eye, the tenseness in his neck had dissolved and the greyness of his complexion had lifted. She asked how he felt, if the treatment had helped, if the pain was diminished, but Mr Sewell expressed any gratitude in a monosyllabic way.

'I'd like you to come again,' Thea advised, 'towards the end of this week, preferably. I'd also like you to see one of our osteopaths for some manipulation.'

'Fine,' Mr Sewell said, 'OK.'

'I'll book you in downstairs,' Thea said, leading the way.

'Thank you, Miss –?' Mr Sewell waited to be informed.

'Thea,' Thea assured him, 'Thea's fine.'

He nodded and left.

'Thea darling! I'm late, I know – I'm sorry, honey, but I've had a bitch of a morning. A total *bitch*. And my back's killing me. Total fucking nightmare.'

Thea's twelve o'clock arrived quarter of an hour late with

his usual flurry of excuses. Because he was a regular, she would overrun her lunch hour to honour a full session for him. 'Don't worry, it's not a problem, Peter,' she acquiesced, 'come on up and let's get cracking.'

'I thought only osteos could do that,' Peter joked.

'*Let's get petrissaging* doesn't have quite the same ring to it,' Thea said over her shoulder as she climbed the stairs.

Peter Glass had been a client of Thea's for a year or so. He came in now for 'monthly maintenance' as he termed it, though he regularly phoned for 'crisis sessions' in between. This was meant to be a maintenance visit but it was obvious from his stilted gait that a crisis now superseded it.

'How are you, Peter?' Thea asked him, wondering how long it would take the serene atmosphere of her room to calm him. Peter was usually busy to the point of being manic – an upmarket estate agent earning on commission only, with a complex love life, a love of material goods and a propensity for changing his car as frequently as his girlfriend.

'Work's mental – good mental. Life's crazy – cool crazy. New squeeze, new Beemer.'

'What's Beemer?' Thea asked.

Peter laughed. 'BMW – Beemer, you know? Like Merc? Alpha?'

'Skoda?' Thea said.

'You don't!' Peter exclaimed.

'I don't,' Thea assured him, 'I have a Fiat Panda.'

'You *don't*!' Peter exclaimed with genuine horror.

'Eleven years old,' Thea said proudly. 'Now, how are you?' She glanced at the clock, knowing that he'd talk at her throughout the session anyway.

'Nightmare,' Peter groaned theatrically but with justification. 'Do you want me down to my Jockeys?'

'Yes, please,' said Thea, skimming her notes on Peter's last session, 'and then face down on the table.'

'How's your love life, babes?' Peter enquired, his voice muffled as Thea started the massage.

'This feels tight.' Thea ignored his question, pressing into his lower trapezius until she felt it yield.

'If I was single, I'd wine and dine you, honey,' Peter told her with an appreciative groan.

'If I was single, I'd turn you down,' Thea responded though immediately wished she hadn't.

'So you *do* have a love life,' Peter commented, 'but do you have a love nest? I can show you some gorgeous properties.'

'You haven't been doing those stretches I showed you, have you?' Thea chastised, glad to change the subject.

'Not enough hours in the day, babes,' Peter rued. 'Stretching takes too long.'

'Peter!' Thea admonished. 'That series I showed you takes a maximum ten minutes, on weekdays only. You can do them *anywhere*.'

'Not long but *slow*,' Peter qualified, 'I mean they feel like they take too long because they're so slow. All that holding and breathing. I don't do slow – not in my life.'

Reluctantly, Thea understood. He was a character, Peter Glass, a wide boy and charmer but self-deprecating and thus likeable. For all his bravura and bullshit, bragging of Beemers and calling every woman 'babes', he was a decent bloke contending with vicious pain.

'You do make me feel better,' Peter told her, knotting his Gucci tie. 'If I could afford the time I'd come to you every bloody week. Twice, maybe. It's only here that I slow down and unwind a little while you untie all those crap muscles of mine.'

'Let's book you in for next week,' Thea said.

'Cool, babes,' said Peter, 'but I may have to cancel last minute.'

*

'Zay say zat avocado makes a lady ripe for lurve. Zay say zat carrot cake makes a lady hot. Zay say zat cheesy crisps make a lady juicy.'

Thea stood in the queue at Pret a Manger, thrilled at the surprise of Saul whispering in her ear, with his improbable accent and bizarre theories on foodstuffs.

'Lady,' he continued, murmuring throatily, his voice an octave lower than his regular English accent, 'zay say zat a lady who likes avocado and cheesy crisps and cake of carrot, she is lady who do much sexy sex.'

'Piss off,' Thea whispered, giggling. Saul stood close behind her and kissed insistently behind her ear and along the curve of her neck. 'Stop it,' Thea hissed, 'we're in public.'

'Exactly,' whispered Saul. 'God, I'm horny.'

'I'm on a short lunch,' Thea apologized, now feeling quite horny herself.

'I'll walk you back,' Saul said, 'as long as the tent pole in my trousers doesn't get me arrested en route.'

It had snowed overnight and though the pavements were clear of it, a dusting still sprinkled the shrubs, iced the lawns and cushioned the benches in Paddington Street Gardens. Dogs trotted through the park with elevated action and children scampered around trying to snowball all spare snow.

'It always seems bizarre to be planning summer issues when it's February and freezing,' Saul commented, 'but that's my afternoon – top beaches and barbecue tips. And a haircut – look at me, Christ!'

'After my morning of men,' Thea told him, 'I have an afternoon of girls – my ballet dancer, two pregnant women and my little old lady. But I'd really better make tracks and warm my hands or I'll lose all my clients.'

'And then you'll come to mine?' Saul asked. 'Movie? Villandry carpet picnic? Rude sex?'

'Reverse order, preferably,' Thea said. She looked at Saul

and bit her bottom lip with coquettish intent. 'Who'd've thought that cheesy crisps were an aphrodisiac.'

Saul took Thea at face value and didn't dare say he'd made it up. 'Let's sneak up to your room for a quickie,' he said instead, 'you know you want it, you dirty thing!'

'You're incorrigible. I'm not remotely tempted,' Thea scolded him playfully, kissing him teasingly with her tongue before flouncing into the Being Well with a provocative wiggle.

'Christ, I need a shag,' Saul muttered to himself, putting beaches and barbecues on the back burner, the haircut on hold.

ADAM

April, Issue 11
Vic Reeves/Bob Mortimer cover

- Why British comedy rocks
- Rock – why British rock is comedy
- Sex – rock hard
- Vinnie Jones – still rock hard
- Travel – Gibraltar, Brighton and Australia – and other famous rocks
- Sport – rock climbing
- Win! Some rocks, courtesy of De Beers

ADAM

May, Issue 12
Emmanuelle Béart/Vanessa Paradis double cover

- It's in the Cannes – the sexiest film festival, now and then
- Secrets, lies and big big bucks – what keeps the film industry rolling
- Muscle in – steroid abuse: coming to your high-street chemist soon
- Sex addiction – bona-fide illness or top excuse
- Air guitar, shadow boxing and imaginary golf swings – good for your health
- Property how-to: it doesn't cost much and it won't hurt your back
- Win! A line in Danny Boyle's new film

Saul sat in Alice's office and they both swivelled in the chairs, Saul tapping a Biro gently against his teeth, Alice furrowing her brow and twitching her lip, while they brainstormed features for future issues.

'How about,' Alice mused, 'sex advice through the eyes of – hang on – a porn star, a sex therapist and a—'

'Housewife,' Saul suggested.

'Brilliant,' Alice said, her fingers scuttling over her keyboard.

'I was thinking,' Saul said, 'the Tour de France for the July issue – *the world's best athletes or drugged-up cheats.*'

'Yep,' said Alice, 'I like it. How's the August issue going?'

Saul twitched his lip. He looked sidelong at Alice, swivelled a complete revolution, rolled up the sleeves on his shirt, ran his fingers through his hair, rubbed his chin and then leant forward. 'I'm going to hear by the end of the week if we've got Bowie for the cover,' he said nonchalantly.

'Oh, Good Lord,' Alice exclaimed, blushing visibly, clasping her hand to her heart. She reached across her desk and grabbed Saul's wrists, her eyes darting around his. 'Seriously?' she whispered. 'Because you know you really must never joke about something like that.' Saul raised an eyebrow in affirmation. 'Oh, Good Lord,' Alice exclaimed. She slumped back in her chair. 'I'm coming to the photo shoot,' she declared. 'Have you told Thea?'

Saul shook his head. 'It's not confirmed,' he cautioned, 'and the shoot will be in New York.'

'Well, I feel a business trip coming on,' Alice proclaimed, 'and I'll need an assistant, of course.'

'I'm far too busy,' Saul declared.

'Not you, idiot boy, *Thea*!' Alice retorted, quietly wondering if an enduring crush on an ageing icon was in any way unsuitable for a married woman. She swiftly decided it was not.

'Anyway, Bowie or not, the issue's coming on fine,' Saul assured her, 'it'll be the biggest yet and the ad team are storming their targets already.'

'Brilliant,' said Alice. 'Bowie. Oh, my God. Right. Yes. Moving on – how about something on relationship dynamics, you know, who has power.'

'Who has the balls, who wears the trousers,' Saul said,

'that's good – I'll try and commission someone like Jeff Green to write it. Oh, Richard Stonehill is putting me in touch with a guy who has a self-build company – I thought that would make an interesting piece.'

'Certainly,' said Alice, 'and Ben from the music division is working on Liam Gallagher. Come on, let's go for lunch. Thea said you had an amazing weekend in Brighton. You were lucky with the weather – May bank holiday is usually a washout.'

Saul gathered his things and followed Alice through the building. He smiled to himself, recalling Thea that previous weekend, stripping off nonchalantly on a quiet spot on the beach. It was only when she was down to her knickers that he clarified it was Bournemouth, not Brighton, that had the nudist beach.

'Saul thinks we'll have Bowie for the August issue,' Alice told Mark as he loaded the dishwasher. 'Can you believe that?'

'Believe what, darling?' Mark asked distractedly.

'That we'll have Bowie for the August issue,' Alice frowned.

'Well done,' Mark said, straightening up and rubbing the small of his back. 'I think I'll take some paracetamol.'

'So I may go to New York for the shoot,' Alice said, though she feared tempting fate by being presumptuous.

'New York?' Mark said, rummaging through his briefcase for painkillers. 'No, San Francisco next week, home via Chicago.'

'I give up,' Alice muttered, turning her back on Mark and her attention to the *Evening Standard*, flipping noisily through the pages.

'Alice,' Mark protested quietly, 'I just really want to knock the Gerber–Klein deal on the head – precisely so there won't be so much travelling.'

'Until the next deal,' Alice said under her breath. 'Actually,

I was talking about *me*, Mark – *I* may have to go to New York.'

'For work?' Mark asked.

'Yes, Mark, we're shooting Bowie for the August issue and he's personally requested I attend,' Alice said with cutting nonchalance, though she was now convinced she'd probably jinxed the deal completely.

'Well, that's a feather to your cap,' Mark said ingenuously, wondering why his wife looked cross when her news was so good. He swallowed the paracetamol. 'John and Lisa have invited us to dinner next Friday,' Mark changed the subject brightly, 'and Leo and Nadia want to know if we'd like to accompany them to the Barbican the following week – *Madame Butterfly*.'

Alice tried to bite her tongue but she missed, snapping at Mark instead. 'Oh, great. Dull dinners with your boss and sodding opera with your dreary clients.'

'Alice!' Mark exclaimed, unprepared for her reaction. 'I thought you liked Lisa – you said she's a marvellous cook. And you've been saying recently how you'd like us to go out more, do things.'

'I'm more than just your corporate wife, you know,' Alice said, unfairly as Mark had never treated her as such. Mark, bewildered that a dinner invite and concert tickets could have such an adverse effect on Alice, started cleaning the coffee machine.

With her back towards Mark, she lowered her voice. 'I'm thirty-two, Mark. I don't want to do boring dinner parties and stuffy concerts all the time.'

'Come on,' Mark said, 'it's hardly all the time.'

Alice turned to face him, her hands on her hips. 'That's true,' she said, 'because the rest of the time you're invariably away.'

'Alice, that's not fair,' Mark objected, 'I work hard because

I work for *us*.' He waved his hand around vaguely to signify their home.

'And I'm just the little wifey keeping your home fire burning?' Alice asked spikily.

Mark ran his hands through his hair, though they were full of coffee grains. He was hurt. But very clear. 'You know what, Alice,' Mark said, 'for me that is precisely one of the joys of marriage – knowing you *are* my home. Wherever I am in the world, whatever time it is, no matter how stressful my day or how hectic my schedule, there's this underlying warmth and security which makes sense of everything – the knowledge of my wife, my home.'

Alice flounced off to bed early, in the spare room, in her old bed. She dreamt of New York and David Bowie; that she and Thea brought roses to the shoot, which liquefied into green gloop. In the small hours, she awoke with her heart racing, acutely aware of the hurt and confusion she'd caused the man who loved her most. She felt ashamed. Mark's love was unconditional and she told herself that she should aim to love him likewise. She waited a while and then tiptoed to their bedroom, to their vast bed and said sorry.

Mark was finding it difficult to sleep. His back hurt, the Gerber–Klein deal was a lingering headache and it pained him that he'd upset Alice. He welcomed her with open arms and a tender kiss to her forehead.

Alice had seemed distracted at Pilates, cutting her session short to sit quietly in the reception area, browsing back issues of *Hello* magazine. Even suggesting the bistro on a balmy May evening had taken Thea some doing. Assessing the menu, she remarked that Alice seemed tired.

'I'm not tired,' Alice said.

'Hungry?' Thea asked, beckoning the waitress.

'Not particularly,' Alice said, glancing at the specials board.

'Oh, my God, are you pregnant?' Thea gasped because Sally had recently announced that she was and *she* looked tired and had gone off Pilates and chips.

'I am most certainly not pregnant,' Alice declared flatly.

'Is it work?' Thea presumed.

'No, Thea,' Alice said, 'it's Mark.'

'Mark?' Thea balked, ignoring the chips, which had just arrived. She stared at Alice who was gazing into the middle distance of the restaurant. 'Alice?'

'Yes,' said Alice, prodding the pasta without looking, 'Mark.'

'What's he done?' Thea demanded, heaping Greek salad onto her fork.

'Nothing,' Alice said despondently, twirling the pasta to such a degree that it unwound from the fork completely.

'Nothing?' Thea repeated, with her mouth full.

'Yes, nothing,' Alice sighed, lifting her empty fork and putting it in her mouth, 'and that's the point. It's just nothingy.' She shrugged. 'All work and no play make Mark a dull, dull boy.' Though she felt instantly disloyal, she was just a little relieved too. 'I'm scared that I'm bored,' Alice confided, looking genuinely alarmed. 'I'm worried, Thea. Actually, perhaps it's not Mark. Perhaps it's me.'

Thea didn't want to hear this and didn't know what to make of it, let alone how to comment. 'Mark is all that you've wanted and he is all that you need, he's what you never had and you married him precisely for his commitment and his soberness,' she told Alice sternly.

'But his commitment is to work and he's so sober it's a bore,' Alice muttered. 'Corporate dinners and bloody opera, Thea, that's the sum of it.'

'What are his workmates like?' Thea asked, trying to be positive.

'Mark doesn't have "mates", Thea,' Alice said, 'he has colleagues and clients. They're fine – I mean, a similar age – but dull.'

'Well, I love Mark,' Thea said warmly. 'Let's organize some evenings together, the four of us. How about salsa? Or that hysterical pub quiz you and I used to go to? I don't know, ice-skating at Ally Pally?'

Alice shrugged. 'Can you honestly see Mark salsa dancing? Do you really think he'd leave work on time for a pub quiz?'

'Come on,' Thea said gently, 'perhaps you're a little stressed yourself – work?'

Alice laughed harshly. 'I have David Bowie as my cover boy – how can I be stressed?'

'Maybe Mark's stress is rubbing off on you?' Thea tried, knowing she didn't sound convincing.

'Mark is ticking along just fine, Thea – it's *me*,' Alice whispered. 'Suddenly he seems so much older than me.' She couldn't say it so she mouthed it, staring at the table. *Boring*.

Thea didn't want to hear this. Mark Sinclair was Alice's salvation, the yin to her yang. Alice, it seemed to Thea, had done the grown-up thing when she married Mark; she'd set the standard and embraced the rules. Alice being unhappy made Thea feel discomfited. That Alice was bored caused Thea to worry. As her best friend, she didn't think twice about reprimanding Alice.

'You need to remember all your reasons for marrying Mark,' Thea told her, 'and you need to remember that your playboy exes actually made you miserable. You need to think logically about marriage, Alice, because by definition, you're in it for the long haul. Of course there are going to be fluctuations in temperature – cold currents, heatwaves, warm periods. Maybe you should look on it as just being a little unsettled at the moment,' Thea concluded, hoping to sound reassuring, 'and know that it'll abate and be fine.'

'I'm starting to feel stifled, Thea,' Alice said quietly, wondering when her best friend had become a meteorologist and marriage counsellor. 'There seems to be no frisson between me and Mark. No fizz. It's all gone a bit flat.'

'Alice, I'm the diehard romantic here but even I can acknowledge that there's more to marriage than raunchy sex or just being in love,' Thea said. 'Anyway, I thought you said frissons and fizz were just phenyl-something.'

'Phenylethylamine,' Alice muttered. She felt irritated. It wasn't as if Thea was even living with Saul, so on what authority could she lecture? 'I mean, of course I want to grow old with Mark – I just don't want to be old while I'm still youngish.'

'It'll be *fine*,' Thea said, because she really couldn't start thinking it could possibly be anything other. She believed in the mystical sanctity of being in love; she didn't like the way Alice dissected it into chemical components, albeit light-heartedly. But just then, Thea prayed for surges of adrenalin and dopamine and that phenyl-something for her best friend, so that Alice could feel love flushed and happy to be Mrs Sinclair once more.

Later that night, after sending a text message to Alice assuring her that everything would be OK and that she was there for her, Thea rang Saul to say goodnight. He wasn't in and his mobile was switched off. She tried again ten minutes later. And then ten minutes after that, when his mobile was back on.

'Hullo,' said Thea, hearing traffic in the background, 'where are you?'

'I've just nipped out for a pint of milk and some chocolate biscuits,' Saul said. Thea was surprised he hadn't come across the milk she'd replenished that morning and the KitKats and Hobnobs. 'Oh,' Saul faltered, 'did you? Thanks. How was Pilates?'

'Good,' Thea said, settling into bed for a chat.

'What was it tonight – Rioja and chips?' Saul laughed, obviously walking briskly.

'Alice seemed a bit tired, actually,' said Thea, 'off her chips. Tell you what, why not call me from the land line in a mo'?'

Actually, it took half an hour for Saul to return Thea's call when it transpired he hadn't nipped to *that* corner shop but actually one further afield.

'Can I ask you something?' she asked him.

'Shoot,' said Saul, clattering around his flat.

'Mark –' Thea started. 'You get on with him, don't you?'

'Of course,' said Saul, 'who wouldn't.'

'But you *really* get on well with Richard, don't you?'

'Yes,' Saul qualified easily, 'Richard's a really good bloke.'

'Is Mark not a good bloke, then?' Thea asked.

Saul paused. 'Mark's more of a nice guy than a good bloke,' he explained.

ADAM

June, Issue 13
1st Anniversary special edition
Beautiful Britain cover

- Celebrate!
- It's a tough job, but someone has to do it: Britain's top-selling men's mag one year on
- *Models, actors, singers, whatever – the best of British*
- Power couples – who has the balls may not be who wears the trousers
- High street or haute couture – who can tell?
- Build muscle, lose fat, eat like a horse, no catch
- She told me she was 16 – and other nightmare scenarios
- Wear it, hear it, read it, see it – cutting edge and lead the pack

All the news-stands at Heathrow Airport were awash with the anniversary issue of *Adam*. Because Alice hadn't been able to justify a trip to New York for the Bowie shoot and because Mark himself had stayed longer than anticipated in the States, he was whisking his wife off to Marbella for the weekend as a consolation prize, a gesture. And also, a celebration – he'd finally secured the Gerber–Klein deal. He'd propped her passport and plane ticket against her toothbrush when he'd left early for work.

Mark picked up a copy of *Adam* and bought it. Alice looked puzzled. 'I bring copies home, Mark.'

'Ah, but I want the pleasure of buying my own. Anyone who's anyone buys *Adam*,' Mark said sweetly, 'it's the ultimate accessory. Anyway, a little subliminal marketing never goes amiss – I can always tuck my copy of the *Economist* inside the cover.'

Alice smiled and went in search of a paperback. She needed a break. They both did.

ADAM

July, Issue 14
Tour de France cover

- Superhumans or simple junkies – peddling and pedalling with the peloton
  - The porn star, the housewife, the sex therapist – three women set you homework
  - Beach buff – crash course to boost confidence and tone
  - Next year, we'll be mostly wearing . . . the fashion industry laid bare
  - I earn, I live, I'm broke – stretch it without feeling the pinch
  - The best – and worst – jobs in the world
  - The house that Jack built – self-build successes . . . and nightmares
  - Win! £50,000 of watches waiting

ADAM

August, Issue 15
Double cover: David Bowie/Iman

- Beautiful couple – Mr and Mrs Bowie, as good as it gets
- A shark ate my homework . . . and my arm – facing near-death with a sense of humour
- All buy yourself – online investing made simple
- Cooking – have her begging for more
- I'm 30 and I know I'll never have sex again
- Liam Gallagher, icon or scally?
- Property – buy or rent, sell or let?
- Scrutinized! New releases – buy it, or don't. Trust us

Alice and Thea were concentrating on Sally's abdomen. Sally sighed and poked herself in different spots. They all stared for a while longer. She stood, shifted around, sat down heavily and placed her palms all over her bump. 'Perform – or I'll dock your pocket money!' Sally growled at her belly.

138

'Was that something?' Thea gasped.

'No,' Sally said. 'But that is! Quick, give me your hands!'

Thea and Alice had their hands against Sally's stomach and stayed that way for quite some time to no avail. 'I know, I'll eat some pickled onion crisps – that usually has the wriglet cartwheeling.' But she'd eaten her way through an industrial supply recently and there were no packets left.

'Let's do the ring test,' Alice suggested. 'Sally, give me your wedding ring – and Thea, let me have your necklace. Then we dangle it over Sally's bump and if it swings back and forth, it's a boy. Circles – and it's a girl.'

'Oh, my God, it's twins!' Thea declared as the ring swung this way and that.

'Flatulence, more like,' laughed Sally.

Alice took the necklace from Thea. 'Seriously,' she said with a face so straight the other two laughed, 'it works – my grandma told me.'

'Your grandma also told you if you ate your crusts your hair would curl,' Thea reminisced, 'but despite living on toast you still had to resort to that terrifying perm when you were sixteen.'

'Shut up,' Alice said, 'watch – the ring is going round and round. You're having a girl. Oh. Hang on. No, it's not. What's it doing now? It's a boy.'

Soon enough, they were swinging the ring over the cat (who was male, according to the ring, though her kittens born two years previously would seem to disprove it), a picture of Prince Charles on the *Radio Times* ('Boy!' Alice proclaimed triumphantly) and Richard's shoes ('*Boy*! See!' Alice laughed). Even the floorboards had gender according to the swing of the ring.

'When are you and Mark going to breed?' Sally asked Alice, telling herself not to panic that the ring didn't appear to move at all when she dangled it.

Alice took the ring and assessed the sex of a cushion tucked up Thea's jumper. 'I don't know,' she said cautiously, 'I mean, when we were engaged we'd talk dreamily of babies and sandpits and Winnie-the-Pooh. When we bought the house we allocated "kids' rooms". But actually, we haven't mentioned it.'

'There again, I've been married to Richard for nearly seven years,' Sally said, 'and you two are still pretty much newly-weds.'

'Coming up to two years, actually,' Alice corrected. She gave Sally back her ring and hooked Thea's necklace around her neck. 'I guess I don't feel ready. I guess *Adam*'s been my baby. I guess you have to have sex to conceive and my husband is invariably in a different time zone and continent to me.'

'Mark would make a lovely father,' Sally projected. 'How about you and Saul, Thea?'

'Us?' Thea said, looking up from a pregnancy magazine. 'We're not even living together, let alone married.' Her glum pout surprised Alice.

'But you've been together for ages,' Sally declared.

Thea shrugged.

'You're not waiting for him to ask, are you?' Sally probed, as if the notion was so old-fashioned as to be far-fetched.

Thea shrugged again.

'Ever the romantic, our Thea,' Alice said fondly, giving her arm a reassuring squeeze.

'So?' said Thea, resolutely.

ADAM

September, Issue 16
Willem Dafoe cover

- The quiet hero – Dafoe defines cool
- Sex – learn the language of talking dirty
- Perfect 'V' – hone your physique in a month
- Divas, sparrows, angels, fruitcakes – female rock goddesses
- Yeah man, I was there: Woodstock, Isle of Wight, Glastonbury
- Big Brother – 130 CCTVs log your daily movements
- Fast-food nation – terrifying facts that'll have you reaching for the alfalfa
- Toys, gadgets and gizmos – we don't need them, but we love them

ADAM

October, Issue 17
The Survivor's Guide. Underwater cover

- How to love and have lust survive
- How to do platonic sex and have the friendship survive
- How to dive with sharks and survive
- How to play the stock market and survive
- How to cook a banquet and have your guests survive
- How to renovate your house – and have the building survive
- How to win a survival course in the Pyrenees

Mark stroked Alice's stomach, turned away from *Newsnight* and tucked a lock of her hair behind her ear. 'When is Sally's baby due?' he asked.

'Couple of months,' Alice told him, her eyes on the vast television screen, 'I think her due date is Boxing Day.'

'You'd look glorious pregnant,' Mark anticipated. Alice was quiet. 'Maybe we should think about trying?' Mark said. 'We are married, after all. And we are ageing rapidly. And we do rattle around this big place. And I don't know about you but maybe the cogs of my biological clock are starting to turn.'

Alice wanted to cry and she hadn't a clue why. She invented a coughing fit and rushed to the kitchen for a long drink of water.

ADAM

November, Issue 18
Mick Jagger cover

- Old enough to be your dad, cool enough to be your mate, rich enough to buy a continent – Sir Mick, we salute you!
- Stay or stray? When love loses lust
- Lizzie Jagger – what *would* her dad say?
- Undercover in Afghanistan
- Armani or Burton – who suits you?
- Fitness – prepare now for your mum's Christmas cooking
- Sex and drugs – don't try this at home
- Money – save or spend: is it worth it?

Kiki had worked in the West End for three years, from the time she came to Britain from Indonesia at the age of seventeen. She liked it. The money was good. Her colleagues were now as close as family. Her clients were mostly fine. Her accommodation exceeded her expectations. She felt she had much to be thankful for because she knew she was much luckier than some. Kiki chose not to take much time off, limiting herself to one morning and one afternoon a week but never a whole day. It didn't seem worth it; her plan was to save and not spend and she didn't hate her job enough to run from it whenever she could. She'd seen quite early on how not much business came in on Monday afternoons and Sundays so these were the times she decided not to work.

In the first year of her life in London, she had spent her Sundays and Monday afternoons too overwhelmed by the scale of the capital city, the pace of it all, to do much else than go from McDonald's to McDonald's, splitting a meal between establishments and giving herself an allowance that stretched to a further soft drink and two cups of tea to fill her free time. It wasn't that Kiki became braver, but as time passed the city seemed smaller; her awe simply dwindled and her penchant for McDonald's ceased altogether. As her English improved and she found *Time Out* fairly easy to read, she took to venturing further afield. She started with the major museums and galleries, then she sought out smaller collections, traversing London from east to west, north to south as she did so.

She went on a tour of the Thames Barrier and walked around Hampstead with a group of strangers and a guide dressed as Charles Dickens. She lay on her back alongside other visitors at an installation at Tate Modern and craned her neck during a walking tour of the financial district. She went backstage at the Royal Opera House and down into the orchestra pit at the Barbican. She pressed the buttons in the Science Museum and rode the small train at Kew Bridge Steam Museum. She walked around a candlelit restored Huguenot property in Folgate Street in reverential silence and sang 'My Old Man Said Follow the Van' raucously at a living Music Hall museum. From fans to dolls, musical to medical instruments, from wine to buses – it seemed to Kiki there was a museum to celebrate everything.

Kiki had never heard the shipping forecast. The radio at work, when on, was set to Heart FM and softly at that. But she'd read about an exhibition called 'The Shipping Forecast' showing at a gallery space within Spitalfields market and, though she didn't know her North from her South Utsire, it was a rainy October Sunday so she decided to go along.

'At school, Alice and I did a project called The Shipping Forecast in our second year,' Thea told Saul. 'It was our first and – if I don't count our David Bowie collage – our last foray into mixed media.' Saul laughed and unfurled his umbrella to protect them both from a sudden squall. 'Don't laugh,' Thea protested, 'we sewed and stuck and modelled and carved all the stations on the forecast. We spent ages on it. And though we spelt German Bight incorrectly and treated Lundy Fastnet as a single location – overall, it looked good.'

'So do those burgers,' Saul salivated as they walked through Spitalfields, 'look at the size of them.'

'Culture first,' Thea said, 'then I'll buy you lunch.'

The exhibition was small; just one photo per location, but the space was cleverly subdivided by walls and screens to create a journey for the viewer. This also served to give a sense of private viewing time in front of each image, the chatter of the market merely a muffled background thrum. Saul was leaving Dogger and Thea was approaching Biscay when Kiki moved away from South-east Iceland.

'Hullo.'

Thea glanced round but the greeting appeared to be directed at Saul. She narrowed her eyes and tipped her head, regarding the girl. She knew her from somewhere. 'Hullo,' Thea said.

'Oh, hi!' the girl exclaimed, blushing. She bade Saul and Thea goodbye and off she went, with the shy smile that had enabled Thea to place her.

'It's clicked,' Thea said to Saul.

'Sorry?' Saul said. 'Great photo, this one of Rockall – look at the quality of the light.'

'The girl – that girl,' Thea continued, thinking the photo Saul referred to was actually quite ordinary.

'What?' Saul looked confused and was moving over to Bailey.

'That girl,' Thea said, 'just then – who said hullo to you and me.'

Saul pointed to the photo of Malin. 'Now this,' he said, still pointing, 'this I like.'

Thea stood alongside him and slipped her hand into his. 'I prefer that one behind there, of Portland,' she said, guiding Saul through with her hands in the back pockets of his jeans.

'She works a couple of doors down from the Being Well – in that dodgy sauna-massage place!'

'Really?' Saul said, peering at the Hebrides.

'You've probably seen her without realizing it,' Thea said, 'en route to visiting me.'

Saul turned away from Cromarty. 'Shall we go for that burger now?' he suggested, putting his arm around Thea's shoulders and guiding her away from Viking back through to the market.

ADAM

December, Issue 19

Julia Roberts as Christmas Fairy cover

- All we want for Christmas is Julia
- Christmas parties – seasonal snogging, festive favours, misplaced mistletoe
- Christmas bonus – mine's bigger than yours
- Christmas crap – we sift through the tat so you don't have to
- Christmas cheer – your round
- Christmas dinner – dos
- Christmas carols – don'ts
- Christmas present – free CD: the year's hottest sounds
- Christmas past – how to do a great New Year's Eve

'Do you know, I've been married for exactly two years and this is the first time I've used this particular Le Creuset casserole,' Alice declared to Thea, peeling a label from the lid.

'Is that because you're a ready-meal kind of girl,' Thea teased her, 'or because you eat out an inordinate amount?'

Alice laughed. 'Actually, it's because I put one of absolutely every Le Creuset product on the wedding list so I simply have had no need of this dish thus far.'

'I assume this corkscrew was a wedding present too,' Thea grumbled, 'it's so state-of-the-art I haven't a clue how to use it. In fact, I'm assuming it *is* a corkscrew, right?'

Alice gave Thea the onions to peel while she wrestled with the corkscrew. 'Bloody thing,' she said at length, 'I'm sure the regular old one is at the back of a drawer.'

'And which drawer would that be?' Thea remarked, eyeing the impressive run of them.

'Your guess is as good as mine,' Alice sighed. 'You rummage through those over there and these here, and I'll wade my way through those and these.'

'Bingo,' Thea said after a good five minutes' clattering,

147

fulminating and rediscovering items Alice had thought she'd lost. She uncorked the Rioja and poured two glasses, adding a slosh to the sauce bubbling gently in a small Le Creuset saucepan. 'When's Mark back?'

'Friday,' Alice said.

'Christ, that's cutting it fine for Christmas shopping, isn't it?' Thea declared.

'That's why he'd better find time to shop in Singapore,' Alice reasoned, 'or else I'll make him suffer for it during the January sales.'

'Did I tell you I'm going to Saul's folks for Boxing Day?' Thea said, sitting herself up on one of the many work surfaces while Alice arranged orange slices and cinnamon sticks on top of the chicken. 'It's weird, in London, and as I know him, Saul seems so self-contained, so independent, at harmony with his environment – as if he's always been this age, living in his pad, doing his job.' She raised her legs so Alice could retrieve a zester from a drawer beneath her. 'Yet back in Nottingham there are graduation photos and junior-school woodwork examples and tennis trophies belonging to someone called Saul Mundy who I don't know. And parents. I find them peculiar too – though actually they're completely normal and really pretty nice. I simply can't connect Saul to them.' Thea shifted slightly so that Alice could check the recipe propped up behind her. 'It's as if seeing him in his family home rids him of some of the identity I associate with him.'

'Mark hasn't changed a jot,' Alice said fondly, shutting the oven door and wiping her hands on her jeans. 'It'll be an hour and a half, shall we have some nibbles while we wait?' Alice and Thea sat and chatted, sipped wine and munched tortilla chips. 'The bloke in my wedding photograph is identical to the photo on his parents' mantelpiece of the twelve-year-old collecting his Junior Chess Champion

148

medal from Peter Purves,' Alice said, stretching out on her sofa and placing her feet on Thea's lap. 'Mind you, I suppose I've known Mark for almost as many years so there are unlikely to be surprises or skeletons.' They chinked wineglasses and suddenly she missed him very much. 'I feel bad,' she confided. 'He goes away and I denounce him – yet then I think of his Junior Chess Champion medal or the way he folds everything away every night and I long for him.'

'Friday is only the day after the day after tomorrow,' Thea soothed.

'I'll probably be a stroppy cow when he's back,' Alice said, resigned, 'poor old Mark.'

'Mark thinks he's the luckiest bloke in the world,' Thea told Alice.

'I think we should do our New Year's resolutions tonight, you and me,' Alice declared, 'because we won't see each other till next year, after all. I kind of wish Mark hadn't booked Paris for New Year's Eve – but there's no way I can complain, let alone cancel.'

Over a fabulous Moroccan chicken casserole with saffron rice and roasted butternut squash, and Christmas crackers from Heals, Alice laid out her hopes for the next year.

'I want to win Publisher of the Year,' she listed, straightening her paper crown, 'I want *Adam* to outsell *GQ*.'

'Those aren't resolutions,' Thea told her, testing the plastic whistle that came in her cracker, 'they're goals.'

'Top of my wish-list,' Alice shrugged, reading the cracker joke and deciding swiftly it wasn't worth repeating out loud.

'What about you and Mark?' Thea asked.

'I suppose,' Alice said cautiously, 'it would be to spend more time together. But then that was my aim last year. I suppose, it's for me to be less narky with him. And to develop a taste for opera.'

'And thoughts of babies, perhaps?' Thea suggested.

'I'm going to see Sally tomorrow,' said Alice, changing track but not the subject. 'I bought the dearest present for baby Juliette.'

'Well, if you do have any thoughts about babies,' Thea said, 'for goodness' sake tell Sally not to tell you her birth story.'

'Shitting a watermelon?' Alice asked.

'With spikes on,' Thea whispered.

'Anyway, I'm not thinking of having babies,' Alice whispered back.

'But Mark is,' Thea said quietly.

Over Marks & Spencer's Christmas pudding and fresh lychees, Thea divulged her thoughts for the coming year. 'I'm going to redecorate my flat – a room a month,' she said, 'and I'm going to go running every other lunch hour. I'm going to do my tax on time and pay my credit cards off each month.' She chinked Alice's wineglass.

'And Saul?' Alice asked. 'Where do you see the both of you this time next year? Will you have wed and bred?'

Thea fell silent. She pressed the back of her fork down hard onto the pudding, squashing it flat. 'Actually,' she said, 'I'm hoping for some sense of planning. A strategy.' She took a second helping of Christmas pudding and ate a couple of spoonfuls thoughtfully before peeling another lychee. 'You know lychees are known as "babies' bottoms" too?' she remarked.

'It still doesn't make me broody,' said Alice, analysing the fruit.

'I don't doubt Saul's love for me,' Thea explained, 'but we never really assess it. Neither of us has a problem with commitment – but we haven't ever sat down and analysed where we're at. We just stroll from day to day, ambling along, hand in hand.'

'It sounds idyllic to me,' said Alice, 'and anyway, you know how it's sometimes counterproductive to analyse a relationship – the whole "let's talk about Us" syndrome.'

'I know. Believe me, from experience, I do know that. But I wouldn't mind hearing Saul proclaim that I'm the girl for him.' Thea shrugged at Alice.

'I know what it is,' Alice said, pouring them both some Cointreau. 'You have no shadow of doubt that Saul is indeed your knight in shining armour. But what you want is for him to behave like one,' she declared.

'Rose between his teeth, bended knee – the lot,' Thea laughed, her fist to the table. 'God, you know me well – if you weren't already married, I'd suggest you and I wed.'

'Would you say yes, then, if Saul asked?' Alice probed.

'I don't need him to ask me to marry him,' Thea said, 'that's not the point at all.'

'You are funny – funny peculiar,' Alice said, 'you're such a sucker for extreme romance and yet marriage just isn't on your agenda, is it?'

'But you're just as funny peculiar,' Thea sparred, 'because you can explain the sensation of love in chemical terms yet you marched down the aisle in a traditional frock with a great big grin on your face.'

'Perhaps it's because my parents set me an excellent example of marriage, but yours didn't,' Alice said.

'Perhaps,' said Thea, 'but fundamentally, I regard being in love as so intrinsically, mystically sublime that the man-made institution of marriage seems irrelevant. I think the awesome aspect of true love is trivialized by signing a piece of paper.'

'Well, I think marriage is an excellent idea,' Alice declared. She thought for a moment. 'I suppose where you don't see marriage as being the point of love, I don't see love as being the point of marriage,' said Alice.

'But you do love Mark,' Thea cautioned, 'don't you?'

'Of course I do!' said Alice. 'Will you please stop going on at me about that.'

The Isley Brothers

'You should practise what you preach,' Alice tells Saul non-chalantly while they pore over contact sheets of a recent shoot with Kate Winslet for a forthcoming cover. She bends over the light box, giving a skilled twist to her hair and fixing it against her head with a Biro to keep it out of the way. She lowers her right eye to the loupe and deftly scans the shots. With a yellow chinagraph pencil, she marks off four or five frames, sits back satisfied and hands the loupe to Saul.

'Can you just remind me what I've preached?' Saul humours her while he inspects the contact sheets even faster than Alice, ultimately agreeing with her preliminary selection.

'Well, the figures coming in for the last issue suggest it was our biggest seller yet,' Alice informs him, while marking the chosen images of Miss Winslet to be cropped, 'and I do believe it was your idea to call it the Romance Issue; that you coined the spine quote: "Warmth can be cool – rock on, Valentine". In a nutshell, the slant on love and all its panoply was your call.'

'Which you tried to overrule!' Saul quips, with a raised

eyebrow. 'You thought the February issue should have a completely sarcastic and ironic take. Which it then transpired *GQ* and *Arena* and *FHM* all took. Boring.'

'Anyway,' says Alice, rather primly, 'you should put your name to it.'

'You're not still on at me to join your sodding staff, are you?' Saul sighs, surreptitiously trying to read one of Alice's memos, albeit upside down.

'Christ no, you'd cost me far too much in annual salary and perks now, Mr Mundy,' Alice exclaims. She regards him contemplatively, her head tipped to one side, her hair starting to escape anarchically from her improvised Biro clasp. 'I'm talking about taking your work home.'

'If you are telling me to work from home, you're hardly practising what *you* preach,' Saul says. 'You give Mark a hard time if he even skims through the *Economist* after seven p.m.'

'Not in that respect, you noodle,' Alice says affectionately, 'I'm simply suggesting that you redirect a little of the focus you laid on romance for February's *Adam*, to your home life.'

'Alice,' Saul says with exaggerated exasperation, 'what the fuck are you going on about? You're talking so cryptically I can't work out if you're telling me off, telling me to work less from your office or telling me to become a torch-bearer for Romance.'

'Yes!' Alice exclaims, triumphant, her hair in a sudden swoosh around her shoulders, the Biro on the floor. 'Romantic hero! That's *precisely* what I'm suggesting. With a capital R.'

Saul frowns and then regards Alice suspiciously. 'Are you talking about Thea?'

'Sort of,' Alice confesses, 'but if you tell her, I'll bloody kill you and *then* I'll sack you.'

'If. I. Tell. Thea. What?'

'It's just I know that recently, privately, she's been hoping for some declaration of intent,' Alice shrugs, 'and Saul, you're bright enough to figure out what I'm on about.'

It was a freakishly balmy late February and Saul eschewed ordering a cab in favour of the bus but soon enough jumped from that at the lights to indulge in a long and cathartic walk home from his meeting with Alice. Figuring out what she was on about was alternately unnerving yet stirring. When the thinking became too onerous, he'd pop into a newsagent to check stock and positioning of the titles he worked for, on occasion phoning the publishers to report his findings. One shop still had their Valentine's Day display up, but all the cards and trinkets were half price. Saul found himself browsing, tempted to buy a card – not because it was cheap but simply because it had a cheery photo of two amorous tortoises which he thought Thea would like. Actually, Saul had given her a large envelope filled with Loveheart sweets for Valentine's Day, though he'd painstakingly removed any with inappropriate inscriptions like 'Big Boy' or 'Hunky'. Saul put the rutting tortoises card back. He checked the magazine stock, repositioned *Adam* to the front of the rack, and walked on. He was a little troubled. Was Thea unhappy? But she hadn't given him any cause to think so. He was gently perplexed. Had he ever given her reason not to trust him or believe in his commitment and affection for her? He was sure that he hadn't. What he did acknowledge was that two years and three months into their relationship, he felt so completely comfortable with Thea being an integral part of his life that he really didn't give the matter much thought any more.

Perhaps that was the crux of it; the rub for Thea that Alice alluded to. Though he always looked forward to being

155

with her – and a night apart was rare now – just then he accepted that he never actually told her so. It didn't occur to him to. Wouldn't it seem contrived? And anyway, wasn't the proof in the sweet pudding of their combined lives? He had as many clothes at her place as she had at his, their social circle was so fully integrated that he would need to concertedly recall whose friends were whose originally. Thea's new Hoover was bought by Saul and he'd retiled her bathroom with as much pernickety pride as if it was his own. Often, she changed his linen as a matter of course, stocked his food cupboards and thought nothing of answering his phone, land line or mobile, if he was out of earshot. So many other signs illustrated a love so legible that surely it didn't need to be spelt out too? Everyone knew Saul and Thea were a team. It was such an oft-pronounced phrase that it sounded as though they were no longer two distinct people; the 'd' was dropped and the words fused: Saulan-Thea. The balance between them was such that little rocked their proverbial boat. They got along too well for that, liked each other so much that they never found reason to disagree, or much point in arguing.

Do I take Thea for granted? Is that what Alice implied?

When Saul finally walked up Great Portland Street it was gone six o'clock. He'd been walking for three hours and his feet were sore, his mind still fugged. Was he doing something wrong or just not doing right enough? He meandered circuitously to his street. From the corner, he looked up and saw that his lights were on. He stood still for a while and regarded the run of his windows, stopping to thoroughly analyse what he normally gave no second thought to. Thea Jessica Luckmore, aged thirty-three, was up there. That was a fact. Five feet four inches high, around nine stones in weight, natural mousy hair, hazel eyes, slightly skew bottom teeth, impressive scars from a vicious dog, favourite colour turquoise, favourite book *Black Beauty*, all-time favourite song 'Cygnet Committee' by David Bowie, favourite film *Jules et Jim*, favourite animal tortoise. Supports Chelsea FC but prefers watching rugby. Electric toothbrushes make her gag. Drinks hot Marmite when she has a cold. Once performed a tap dance on *Blue Peter*. All facts he knew off by heart. At that very moment, she was in his flat. Probably watching the early-evening news or taking a shower. Or perhaps she was just sitting quietly letting the physical tensions she'd massaged from her clients all day ebb away from her. Saul walked a few paces closer but stopped again, looking up at his flat.

I don't know what she's doing up there, actually, but the fact is that I much prefer returning home to a flat full of Thea than one devoid of her. She is part of my world. She is synonymous with Home. She lights my life. She makes my space personal. She defines it.

He continued to loiter on the corner, engrossed in thoughts about light bulbs. They were on in his flat and, as if in a cartoon strip, Saul envisaged one suddenly sparking into light atop his head. As if he'd just had the best idea in the world. Like the answer to life itself had clicked on. How many feminists does it take to change a light bulb? Just one, actually – and I don't think that's very funny. How many Theas does it take to change a light bulb? None, actually. Saul had systematically gone through her flat just that weekend and replaced the lot.

February may have been unseasonably mild but Saul acknowledged it was downright deluded to have the Isley Brothers' 'Summer Breeze' soaring through his mind. Over the years, when discussing his Desert Island Discs with friends or compiling his Top 8 by himself in the bath, it had been the only mainstay on his list. It was one of those songs that in his head he sang perfectly but out loud, when he so wanted to put the power into his voice that the song instilled in him, the result was discordant and cringeworthy. Just then, though, it wasn't the summer breeze per se, nor the bizarre notion of having jasmine in one's mind; it wasn't the sweet and melodious tune nor the joyous vocals. For Saul, the immediate connection was with a man returning home; knowing from the mere hang of the curtains, from the little light shining in the window, that his love was there, with her arms reaching out to hold him, to make his world all right. More than all right. The blissful domesticity of it all. What more could a man want?

> *And I come home from a hard day's work*
> *And you're waitin' there*
> *Not a care in the world*
> *See the smile a-waitin' in the kitchen*
> *Food cookin' and the plates for two*
> *Feel the arms that reach out to hold me*
> *In the evening when the day is through*

Saul takes the stairs, two at a time, music filling his soul, mirroring his feelings, reverberating around his head, providing the answer. He bursts through the door and Thea looks up. There she is. There she is. Sitting on the sofa with her feet on the coffee table. Painting her toenails. Wearing a T-shirt of his, inside out. A mug and a screwed-up KitKat wrapper by the bottle of nail polish. *The Simpsons* on the television with the volume turned down. David Bloody Bloody Bowie on the stereo.

'Hullo,' she says, 'I'm painting my toenails. It's a freebie from Alice – it's Chanel. I've cooked us something delicious. It'll be ready in an hour. How was your day?'

Saul doesn't know what to say because he hasn't a clue where to start or how to say it. The Isley Brothers desert him. All he can do, just now, is nod and say hi, kiss the top of her head and kick himself, as he passes by on the way to the fridge for a beer.

'Are you all right?' Thea asked him, a couple of hours later. She regarded him with a softly suspicious expression.

'Fine,' Saul assured her. 'God – why?'

'I don't know,' Thea said lightly, 'you've seemed a little pensive and you keep looking at me when you think I won't notice. Makes me think I have a Biro mark on my chin or a stray bogey.'

Saul drew her against him, enfolding his arms around her, and gently placed his lips to her temple while they watched the nine o'clock news.

He slept fitfully that night. They'd had intercourse by frantic fucking rather than refined lovemaking more akin to his earlier mood. He should have been worn out after that, drained after all his thinking on top of a long walk home. But he'd drift off then wake up, every hour or so. At two a.m. he awoke to the Isley Brothers playing again and again in his head. Be quiet. At four a.m. he woke again because he could no longer hear the Isley Brothers, his heartbeat drowned it out. And Alice. Oh shut up, Alice. I can think for myself. By five a.m. Saul had reached a turning point.

I'm confident I haven't done anything wrong – but perhaps, just perhaps, it really is time to do the right thing.

The notion made him feel exhilarated and terrified and like waking Thea right there and then. However, at some point, he must have slumped down into a soundless, dreamless sleep because when he woke with start at eight o'clock, he felt exhausted and fuggy and, as a consequence, noncommunicative.

'See you later, grumpy,' Thea said, kissing his cheek as she left for work.

* * *

Shall I email her?

Ask her by text message?

But not over the phone.

Should I write a love letter or dictate a message to a florist and have it sent in someone else's handwriting with a huge bouquet?

Shall I just stride into the Being Well, burst in on her and ask her outright?

Perhaps I should whisper it to her while we make love?

Or ask her nonchalantly after we've had sex?

I could do it over dinner – a ready-meal or after sausages at the Swallow or even a table at Sheekey's?

I could call to her from my window when I see her approach.

Ought I to whisk her away and do it on some glorious bridge in Venice or Paris or Las Vegas even?

Blag an Aston Martin DB7, take her for a spin and then ask?

Should I run any of this past Alice?

Or Ian?

Should I let Barefaced Bloke do the talking for me in my piece this Sunday?

How about a singing telegram?

Balloons in a box?

Icing – literally – on a cake, spelling it out?

First thing in the morning? So how about tomorrow?

Last thing at night? What about tonight, then?

No time like the present? Then fuck it – why don't I just jump on my scooter and nip up to Crouch End right now?

Serenade outside her Gothick tower?
Rapunzel, Rapunzel – I have something to say.
Did David Bowie say anything on the matter? Hang on,
I'll just do a Google search to find out.

But what will she say?
What will she say?
And will she say yes?

Crowded House

It's raining. It's pouring. It's bucketing down cats, dogs and hailstones on a day when really it shouldn't. It is the first day of spring and it also happens to be Juliette Celia Stonehill's baby blessing. Her daddy is pissed off because he hired an awning, paid caterers, organized everything impeccably but forgot to even hope the weather would be fine. Her mummy is in a bit of a flap because she doesn't know quite how to position sixty people on the ground floor of a Highgate terrace house.

'Sally!' Thea pipes up. 'Brainwave – you, Richard and Baby Ju stand on the landing at the top of the stairs, god-parents on the steps below, then close family for the few steps down and then we'll all shove and scrum around the lower steps or out in the hallway.'

'Genius!' Sally exclaims. 'But – oh.'

'What?'

'Come with me a sec – you stand at the bottom there. Now, look up at me standing at the top from different angles and check you can't see up my skirt.'

'Great knees, Sally – but that's all you're giving me.'

'Cool, great. But – oh. Do you think it's rude to ask

162

everyone to take their shoes off – the carpets are new?'

'Yes – but no one would put it past you to.'

'OK, everyone! Everyone. We're having the ceremony on the stairs and can you all take your shoes off, please. Pass it on. Pass it on, Thea – can you spread the word?'

When Saul Mundy had split from Emma all those years ago, one of the things that upset her most was the fact that he didn't cry. One of the things that made the ordeal easier for Saul was an inkling at the time that Emma was actually charging her waterworks with a torrent not entirely commensurate with her distress. He'd since written a couple of pieces as Barefaced Bloke on the whole subject of men and tears. He'd focused on the tears shed and embraces shared by grown men when Spurs lost to Arsenal in the last minute. Another time, he claimed that contrary to popular belief, heterosexual blokes cry frequently and easily. The perfect trigger of Bruce Springsteen songs, for example. Whisky, in certain amounts. *Raging Bull* and *Chariots of Fire*. Wrestling with IKEA shelving. Getting pubic hair caught in a zip – not necessarily one's own. Zip, that is.

Saul himself did not subscribe to stiff-upper-lipness yet he did not cry often. Recently, Springsteen had got to him. And Spurs losing, of course. But that day, the first day of spring, in his socks at the Stonehills' house in Highgate, he did. It was as if all the most cherished components that made up his world were colliding – yet on impact they were cloaking him in cloud-soft warmth and affirmation.

Life is really, really good. I am thirty-five years old and that baby girl is so tiny and beautiful. And her very existence makes sense of all the things we take for granted and don't bother to think about or don't treasure and acknowledge enough. Sex is fun but baby making is what it's all about. And my friend Richard made that little Juliette. And

163

*he wasn't a friend until I met him through the woman I love.
And I met him because she'd given him the jacket I'd lent
her up on Primrose Hill one November afternoon that seems
an age ago.*

'Saul?' Thea whispers. 'You OK?' He turns to look at her
and nods and grins with eyes that are bloodshot from the
pressure of welling tears; his nose crackling with snot. Thea
looks simultaneously embarrassed but moved. 'Shh!' she
hushes because Saul's sniff makes heads turn away from the
action on the stairs. She hands him a tissue, which Alice has
passed her with a nudge and a raised eyebrow.

'Soft git!' Alice whispers carefully to Thea. Thea giggles.

'Saul,' Thea finds him knocking back champagne as though
it's lemonade, 'you OK?'

'Fine!' he declares. 'Thirsty.'

'Were you OK?' Thea asks him tenderly, putting her arms
around him. 'Back there?'

'Back there?' Saul frowns, feigning confusion.

Thea tips her head to one side and regards him quizzically.

'Champagne?' he offers.

'Piss off!' Thea retorts. 'You know champagne and I don't
mix. Evil stuff.'

'You would think that after a lifetime as a hack, he could
take his drink by now,' Thea apologized to Sally an hour
later while Saul swayed around the hallway, peering at framed
photos unsteadily.

'Don't worry about it,' Sally laughed, 'take him home and
put him to bed with a bucket nearby.'

'Thanks,' said Thea, rolling her eyes, 'Mark and Alice are
giving us a lift.'

'Thea, is everything OK there?' Sally lowered her voice.
'Alice seems a little – I don't know. Distant? Preoccupied?'

Thea thought for a moment. 'She's fine,' she said, 'she's Alice. Mark's been abroad a lot and she's feeling a little – needy.'

'We need to make tracks,' Alice said, her coat already on, 'Mark's got to go into the sodding office.'

'You could stay? Cab it home later?' Thea suggested.

'I think I'll just catch up on a little work myself,' Alice said flatly. 'If you two still want a lift, we're going now.'

'Bye Alice, bye Mark, bye Thea,' Sally kissed them all and waved them off from her doorstep. 'Bye Saul. Oops – easy there, tiger. Christ, is he all right?'

'Fuck bollocks, my knee. Ouch. Wank,' Saul fulminated in a stagger towards Mark's very nice Lexus.

Although Thea focused on Saul for the journey over to Crouch End, noting with alarm a green-tinged pallor permeate his face by the top of Coolhurst Road, she was also able to observe her best friend gazing out of the window in a quiet world of her own, a downward sigh to her shoulders. Just then, she wished she was sitting with her arms around Alice, rather than serving as a buttress to the slumping Saul. Thea also noticed that Mark drove with deliberate attentiveness to the route and road sense, thereby counteracting any chance for chat.

He's probably just worried Saul will throw up on the cream leather, Thea told herself, *or thinking about the hassles awaiting him at the office, perhaps.*

Thea put Saul in her bed with a bucket at the side and a jug of water and a packet of Nurofen on the bedside table.

'I love you, Thea,' he slurred while she bustled around him, undressing him and plumping pillows, 'I really love you and want to get you for ever.'

'Now, let's go and have a pee, yes?' she said in a matronly manner. 'Come along.'

'I don't want to have a pee,' he mumbled petulantly.

'Come on,' she said as she hauled him through to the bathroom and pulled down his boxers, 'have a nice pee.'

'I don't want to have a pee,' said Saul sulkily while it gushed out with Thea's guidance.

'Now let's get you into bed.'

'I don't want to go to bed,' Saul objected, bashing his shoulder into the door frame but appearing not to notice. 'Come for a cuddle? A nice shag?'

'Have a snooze first,' Thea cooed, thinking just then that she really did not want to cuddle let alone shag this beery leery lump.

'I don't want to have a snooze,' Saul pouted as she shoved and pushed him to a safe place at the centre of her bed.

'Do you feel OK?' Thea asked. 'Because there's water right here – and a bucket just there if you don't.'

'I feel very OK,' Saul muttered with his eyes closed and a frown he couldn't correct. 'Room going dizzy.'

'Oh shit,' Thea whispered under her breath while closing her nose to his. She flicked his cheeks and shook him. 'Saul. Saul! Open your eyes and sit up. Now. Hey you! Up!'

Saul's eyes opened in sluggish succession and he lumbered himself up into a seated position of sorts. He brought his face in the approximate direction of where he thought Thea's voice had come from and, finding she had quite a few faces, he tried to keep his glazed eyes anchored to some of hers. She didn't really know his face at all just then and she wasn't sure whether she was amused or actually a little repelled. 'I love you, Thea,' Saul slurred, his eyes welling, 'marry me, Thea, marry me.'

'Drink some water, Saul,' Thea said, 'here – sip. That's right – it's a lovely pint of beer. Sip some more. OK. Do you feel OK? Sip some more. Do you want to pee again? Yes? Right, come on then. No, you can't pee in the bucket. Oh

Christ. No no! Not on the carpet – in the bucket, then. There. Good boy. Finished? Good. Oh shit, not finished – careful! OK, now back into bed. More sips of water. I mean beer. Little sips. Don't gulp. I'm going to wash out the bucket and bring it back. Are you going to puke? No? Well, I'm going to bring the bucket back just in case.'

'I love you Thea and I want to live with us for ever and ever.'

Thea patted his forehead and went to rinse out the bucket and replenish the glass of water.

Saul had been so drunk he couldn't remember a word he'd said to Thea. Saul had been so drunk Thea hadn't bothered to believe a word he'd said.

Peter, Gabriel

'Thea? Sorry to phone so early – it's Mark.'

'Hullo, Mark – I was up actually. I slept on the sofa – Saul's sleeping it off in my bed, drunken bum. Is everything OK?'

'I've done something to my neck – that's why I'm ringing so early – I just wondered if you could squeeze me in? I'm in pain and I can't move it much.'

'I don't have my appointments diary – I'll be at work at nine – I could call you then? I can assess you but you may need an osteo.'

'*Nine*? Oh. It's just I have a meeting and I was wondering—'

'Oh. Yes, of course. Can you make eight? In fact, I could probably be there for seven forty-five.'

'Thanks, petal.'

'Don't be daft! Oh, is Alice there? Can I have a quick word?'

'She's still asleep, Thea. My neck – you know – anyway, so she slept in the spare room. So as not to disturb me, you see.'

'Sometimes spasms are only partly physiological,' Thea advised Mark gently as she assessed his predicament an hour later. 'The pressure of stress can greatly exacerbate even mild twinges.'

'There's a fair bit going on at the moment,' he told her. Thea nodded.

'At work,' Mark added, lest she should probe.

Thea nodded again. Over the years, she'd found that simply nodding whilst looking down at her notepad, pen poised, often encouraged her clients to elaborate with greater honesty than if she asked them outright. She looked down at her notepad and waited for a moment before nodding again. But Mark said no more.

'I would really like you to see one of our osteopaths,' Thea recommended, 'Dan and Brent are both excellent. But you have to promise me not to cancel – I know you're busy but believe me, it's a false economy to turn your back on the odd hour of osteopathy. I can ask the guys if they can schedule you in for an early or a late. Failing that, I'll ask if they know of a practitioner nearer to your work.'

'Thanks, Thea,' Mark said, 'I appreciate it.' He bent down gingerly to pick up his briefcase.

'Lower yourself, don't bend! Lower like a child does – they squat, keeping their backs straight, they never stoop. And lift like a weightlifter – face straight ahead.'

Thea insisted Mark put his briefcase back down and they made a few practice lowers and lifts. He marvelled at the simplicity but efficacy of the technique. He did it again. 'Christ – thanks, Thea.'

'No problem,' Thea smiled, 'and don't roll your neck like that!'

'Sorry,' Mark said sheepishly.

'Buy a packet of frozen peas on your way to work, wrap it in a towel and plonk it on your neck,' Thea suggested.

'Peas?'

'Sweetcorn will do too. And take it easy, please,' Thea

said gently, 'or just a little easier. At work and at home.'

However, by then Mark had put his jacket on and his guard up.

There was nothing a good full English breakfast couldn't cure and though Saul had woken with a cracking hangover, two sausages, eggs, beans, bacon and fried bread later he felt revived and clear-headed. He'd just go back and tidy Thea's flat and then make his way into town. As miserable and rainy as the previous day had been, it was now a sparkling spring day. With the aesthetic wizardry of sunlight and clear skies on a March Monday, Crouch End resembled a bustling, self-contained, relatively picturesque market town. Strangers greeted one another cheerily, mothers promenaded cutting-edge buggies boasting babies resplendent in bright knits and cute hats, pensioners dawdled happily, catching up on the price of this and the cost of that and wasn't yesterday's weather *atrocious*. Pairs jogged to and from Priory Park, shopkeepers stood outside their premises grinning at nothing in particular and friends gossiped as they made their way to Banners for smoothies and comfort food. Saul thought how Hollywood would pay big bucks for such a scene; quintes-sentially English due to the balance of local architecture, local colour and local characters. As if on cue, a talented young television actor passed by Saul and said 'All right, mate?' as he went. 'Hiya,' Saul replied. He was in a very good mood.

Peter Glass wasn't. Peter Glass was actually in a full-blown foul temper. He'd invested hours each day, over a number of weeks, in a potential buyer who that morning had pulled out at the last minute without so much as an apology, let alone an explanation. So the luxury trip to the Seychelles was off. And so was upgrading the Beemer.

'All right, babes?' Peter said to Thea in a hollow voice

170

and with a face like thunder. 'If you can massage away the aggression I feel, I'll pay you double.'

'You don't need to pay me double,' Thea assured him, 'just lie down and I'll let your body guide me. Trust me. Try to clear your mind. Try not to talk.'

'I could fall asleep,' Peter murmured, an hour later.

Thea looked at her watch. She had an hour's space before her next client. 'Just relax for a while, Peter, I'll come back in a mo'.' Actually, Thea returned forty minutes later and gently woke him up.

One ballet dancer, a pregnant woman and a tennis coach later, Thea's last client for the day is Mr Sewell. She has continued to call him Mr Sewell though he is now a regular client and even occasionally divulges quite personal information with no warning and certainly no prying on her part. Recently, he'd expressed his concern that his neck felt no better though he was much happier in himself having returned to his wife. On his last visit, he'd actually started reciting lines from the new Ricky Gervais television series and had laughed so much the bed had shaken.

Souki meets Thea on her way down to the waiting room. She's holding a latte and a muffin. 'Mr Sewell is here,' she says, 'and so is Saul. With coffee and cakes for us all, bless him.'

'Hullo, Mr Sewell, would you like to go on up and get ready,' Thea says, giving Saul the same nod she gives all her clients, 'I'll be with you in a moment.'

Saul waits for Mr Sewell to disappear upstairs. Thea could murder that muffin. It had been an early start and a long day.

'I'm starving,' she says. She approaches Saul who is offering her the cake. He snatches it back as she's about to take it. 'Hey!' she protests.

'Say yes!' Saul says. 'If you say yes, the muffin is yours.'

'Yes?' says Thea. 'Whatever – yes *please*.'

'But you don't know what you're agreeing to!' Saul exclaims.

'I'm so hungry I'd agree to anything,' Thea assures him.

'Really?' he says, a veritable twinkle to his eye. Thea nods, literally licking her lips. Still he holds the muffin aloft. 'Would you say yes to a Gimp Mask and PVC crotchless knickers?'

Thea regards him as if he's mad. 'Yes, yes, now give me the sodding muffin – I'm going to be late for Mr Sewell.'

'Would you say yes to moving in together?' Saul says, offering her the cake.

Thea's heart leaps into her mouth while her stomach somersaults and Saul's proposal fills her head. Suddenly, there is no room for cake. And she can't find her voice and time stands still and poor Mr Sewell is in his underwear, face down on the bed in the room at the top.

'Well,' Saul says, 'are you going to say yes?'

Thea stares at him.

'Is that a yes?' Saul asks, jiggling the cake temptingly.

Thea gulps.

'Live with me, be with me,' Saul implores, 'let's move in together, live with each other for ever and ever. Live happily ever after.' He picks out a chocolate chip. 'Say yes – and the muffin is yours.'

Thea blinks, grins and nods. Yes, she mouths. 'Yes!' she laughs.

'Fantastic,' Saul says, 'and all for the price of a muffin.' He turns her around to face the stairs. 'Back to work, missy,' he laughs, giving a gentle shove to her bottom, 'see you later.'

Thea is five minutes late for Mr Sewell.

'Sorry to keep you,' she apologizes quietly. She puts the muffin down on the table. She knows that she'll be in a quandary whether to eat it or keep it for sentimental posterity.

'Now,' she says to Mr Sewell, 'how's that back of yours?'

'Not bad,' he says, lifting his head a little, 'how are you?'

It's the first time Mr Sewell has ever asked Thea anything remotely personal. She's slightly taken aback. 'Oh, fine,' she breezes, 'I'm fine, thank you.' She lays her hands lightly on Mr Sewell's back, closes her eyes and inhales deeply. She controls her exhale while she moves her palms up his back to his neck, strokes out along his shoulders, sweeps down and up his arms, squeezes along his upper arms and then swoops her hands back over his shoulders and down his back. He sighs with relief and pleasure. His body feels good to her. Much softer and more receptive than on his last visit. It's an easy massage to give.

Cohen & Howard

Alice held Thea very close as she embraced her. And when she sensed Thea was ready to pull away, she held her tighter still. 'Good,' she said, 'I'm so pleased. It's the right time. It's brilliant news.'

'Do you think I'm doing the right thing?'

'You have to ask?'

'Are you happy for me?'

'You have to ask?'

'You do think that Saul is The One For Me, don't you?'

'You have to *ask*?'

Alice and Thea gazed at each other, manic excitement manifest and contagious in their dancing eyes and slight breathlessness.

'So,' Alice said, 'there we have it. We're all grown up, you and I. God, I'll probably be pregnant by your house-warming party,' Alice said with a slump to her shoulders, 'and I'll be confined to wearing some God-awful kaftan and support tights.'

Thea looked at her thoughtfully. 'I wasn't really thinking of house-warming parties. But are you really thinking about pregnancy?'

'I can't see how my marriage will survive if I don't,' Alice reasoned, a little darkly.

'Shit,' Thea exclaimed, 'don't say that. You're not serious? I mean, I know you've been low – ambivalent even – but we've talked through it all, haven't we. Time and again. Surely you are not considering a baby to hold the answer?'

Alice was quiet. She regarded Thea with a meekly apologetic pursing of her lips. 'I'll never forget your mother begging you to be the glue to keep your father from leaving. How old were you? Fifteen?'

'Fourteen,' Thea corrected.

'When did you last see him?' Alice asked.

'Three years ago?' Thea estimated.

'It's interesting,' Alice said quietly, 'how divorce affects a child by shaping their attitude towards love as adults. Many become totally averse or utterly cynical to long-term relationships. You come from a pretty poor example of marriage and yet it seems it's given you the determination to truly believe in lasting love. It would make an interesting article for *Adam* – how *blokes* are affected by their parents' relationships.'

'Well, it seems you and I have struck lucky with Saul and Mark then, as they both come from good stock,' Thea mused.

'You make them sound like prize rams – in fact, you sound like your mother!' Alice laughed. Her expression changed, she placed the back of her hand against Thea's cheek. 'You have always imposed somewhat fairy-tale proportions onto love and eternity. I know I tease you. And sometimes, it *has* landed you in a pickle. But ultimately, I think it's your greatest strength. I may rib you for being a hopeless romantic but actually I admire you for it.'

'You don't mind that I don't believe in your theory that your phenyl-something is the cause of love?' Alice laughed and shook her head. 'When I was little,' Thea said cautiously,

175

'the only way to block out the noise of the rows, the only way to put something pretty into my life, was to lose myself in this imagined world of heroes and heroines triumphant in love.'

'Well, now you have your hero in Saul,' Alice said conclusively.

'And you have yours in Mark,' Thea said, adding a note of warning to her voice. 'Do not use a baby as glue, Alice, please.'

Alice regarded her wedding ring thoughtfully. 'Glue, Sellotape, Velcro,' she said quietly, 'some type of weather-tight bonding is needed, that's for sure.'

'Bonding,' Thea said, musing over the word. 'It'll be within you, within the home itself,' she said decisively, 'you'll just have to patiently seek it out.'

'And there ends our correlation between love and sticky stuff,' Alice proclaimed. 'There are only so many metaphors a girl can take in her lunch hour.'

'Love *is* sticky stuff,' Thea shrugged with a wink, 'if we're talking fellatio.'

With his sharp suit, loud tie and verbal swagger, the estate agent at Cohen & Howard reminded Thea of Peter Glass but as Saul didn't know Peter Glass, and as Thea assumed that all estate agents were probably alike, she didn't comment. Just then, with the agent slicking back his already product-laden hair and rolling a fat Mont Blanc pen avariciously as if it were a cigar, Thea wondered whether they should have consulted Peter instead. He'd been in that morning. On a roll. Deposit paid for Seychelles ultra luxury. Upgrading the Beemer to a Merc. Taking a new girlfriend to Chinawhite. Hardly aware of the crick to his neck.

'Miss Luckmore,' the estate agent was saying, 'will Cohen & Howard be handling the sale of your property too? We do have an office in Muswell Hill – and market share in N10, N8, N22.'

'We would consider it,' Saul butted in, enunciating his vowels an octave lower than Thea had heard before, 'for a drop in your commission to 1 per cent, bearing in mind that you'll be handling the sale of my property and most probably arranging our purchase too.' Thea didn't mind that Saul had answered for her. She found it quite touching. Plus he was saving her 1.5 per cent which would probably pay for an IKEA kitchen. 'If we can agree on such a commission,' Saul was saying, 'you may have both premises to market.'

'Immediately?' the agent asked with a lip-lick of gleeful anticipation.

Saul and Thea looked at each other. Saul raised an eyebrow and a smile broadened. Thea bit her lip – not with reservations but to quell a rising chirp of excitement. 'Immediately,' Thea told the agent.

She and Saul left the office with a clutch of property particulars and, with arms linked and a skip to their stride, headed for Patisserie Valerie on Marylebone High Street to peruse the details over coffee and cake. For a day devoted to the exposing of fools, April 1st for Saul and Thea was proving to be a day in which they were making some very wise moves. Saul put his arm around Thea's waist and pulled her close to him, giving her a smacking kiss to her temple. She beamed up at him. 'I'm so excited!' She started babbling about Shaker-style kitchens and granite worktops and Smeg fridges in retro pink. She enthused about Purves & Purves for rugs, that she'd seen Mies van der Rohe style Barcelona chairs on the web for a bargain. With a footstool and no delivery charge. Perhaps in cream. 'Designers Guild for fabrics!' she exclaimed. 'And can we buy a superking-size bed? I love Farrow & Ball paint colours.' She was hopping and weaving in her excitement. 'Bridgewater!' she beamed, standing outside the eponymous shop. 'Oh my God, I *adore* her crockery.' A few steps later, Thea was darting over the road and pulling Saul into the White Company. 'Divine!' she repeated as she ran her hands lightly over the stacks of linen. 'Let's make the bedroom a peaceful haven of muted tones. Mushroom. Ecru. Flax. Calico. Vanilla.'

'His and Hers waffle towelling robes?' Saul suggested, twirling one against himself, his gentle sarcasm totally lost on Thea.

'Actually,' she replied artlessly, 'the Conran Shop's the place for bathrobes – we could look at prices after we've had tea.'

Even an old-fashioned homewares shop caught Thea's attention as they strolled on and she enthused about their exhaustive range of Vileda mops and accessories. Jabbering on about cream carpets, Venetian mirrors and terracotta chimineas for patios, she danced in front of Saul so that he almost tripped, wrapping her arms around his neck and standing slightly on tiptoes to kiss and kiss him some more. Calmly, he encircled her waist with his arms, lifted her up and continued to walk towards Patisserie Valerie while Thea laughed and embraced him as he carried her.

'Oh here, this is for you,' Saul said. 'It's only silver – but I thought it was very you. The jeweller is Ian's sister.'

Outside Waitrose, Thea looked at the ring. It was inscribed.

∞ *I have spread my dreams under your feet* ∞

'*Tread softly because you tread on my dreams*,' Thea said quietly, completing the stanza. She loved that Yeats poem. She looked at Saul, elated, awash with love and brimful of excitement for their future. Their dreams were shared, their future spread ahead. For Thea, not even the most sumptuous wedding in the world, or the most gorgeous flat on the market, or the most expensive ring from Tiffany, could actually better the dizzying happiness she felt just then.

'Well done, mate,' Richard said to Saul, slipping his racquet into its cover.

'But you *slaughtered* me,' Saul laughed as they headed from the court to the showers.

'I meant about Thea, you prat!' Richard said with a friendly shove. 'Sally told me you're buying a little love nest together.'

'We've signed up our flats with Cohen & Howard,' Saul called over the shower cubicle.

'Wise,' Richard affirmed. 'Did they drop their commission?'

'You bet,' Saul said, 'I mean, both properties should be a doddle to sell. And we both bought at the right time.'

'Well, if you need an architect,' Richard laughed.

'Discount?' Saul joshed, grabbing a towel and throwing one to Richard.

'Yeah, right,' Richard laughed. 'Anyway, what are you looking for and where?'

'I thought I'd have a tough job suggesting Thea relinquish her Crouch End affections,' Saul mused, 'but actually she's really into the idea of central London.'

'There are some great developments near Covent Garden,' Richard informed him, 'the Drury Lane end. I know of one not yet released – I could try and organize a viewing.'

'That would be cool,' Saul thanked him, 'I know Thea likes the idea of Bloomsbury too. But she's seen too many Merchant Ivory films.'

'I have to say, the area you're in at the moment is fabulous,' Richard commented, heading out from the changing room.

'I'll drink to that,' said Saul, clanging shut the locker and following him out of the changing room.

'You'll drink to me trouncing you at squash first,' Richard

laughed over his shoulder, as they headed for the bar, 'and then we'll drink to you and Thea.'

'And then we'll wet your baby's head,' Saul elaborated.

'And then we'll raise a glass to my wife,' Richard said.

'I can't believe we haven't been out to celebrate Juliette's birth,' Saul marvelled, 'we must be talking four months or so.'

'Christ, I had to negotiate hard with Sally, let me tell you,' Richard sighed. 'I get tonight off only on the guarantee of a midnight curfew and the assurance of only mild wooziness as opposed to utter inebriation. *And* she's factored into the equation a lie-in on Saturday *and* her own night out with Thea and Alice next Wednesday.'

'She drives a tough bargain, your wife,' Saul commented, raising his glass to her nonetheless.

'I have my two beautiful girls,' Richard declared with a happy shrug, 'they have me wrapped around their little fingers – but I'm a pretty happy captive.'

Hullo, little home. Hullo, my little slice of Lewis Caroll Living. I've entrusted you to some wide-boy estate agent with a dodgy goatee beard. Lance from Cohen & Howard's Muswell Hill office. He says you'll be a breeze to sell. And I have no idea why I feel guilty. Like I'm abandoning you to some unknown fate, like I'm turning my back on you after all the security you've given me. But I like to think of some other Thea chancing upon you, living here and loving it until life moves her along too. Saul says I mustn't become emotional about selling. I walloped him for that – what a daft thing to say. Of course it'll be an emotional process. Do you know he says it would be better for me not to meet potential purchasers? He ganged up with Lance on that one. Saul says he knows me, he says if potential purchasers don't live up to my exacting expectations, I won't sell to them even if they offer the asking price. But to me, that's obvious – to him, that's daft. Lance looked horrified.

This home is an extension of me – an expression of who I am and how I've been; a living photo album, an entire diary of my last five years. All the things these walls have seen! All the comfort I've felt here, the safety of it all – the stains from my tears, the marks of my happiness. I could write a novel about it! I can't possibly sell to someone who won't love this place as I have. I'll always love Crouch End and my memories of my gorgeous first flat will remain vivid and cherished. I was very, very happy here. When I was a single girl. All that time ago.

The first person who walked through Thea's front door made an offer within twenty-four hours. The second person who viewed the property half an hour later, made an offer the next day of the asking price. Lance warned the third person before they went to see the flat that he'd already had two offers within twenty-four hours of the property being on the market. That person saw Thea's flat and offered the asking price there and then, before they'd even stood in the hallway with all the doors closed for maximum Lewis Carroll impact. Thea didn't quite know why she declared she needed a night to think about it. And nor did the potential purchaser, who promptly raised his initial offer of the asking price by a full five thousand pounds, guaranteed a speedy exchange of contracts and volunteered details of his lawyer, his surveyor and his mortgage company. 'Let me sleep on it,' Thea pleaded with Lance.

'Well, sweet dreams, darls,' he said to her, 'but you'd better get an early night because I'm telling you, they'll be on the phone as soon as the office is open tomorrow morning.'

That evening, Thea thought how Peter Glass calling her 'babes' was more classy, more genuinely affectionate than Lance's 'darls'. But she couldn't let that influence her decision.

She just wanted a night all alone in her home before she gave the go-ahead. She sent some goodnight kisses in a text message to Saul but it was to Alice that she sent a text: fuck fuck fuck do i sell sell sell??? Tx

The reply was immediate: yes yes yes Axxxxxxxxx bloke = nice gay guy who sez flat is DIVINE! Thea sent back.

sounds perfct! ;-) Alice wrote.

r u watchng ER? Thea texted back

yes! Alice replied, Carter damn cute

Luka cuter! Thea responded.

fone during ads? Alice wrote.

k xxx texted Thea.

'So, basically, if I accept the offer the whole thing could be done and dusted within a few weeks.' Thea switches the phone to her other ear and changes the subject after a lengthy and thorough dissection of *ER*.

'Look, I know this purchaser isn't in a chain and he's offering top dollar and he's a nice sensitive gay bloke who loves your colour schemes and is into the whole Rapunzel vibe, but don't be pressurized to rush it through,' Alice advises her, tucking the phone under her chin while she runs a bath. 'You and Saul mightn't find somewhere for ages.'

'Yes, but I can move into his place,' Thea theorizes.

'True, but all your stuff would have to go into storage and it is *his* place,' Alice reasons, 'I mean, it may be cool and funky but it's not big.'

'True,' Thea agrees, 'true.'

'You should go for a speedy exchange of contracts,' Alice recommends, 'and then a slightly longer completion – at least that way you have the security of the purchaser's deposit.'

'Makes sense,' Thea agrees, 'I'll sleep on it. Anyway, how are you? Are you packed?'

Alice groans. 'No,' she sighs, 'I mean, what the fuck am I meant to take?'

'I don't know,' Thea says, 'what does one wear on an all-expenses-paid management-bonding trip? I've never been on one – it's not really a perk in my line of work.'

'It's hardly a perk,' Alice groans, 'it's a pain. I mean, we managers all know each other well enough anyway. Why we have to traipse out to France for five days I don't know. I'd get more of a feel-good factor from a hefty bonus or an increase in holiday entitlement.'

'Well, at least you can shop,' Thea says.

'We're in the middle of fuck-knows-where,' Alice says sulkily, 'the nearest town is Arles which is more famous for Van Gogh or Cézanne or someone, than for Prada.'

'Well, at least you may come back with a tan,' Thea says.

'I looked at the weather forecast there just today. *Il pleut.*'

'Come on, Alice,' Thea says, 'it'll probably be a laugh.'

'They've told us to pack "cagoules" – the closest I have is my Agnès B mac and I'm *not* taking *that*!'

'I have a cagoule,' Thea confesses cheerily, 'you could borrow it if you like.'

'Is it repulsive?' Alice asks.

'Fuck off! It's Berghaus, it's cutting edge and it cost a lot.'

'Could I borrow it then?' Alice asks a little sheepishly. 'That would be great – oh, but what colour is it?'

'Black and red,' Thea tells her and Alice can sense she's raising her eyebrows.

'Well, my walking boots are black Gore-tex,' Alice muses.

'See, you *can* be colour coordinated *and* appropriately dressed,' Thea concludes.

'Languedoc, here I come,' Alice says with negligible enthusiasm, 'whoopee-doo.'

'When do you leave on Friday?'

'Some ungodly hour,' Alice moans, 'back next Tuesday. I

can think of better ways to spend a long weekend, but there you go.'

'Text me while you're there, won't you?' Thea says.

'If I get a signal in the middle of Cézanne country,' Alice says darkly.

'Is Mark away anyway?'

'Ironically, no – so it's his turn to rattle around the house on his tod,' Alice says with a note of triumph. 'Listen, can you give that cagoule to Saul – he's coming in for a meeting on Wednesday so he could bring it in for me.'

'No problem,' Thea says, 'and Alice – shall I accept the offer then?'

'Yes, yes, you should,' Alice says encouragingly, 'it's time to get the ball rolling, Thea my dear. Time to trade in your little bit of Lewis Carroll Living for something more grown up.'

Alice envisages Thea sitting there, curled on her sofa, looking around her flat, nodding reflectively. She'll text Thea before she goes to sleep, she decides, tell her again that she should go for it. That it's the right decision. That she'll be quids in, in every respect. For now, Alice will drizzle an extravagant amount of Penhaligon's bath oil into her bath and luxuriate – after all, she may well be restricted to lukewarm showers in the depths of Cézanne country.

La Grande Motte

The group flew into Montpellier airport. All of Alice's colleagues had packed rucksacks, two or three even opting for a size small enough to pass as hand luggage. Because it had been traumatic enough for Alice to pack a cagoule, there was no way she was going to forsake her Mulberry grosgrain holdall for a backpack. Her bad mood blackened when her luggage arrived on the baggage reclaim damaged. Off she flounced to the baggage-handlers' office to complain.

'Come on, Alice,' Steven Hunter from the music division called over to her on behalf of the group, 'the coach is waiting.'

With her hands still stroppily on her hips she spun on her heels and glowered to all asunder. 'Coach? *Coach*? Oh, for Christ's sake.'

However, she was happy to concede that with its air conditioning, the lounge-style seating, various refreshments and superb suspension, the coach was a far cry from that which she was expecting: the juddery, slurching vehicles upholstered in the colours of vomit she recalled from school trips. Her appeasement was short-lived and her lifted spirits dove again on arriving at the hotel.

'It's not a hotel,' she hissed to Jeanette Baker from the lifestyle division. 'It makes Center Parcs look like Gleneagles.'

'You're such a snob!' Jeanette teased her. 'Who cares if it's Butlins de la Camargue – the plonk'll be plentiful and we'll be happy campers.'

Alice raised her eyebrows at herself and smiled. 'Do you reckon we'll have mini-bars in our rooms?'

'Rooms?' Jeanette exclaimed. 'You do know we're having to bunk up?'

'Bunk up?' Alice asked.

'Share,' Jeanette elaborated, 'in groups of three.'

Alice laughed heartily and gave Jeanette a jocular nudge. While the lady with the clipboard who'd accompanied them from the airport bustled through to the hotel reception, Alice coolly took stock of the situation. The group consisted of twenty respected managers each on a high and esteemed rung of their company, all justly honoured by PPA, BSME or ACE awards, soaring circulation figures and massive advertising revenue to their credit. In addition, most were married, all were in their thirties or beyond, on top salaries with share options and positions on the board. Of course they were going to have their own rooms, with mini-bars and satellite television.

Oh no, they weren't.

'I thought you were joking,' Alice almost wept to Jeanette, an expression of pleading panic furrowing her face.

'Well, I have my iPod and speakers and Jacquie Duckworth bought duty-free gin and two hundred Marlboro Lights – so our dorm will be rocking,' Jeanette tried to enthuse.

'You bet,' said Jacquie, her duty-free carrier bag clanking in proof. 'Who needs a mini-bar?'

'You're on!' said Alice, hoping her enviable collection of

Bobbi Brown cosmetics would be seen as a valid contribution.

'No, you're not,' Ben Starkey butted in darkly, 'they've already designated who's in which room.'

'You are *joking*!' Alice exclaimed hoarsely, while Jacquie almost dropped her fags and lost her bottle.

'He's not,' Jeanette said glumly, trudging off with the publisher of the crafts titles and the director of circulation.

The accommodation was set in the grounds, in rows of gaily painted breeze-blocked cabins, optimistically called chalets. As Alice trudged towards hers, she was suddenly aware of the natural beauty of the landscape and that it was quite at odds with the ugliness of the hotel complex. The sea could be heard but not seen and the big sky of the Petite Camargue, by then streaked with a colour close to apricot, seemed somehow higher and lighter than that above London. Beyond the hotel grounds, inky pine forests fringed the dunes that led to the coast and a distinctive salty tang from the lagoons and marshes permeated the air. However, Alice's appreciation of her new surroundings was negated on arriving at Chalet B27. Pea-green on the outside, the breeze-blocks inside had been painted the colour of lemon curd, jumping to a hue close to tomato ketchup in the bathroom. It was by no means cramped, in fact it was spacious, with an additional toilet and a large hallway doubling as a lounge with peculiar seating modules made from foam blocks covered with bright fleece fabric. However, in the bedroom Alice felt irritated by the organization of space. Why insinuate that the three beds were afforded privacy by placing them at acute angles, partially screened by ugly furniture? Why not just build stud walls and be done with it? Alice rarely smoked and gin was not her tipple, but as she attempted to unpack how she craved a swig from Jacquie's bottle, a lungful of Marlboro Lights.

*

'Gosh, three coat-hangers between us,' Anita Farrell remarked as if it were a scandal. 'Luckily for you two, I only brought casual clothing so you can share my hanger.'

Alice smiled fleetingly at Anita, who was placing well-worn slippers by the side of her bed. Then she glanced at Rochelle who was arranging framed photos of her horse on the chest of drawers.

Christ and Double Christ.

Alice was in a sulk.

Why wasn't she sharing with Jeanette and Jacquie? How on earth would sharing rickety wardrobe space with a fifty-year-old equestrienne and a slipper-wearing spinster editorial director of the business periodicals augment her career? In what way was any of this going to affirm her affection and fidelity for the company? And how were *Adam* and *Lush* and the rest of her titles to benefit from their publisher spending a week in a ghastly hut with two of the dullest women in the company?

'My church is holding a forum on how the media corrupt our youth,' Anita was saying as she stacked a pile of increasingly khaki clothing on a plastic chair, 'teen mags, lads' mags and the like. Would you be interested in speaking, Alice? Defend *Lush* and the like?'

Christ, Christ and Triple Christ.

'You see,' Rochelle sighed, loading an excessive amount of thick socks into a drawer, 'that's where ponies come in. Did either of you read the research conducted for our Christmas issue of *100% Horse*? It established that youngsters who ride are far less likely to play truant or misbehave. To love a sport at an impressionable age, to embrace the responsibility of caring for an animal – is proven to keep them out of trouble. The readership of *Pony World* is now over 75,000 – so encouraging, don't you think?'

Good God Almighty.

'Rochelle,' Anita fizzed, 'you could be on the panel too! You and Alice could go head to head!'

Sweetest Jesus H Christ.

'When I was a kid,' Alice said to the middle of the room while she attempted to load two Whistles skirts, a Nicole Farhi shirt and a Brora cardigan onto a single hanger, 'I used to ride regularly. I was madly in love with a pony called Percy but for me the main point of it all was snogging Nathan Jones behind the tack room and smoking John Player fags on the muck heap with my best mate Thea.'

Supper, eaten at long refectory tables, preceded something called 'Orientation', according to the printed itinerary handed out with the hors d'oeuvres. Alice sat at one end with Jeanette and Jacquie in a conspiratorial huddle, planning the best time to convene for gin and cigarettes. Their spirits rose with the arrival and constant replenishing of ceramic pitchers of quite palatable rosé table wine throughout the meal.

'What's Orientation, do we think?' Jacquie asked.

'Probably some character-building mountain hike,' groaned Alice.

'In the dark,' Jeanette added.

'But it's in Conference Room B,' Jacquie pointed out.

'Perhaps it's an emotional workshop to scale the metaphorical mountains we've encountered in our working lives,' Alice said.

'Well, we'd better prepare our mind-set then,' said Jeanette, sloshing more rosé into their glasses. They drank to each other, they drank to workshops and mind-sets, they drank to orienteering and orientation. By the time they headed for Conference Room B, they were incapable of walking a straight line, unable to follow arrows and thus couldn't find Conference Room B at all.

It must be here somewhere.

If only they'd taught us orientationeering before supper.

We could always just nip back to mine and have a tiny sip of duty free.

Yes, that is a good idea.

After all, when they realize we are lost, that's where the search party will first look.

Exactly – so we probably won't miss too much orientaling anyway.

Exactly.

Good plan.

Cool.

As the three of them staggered off in the vague direction of Jacquie's cabin, Alice thought how this wasn't too far off a school trip after all. St Trinian's for big girls. Mallory Towers with booze. Just then, she had to concede it might just be a bit of a giggle.

Paul Brusseque

Alice was the last one on the coach the next morning. She didn't dare take off her sunglasses though the day was quite dull. She mumbled an apology to a pair of male feet clad in high-performance hiking boots. She noted Jacquie curled almost foetally in one seat, a decidedly pale Jeanette staring vacantly ahead in another. She saw Anita and Rochelle sitting together, lowering their eyes to their laps as she passed. She found an empty row towards the back, slumped down, closed her eyes and prayed for the Nurofen to kick in. A twangy Australian voice disrupted her need for absolute silence. She assumed it belonged to the hiking-boot man but there was no way she was going to open her eyes to verify this.

'Right guys, we're off to Mont Saint Victoire this morning – immortalized in the paintings of Cézanne. But we're not going to sit there with our watercolours, we're going to climb the fucker.'

'Just you try and make me,' Alice muttered under her breath.

Alice was the last one off the coach. A surreptitious glance around revealed that most of her colleagues – in fact everyone but her, Jeanette and Jacquie, were dressed appropriately for a walk up Cézanne's mountain. Alice, though, was wearing a denim skirt, a velour hooded top the colour of bubblegum and a pair of beige Hogan trainers with no socks.

'OK guys, let's go!' enthused the bloody Australian.

'I'm not a guy,' Alice said to herself, pinching the bridge of her nose to see if that alleviated the throb in her skull, 'so I'm not going.' She turned to face the coach and saw the driver tucking into a hunk of baguette, with slices of ham the size and texture of chamois leather draped over his knees. Her stomach lurched.

'Excuse me?'

Christ. The jolly Antipodean.

Alice turned. 'I'm not going to walk up your mountain,' she said politely to his feet, 'I'm feeling a little fragile. And anyway, none of my mags have anything to do with hiking.' The hiking boots gave one irritated tap. She travelled her eyes up over the laces to ribbed socks rolled down. Above those, tanned shapely lower legs with a masculine smattering of coarse hairs.

'What's your name?'

'I beg your pardon?' Alice balked, looking up a little further and seeing a pair of knees, one of which was grazed.

'Well, Ibegyourpardon, I always find that a stroll in the fresh air clears a hangover far more thoroughly than sunglasses and a sulk.'

Alice's eyes travelled over a pair of thighs so shapely they'd be termed 'thighs to die for' in *Lush* magazine. She stopped for a moment at the jagged fringe of frayed denim shorts.

Then looked upwards; over a lean torso clad in a faded T-shirt lauding some obscure rock band, skimmed over tanned forearms, on up to broad shoulders and a strong neck.

'Come on,' he urged quietly, 'it's more of a stroll up an easy incline. And if it *is* too much for you, we'll do some team bonding and make a stretcher from twigs for you, hey? Deal?'

'Oh fucking hell, deal deal deal,' she muttered. Finally, she established eye contact and found herself ensnared by a pair of eyes the colour of cypress trees. She flashed a lascivious smile in automatic response. Miraculously, her hangover was lifting already.

'Who are *you*?' she asked.

'I'm Paul Brusseque,' he said, extending his hand, 'I'm your group's guide.'

Alice was very tempted to remark to Anita, whom she overtook as she strode on to contrive a position closer to Paul for the hike, that there is a God after all.

'Teacher's pet,' Jacquie hisses at Alice with a wink.

'Thought you were married!' Jeanette remarks with an arched eyebrow.

'Fuck off!' Alice retorts, blushing a little.

The afternoon's session, back at the hotel, was a crashing disappointment. Alice had turned up early with a careful slick of mascara and a subtle change of clothes only to discover that the workshop was being taken by a large Belgian psychologist with a peculiar moustache-less beard and an annoying habit of interspersing '*non?*' throughout his sentences. She skimmed through the itinerary and wondered if Paul would be umpiring the pre-supper rounders match.

He was.

Alice had always been good at rounders at school. She and her team were delighted to discover that almost fifteen years later she could still bat magnificently and field like a dream. She was the centre of attention, a place she knew she thrived in. It seemed to her a while since she'd been there and, as she sat at the refectory table talking left, right and centre, she thought how much she loved it. It suited her: she became wittier and more energized. Her words were hung upon, her anecdotes were laughed at, she had something to say about everything and everyone wanted to hear it. She felt popular and attractive and she simply didn't have time to listen all the way through Mark's chatty message on her phone. Everyone was meeting at the bar for the evening. Including the Bearded Belgian and including that Paul bloke.

It was as if cogs of concupiscence, recently dormant, started slowly to turn again in Alice; oiled by bottles of Kronenbourg beer and lubricated by frequent eye contact from Paul Brusseque. She'd absorbed the information that her colleagues' polite chat revealed about him. He worked there each spring and summer and then did the ski season. This was his third year. No, he hadn't been to England but he'd like to. His mum was Australian, his father was French. Originally he was from Cairns and this year would be his first trip home since he left for Europe at the age of twenty-six, three years ago. He was the 'outward-bound bloke' – Fritz the Belgian shrink conducted the formal workshops. And yes, he had a heap of physical activities in store for them. Pont du Gard the next day. A cathedral at Les Baux the following day. Yeah, he lived on site – in a chalet just like the ones guests had, but painted just white. The pay was pretty cool. The region was pretty cool. Hiking the petticoats of Mont Saint Victoire on a weekly basis was pretty cool. Arles and Nîmes were pretty cool towns. Carcassonne was awesome, Montpellier a bit of a dump. The French in general were a pretty cool nation. France on the whole was awesome. French food was fantastic. And French beer was just the best.

'And how about the French ladies?' Alice asked casually but with slyly lingering eye contact.

Paul regarded her levelly. 'Some are pretty cool,' he said, 'some, however, are *hot* – so liberated.' A bolt of desire struck Alice but she quickly swept all evidence behind a coquettish smile. 'You married?' he was asking. Alice wanted to say no. She ought to say yes. But nothing came out. 'That's some fuck-off ring,' Paul commented.

Alice looked down and wished she wasn't wearing it. 'It's fake,' she lied.

'So you're not married?' Paul asked.

'I didn't say that,' Alice said haughtily and saw how it made his pupils darken, 'I said my ring was a fake.' She took a consciously lingering sip at her bottle of beer. 'The real one is in the safe at home.'

Paul held out his hand and raised an eyebrow. Without batting an eyelid, Alice took off the ring and dropped it nonchalantly into his hand. He assessed its weight and held it up to the light. He placed it back on her finger, his thumb travelling suggestively to the centre of her palm as he did so. 'Your husband must earn a fair whack,' Paul commented, chinking his bottle against hers.

'I'm very lucky,' Alice acquiesced.

'He's the lucky one,' Paul said, regarding her squarely and with no ambivalence.

In his terms of engagement, there's probably a rule of involvement.

Alice walks back to her room.

Some code – both contractual and moral. Like teachers and pupils. Liaisons with clients is probably forbidden. It'll be a sackable offence, no doubt. However, there's probably a fine line drawn and delineated in his job description – and his nature – when it comes to flirting. Flirt all you can and thereby boost morale. He's probably being paid to flirt. He's probably been told to pamper my self-esteem.

Somewhat unsteadily, she slips her key into the lock.

Well, I can't remember the last time I was flirted at. And it's certainly one big, long-overdue ego boost. And I liked flirting back. It's fun. I feel bright and sparky and attractive.

Momentarily, she considers going to find Jacquie or Jeanette for a gin and a gossip. But she knows this would be inappropriate, unwise even. It is late anyway. And though she gets on well with them, they aren't exactly close friends, just the closest she has out here, far from home. She looks at the key in the lock. She takes her mobile phone from her pocket. Perhaps she'll just give Thea a quick call.

And say what? Was there actually anything to say?

I haven't done anything and I have no intention of doing anything. So why do I feel precariously close to the edge of my comfort zone? I'm married after all – and that's life's greatest anchor, isn't it? I'm hardly going to lose my head to some bloody outward bounder. An outward bounder and a cad, no doubt. And I'm out of bounds.

She brought up the blank screen on her phone and wondered what to text Thea. She tapped in H. *Hullo? Help? How are you? Having a great time? Having a harmless flirt? Horny bloke – what'll I do?* She deleted the H and switched off her phone.

Harmless flirting can't hurt.

It depends how secure is the base you've come from, Alice. You're a married woman, not 100 per cent happy. Flirting may well be unwise.

Pont du Gard

Paul surreptitiously and adeptly fondled Alice's backside the next morning as she disembarked the coach on arrival in Nîmes. She was so surprised, all she could do was gawp.

'Ever wondered where your jeans come from?' he asked her.

'Whistles,' Alice informed him, appalled that her blush had yet to subside.

'In the nineteenth century, they started producing a hard-wearing cloth right here in Nîmes,' Paul said casually, 'then Levi Strauss started importing it to California, this *Serge de Nîmes.*'

'De *Nîmes*!' Alice exclaimed as the penny dropped and Paul helped himself to another furtive feel. '*Denim*!' At once, Alice justified Paul's precocious assault on her bottom. He was just trying to make a point. Quite well, actually.

Paul addressed the group, informing them to meet back at the coach in two hours to head on to the Pont du Gard. 'You want to get a coffee?' he asked Alice.

'No, thanks,' Alice said, practising what *Lush* preached about playing hard to get. She flounced off with Jeanette and Jacquie; an obvious wiggle to her denimed derrière for Paul's benefit.

Alice's stomach had flipped with an excited butterfly or two at Paul's lip-licking smile when she boarded the coach later; however it lurched and her spirits plummeted when she caught sight of the Pont du Gard. Was her knowledge of world-famous architectural landmarks really that poor? Had her History A level meant so little? How could she forget Agrippa's monumental aqueduct? And now, apparently in the name of character building and team bonding, they were going to have to walk its length.

'OK, guys,' Paul held the coach's microphone like a rock singer, 'here she is! 275 metres long, almost 50 metres high and built to transport 20,000 cubic metres of water daily into Nîmes – the Pont du Gard! Watch your step – we're walking right on the top – there are slabs over the channel where the water once flowed, but there are no railings. My advice? Don't look down!'

'I don't do heights!' Alice hissed at Jeanette and Jacquie. 'I'm not walking across *that* – I can't. Seriously. I feel sick just looking at it.'

The previous day, Alice hadn't felt like traipsing up the lower slopes of Mont Saint Victoire because she'd had a cracking hangover and had yet to spy the aesthetic merits of Paul Brusseque. Today, she had been actively looking forward to the day's activities, to banter and eye contact with Paul. However, she was now genuinely alarmed. She didn't want to walk this bridge at all. She did not have a head or the guts for heights.

She had presumed the day would be spent doing things that made her happy, that she could do well at, that would enable her to show off. Like rounders, or being the life and soul. However, now she was faced with a dilemma. If she admitted to her terror and therefore saved herself the trauma of walking across the bridge, she'd thereby deny herself the company of Paul Brusseque. And possibly jeopardize her standing in his affection. But, if she opted for his company and walked the sodding bridge, she'd be a gibbering wreck – which was not a feeling she wanted to feel, nor an image she wanted to project.

'I'm not doing it,' Anita announced, happily decisive, 'no way, José! I had an operation on my knee a couple of months ago.'

'I'll keep you company, I don't mind,' said Alice with hastily deployed altruism. 'I'm staying with Anita,' she told Paul, mouthing that her colleague was scared.

'Anita, do you need Alice to stay with you?' Paul asked because he'd already sensed Alice's anxiety.

'Crumbs, no,' Anita said, 'I'll be fine!'

'Are you sure?' Paul asked.

'Absolutely,' said Anita, 'I have my book to read.'

'Come on, Alice,' Paul said nonchalantly.

With her mind working overtime yet unable to hatch an escape route, Alice followed Paul, feeling sick but desperate to hide the fact.

'See up there?' Paul stopped and came close behind her, pointing ahead so that his inner forearm lightly brushed her cheek. 'Can you see the phallus? Look between those two arches. See it?' Alice looked but her nerves were such that she couldn't make out anything other than the horrible height of it all. 'The Romans carved it as a symbol against bad luck,' Paul told her. Alice made a strange noise in her throat and turned it into a laugh she intended to sound breezy and not too fake.

Alice is 50 metres above the river. And there are no railings. And there are regular, large gaps in the stone. And everyone else apart from Anita is walking across – albeit some more gingerly than others. But they're all making that journey. Alice can't. She simply can't. And now Paul is coming back with an outstretched hand and a sympathetic but strong voice urging her to make that first step. Come on, lady, you can do it, you *can*.

Alice takes a step and freezes. She's going to faint. No, she's not. First, she's going to throw up. No, she's not. She's not going to hold his hand. She doesn't want to hold his hand and she doesn't want to be on this bridge no matter how famous and iconic it is. She's scared, really terrified.

'Face your fear,' Paul implores her, 'come on, hon. Face your fear – and trust me. I'll take you there. You'll feel so fucking great. Let's do it. Go!'

'No, I can't.'

'Oh, you can – you're a strong woman. You can do it.'

'I don't *want* to.'

'*I* want you to.'

'I don't *care* what you want!' Alice declares, suddenly absolutely sure of what she wants. 'I can't and I don't want to and I'm not going to do it. All right?'

Cautiously, she turns away, tears of fear, humiliation and relief catching in her throat. She's shuffling away gingerly; hating herself, hating Paul and his stupid motivational speak, hating herself for wanting to impress him, hating herself for being too weak to. Face her fears? Why the hell should she do that? Just so she can impress some brawny Australian tour guide? Perhaps owning up to one's fears, admitting to one's limitations, is a strength, not a weakness anyway. She's afraid of heights, everybody. *Compris*? She's *happy* to be afraid of heights. She loves her vertigo, OK?

'Don't give up, Alice,' Paul has come after her again, 'you're made of stronger stuff than that.'

Alice turns and regards his beautiful, tanned face. 'Will you just fuck off!' she growls. 'Just leave me alone.'

She takes refuge by a crop of pine trees nowhere near Anita. It is quiet and the air is warm and fragrant. Her back is turned towards the aqueduct. If she's so relieved not to be walking the Pont du Gard, why does she feel so wretched?

Flamingos look peculiar when they fly; crooked and too rigid to be aerodynamic, surely. In fact, until Alice had seen them fly, she had assumed the birds to be flightless. Like emus and boobies and dodos. She'd always thought of flamingos as comedy birds with their clonking great beaks, one-legged stance and synthetic colouring. Actually, she hadn't thought about them much at all, until just then, sitting on her own by a Camargue lagoon just outside the hotel's perimeter; the glass-wort and tamarisk of the whispering marshland providing a protective screen behind which she could indulge in her bruised mood. Flamingos flew purposefully overhead, animating a dusk sky streaked with a colour identical to their plumage.

'Artemia.'

It was Paul's voice and she felt his breath on the back of her neck. He sat down behind her. She hugged her knees close to her chest while he stretched his tanned, shapely legs either side of her.

'Artemia,' he said again, 'they're flamingos' favourite snack – a mollusc that gives them their awesome colour. Do those birds look like crazy fuckers or what!'

I think I'm on the verge of being a crazy fucker quite literally, Alice remarked to herself, though the balance just then tipped a little more towards foreboding than excitement. But her gaze was drawn magnetically to the athletic splendour of Paul's legs and her stomach somersaulted as she recalled the sensation of his grope through her jeans to her bottom and beyond. In an instant, she theorized that she was miles from home, no one need know, and it wouldn't mean anything anyway. The notion of sex with this man shot her adrenal glands into overdrive and her scales of morality and reason tipped suddenly again. Caution and misgivings were now outweighed by pure and reckless desire. Rapidly, she justified that a rampant one-night stand with this stereotypical sex god might even be a rather good thing, a necessary elixir. Mightn't it restore the self-confidence she'd lost over recent months? Couldn't it redress the sexual imbalance that had gone untended at home? Wouldn't it put the spring back in her step? She'd be a nicer person for it. Absolutely everyone would benefit.

So Alice turned a blind eye to Mark smiling sweetly in her mind's eye and replaced it instead with an image of him in Marbella, with his sunburnt forehead and his legs paler and half the size of Paul's. She glanced down again at Paul's legs, regarded his hands with their shapely fingers, his bangle of Mexican silver, the provenance of which most probably involved some daring adventure or other.

Alice turned deaf ears to the clangorous warning bells. Her memory failed her when it came to her marriage vows. Instead, she leant back against Paul and while he gabbled on about molluscs and tamarisk or whatever, she wondered just when they would fuck.

Not that night, it transpired, though their verbal foreplay had been such that if Paul had suggested a shag in the corner of the bar Alice would have complied. Instead, people and particulars provided obstacles. Alice was sure if she'd told Jeanette and Jacquie that she wanted to bed Paul and could they please leave, they'd have done so. But there was absolutely no way she was going to tell a soul. And so Jeanette and Jacquie flirted with Paul themselves, apparently oblivious to the frisson reverberating between him and Alice. Furthermore, the bar was full of her colleagues and his; the pair of them could hardly leave without being noticed. And where would they go anyway? Back to Alice's chalet where no doubt Anita was saying her prayers and Rochelle was text-messaging her bloody horse? Or back to his which he shared with the weirdy-beardy Belgian psychologist who'd have a field day analysing their ravenous coupling? Instead, they had to settle for eye contact of burning intensity, sign language of moistened parted lips, secret signs of fingers touching fleetingly as beer bottles were reached for. Their gaze lingered for dangerous but thrilling seconds. They synchronized their trips to the toilet so that they could brush past each other. Alice stared at herself in the mirror after one such rendezvous, looked hard at her reflection. She glowed. The proximity, the inevitability, of sex with Paul was intoxicating, made all the more so by the hassles and logistics blocking their way.

Alice strolls back to her cabin, alternately whistling and humming, a comely but conscious wiggle to her walk. She looks over her shoulder once or twice to see if Paul is following. He isn't. It's simultaneously frustrating yet thrilling. She is drunk on this cocktail of anticipation and desire. She closes the door to her cabin after a long loiter and a last look down the path for Paul. The bedroom lights are off and she tiptoes around, giggling to herself. She tries to locate her mobile phone, fumbling around her possessions in the dark. She finds it and gets into bed, switching it on under the pillow so as not to waken Anita or Rochelle. Two text messages flash up. She replies to Mark's with a brief goodnight. She opens Thea's.

omigod! acceptd offer on my flat!!!! u ok???? Txxxxxx

Alice sends one back replete with congratulations and kisses. Then she lies in the dark and tunes into how high she feels. She and Thea were often at their happiest at the same times. Thank God, though, that their crises never collided.

Good for Thea. Moving on. It's the right time. She's found her Mr Perfect – someone she can both be madly in love with and deeply lust for and Saul feels the same.

Alice's phone vibrates through another text. It's Thea.

thanx! am taping ER 4 u . . . !! xxxx

Shall I creep out and phone her? How can I text across all that's happening? But God I'd love to share the thrill of it all with her.

Another text message buzzes its arrival. Thea again.

howz u? bored of brie & team-bonding bollox? don't despair – home v soon!!

It struck Alice like a bolt of lead. The next day was the last.

And we're off to some bloody cathedral. It's now not only a case of when I'll screw Paul, but where?

Les Baux

'I can think of better ways of spending my last day than traipsing around some stuffy old cathedral,' Alice murmured to Paul, consciously perking out her breasts and licking her lips lasciviously as she brushed against him on leaving breakfast.

'Get on the coach, wench,' he all but growled, hooking his finger in the back of her skirt as she passed, affording himself a tantalizing glimpse of her underwear.

The coach trundled the party into the heart of the Alpilles, to the Val d'Enfer and the eerily beautiful village of Les Baux. As the group set off on foot, Paul discoursed on how this area, this Hell's Valley, was the inspiration for Dante's *Divine Comedy*. Alice looked around her, captivated by the stunning natural forms, some eroded into strange tortured shapes by the wind, others carved and hacked into stark angularity by the quarrying of dark red bauxite rock and creamy limestone.

Paul stopped. 'No doubt many of you guys reckoned there were better ways of spending your last day than traipsing around some dull old cathedral.' He looked around the group, skipped over an offended Anita to linger his gaze on Alice. 'Well, I'm telling you this is like no cathedral you'll ever have seen but it's a religious experience you won't forget. Welcome, guys, to the Cathédrale d'Images.'

It had been a quarry. But now it was more than a quarry. It had been used as a filmset by Jean Cocteau but it was so much more than a stage. The Val d'Enfer had inspired Dante but it was so much more than a backdrop. Cathédrale d'Images was like a vast gallery, a huge exhibition space, yet the pictures were transitory and did not actually exist at all. The group walked through and down, deep under the mountain, into a gigantic hall sectioned by megalithic columns left by the quarrying as structural support. Every surface had now become a natural screen for the projection of constantly changing images up to 20 metres in size, above, below, side to side, over there, over here, over everyone – 3,000 images. This wasn't an exhibition, this wasn't *son et lumière*, this made IMAX seem singularly unimpressive.

Underfoot, the limestone had been long since ground into a silt-soft powder as fine as flour, as light as goose down, as deep as a beach. Instinctively, many of the group took off their shoes and shrugged off preconceptions and inhibitions. Alice included. All around, images of Africa burst out against the bare rock face, whilst African music both melodic and intensely rhythmic drowned any other sound or the need to talk. The effect was mesmeric, hallucinatory almost. If the purpose of a cathedral is to suck a visitor deep into its very message, then this disused, recycled quarry was a cathedral indeed. Where was Alice? In Africa? In France? Was she hearing with her eyes and seeing with her ears? Why hadn't she been anywhere like this in her thirty-three years? Her body began to sway to the hypnotic drum-heavy soundtrack and she sashayed her way, trancelike, through the halls. Sometimes, she was completely alone, images drenching her. Sometimes, she found herself amongst people – her colleagues, strangers, all sharing the space and the experience and moving to the rhythms instinctively. Savannah and fabric and faces and dried river beds and wildlife and blood-red skies enveloped her. She caught sight of Rochelle, dancing quite bizarrely all by herself, but Alice had no inclination to laugh or cringe. Paul was right. This was a cathedral in so much as it was an awe-inspiring space where all who entered experienced an intense and spiritual headiness. Paul was right. Where was he?

He's behind me, he's to my side, he's in front of me. An image of a huge tribal chief swathed in robes the colour of sunburst is superimposed over him. Paul's face is red and yellow. Now there's a flame tree all over him. And now he's up close against me. His lips are hovering near mine. Touch down. Tongue. I'm kissing Paul. And his hands are all over my body, they're squeezing my boobs and fondling my bum and travelling up and down my back. And mine are grappling and groping him. God, his biceps, his six-pack, his tight bum. We're swaying and pulsing to the music, which is deafening and divine. Christ, I'm turned on, not just by his lip–tongue talent, nor the tantalizing bulge of his hard-on or the fact that he's pinching my nipples and nuzzling my neck. It's more. It's the energy of this place. It's the strange contradiction of stone that is soft, powdering its way between my toes. It's the thrumming tribal beat. It's the sultry, rich, ever-changing colours. It's like being stoned. I suppose, in this derelict quarry, we are stoned in a sense. Actually, it's better than being stoned. It's more real. My senses are in overdrive. I'm gorging on Paul's mouth like I've been half starved. I have no idea if people can see us. I don't care if they can. I want to stay in this moment. I want to be in this place.

The wink wink nudge nudging started on the coach. It was as if the unbridled unity the group attained inside the Cathédrale was decimated by the startling sunlight and sudden heat which confronted them on leaving. As if, by shielding their eyes from the sun, they hid from the unexpected spirituality they'd just encountered. As if it was suddenly unseemly for publishing and editorial directors to be seen barefoot and blissed out when they were normally known for their professional poise and thrust. No matter how at ease they had felt within the Cathédrale d'Images, it was a comfort zone they could no longer access once the reality of the day outside had hit them. And so the whispers started. Alice was dismayed. How could something that had tasted so good and felt so right have negative ramifications so quickly? Even Anita seemed to be having a good old gossip with Rochelle as they stood in line to board the coach.

'And what do you have to say on the matter?' Jeanette whispered, slithering into the seat next to Alice, raising an eyebrow while elbowing her in the ribs.

'Yes,' Jacquie said, popping up from the seat in front, 'what's your take, Alice?'

Fuck. Is that it then? Is that where a trance-like snog in some spaced-out quarry gets me? Does my perceived crime really warrant my reputation being compromised? Christ, it was only necking and a bit of a grope – it's not as if we got down and shagged. God, if only we'd've fucked at least it would have made this bit slightly more worthwhile. Hell's Valley indeed.

'Consenting adults,' Alice declared in an uninterested voice. 'People shouldn't judge so sweepingly nor condemn so quickly. Perhaps the behind-the-scenes situation justifies the visual dramatics – you know?'

'Blimey, Alice!' Jacquie said. 'You do surprise me.'

'Me too,' Jeanette agreed. 'After all, she's your main rival at work – and you need him on your side. We all do.'

'God knows I do,' Jacquie sighed, 'but not enough to perform *that* on!'

Alice stared from one woman to the other and as the pennies began to drop like a one-armed bandit spewing the jackpot, she wondered how best to backtrack.

'Isn't she married?' Alice hedged her bets, trying to come

across as knowing exactly who – never mind what – they were on about.

'Clare?' Jacquie exclaimed in a whisper. 'Didn't you hear Clare called off her engagement? Even though the Vera Wang was already on order.'

Clare! They're talking about Clare Cabot. Christ alive!

'He's married too, isn't he?' Alice went for broke, now keen to know just who it was that Clare had done what with in the depths of the quarry.

'Geoff is more than married, Alice – Christ, his baby can be only a few months old. A few weeks even.'

Geoff – they're talking about Geoff. Bloody hell, Clare and Geoff. Who could've seen that coming?

'I like Geoff,' Alice mused, gazing out of the window as the coach ambled off. She wondered whether she'd ever return to Les Baux. Perhaps the experience should be left as a one-off so as not to dilute the impact.

'Everyone likes Geoff,' Jeanette whispered.

'That's the point,' Jacquie agreed.

'What on earth possessed him to go for *her*?' Alice joined in, for safety's sake.

Yet I do know what possessed them. I empathize. La Cathédrale d'Images possessed them. As it did me. But Clare was caught and I wasn't.

Now that it transpired Alice hadn't been seen, but so easily might have been, her desire for Paul increased tenfold and the danger of being caught made the notion of sex with this man all the more irresistible. It was all she could think about. However, the afternoon was timetabled relentlessly with the Belgian's motivational workshops and role-playing exercises; the evening was centred around the team dinner; their plane was leaving first thing the next morning.

Well, no doubt Beard Man from Bruges will be harping

on about believing in the Power of Me. So why don't I just practise what he'll be preaching – I ought to account for my actions and Access the Impact I have on others. Right then. If the point of this trip is to inspire me, I can think of something far more motivational than one of Fritz's daft exercises. I'll be role-playing all right, just not in Conference Room B. If there's one thing that's guaranteed to make me feel good about myself, that will make me think this trip has been worthwhile, that it's given me something positive and memorable to take home, it'll be rampant sex with Paul Brusseque. Surely all managers of my calibre should be encouraged to take matters into their own hands as we see fit? And what matters to me is getting hold of Paul's throbbing cock. See how we fit.

Alice told Anita and Rochelle that the experience of Les Baux had given her a migraine for which the only cure was to lie down, undisturbed, in a darkened room. She told Jeanette and Jacquie she was faking a headache to skive off the afternoon's sessions and she'd meet them in the bar at six. She told Paul she was playing hooky from the afternoon's workshops and to meet her in her room in ten. She told herself that all of this was a very good idea. So she set about tweezering renegade hairs from her bikini line, applying a little perfume in strategic places and putting on fresh underwear, a swipe of mascara and a dirty, dirty smile.

Paul takes off his watch and puts it in his bedside drawer. He washes his hair, showering the limestone from his legs and feet. He must have made over fifty visits to Les Baux over the past three seasons, but still the place captivates him, simultaneously charging and challenging him physically and emotionally. This year's theme of Africa is the best yet, he feels. Last year it was the Seven Wonders of the World. The year before, Ancient Greece. But there is something about this year's display, the entrancing clash of the primitive and the opulent in sound and vision alike. Just as there is something so compelling about Alice – last year he'd had a couple of clients who'd done all the pursuing. Sex had been easy and both women had automatically tipped him handsomely which alone was an unexpected and rather welcome bonus. Getting paid to come when the women were gagging for it anyway – it was as close to being a porn star as he'd ever get. The year before that, his first over here, he'd bedded that older woman – and had then had those pointless few months supposedly dating Nathalie from the tennis club.

Paul dresses. He wonders what state of undress he'll find Alice in. He grins at the thought of her, spread-eagled on a bed, perhaps. He considers how she has everything he rates – looks, intellect, success and spirit. But she's off back to England tomorrow. Paul is horny as hell, as he has been for the last four days. He puts on new boxer shorts and a fresh T-shirt. Hand relief has provided him temporary respite the last few nights but the sight of Alice each morning has tipped him into a dither of desire all over again. And now he's been summonsed. The imminence of sex, after a couple of celibate months, is stirring his cock already. He checks his reflection and he's looking good.

He knocks and waits for an answer, as if unsure whether anyone is home.

'You're polite,' Alice teases, because she was half looking forward to him bursting in and ravishing her without so much as a greeting. She is in a white T-shirt and jeans. Barefoot and braless. Her nipples are precociously erect and her arse is tantalizingly pert. She smells good and looks great. And his cock is hardening by the minute. Yes, they have all afternoon, but what he actually wants is to fuck her right

209

now and empty the throbbing sack-load of expectant sperm amassed since that morning.

'You're happy to see me,' Alice remarks, eyeing the bulge in his shorts.

'Nah, it's a gun in my pocket,' he quips back.

'Well, take off your holster, cowboy,' says Alice, 'and let's fuck.'

If Alice was to document it all, she'd reprimand herself for a glut of clichés. But actually how else can she describe being wetter than she's ever been? That her sex is throbbing for him? That her lips are engorged with the anticipation of being kissed and her heart is racing from the fire of his intense gaze? Similarly, the simple fact is that his straining cock *is* rock hard, his butt *is* firm and his abs *are* rippling. Her breasts are indisputably heaving and her sex is oozing with the honey he can't lap enough of. They are devouring each other as if their hunger is insatiable.

God, this is kinky. Mark stays a decorous and hygienic distance from my bum on the occasions he does go down on me. It's fantastic that my breasts are tits again, to be man-handled greedily. I can't even recall Mark's term for my genitalia but Paul has just said 'Christ, you have a cute cunt.' I need this – I've missed this. How refreshing to be fucked senseless rather than being made love to conscientiously.

'God, you're a horny bitch,' Paul pants, tonguing her ear lobe and sucking his way down her neck, up her chin and deep into her mouth.

'You're a pretty good fuck yourself,' Alice reciprocates, licking the salty dampness from his torso as she slithers downwards to feast on his cock. His balls are shaven. She is surprised. She likes it. She wants to writhe, she wants to show off and she contorts herself this way and that, taking charge and initiating positions and the pace. Now she wants to be supine and subservient, revelling in this man driven wild with his desire for her. He flips her onto her side and he plunges into her from behind. He hauls her top leg over his waist, her body stretched out to his touch. Craning her neck around, they suck at each other's mouths while he fondles her tits and slips his fingers between the lips of her sex, finding her clitoris and rubbing gently until she's on the brink of orgasm.

'Don't come,' he commands. He pulls out and his lips are feathering over her nipples infuriatingly lightly. Now he's not touching her at all – he's between her legs staring intently at her sex. Alice gives a playful buck of her hips and he takes his face down to her, dabbing his tongue tip gently over the outer lips of her sex. She writhes and spreads her legs, thrusting to glue his mouth to where she wants, but he resists.

'Fuck me, you bastard,' she hisses.

Suddenly, he's sucking her clitoris and plunging a finger deep inside her sex, another up her anus, and the mind-blowing orgasm she's been craving racks her body. While she continues to shudder with spasms of pleasure, he squats over her and she takes his cock in her mouth before he pulls out and pumps his come all over her stomach. Alice takes her fingers down to the sticky lake of his spunk and massages it over her belly. Then she sucks at each finger while remaining eye locked with him. She feels as though she's just starred in her own private porn performance. And she's loved every minute of it. What a great idea this trip was. Look what she has to take home with her!

It wasn't possible for Paul to grab any time with Alice the following morning. When she boarded the coach, he could only shake her hand and say 'Well done.' Just as he shook everyone's hand and congratulated them. He waved them off. He couldn't tell who waved back behind the tinted glass.

He reckoned he'd go down to the beach for the day, unwind and prepare for the arrival of the next group the following day. The group had presented him with a cool pair of O'Neill shorts – he wanted to try them on. April was warming up by the hour and the delicate fragrance of spring was being usurped daily by the denser scent of summer. Waiting for him at reception was a note from Alice. He took it with him, unopened, to the beach.

> *Dear Paul,*
>
> *No doubt you're already poncing around in your snazzy new shorts – for the record, I did not contribute to the whip-round for you. I wouldn't want you to think that I was paying you for services rendered – I wouldn't want you to feel like a whore . . . So, here's my mobile phone number – be sure to phone if ever you find yourself in London. I'll be only too pleased to play hooky from work and entertain you in my own inimitable way . . .*
>
> *Alice Heggarty*

The note made him laugh, made him long for Alice. He'd look up 'inimitable' later. First, he'd work on his tan and ponder the logistics of a trip to London some time soon.

Le Retour

Alice could have gone straight into work but she didn't want to, though they arrived back by lunchtime. She could have spent the afternoon at home, reacclimatizing to her life, but she didn't want to do that either. She should have gone to Thea to confide and be guided, but she didn't want to, not yet. What she wanted to do was to be by herself, accountable to no one, for a precious few hours more. She wanted to indulge in memories of the last few days; conjure the look and the taste and the feel of Paul. Transport herself back to Les Baux. Just for a little while longer. Not to daydream. Simply to remember.

So Alice whiled away her afternoon in an Internet café off Tottenham Court Road. She surfed the sights and facts of the Camargue, of the Pont du Gard, of Arles and Nîmes, of Les Baux and flamingos. She visited the O'Neill website and clicked on the same pair of shorts they'd bought Paul. She found the hotel website and clicked on every picture, analysing the tiny, pixillated figures. It was stupid to check the tariff page she told herself as she did just that. She Googled Paul's name but found nothing. He really ought to be nothing, she told herself. It wasn't as if she'd be going back, or would ever see him again. He had to have no role in her memory other than as a one-afternoon stand, a fantastic shag with no strings attached, guilt-free sex, a zipless fuck and best forgotten.

In his closing debrief, Fritz had told the group to 'take what we give you and turn it into new tools for your trade'. She'd do that, she would. She could apply it to her life in general. She wouldn't be deifying Paul. She wouldn't long for him or allow the tricks of memory and the mundanity of everyday life to transform him into anything other than a Franco–Australian beefcake she'd shagged. She'd turn the event to her benefit, she'd make sure she was eternally grateful it had happened. After all, her sexual thirst had been quenched and the spring to her step, the glint to her eye, her verve and her smile, had been restored.

Mark arrives home with a bunch of flowers and a legibly excited smile.

'Hullo, you,' he coos, embracing his wife. 'God, I missed you – I did try to ring.'

'No signal,' Alice shrugs, hugging him back and thinking to herself that he's had a disastrous haircut.

'Did you have a great time?' he asks, taking off his jacket, loosening his tie and top button, rubbing his temples and pinching the bridge of his nose. What a day. Good to be home.

'It was fine,' Alice shrugs again. 'You know these courses – part outward-bound, part bullshit-waffle assertion techniques. We were timetabled to within an inch of our lives.'

'Was it as dull as you were expecting?' Mark asks, leafing through the post and leaving it all unopened.

'I guess not,' Alice says, 'but you'll never guess – they made us share rooms! Can you believe that? Three hangers between us!'

Mark laughs as he selects a good Rioja and hunts for the state-of-the-art corkscrew. 'Well, you look gorgeous, Wife – look at you. You really do. The outward-bound bit must have done you good. All that fresh air and exercise. God knows I could do with some.'

'It was all very picturesque. Like a Stella Artois advert. And actually the workshops weren't too hug-a-tree or primal-screamish. But I didn't walk the Pont du Gard,' Alice admits sheepishly, 'I was too scared.'

'I don't blame you,' Mark says. 'I've done it – and it's pretty hair-raising.'

'You've been?' Alice is stunned, appalled, intrigued.

'During my gap year,' says Mark, still going through end-less drawers in search of the corkscrew.

'Did you go to Les Baux?' Alice asks, almost accusatorily.

'Don't think so,' says Mark who's found the corkscrew. 'Was it good?'

'So-so,' Alice shrugs, 'no big deal.'

What?!

When Thea and Alice saw each other a couple of days later, they were each fizzing with excitement, gabbling unexpurgatedly, demanding that the other listen to me me me.

'So the estate agent reckons my buyer will be ready to exchange contracts in the next couple of *weeks*! We're looking to complete perhaps a month or so after that. And this place Saul and I have seen is just amazing.' Thea looked to Alice for a reaction. Her friend was grinning, eyes dancing, stuffing a chocolate éclair into her mouth. Good. 'It's duplex – with a roof terrace! It's like something you'd see on *Grand Designs* – beautiful flow of space and just the most incredible fixtures and fittings. You are going to die when you see the bathroom! And the kitchen is my dream kitchen. The views – oh my God – just you wait!' Alice glowed with excitement, which delighted Thea and spurred her to continue. 'There's just a one-bed flat beneath and guess who lives there? Guess! Rene Overton!'

'Who?'

'Actually, I hadn't a clue who he was either,' Thea laughed into her tea, 'but we're reliably informed that he's the definitive hairdresser to the stars.'

'So you'll be popping down, not to borrow a cup of sugar, but rather his ceramic straightening irons?'

'My hair's too short for those, silly,' Thea hooted, 'but I *am* hoping that he likes nothing better on his days off than to pop up to the flat above for a quick blow-dry!' Alice and Thea guffawed excessively. 'I'm also hoping never to have to pay for hair products again,' Thea continued, 'so the whack of our mortgage repayments will be beautifully balanced by freebie haircuts and industrial-sized bottles of shampoo. As long as our offer is accepted. Anyway, so the king of hair is on the first floor and the ground floor is a snazzy interiors company.'

'So you're thinking free sofas too?' Alice laughed. 'You could offer your home as a kind of living showroom – in return for full furnishing.'

'Genius!' Thea exclaimed and they chinked teacups and agreed to share another éclair. 'So tell me about France? Was it OK in the end? Oh! I've got the *ER* tape for you – here.'

Alice regarded Thea, twitched her lip and let a lascivious smile spread. 'It was – interesting,' she said, rolling out the word with cunning. 'Have you heard of a place called Les Baux?'

'No?'

'Cathédrale d'Images?'

'No.'

'It's this place, this space – I don't know how to describe it. Dante loved it, Cocteau loved it. You'd love it. It's a defunct quarry – and you walk around while all these massive images are projected all around to amazing music.'

Thea regarded Alice, alarmed. 'You haven't gone all trippy-hippy, have you?'

Alice threw back her head and laughed. 'No, of course not! But it was undeniably atmospheric and intense. And had a bizarre impact on us all. *Anyway*, Clare Cabot – you know, my nemesis – shagged Geoff Sprite. Practically there and then – regardless of their audience.'

'You are *joking*?' Thea gasped. 'Blimey! Talk about scandal – *outrageous*!'

'And I shagged our guide.'

'What?!'

Alice bit her lip, glanced away and then dragged sheepish but sparkling eyes back to Thea. 'This absolutely gorgeous bloke called Paul,' Alice confessed, her brow furrowed above her excited whisper, 'divine looking – the sort of physique you see on a Calvin Klein underwear ad. Incredibly handsome – half French, half Australian – a real mountain-climbing, nature-loving, sex-god stereotype. Bit of a toyboy actually – not even thirty. Does the ski season half the year. Anyway, so we're in the cathedral – *cathédrale* – and there's this thrustingly sexy rhythmic music and all these images of Africa. And Paul and I have been flirting since I arrived and it's obvious he fancies me. And I don't mind saying it made me feel really fantastic. What a boost – attention like that can certainly restore a girl's pout and wiggle! So, there I am, walking around this quarry with the sights and sounds of Africa and watching my colleagues dancing. It's like everyone was stoned (*stoned*? *Quarry*? Do you see!). Anyway, suddenly Paul's there – there's been all this chemistry, days of lingering looks and lip licking and brushing past each other accidentally-on-purpose. And he's there, Thea, right up against me. And he just starts fondling me and snogging me. Real snogging – like we used to do at

218

teenage discos. Greedy, lust-drenched tonguing and groping. It was incredible.'

'*What*?'

Alice regarded Thea. 'Then I shagged him!' Immediately, she covered her face with her hands and groaned.

'Alice! You did *what*?'

Alice peeped at Thea through the cage of her fingers. 'When we returned to the hotel. I bunked off to bonk, basically.' She placed her hands in her lap, chewed at her lip guiltily. 'We snuck off and had the most rampant, filthy, abandoned wild sex of my life!'

'What?'

'Stop saying *what*!'

'But Alice!' Thea protested, her eyes skittering over her best friend's face trying to detect a lie, obvious elaboration. Anything but the dance and sparkle that met her gaze.

'What!' Alice exclaimed, her face twitching between shame and triumph.

'You're *married*!' Thea exclaimed. 'That's what.'

Alice looked at Thea. She had thought Thea would be surprised – stunned, perhaps – but still she had expected her best friend's approval. She was taken aback by Thea's frown. 'So what?' Alice said, with a defensive jerk to her shrug.

'But what about Mark?' Thea asked quietly.

'What about him?' Alice replied evenly. 'He's hardly going to find out, is he. I'm not likely to leave Mark for some tour guide, am I – albeit one with an incredible dick and the last word in sexual athletics. Come on, Thea – get off your moral high horse! I had a one-night stand! That's all! And do you know something? I don't regret it and I don't feel guilty. It's what I needed and I feel fucking great. It completely boosted my self-esteem. There will be no repercussions.'

Thea sipped her tea. It was lukewarm and she grimaced as she swallowed it down. Despite that, she sipped again to give her time to think because, just then, she really didn't know what to say. Thea was gutted by her friend's behaviour. She wanted to whack Alice, to scold her, to say what the hell were you thinking, why the hell did you do that, don't you dare get a taste for it, don't you ever do it again. But she didn't. She couldn't. Just look at Alice – just look at her – gone is the pale complexion of late, the dullness to her eyes, the slump in her demeanour, the fatigued gazing into the middle distance, the disillusionment with her lot. Look at her now – she looks as though she's spent a fortnight being pampered at a world-class spa, she looks as though she's won the lottery, she looks as though she's mid-leap from Cloud 8 to 9, she looks as though she's having the time of her life. She's beautiful and centred and exuding delirious happiness. She's radiating the glow of a well-laid woman.

'You're wicked, you are,' Thea decided to say, acting bright and breezy, though privately it irked her to have to do so, 'you're a slag!'

'I know!' Alice said, surfacing from giggles to sigh at the memory of it all. 'I tell you, if you had to choose between Paul Brusseque and Brad Pitt? No contest whatsoever.'

'And if you had to choose between him and Mark Sinclair?' Thea said with a sternly arched eyebrow.

'Fuck off!' Alice barked defensively, trying to cover it with a beguiling pout. 'It was a one-night stand – that's all. A common, simple, one-night stand. Christ, stop giving it more gravity than it deserves. Anyway, I'm telling you, Miss Sanctimonious – if you were faced with someone even half as horny as Paul Brusseque, far from home and safe in secrecy, I'd defy you not to drop your knickers too.' Alice sucked in her cheeks slightly, as if challenging Thea to retort, to deny if she dared.

'But I have Saul,' Thea said firmly. 'I wouldn't want to.'

'When temptation confronts you, believe me you are a

helpless, happy slave.' Alice lowered her voice ominously and wagged her finger with detectable superiority.

It was as if, by being flung far from Alice's conscience, thoughts of Mark were assaulting Thea's. She couldn't rid an image of him from her mind's eye. It was irrelevant that he would not find out about his wife's adultery – still Thea's heart bled for him. She felt like an accessory to Alice's crime. And Thea decreed it a misdemeanour absolute. She deemed sexual fidelity and true love to be inextricably bound. For the latter to exist, the former was unconditional. No one would ever love Alice as much as Mark – and Thea believed he should be loved right back. Just then, Thea didn't know which was worse – the fact that Alice had been unfaithful to Mark or that, as a cuckold, he was to be pitied. On Mark's behalf, Thea felt the humiliation and bewilderment she hoped sincerely that blessed ignorance would keep from him. It was horrible.

'Are you OK?' Saul gently tucks Thea's hair behind her ear. He's concerned – she's been withdrawn all evening, chewing at the skin around her fingernails, fiddling with her ring, frowning suddenly, even wincing once or twice.

'Fine,' Thea nods with minimal eye contact though Saul notes a gauze of sadness clouding her eyes, 'just tired.'

'You sure?' Saul presses because he's rarely known Thea in anything other than her sunny, happy state. Especially recently – she's been infectiously euphoric. He doesn't like to see her unhappy but he doesn't know how to help and it is not his style to pry.

'Honestly,' she says, but unconvincingly because he knows she's trying to inhibit further probing, 'I'm done in. Sometimes, giving massage can invigorate me – sometimes it utterly depletes me. I think I'll go to bed.'

'OK,' Saul says, placing his hand tenderly across her forehead, then tapping the tip of her nose with his finger. 'If you look in my bag, I bought you the new issue of *Grand Designs*.'

'Thanks,' Thea says and she takes the magazine off to bed, grateful for distraction. That's what she'll think of – sinks and fabrics and flooring and ways with light. Not Alice, she won't think of Alice. Or Mark. She'll think about setting up home with Saul. And she smiles at the knowledge that absolutely no one, from Brad Pitt to this Paul Brusseque, could tempt her from Saul.

txt sex

It's peculiar – I almost feel like writing an anonymous piece for Adam on the merits of infidelity. I want to evangelize the effect that a one-night stand has had on my life. I want to stand up and defend what our society denounces as morally reprehensible. It's not. I was miserable before – doubting the point of marriage, questioning my choice of husband, negative about my lot, pessimistic about my future. And it all came down to sex! Just sex. That instinctive, carnal interchange. Simple sex – that's all. I'm sure of it. One dose of pure sex and I'm cured! Now I'm happy with my husband, my energy and optimism have returned at both work and play and best of all, I feel happier and more centred in myself than I have done for months.

When Alice felt buoyant, everyone in contact with her was dusted with her jauntiness and vigour. Her team produced work worthy of awards and Mark reaped the benefits of his wife's excellent mood. She was spirited yet affectionate, effervescent but considerate. She didn't glower when he said he'd have to go to Singapore and Tokyo the following week, instead she came home with potions and tonics from the naturopath to alleviate all primary and secondary symptoms of jet lag. Their lovemaking was back up to twice a week and Mark noted with some pride how she wanted to prolong each session, how her eyes were closed throughout as if in utter appreciation of their coupling.

It lasted a week. Then the first text message arrived. And by replying to it (initially she justified it would be impolite not to at least answer, but if she was honest, she fired back her reply in anticipation of another response) Alice somersaulted down into the murky depths of secrecy, lies and betrayal.

'Is that your phone?' Mark said, while ripping something out of the *Financial Times* and tucking it in his suit jacket. 'Bloody hell, it's almost midnight – who's texting you at this time as if I couldn't guess?'

'It's just Thea – fretting about her house sale and stuff,' said Alice, not knowing quite how she was controlling herself, having seen that the number was overseas. 'I'd better reply – I know how stressful the process is.'

'Why don't you just ring her? Your thumb will get RSI!'

'Saul's probably asleep – that'll be why she's texting,' Alice said with a mock yawn. 'I'll go and have a bath and reply.'

'Tell her we thoroughly recommend our conveyancing lawyer.'

'I'll do just that.'

With enormous restraint, Alice resisted running to the bathroom, sauntering away instead with credible nonchalance. As the bath ran, she sat on the edge of the tub and read the message, her stomach flipping with a swarm of manic butterflies, her heart galloping in her throat.

`it's late. lying here thinking of u and ur wet pussy. PB x`

Alice wanted to squeal and squeak and run around whooping 'It's from Paul, it's from Paul!' What should she say? How should she reply? Should she reply? Or ignore? Should she text Thea and send her four or five possible responses to choose from? Shit – the bath is almost overflowing.

Alice sat in the bath and read Paul's message over and over. Giggling, her thumb set to work.

pussy wet thnkng of u

Did she dare? Did she dare say that? Did she dare send it?

She did.

Come on, come on – reply, damn you!

Come
       on!

                        Replyreplyreply.

Yes!

rock hard – where r u?

She gave a joyous shriek.

'Alice?' Mark called through the door. 'Are you OK?'

'What? I'm fine – I'm fine. It's just Thea being daft.'

in bath – v soapy

She waited a decorous few minutes before sending it.

'Alice?'

Oh for fuck's sake, Mark – what?

'Yes?'

'I wouldn't mind coming in and doing my teeth and stuff.'

Shit, the next message had just buzzed through and she was desperate to read it.

'But the door's locked,' Mark continued.

'God, can't I have a bath in peace,' Alice protested. 'Look, I'll be out in two minutes – all right?'

She heard Mark pad away. She felt relieved rather than guilty. She looked at her phone.

u horny bitch

Paul was right. She was. She was horny. Very excited and

extremely horny. Just then she was horny enough not to care that she was a bitch.

Five pence was the cost of it. It occurred to Alice that a 5p text message had bought her an affair. But she didn't stop to think that it might be at the price of her marriage. It was just harmless texting, after all. Virtual sex. Not real. No one need know.

But it wasn't long before Alice was living from text message to text message, becoming decidedly fractious in between. Her moods, a pendulum swinging erratically between high spirits and furtive anticipation; her spiky frustration affecting everyone in spitting distance. She could be impatient and surly at work and short-tempered and snappish with Mark, or inspiring and energetic with her team and affectionate and vivacious at home. It all depended on whether she was owed a text from Paul or not. No one around her could figure out what the problem was and whether or not it lay with them. Because they did not know where they stood, so they tiptoed around her and tried their best to please her.

Thea was dismayed when Alice handed over her mobile and told her to scroll through. 'You said it was just a one-night stand.'

'It was,' Alice frowned, snatching back her phone and gazing at the screen as if a photo was lodged there. 'God, stop taking everything so seriously, Thea,' she said, 'they're just silly, sexy, harmless texts – but Christ they make my day.'

Once more, Thea felt compromised between her own personal morality and Alice's infectious energy.

'They must be costing you a fortune,' Thea remarked.

'I've started buying those text bundles the phone companies market at teenagers!' Alice exclaimed, her face one lascivious expansive grin.

'Let me see that last one again,' Thea requested because

she felt it was expected of her. Though she didn't want to encourage Alice, she knew her duty as the adulteress's best friend was not to alienate her either.

And when Mark flew off to Singapore and Tokyo on business, then the phone sex began. In the house alone, with no intention of asking Thea's approval, permission or advice, Alice phoned Paul. And the outright dirtiness of the text messaging was replaced with naughty giggles and coy referencing and then, surprisingly, five minutes of chit-chat. On a nightly basis.

'He's just a friend,' Alice justified to Thea, having thrust her mobile phone at her friend's ear so she could hear his voice. 'We're just mates.'

'"Mate" being the operative word,' Thea couldn't resist saying. 'You fucked, remember.'

Alice physically swiped the air dismissively. 'He lives in Fucksville France!' Alice breezed, as if Thea's insinuation was ludicrous.

u awake? can u spk? u alone?

Yes, Alice was awake but no she couldn't speak because Mark and she were just about to sit down to supper.

'I'm just going to the loo,' Alice told Mark, surreptitiously slipping her phone into her back pocket. 'Can you stir the sauce and switch the rice off in a couple of minutes?'

'Wine? White?' Mark asked, starting the interminable search for the sodding corkscrew.

Alice locks the toilet door.

not alone — hows u, big boy?

coming the reply announces.

Alice laughs as she sends her reply: u dirty boy — u'll go blind!

coming over he sends back.

Before Alice has the chance to absorb the information let alone formulate a response, a barrage of messages arrives on her phone.

```
to london
   next tues
      3 nights
         get ready, baby - gonna make u sore
```

Oh
  My
    God

Sitting on the closed toilet seat, Alice is utterly stuck for text words.

She switches off her phone without replying and leaves it on top of the cistern in irrational fear of Paul suddenly materializing from it like a genie from the lamp.

Oh
  My
    God

Table for Four

'I can't remember it being this much hassle when I bought my flat five years ago,' Thea declared with a sorry pout around the table.

'You were a first-time buyer,' Mark said soothingly, asking the wine waiter to bring whichever red he'd recommend.

'But it's not like I'm in a chain,' Thea protested, 'my problem is that my buyer is a bloody lawyer and he's being exasperatingly finicky. We could be on the verge of exchanging contracts but he's not going to unless a structural surveyor has checked some minor detail or other.'

'Has your offer been accepted on the place you like?' Mark asked Saul.

'No – we've upped it but they're sitting on it,' Saul told him, squeezing Thea's wrist supportively.

'It's Sod's Law – and it's down to the bloody postcode fiasco. Thea's trying to sell in a buyer's market and yet you're trying to buy in a seller's market. All in the same city,' Mark observed. 'Thea darling, if you sell before you buy, you can always store your stuff at ours.'

'Thanks,' said Thea glumly because it was of little consolation just then. 'They say that moving house is the most stressful thing we encounter after death and divorce.'

'Better not die then – and keep cohabiting, rather than marrying,' Mark laughed. He looked over at Alice who was gazing at her lap. 'Are you OK, darling?'

'What?' She looked up and around the table as if she was startled to find herself there with them. 'I'm fine. I'm fine. Just hassles at work – just had to text one of my editors.' She brandished her mobile phone and then dropped it into her bag. Thea looked away from Alice's fleeting smirk. 'Have you exchanged yet?' Alice asked her. 'Wasn't it meant to be this week?'

Thea groaned, put her head in her hands, looked up and glugged gratefully at the glass of wine. 'Don't ask!' she said hoarsely, and then proceeded to repeat in great detail the stress and minutiae.

'Did you get my text?' Alice asked her, as if she'd not heard a word of Thea's rant.

'What text?'

'About my client?' Alice said.

Thea checked her phone. 'Oh, it's here – I hadn't seen it.'

`lover boy's coming 2 UK nxt wk ! ! ! ! ! ! !`

Thea read it and read it again. What on earth was she meant to say? Right then? Right there? In an upmarket restaurant with her best friend's husband in eyeshot of her mobile phone. 'Right,' she faltered, 'right.'

'He'd like to see you,' Alice carried on blithely while Thea prayed that Alice's expression of triumphant glee was legible to her alone.

'OK,' Thea nodded slowly, 'OK.'

'Who's this?' Mark asked.

'Paul,' Alice announced lightly, as if jogging Mark's memory that he knew him too. 'I think Thea should assess him.'

'Paul Who?' Saul asked.

'He's not part of the *Adam* team,' Alice replied dismissively, 'different department.'

'What's his problem?' Mark asked politely.

Thea couldn't believe it was she who was starting to redden. Surely it should be Alice. But Alice was having great fun with her hidden meanings. 'I've told him to be careful. I've told him he'll be flat on his back by next week – so I really think he'd benefit from Thea's evaluation.'

Thea's appetite slumped. Luckily for Alice, Mark and Saul presumed Thea had lost it under the pile of faxes and hassle swamping her from the sale of her property.

'Alice was in high spirits,' Saul remarks, peeling off his clothes and slinging them onto the floor.

'Manic, I'd say,' Thea asserts, picking up Saul's clothes and adding them to a pile she's sorted to be washed.

'Are things OK with her and Mark?' Saul asks cautiously.

Thea pretends not to have heard as she heads off with the laundry to the kitchen to load the washing machine, hoping to buy herself some time in which Saul might forget his question. He's in bed, when she returns, reading *FHM*.

'New issue?' Thea asks.

'Do they?' Saul looks up.

'Pardon?'

'Issues – you said Alice and Mark had issues.'

Thea laughs unnecessarily. 'No, no! I asked if that *FHM* was a new issue!'

Saul looks at the front cover and nods. Thea climbs into bed, faces away from him and yawns exaggeratedly at how tired she is. Saul puts down *FHM* and spoons up against her back. 'Don't tell me you're turned on by some soft-porn pics in a bloody lads' mag!' Thea exclaims, feeling Saul's hard-on nudging hopefully at the small of her back.

'Don't be daft,' he murmurs, nuzzling her neck, 'it was

the sight of you doing the laundry in the buff. Your gorgeous peach of an arse.' And he is burrowing under the duvet to the object of his desire, kissing her buttocks and unexpectedly spreading her cheeks for a long lick downwards. Thea is pleased to close her eyes and swim into the physical sensations Saul is crafting; to propel herself away from the stress of selling her flat and the disquiet over her best friend's behaviour.

Sometimes, Thea likes to be dominant during sex with Saul; she'll initiate it and call the pace and the positions. At other times, she craves utter synchronicity – that he desires her as much as she does him, that he wants to take her from behind at the exact moment she flips herself over, that she wants to suck his cock without needing to be asked, that their orgasms occur within milliseconds of each other. But there are also times, and just now is one of them, when what she needs is to be made love to. She wants to consciously detect that Saul loves and desires her absolutely, venerates her, to the exclusion of all other thoughts and all other people. And so Thea lies in his arms, being licked and kissed and adored and wanted.

Post-coitally, with Saul on his back panting himself back to a normal heart rate, Thea snuggles against his chest. She cups her hand lightly over his cock still semi-hard and twitching lazily. 'God, that was good,' Saul declares. Thea smiles. Good.

'Saul,' she says in a quiet, little-girl-lost voice she is not in the habit of using blithely, 'promise me we won't ever be like that.' He twists his head down to look at her and she gazes up at him, with a beguiling bat of her eyelashes. 'Like Alice and Mark,' she says very quietly, all wide-eyed and winsome.

'I thought there was something up,' Saul declares. 'What's going on with those two?'

'I don't know,' Thea evades, 'nothing, probably. You know

232

Alice. The point is, I never want us to loiter on that plateau of complacency.'

Saul kisses Thea on the forehead. 'I know what you mean – it was as if Alice was unaware that her husband was dining with us at all. They converse without really communicating – they didn't really chat to each other. They just made up the numbers for a table for four.'

'I just want you and me always to stay close – and always truly feel *in* love,' Thea declares. She kisses Saul back and turns to fall asleep, feeling a little happier and safer.

P.I.C.

'Cover for me!'

Thea's heart dropped and she felt like hanging up the phone. She'd become reluctantly resigned to such a call from Alice, which wasn't to say she hadn't been deludedly hoping Alice might say Paul had changed his mind, or he was staying in Lancashire, or she'd changed her mind and was ignoring his calls.

'Cover for me?' Alice implored. 'Please! Come on – you promised. You must honour our promise to be each other's P.I.C.'

Thea suddenly deeply regretted that fateful school day in the second year when they had snuck behind the science block to smoke – daring each other, declaring they'd be each other's Partner In Crime, swearing solemnly that if one was caught the other would go down with her. But neither was caught and they puffed their way through the packet of Sobranie Cocktail cigarettes over the next eight lunch hours. And after that, when it came to anything which implied risk or wrong, Thea and Alice committed to being each other's P.I.C. I'll do it if you do it. Come on, let's try it! I won't tell if you won't. We'll say it was *both* our ideas! The difference

234

now was that this was the first occasion in eighteen years that the P.I.C. was acting merely as lookout rather than collaborator.

'It would be the one bloody week Mark isn't travelling,' Alice bemoaned, 'so cover for me, Thea. You *have* to.'

'When?' Thea asked out of a sense of duty, an unwilling partner in a crime she did not want committed.

'Tonight! Tomorrow night! The night after!' Alice's effervescence and excellent spirits were seductive and Thea had to sternly remind herself of the deplorable cause of Alice's mirth.

'What's your story?' Thea sighed.

'Pilates tomorrow night – with you. And some late-night preview shopping thing at Heal's on Thursday night – with you. He flies back Friday afternoon.'

'When does he arrive?'

'Late tonight,' Alice enthused.

'You're not going to climb out of your window and steal away to him tonight, are you?' Thea asked flatly.

'No, I'll just about resist!' Alice laughed.

'You *so* owe me, Mrs Sinclair,' Thea told her.

'I think I ought to be Miss Heggarty for the next three days, don't you?'

'I wouldn't mind going to that Heal's thing anyway,' Thea justified. 'Saul and I could look at dining tables.'

'I made it up, silly!'

'Alice,' Thea cautioned, 'are you sure you're doing the right thing here? Isn't it bloody dangerous?'

'Yes,' said Alice, 'it *is* dangerous but I have to do it – I feel compelled to – so in that respect, it must be right even if, on paper, it's wrong and dastardly. I have to rid it from my system.'

'I thought the one-night stand had done that,' Thea reminded her.

'So did I,' Alice said darkly. Then she brightened. 'Guess what!'

'What?'

'I'm going to play hooky from work tomorrow afternoon and Thursday morning.'

'Christ, Alice,' Thea exclaimed, 'you really need to tread carefully.'

'Oh shush, Thea – you know you'll be gagging for details!'

And that was it. That was just it. No matter how greatly Thea deplored Alice's actions and despaired at her abhorrent lack of morality, she did indeed crave details. The whole scenario was car-crash horrific, but like a terrible road accident, one is compelled to look. Because it's bizarrely life-affirming to gasp and recoil from something so appalling you can't believe it's real. And it's sobering to think thank God that's not me. And it's chastening to think I hope it never happens to me.

Miss Heggarty and Mr Brusseque

Alice's first thought was Christ, what on earth am I thinking, let alone doing? This isn't me. This really isn't.

However, her need to live out her fantasy as a foxy temptress, to fulfil her desire for debauchery with the rock-climbing, nature-communing sex god, overruled her crashing dismay at where the dirty deed was to happen. Paul had given an address in Clapham – 23a Blanchard Road. It was the 'a' that unnerved Alice most. As the taxi stuttered its way along Blanchard Road, with the driver and Alice craning to see numbers, she kept her hopes up. The road was pretty. And quiet. That was a good start. The fare was expensive and Alice justified it would be money well spent.

'Number twenny-free, darling.'

Alice noted the scruffy front door and numerous bells and hoped they were but an ironic façade to a *bijou* residence. Perhaps the beer bottles and takeaway cartons tossed aside in the front garden were there as a cunning foil to would-be burglars. As she rang the bell, she lowered her expectations and just prayed that there wouldn't be batik bedspreads pinned up as wall hangings, or Jim Morrison looking down in his Jesus-like way from posters Blu-Tacked to the backs of doors. Please no CND symbols graffitied with marker pen onto the fridge door. And dear God, no patchouli joss-sticks.

You're a snob, Alice.

No, I'm not – I've merely outgrown the 'dope-smoke digs' thing.

Been there done that?

Exactly (though I've never used a bedspread as a wall hanging).

But now you're a married woman of thirty-three living very nicely in Hampstead.

Exactly.

Sloping off work for a little light adultery in the afternoon.

When Paul saw Alice through the spyhole, he hovered and stared. What a great suit. He watched Alice grow impatient, saw her looking with certain disdain around her. He grinned. He'd give her something to moan about. And just then, the expense of his trip over to England, the negotiation it had necessitated at work, the lies he'd told to Brigitte, whom he'd just started seeing, were all worth it.

'It's not the Ritz,' he said as he opened the door, brandishing his easy smile and looking Alice up and down like a tipster evaluating a racehorse, 'but the sheets are clean and no one's here.'

'I could've booked us into a nice hotel for the price of the taxi fare!' Alice pouted, brushing past him and finding herself in a communal hallway badly in need of a Hoover. She primly offered her cheek for the kissing but Paul took her chin between his finger and thumb and turned her face towards his, sinking his mouth over hers, their tongues suddenly in a whirl.

'Let's fuck,' he murmured. Alice's desire to be in bed with him was so strong that she didn't notice the scruff of pizza flyers and general detritus littering the hallway, the rude waft of other people's cooking. It may as well have been the Ritz, for all the attention she gave the surroundings. The flat itself was unkempt with drab, tired furniture and unforgivable features such as the paper lantern with a glaring rip in it, a plate with dried HP Sauce left on the sofa. Alice did note that there were no ethnic bedspreads on the walls and for her, just then, this fact alone both rose-tinted the rest of the flat and justified her illegal exeat from her marriage and her career that afternoon. So, on a mattress on the floor, under two sleeping bags zipped together, Alice romped the afternoon away with her lover.

It was only when she awoke with a start from a doze she couldn't recall slipping into, slightly chilly and aware of the irritating sound of Paul's semi-snoring, that it struck her she was on the other side of London to where she lived and worked and that her surroundings were categorically unpleasant. On any normal Wednesday, she'd be making her way home by now. An image of her sumptuous bathroom, the luxurious fluffy weight of her Egyptian cotton bath sheets came to mind. With it came a stab of guilt. But if she felt guilty it meant she was in the wrong and she wasn't prepared to own up just then. The best thing to do was to put it all out of her mind. And the best way to do that was to give herself something else to think about. So she rolled over and started to kiss and caress Paul. Soon enough they were fucking again and all thoughts of work, marriage and scuzzy bedrooms were flung far from her conscience.

Every time the phone rang, Thea jumped, fearing it was Mark wanting to know if she'd seen his wife. What was tonight meant to be? The Heal's do or Pilates? Saul assumed that Thea's tetchiness was due to her anticipation that the phone would be the estate agent ringing with news, bad or good. She didn't tell him but she was almost relieved when it turned out to be the vendor's agent turning down their revised offer on the new property.

'Come on,' said Saul, 'let's go out – let's go for a few drinks, perhaps a stonking hot curry, and not think about bricks and mortar.'

But Thea worried they might bump into Mark, which was highly unlikely as he wasn't that partial to curry. 'Let's catch a film instead,' she suggested, thinking that she'd be safe in a dark cinema.

'Good idea,' said Saul, 'Arnie's new film would be a welcome distraction. Let's go.'

However, Thea suddenly thought what if Alice needed her? What if all had gone horribly wrong in Clapham? What if her phone didn't have a signal in the cinema? She couldn't risk that. 'No,' she flummoxed, 'curry. Let's go local.' Saul was now a little irritated but it was nothing a karahi chicken couldn't soothe.

As Alice took a taxi all the way back to Hampstead, she began a text message to Thea but stopped mid-word. What was she meant to write? State the obvious – been shagging non-stop and now walking like John Wayne? Perhaps theorize instead – orgasms this good cannot be bad? Instead, she pressed the speed-dial button to phone Thea. But what would she say? We fucked until suppertime and then I tried to have a shower in a bath with scum-marks and one of those rubber shower attachments you bung onto the taps like a milking machine? Was she to tell Thea that the flat was rented by a bloke who was a friend of a friend of Paul's? That some bloke had arrived back at some point and was quietly rolling a joint on the sofa next to the plate with the dried-on sauce when she and Paul surfaced? Which precise details of the afternoon were worth recounting? The only people who knew of her whereabouts were she, Paul and Thea. And they all knew the purpose of the afternoon was solely sex and no matter how mind-blowing the orgasm, the mechanics of sex were pretty straightforward.

All this thinking had passed the journey. Her cab was already travelling through Camden. She decided she'd send Thea a short text before she went to bed, confirming lunch the next day. Please don't let Mark be at home.

Please don't let this be a day when he doesn't have to stay late for some conference call or other.

Thea thought how Alice's teenage fluster and giggle the next day were actually quite endearing. If this Paul bloke was good for anything, it was reinstating her best friend's bounce and spirit.

'God, I can't wait for you to see him!' Alice declared, drumming her fingers on the restaurant table in the safe territory of Maida Vale. 'I'm telling you, he's more gorgeous and sexy than *anyone* you'll ever have seen – in reality or on screen. Honestly!'

'Shut up, you idiot.' Thea poked her. 'You sound like a teenager.'

'He's here – here he is!'

Thea was desperately disappointed. She was a firm believer in beauty being much more than skin deep. But she had to admit that Paul was quite spectacular looking, in a rugged, Timberland-branded sort of way. Not really her type at all – but unquestionably attractive and obviously smitten with Alice. He shook her hand and took Alice's in his which made Thea feel awkward.

'Are you enjoying your trip?' Thea asked him with a stern edge that made Alice kick her under the table.

'Very much,' he said, ruffling his already tousled hair.

'What have you done?' Thea probed, moving her legs out of kicking distance. 'Where have you been?'

241

'Oh, you know, mainly hanging out in Clap Ham.'

His enunciation of the silent 'h' struck both Thea and Alice but while Alice thought it sweet, Thea let it irritate her supremely.

'You haven't seen the sights then?' Thea challenged him.

'Like Bucking Ham Palace, you mean? Or Saint Paul's Cathedral?'

Silent 'ai', you prat.

'Any of the galleries?' Thea persisted, holding Alice's glare. 'Our glorious parks?'

'Not this time,' Paul said, throwing a furtive smirk over to Alice which Thea intercepted. 'I'm on a tight schedule, you know? Perhaps next time, though.'

'Next time?' Alice exclaimed.

'Next time?' Thea challenged.

'Hey, the trip over was a doddle – why not!'

Alice excused herself and went to splash cold water on her face. Thea and Paul glanced at each other awkwardly.

'So,' Paul said, 'is her man a bit of a bastard then?'

'Who?' Thea shot. 'Mark? A bastard? He's one of the nicest people I know.'

Paul seemed surprised. 'Well, she's obviously not getting what she needs.'

Alice returned before Thea had the chance to respond. 'We could, if you like, go for a stroll in Regent's Park this afternoon,' Alice said to Paul, 'if you felt the need to authenticate your trip.'

Paul shrugged before a thoroughly licentious expression suffused his face, which Alice found thrillingly contagious.

'Thea,' Alice said without taking her eyes off Paul, 'are you staying at Saul's tonight?'

Thea had been busying herself with her French fries. 'Yes, why?'

'Perhaps I really ought to go and *water your house plants*,'

Alice said, licking her lips at Paul whilst trying to locate Thea's legs to nudge with her foot.

'Sorry?' Thea knew exactly what Alice was implying but was so taken off her guard as to feel downright insulted.

'Perhaps you'd like me to *stack your post*?' Alice elaborated, slithering a coy giggle over to Paul. '*Do your laundry*?'

'Alice, are you asking to borrow my flat to shag Paul?' Thea barked, hoping to shock some sense of decorum into her and embarrass Paul.

'We'll leave it spick and span,' Paul told her, obviously rubbing at Alice's leg under the table.

'Please?' Alice pleaded with her most winsome, beguiling pout.

'I have to go, I have a client in twenty minutes,' Thea declared, leaving with a blatant glower. Alice stood up to go after her, prepared to demand her door keys, when she saw Thea had left them on her plate already. In a splodge of ketchup.

Alice licked off the sauce with wholly unnecessary suggestiveness. 'Let's go and see the sights of Crouch End,' she declared, snogging Paul while a waitress cleared the table.

Loggerheads

Thea was appalled, incensed and insulted. Poor Peter Glass received a massage so vigorous he was virtually winded and Thea's final client was given a perfunctory forty minutes before being told he was much better despite leaving her room with the stilted gait he'd entered with. Later, Thea snapped at Saul, 'Tell them this is our final offer and they can take it or fucking fuck off.' And then, when she saw she'd missed a call from Mark, she burst into tears.

'Baby,' Saul tried to soothe her, 'baby, what's up?'

'Nothing,' Thea cried.

'Tell me,' Saul said, through lips pressed to the top of her head.

'Alice,' Thea sobbed.

'What's wrong with Alice?' Saul asked, remembering he hadn't seen her in the office that afternoon. 'Is she OK?'

'We've fallen out,' Thea whispered. She felt a sudden stab of acute loneliness at the fact that Alice was actually very happy and utterly unaware that they'd fallen out.

'About what?' Saul said, wiping Thea's nose for her. But Thea didn't want to tell him. She'd been sworn to secrecy, after all. And a part of her could not betray trust placed in her. Another part of her simply didn't want to reveal the crime, the sin, to Saul. He liked Alice. He worked with her. He liked Mark too. It was so hideous she didn't want to talk about it. She didn't want to say out loud that she hated her lifelong best friend for behaving in a manner which threatened to undermine all they were meant to hold sacred, all they were supposed to be striving to achieve. This wasn't playground gallivanting or youthful experimentation. It was full-on promiscuity. It was dangerous and deplorable and Thea didn't want it to be happening. It made her feel unsafe. Why wasn't Alice behaving?

'What about?' Saul repeated.

'Just stupid,' Thea said, wiping her nose gratefully against Saul's shoulder, 'nothing.'

'It'll blow over,' Saul said, kissing her forehead, 'these things always do. She's your best friend. I bet you she texts you before she goes to sleep tonight. Now, am I really phoning the estate agent declaring our final offer or the vendor can fucking fuck off?'

Thea smiled. 'I love you Saul,' she said with a crackling sniff. 'I'd never do anything to hurt you – even if you might never know about it.'

Saul gave her a puzzled smile. 'Thanks, baby,' he said, 'ditto.' Thea leant towards him and cupped his face in her hands, kissing his mouth with tenderness. 'I'm going to phone the agent,' he said, kissing her back. 'Are we agreed this is our final offer then?' Thea had her eyes closed. She nodded. She did so love Saul. Her home was with him, wherever that might be.

Thea's Twelve O'Clock

'Hullo. I brought your keys back. And a latte.'

'Alice, I don't have time for this – my twelve o'clock is due any moment.'

'I *am* your twelve o'clock, silly.'

'What? You? Why?'

'Because I'm not due in at work until this afternoon and I've just said goodbye to Paul and I could do with a massage after all the vigorous indoor sport I've been doing.'

'Well, you're not having a freebie.'

'I paid in advance, actually. Are you OK, Thea? Has something happened? Is it the flat?'

'Alice, just undress and lie face down on the table. Are you in pain or discomfort anywhere?'

'Not specifically. But I *have* been shagging Paul in a furiously athletic way. And I suppose I have been burning the candle at both ends.'

'Is there any tenderness?' Thea asks, loading the question with ulterior meaning.

'Nope!' Alice declares, rather triumphantly.

'Is there any tenderness, Alice? Any tenderness at all?'

'None whatsoever,' Alice says, 'unless you can locate something I can't feel.'

Thea regards Alice's body, supine and undeniably beautiful. And she is filled with an emotion just short of pure loathing.

'Lie face down, please,' Thea says as she slips off her clogs and pads over to the table. She gazes down at Alice until Alice can feel Thea's calm, measured breathing trickle over her skin. Thea is centred and ready to begin. She knows just the type of massage that would do Alice good. She won't bother with effleurage – the basic light and soothing stroking techniques she'd normally start and end a session with. Effleurage is best used for the reduction of pain and for its relaxing properties. Well, Alice doesn't seem to be in any pain and appears totally at ease. Nor does Thea feel Alice would benefit today from petrissage, the compression or kneading method primarily used to stretch and release muscular tissue – hadn't Alice bragged that shagging Paul had given her a full body workout? Alice certainly doesn't require any lymphatic massage and Thea feels friction methods won't be needed – there's enough friction already. Perhaps some invigorating percussive movements might be useful – hacking, pounding, cupping and flicking could serve Alice well today. Mainly, though, Thea is going to treat Alice with skin rolling – whether Alice considers this a treat will be interesting.

Using a method akin to hand rolling a cigarette, Thea pinches up a sausage of Alice's skin and uses her thumbs to roll it up and over her fingers. The sensation is like being pinched, pulled and scorched. And because the technique is a rolling motion, there is no break, no hands off. Initially Alice says nothing because she assumes it is good for her and assumes the discomfort will lessen. But the discomfort turns to pain and the pain has no let-up.

'Ouch!' Alice gasps. Thea continues to roll her skin, all

the way along her back, her waist, her shoulders, her neck.

'Jesus, Thea!' Alice cries out. 'It feels like an inside-out Chinese burn.'

'Just relax,' Thea says in a soothing tone belying the frown Alice can't see.

'Thea – ow!' Alice protests but Thea continues, rolling Alice's skin over and over.

Let me do a weaselly little roll-up. How about a nice thick Vienna sausage? Now I'll roll a joint – carefully and slowly and tightly. Right, I think it's time for some cocktail chipolatas. Another skinny roll-up now. A nice fat Churchill cigar. How about I try to turn your skin right over? As far as it'll go.

'Thea! You're killing me!'

'I'm not killing you,' Thea declares with derision, 'I'm merely working from basal layer to skin surface. I'm using a variant of connective-tissue massage – it is believed that the surface tissues, being a continual membrane, connect to the brain and that one's emotional state can affect the tissues and vice versa. So I'm just seeking to unravel, smooth and repair the myo fascia, OK?'

'But it hurts.'

'Rubbish. Think of it as a powerful neurofascial effect.'

'But I don't know what that means.'

'Alice, stop being so wet. Just lie there and think of England then.'

Thea starts using the technique on Alice's upper arms. Alice twists away. The soreness makes her eyes smart. 'Stop it, all right? I've had enough. Thanks, Thea – OK. You can stop now.'

'Just let me find a couple of trigger points,' Thea says with deceptive gentleness. Alice heaves out a sigh of relief as the skin rolling ceases. And then yelps. She can't define where Thea has just pressed but pain scores at her temples.

'Oh dear,' Thea says, 'I'd say you need further treatment

there.' She presses elsewhere and the pain is referred as a stab down Alice's leg. She finds another point and Alice's eyeball feels as though it's been sliced. 'Gosh, Alice,' Thea says, 'I'd suggest intensive therapy. You're in a mess.'

'Seriously, am I in a mess?'
   'Yes.'

Alice sits up. Her eyes are watering and her brow is furrowed. Her back feels as if it is covered in seeping blotches, bruises and weals. 'Can I get you struck off some register?' she asks reproachfully as she dresses. 'You're a total sadist!'

   'Can I have *you* sacked from *your* job?' Thea retorts over her shoulder, tidying away towels and laying a fresh swathe of paper sheeting over the bed.

   'Well, I may give my staff the odd headache but I don't inflict physical pain,' Alice laughs, 'so under what grounds?'

   'Playing truant to play truant from your marriage,' Thea declares, hands on her hips. She's batted her shot with conviction and she is primed for any volley back. Alice stares at her but Thea outstares.

   'Thea, is there something you want to say?' Alice asks, bristling.

   'Yes, there is,' says Thea, relieved to be invited to let rip. 'I think you're out of order and I'm mad at you for risking all that you have. You're behaving like someone we'd hate. I'm not even going to go into you asking for the keys to my flat.'

   Quite suddenly, Alice looks as though she might cry and Thea hopes she will. 'Stop giving me a hard time – you have no right to.' Alice jumps to the defensive, hugging herself and rubbing her upper arms as if Thea has just rolled the skin there again. 'Just because you have it all with Saul – all the loving and all the passion and all the dreams. Don't be so fucking patronizing. You have no idea what it's like. I'm miserable – I can't believe you can't see that, you're meant to be my best friend. I've been miserable for months – you of all people should have known.'

'You have nothing to be miserable about,' Thea announces, now as outraged by Alice's poor defence as by her immoral deed itself. 'Stop trying to come across as the victim. You just got bored.'

'You know what,' Alice spits back, 'you're completely right. Bored is an understatement. Money can buy all the luxury that surrounds me but my body and my soul ache for attention.'

'For Christ's sake!' Thea has to clench her teeth to bite back yelling. 'Mark is madly in love with you. He worships you. You know that. It's why you bloody married him. How can you jeopardize that?'

'Don't you dare go all sanctimonious on me,' Alice warns her.

'I'm not,' Thea says coldly, 'but look at the facts. It's shocking. You've been married less than three years and you're behaving like a slag just because you get sulky that Mark works hard, travels a bit and you can't work the home cinema or find your ridiculous corkscrew.'

'Don't insult me,' Alice barks. 'It wasn't me who put that corkscrew on the wedding list.'

'I'm *so* glad you've brought up the wedding,' Thea says with infuriating calm. 'You can remember who chose what on the list but you can't remember the vows you made to Mark.'

'Whose side are you *on*?' Alice asks with genuine alarm.

'Mark's,' Thea proclaims. 'No one will ever love you more, keep you safe, look after you, put up with you, the way he does. You're an idiot, risking all that you have for some beefcake's dick.'

A fat oily tear oozes from Alice's eye and slicks a slow path down to the tip of her nose. She whispers something.

'Speak up!' Thea demands.

'I know,' Alice croaks. She wipes her nose on the back of her hand. 'Do you know the barrenness of being worshipped by someone you are not in love with?' Alice looks up at her. Thea is stuck for words. She wanted this to be the great reprimand, she wanted to dish out just deserts, to give Alice the ticking-off of her life. 'You're right, Thea, I'm an ungrateful cow. I hope to God Mark never finds out. He doesn't deserve this.' Alice is teary and holds her arms out to Thea, like a child craving a mother's embrace. 'And you're right, Thea, I've turned my back on it all for the transient physical ecstasy of being fucked by a hunk of brawny beefcake. But I can't help it. I crave it. This kind of attention is what makes me tick. I don't think I can survive without it.'

'You said it was just a one-night stand.' Thea squares her shoulders and folds her arms.

'Will you just stop judging me,' Alice shouts. 'You have no idea. You don't know what it's like. Just piss off, will you.'

'You're insane,' Thea laughs harshly. 'Don't bloody come to me when it all goes horribly wrong.'

'Sod off, Thea,' Alice hisses, 'don't flatter yourself.'

Thea's Six O'Clock

It has been a long day. Thea and Saul still have not heard from the estate agent whether their final offer has been accepted, and Haringey council still haven't confirmed the last of the local searches which means Thea won't be exchanging contracts on her old flat this week. Most of all, she's depressed about Alice. For all the vehemence of her disapproval, Thea can still empathize with her best friend for what she's suffering, no matter how twisted she considers her dilemma to be. But Alice stormed off earlier and Thea didn't go after her and they've never fallen out like this before and Thea isn't sure what the etiquette is now.

She has one final appointment. Mr St Clare. Souki has written 'n/p' by the name and Thea wonders if she actually can muster the energy to go through the necessary rigmarole of note-taking, assessment and judging the bony landmarks of a new patient. She slumps her way down the three flights of stairs and fixes a smile on her face before entering the waiting room. Oh bloody bloody hell. Mark is there, looking decidedly pale. Or is that just in comparison with bloody Paul and his bronzed sex-god looks?

'Mark!' says Thea as if it is a lovely surprise and what on earth could he want.

'Hullo, Thea,' he says, rising.

'Er, Mark, the thing is I have a six o'clock booked,' Thea says kindly. 'Is everything all right?' She doesn't know if Mark even knows that Alice has been in for a massage.

'I *am* your six o'clock,' Mark tells her. 'I tried to call your mobile last night but there was no answer and I didn't want any favours like last time so I decided to book myself in officially.'

'St *Clare*,' Thea says. 'They misspelt Sinclair so I didn't click.'

'It's my neck again,' Mark explains, 'see?' He turns his head with good range to the right but can judder only half the distance to the left.

'Come on up,' Thea says. 'Let's see what's going on. And we'll figure out what we can do.'

What Thea would actually like Mark to do is to see Dan or Brent, one of the osteopaths, but both are fully booked a week in advance and actually their therapy might not be quite appropriate today. But there is work she can do on Mark in the meantime. She considers the knot Mark has in his rhomboid muscle and a stiffness around the thoracic, both of which are contributing to the soreness and stiffness he feels in his neck. Under normal circumstances she'd do a deep and lengthy focused palpation with her thumb or finger precisely into the tender nub of the problem which, though intensely painful, usually results in immediate relaxation. However, part of her innate skill as a masseuse is to read her client's situation. And Mark is an open book to Thea, not that he knows it. Thea feels that what he needs today, more than anything, is a simple laying-on of hands; some classic TLC. She needs him to leave her room feeling soothed and relaxed.

'Just pop on the table, Mark,' she says softly, 'and lie face down.' She heats a little geranium essential oil in the amphora and checks that the room is warm enough. She walks over to Mark and stands alongside him. She inhales and exhales and inhales again. She closes her eyes and exhales in a long, controlled, silent breath. OK, Mark, this is for you.

Touch down. Thea places both hands on Mark's back and presses lightly; she begins to rock his body from side to side, from one hand to the other. She keeps the rhythm gentle and consistent and soon feels him yield and allow his body to travel under her guidance. Then, with Mark relaxed and tuned, Thea sweeps her hands gently from the base of his back up and around his shoulders, down again, around again. The effleurage soothes Mark to the extent that Thea can actually see the space between his ears and his shoulders lengthen as he relaxes and lets go. She kneads him sparingly. All she wants to do is instil in him a sense of calm, a feeling of well-being, make him subliminally cosseted by the care and comfort one human can dispense to another. Sometimes, when Thea massages, she experiences negative energy or tensions travelling from her client and into her, leaving her quite enervated. From other clients, the massage can even be mutually invigorating. But from Mark today she detects so little energy of any persuasion that she simply takes to stroking him. As her hands travel their persistent warmth wisely over his body, she closes her eyes and envisages sending affection and hope down through her arms, through her fingers to be absorbed by him.

'Mark, when you're ready, turn onto your back,' Thea tells him, leaving her hands on him constantly. She covers him with fresh towels and walks her way to the head of the table, keeping a hand on him all the while. His eyes are naturally half closed and she's pleased. She rests his head slightly to one side into her hand. 'I'm going to apply a little pressure just with my fingertip to a point near your sternocleido-mastoid attachment,' she tells him, doing just that. 'It'll feel nice when I release,' she says, and it does. Then she straightens and cups his head in her hands, placing her fingertips at the base of his skull. 'I'm going to do the same to points in the sub-occipital region,' she tells him. She judges the length of his exhale to be directly proportionate to the tension she's released. Good.

Thea strokes along his neck, down over his shoulders and along the top of his arms. She runs her hands over his scalp, uses her fingertips to walk the skin lightly along the skull, tugging at tufts of his hair like a troupe of industrious fairies on a mass weaving mission. Then with the lightest touch, she changes pace and position and treats the acupressure points on his face in a calm and measured way. She stands and tugs each of his arms in turn, stroking downwards until she reaches his palms where she massages carefully before rubbing along the length of each of his fingers to give a sudden, light fling to each fingertip. To Mark, it feels as though Thea has guided his entire deposit of stress and tension down each arm, and coaxed it out of him. He's sure that if he looked to either side of the bed, he'd see little piles of the negative stuff.

Thea has worked on Mark for over an hour and a half and he's so still he looks dead. She wants to cry. She bites her cheek hard. 'OK?' she asks, implying that, should he say 'not quite', she'd happily work on him some more. Mark is too relaxed to find his voice but he thinks he's given the semblance of a nod. 'OK,' Thea confirms, 'you take your time. As long as you like.' She tiptoes from the room.

When she returns a generous quarter of an hour later, Mark is sitting in one of the plastic chairs, in his suit, tie neatly knotted, briefcase propped against his leg.

'How do you feel?' Thea asks him.

'I tell you, Thea,' Mark says, shaking his head in wonder, 'that was just what I needed.'

'Good,' Thea says, 'but you should have a little osteo too.'

'Can't you teach Alice how to do that?' Mark asks her, laughing. 'Go on, do me a favour.' Thea doesn't think it funny at all, but she's not going to show it so she gives Mark a kiss and tells him to book in with Dan or Brent. As she tidies her room, she reflects on the bizarre parity. Alice doesn't ever think of giving her husband a massage though he'd love it. And Saul never wants Thea to massage him, because he says he simply doesn't get it.

Cold Shoulders

It was strange for Thea to experience something as momentous as exchanging contracts yet have no Alice to effervesce and celebrate with. And it was peculiar for Alice to be totally disinclined to contact Thea though she knew she could well benefit from her advice and support. As high as Thea felt, Alice was low. This zipless-fuck concept wasn't as carefree and uncomplicated as she'd planned. She was unnerved that her sassiness could have been so easily replaced by irritable insecurity directly accountable to the time it took Paul to send a text, to the length and tone of his abbreviated words. She'd even started feeling jealous of Paul's new groups, imagining some gorgeous woman or other sashaying across the Pont du Gard in front of him, or seducing him in the Cathédrale d'Images, or sharing knowledge about the dietary preferences of the flamingo. And though she'd urge herself to practise what she preached, or obey the editors of *Lush* at the very least, she often found herself forsaking the 'play hard to get' or 'treat him mean, keep him keen' philosophies to send Paul texts that sometimes simply said did u get my last txt?? Her mood towards her staff depended entirely on whether or not Paul had replied. If she was awaiting a response, she was impatient and unfocused. If he replied, she fizzed with energy and creativity. Mark, though, bore the brunt of the length and frequency of Paul's messages. If Alice was expecting a reply, she was sullen and distracted. If his reply was of pleasing length and raunchy content, she'd be offhand with Mark because she resented him for not being Paul. If Paul's text was short and mundane, Alice was even more moody with Mark, begrudging him for being all she had.

Alice needed Thea, she knew how she'd benefit from the two of them 'workshopping' her dilemma through, blasting away unreasonable misgivings, deciding on a constructive way of thinking, a realistic path forward. More than that, Alice just missed Thea. It was lonely confiding to her own reflection; she couldn't give herself any astute answers and if she didn't want to hear certain advice, she could just turn away from the mirror and strop off. Without Thea, Alice didn't have the confidence or the motivation to confront the state of her relationship with Mark, the situation now developing with Paul and what to do with one, the other or the both of them.

Thea quite simply missed Alice; she wanted to have a second opinion when she browsed around the White Company store on Marylebone Road, she wanted Alice to take her to that place she knew near Westbourne Park that did stunning antiqued mirrors. However, Thea was still bristling with indignation that Alice should behave like a careless tart. And Alice was exasperated at what she perceived to be a sanctimonious arrogance and complete lack of understanding on Thea's part. How could they be best friends if their moral codes were indecipherable to each other? What connection could they truly have if their ethics and standards were so diametrically opposed? There was absolutely no attraction in such opposites. The only comfort to Alice was that, despite feeling detested by Thea, she knew her secret was safe. Even through the silence and dislike, she knew Thea was unwaveringly loyal. She doubted whether Thea would even confide in Saul.

Mark and Saul both knew their partners had fallen out. But neither of them knew the reason. Even without a reason, it seemed so daft for two grown women, two childhood friends, two soulmates, not to be speaking. But when Mark tried to ask Alice, and when Saul asked Thea, both men were given such short shrift that they decided not to mention the friend until she was back in favour again. Mark, who came back to Thea for another massage on the osteopath's advice, dared to begin: 'Thea, why aren't you and Alice—' at which point it felt as though his skin was being pinched into corduroy and he thought better of finishing his sentence. Certainly, he didn't dare voice his concern for his marriage to Thea. Anyway, if she wasn't on speaking terms with his wife, she probably wouldn't know why Alice's temper was as it was. Saul, over a brainstorming lunch with Alice, filled her wineglass for the third time and said, 'When the fuck are you and Thea going to kiss and make up?' but Alice had narrowed her eyes and shot steel-cold daggers which told him most emphatically to back off.

Sally knew her two friends weren't speaking but neither Alice nor Thea would tell her any more than a non-committal shrug would permit. Pilates became a place where Alice and Thea, if their sessions had to overlap, tried to out-Pike, out-Elephant, out-Mermaid each other. Sally could only watch – and actually wish her roll-ups were half as good as Thea's, her Swan-dives anywhere near as fluid as Alice's. So everyone around them kept quiet about the situation though they all thought it was bizarre and really quite childish.

Black Beauty

It was one of those balmy May days when the dull drag of winter is forgotten and the promise of summer is at last plausible. Under opalescent skies of Wedgwood blue, gluts of flowers burst from bud and juicy foliage unfurled in a gloss giving the air a clean freshness and warmth that could be tasted and smelt. The day had a clarity which bestowed splendid humour and a spring-cleaned *joie de vivre* on everyone. Alice strode into work in a fabulous mood actually dictated more by the weather and the wearing of sandals for the first time that year, than the kinky message from Paul which had just arrived on her phone. Saul had rattled off an article for the *Evening Standard*, filed his copy for the *Observer* early and banked a number of long-awaited cheques, all ensuring a smile of the broadest dimensions. Mark arrived at work to be called into a meeting with the CEO, VP and MD where he was promoted, given a whopping pay rise and the assurance of more staff and less travel. Thea awoke alone in her flat and turned her face towards a kiss of sunlight filtering in through a gap in the curtains. What a gorgeous day, she thought, what a gorgeous day.

*

'Morning!' It was Saul.

'I'm on the bus!' Thea tried to whisper into her phone while steadying herself over the bumps and lurches of Kentish Town Road. 'Let me phone you when I'm at work.'

'Is the bus crowded?' Saul asked.

'Yes,' Thea bemoaned, 'standing room only.'

'Do you want to give your fellow passengers something to smile about?'

'Saul,' Thea chided softly, 'let me phone you when I'm at work. It's ever so jolty.'

'Thea – our offer has been accepted. We stand to exchange and complete simultaneously – in a month.'

Suddenly, the pretty passenger with the gamine crop was jumping for joy and whooping with delight, proclaiming 'We've got it, we've got it!' breathlessly to everyone. 'Our offer's been accepted!' she was singing. 'We're buying this great flat!' Her fellow passengers grinned at her spontaneous emotion. Just as Saul anticipated they would when he envisaged her reacting in precisely the way she did.

Thea out-talked Peter Glass when he came in for a session at ten. He knew the development Thea spoke of and assured her that the agreed purchase price was a good one. He couldn't really comment on her tumble of ideas for a colour scheme on a theme and variations of taupe but he let her gabble on in the hope that she'd soon return her undivided attention to his frozen shoulder.

'Well, good morning, Gabriel!' Thea greeted a somewhat taken aback Mr Sewell an hour later. 'And how are we, this gorgeous day?'

'I'm fine, Miss Luckmore,' he said rather pointedly which went unnoticed by Thea who practically skipped her way up to her room.

'Come on then!' she smiled expansively at Gabriel. 'Hop on the bed and let's have a look at you.'

I know we haven't exchanged – and I know the process might be beset with hassles and stress but sod it, I have a good vibe and a long lunch hour and it's a beautiful day so I'm going to stroll all the way to the Ruth Aram shop and buy something gorgeous for our new home. A lamp maybe! Perhaps something funky and functional for the kitchen! Or a stunning piece of ceramic just because it's beautiful!

She phones Saul to see if he wants to join her, perhaps even squeeze in a celebratory sandwich lunch somewhere, but his phone is off and she imagines he is either up against a deadline to extol the new generation Bluetooth for *T3* magazine or perhaps out of range in some picture editor's office.

No! No, he's not! He's not doing Bluetooth or pictures because there he is! Just ahead of me! Over there! Saul! Saul! O most auspicious day!

Saul is wending his way down Berwick Street ahead of Thea. The scamp and bustle of the market absorb Thea's voice so she attempts to pick up her pace and weaves between stall-holders and browsers to try and catch up with him. She sees him turning left.

'Hey! Saul – Mr Mundy!'

He hasn't heard. And there's a bloke riding a moped on the pavement sending pedestrians scattering like skittles. Thea skips her way on and off the kerb with the deftness of Gene Kelly in *Singing in the Rain* only it's not raining, it's gloriously sunny. She turns the corner just in time to see Saul disappearing into a doorway some yards ahead.

Damn. Quick. Let me try his phone again. Bugger – still off. He must have gone into some meeting. Bluetooth and pictures or what have you.

Momentarily disappointed, Thea decides she'll stroll along this street anyhow because it won't be too much of a detour and, although it's mostly sex shops and dodgy video clubs, there may be some interesting shops further along.

Here. This is where Saul is having his meeting. In here.
Strange.
Doesn't look like an office.
There's no front door!
Well, there is, but it's been propped open. But there's certainly no sign of a reception area with a cold-water dispenser and the company logo on laser-etched glass. The open doorway reveals just a bare hallway and a staircase, with gloss paint chipped like a tart's fingernails.

There are two signs taped to the door jamb, each beneath a buzzer.

BLACK BEAUTY 1ST FLOOR

MODELS! top

Thea stands at the threshold and backs away. How odd – because she's sure this was where Saul went. Positive, in fact. Perhaps it's all very C. S. Lewis, she thinks to herself – you go in one place and come out quite somewhere else. She checks the buildings to either side. One is a minicab office with a sleepy Ugandan sitting on the doorstep with a clipboard on his knee. The other is a business selling perspex of all colours, thicknesses, shapes and sizes. It's closed, though. *Back 1 Hour* the note says. No, this building in between is definitely where Saul went in.

Thea hovers back outside the building. Black Beauty and Top Models. Fleetingly, she imagines Kate Moss and her pals sitting upstairs watching daytime television and the thought is so incongruous she grins. But anyway, it's 'MODELS! top', not 'top models', so Thea lets the image go.

All it says is 'BLACK BEAUTY 1ST FLOOR' and 'MODELS! top'. But there must be someone else, another business, in there because Saul's gone in.

'Excuse me.' Thea approaches the Ugandan, relaxed on a rickety chair, tapping a Biro on his clipboard.

'You want a cab, lady? Where you going?'

'No, thanks. I'm just. Do you know what else is in that building?' Thea asks. The man glances and shrugs. 'Is there a small studio or company that makes gadgets?' Thea asks. 'You know, boys' toys and the like?' The minicab man chuckles. 'Is there something to do with publishing in there?' Thea persists.

'No. Just the girls,' the man tells her, 'just those girls.'

'Oh,' says Thea, frowning. How peculiar. She stares at the building. There's probably a writer's tiny garret right at the top. Saul's probably gone to commission some freelancer or other. 'Is there a tiny office right at the top?' she asks. The minicab man shrugs and shakes his head. Thea reads this as the man not actually knowing the answer. The perspex shop is still closed. Maybe they have a small storeroom in the next building and Saul needs some perspex.

BLACK BEAUTY.

Wait! Oh my God, Black Beauty!

Thea spins an explanation so plausible and heart-warming that she starts swooning at Saul's thoughtfulness.

He's researched it! It's some book specialist devoted to Anna Sewell's great tome! He's buying me a first edition!

Is he?

Is he, Thea?

Is that what he's buying in there?

She sees that the minicab man is putting his chair inside and shutting up shop, walking off towards the market. The street

264

is quiet. There's another man, sauntering up the street, jangling a bunch of keys. Perspex for sale. What kind of a trade is that? How much perspex must you sell in a day to make a living? How long has Thea been there? She has no idea. How long has Saul been in there? She just can't figure it out.

'Exuse me,' she approaches the perspex man as he's unlocking the shop door, 'what's next door?'

'It's a house of ill repute, my dear,' he says theatrically, lightly.

'And what else?' Thea asks. 'Are there any writers in there too? Or small quirky businesses? Anything with anything to do with magazine publishing?'

'No,' the man says, 'just the girls. Try a couple of streets along – there's a few book places and the like around there.' He enters the shop. Thea remains on the pavement. She's starting to feel sick and confused. Come on, *think*. There *must* be an explanation. Why is Saul in there? What's he doing? When is he coming out?

BLACK BEAUTY 1ST FLOOR.
MODELS! top

Where is Saul? Where is he? First floor? Or on top?

There's only so much thinking Thea can do because, after all, there's only the girls in there. And Saul. In painfully slow motion, Thea's life is beginning to fragment into splintered images and fractured memories, half-formed theories and hastily rejected signs and clues, all of which wreak havoc with her ability to acknowledge fact.

* * *

A door closes. Footsteps are descending the staircase. Thea fears she's rooted to the spot and yet suddenly she finds herself inside the perspex shop. Her heart pounds in her throat and head at different rates. Some force hauls her stomach against her spine and evaporates all the moisture in her mouth. Her conscience rails; she yells at herself you horrible cow! how dare you cast aspersions at Saul! how dare you think he could do something like that! something like that to you! look! see! it's not Saul! of course it's not Saul – it's a complete stranger! just some sad old fat bloke in his sixties who lives with his mum in Purley and has never had a girlfriend.

No.

It *is* Saul. It *is* Saul. It *is* Saul.

Thea watches Saul saunter past through her fractured perspex veil. Saul, distorted through this prism of shards and sheets and panes and panels in jewel-like colours and degrees of transparency. Everything is twisted, fragmented; like a Cubist painting. What is real? How do you piece it together? How can the meaning be deciphered?

That was Saul.
    It was him.
    It really was.
    He wasn't casting furtive looks to either side. He didn't skulk away incognito. His head was high and he looked pretty happy.

'I need to use your toilet.'
    Mr Perspex has never had a customer ask before and this one doesn't even seem to be a customer but Mr Perspex shrugs and tells Thea it's out the back. She vomits. She throws up everything she has inside her. She flushes it away but sud-

denly there's more. She flushes again before another churning spasm scorches her stomach and burns her throat as she hurls bile down into the toilet. Flush it away. Flush it away. She heaves and retches but at last there's nothing left. Physically, it's a relief yet still she feels desperately sick.

Nothing's left. There is nothing left.

Alice?

```
u there, Mr B?
```
   Yes, he is!
```
howz u? I miss u, u mad sexy bitch! ☺
```

```
miss u 2 ☹
```

'Who are you texting, Alice?'
   'No one – I mean, it's just a work matter, Mark.'
   'Do you fancy Thai?'
   'Sorry?'
   'Thai – takeaway?'
   'Yes. Sure. Whatever. Just give me a minute, would you,
Mark?'

```
bad timing, txt u L8R xxxxxxxxxxx
```

'Sorry, Mark. Now, what were you saying?'
   'Do you fancy Thai?'
   'I'm not hugely hungry, actually.'
   'Well, there's nothing in the fridge.'
   'I've been busy!'

'I'm not criticizing you, Alice – I just said we've nothing in the house so do you fancy popping out for a meal or ordering a takeaway?'

'Oh. OK. Sure. Order plenty and I'll have a nibble.'

'OK. Unless you'd rather go out?'

'No – takeaway is fine. Just get a takeaway.'

```
u there, big boy?

  yes - thnkng of ur hot bod . . .

  my hot bod v v slippry! .

  me hard & horny - wanna suk?

  yum yum cum! come 2 me! come 2 uk??!!

  luv 2 but me skint

  but I want 2 play with my toyboy . . .

  can u fone?

  no - not now - not poss xxxxx
```

'Here we go – I ordered way too much. Are you all right, Alice?'

'Sorry? Yes, I'm fine. Just thinking about work actually.'

'I popped into Blockbuster too.'

'I have some work to do – do you mind if I disappear for an hour or so?'

'No – of course. Here, let me do you a plateful. There you are, darling.'

'Thanks, Mark.'

```
I cld send u tix . . .

  wots 'tix'?

  TICKETS - idiot! u r all balls, no brain!!
```

```
Easyjet/Eurostar etc

but I'm broke Alice!

am sure u can thnk of ways 2 recompense
me, Mr B

cld fuck u til you beg for mercy . . .

hmmm that'll do nicely!

seriously, Alice - u serious?

v serious - will research & fone/txt u 2moro
xxxxxxxxxxxx

xxxxxxxxxxxx
```

'How did it go?'

'That was delicious.'

'How did it go? The work – all done?'

'Oh. Yes. It's fine. I just wanted to try to sort something out. Mark – have you any trips booked in the near future?'

'I'm not sure. Why?'

'Oh, nothing. It doesn't matter.'

'I know what you're after – a holiday! Good call, Alice – we haven't been away for ages. Tell you what, I'll mention it tomorrow. What a great idea. How about the Maldives – ultra luxury.'

'But are you going away on business at all? Soon?'

'I don't think so – no plans to. Anyway, you know what – sod it! I'd cancel!'

* * *

```
u there? X
```

When Alice's phone buzzed a message through two hours

later, her heart skipped but then slumped at not seeing Paul's name flash up. Her heart then picked up its pace a little when she saw it was from Thea. Alice read it and then deleted it.

I am here, Thea. But I'm not quite ready yet, lady.

Thea?

'Hi, babe – just me. I'll leave a message on your land line. Call me when you get this. Bye!'

```
lunch 2day? Film 2nite? Sx
```

'Oh, hi hon – it's just me – I'm wondering if you've lost your mobile? Anyway, give me a call as soon as you can. Bye.'

```
earth 2 Thea, earth 2 Thea . . . Wheres u????
Fone me!! Sxxxx
```

'Hullo, babe – have you been abducted by aliens? Fallen down a well? Run away? I'm slightly worried now – give us a call. OK. Bye.'

```
r my txts arriving - is your fone on the
blink?? Sxx
```

'Er. It's just me – Saul – I think you've probably lost your mobile but I'm leaving this message anyway and I'll call your land line again. If you pick up this message, can you phone me, babe? Speak to you soon, bye.'

'Thea, it's gone lunchtime now – can you please phone me as soon as you get this message? Love you.'

'Alice? It's Saul. Yes – I'll be in around three-ish. Listen, I don't suppose you've heard from Thea, have you? No? No – no reason – I think she may have lost her mobile, that's all – daft thing. OK, I'll see you later – yes, I'll bring them in with me.'

'Thea, it's Saul – if you're there can you pick up, please. I popped into the Being Well but you're not there and they don't know where you are either. Can you phone me as soon as you get this? Or text. I'm at home – but the mobile is on, too. Speak soon. Love you.'

'Hi, Alice – it's Saul again. Listen, do you mind if I cancel the meeting – Thea's not at work, there's no answer on her mobile or at home and I'm worried now. Pardon? I saw her two nights ago – I spoke to her yesterday morning and told her about the offer being accepted. She was giggling on the bus. I haven't heard from her since. What? Yes – the offer on the place we like, it's all going ahead. Listen, I think I'm going to go up to Crouch End – I have keys. Is that OK about the meeting then? Cool. Yes. Tomorrow's fine.'

* * *

Shit. Thea's text late last night. Alice grabs her phone and fires off a message.

u ok?

After two minutes too long, she sends another.

```
u ok? Axx
```
Thea could cry with relief. Help is at hand. Alice is there.
```
no. Tx

u at home? Axxx

yes - can u come?? need u, v v much Txx

k. on my way - so is Saul
```

Saul? Coming here? No no no! Shit. I don't want to see him. I've got to go.

When Headfuck Boy had dumped Thea, her heart had been broken and the pain had been terrible and exquisite but in a cathartically Brontë-like way. However, Saul hadn't broken her heart. If he'd wilfully broken her heart, at least she could hurl herself into a romantic vortex of grieving, sobbing and deluded hope. Instead, Thea was lumbered with his insidious secret and it was asphyxiating. A broken heart was a walk in the park compared to this. All she'd been able to do for twenty-four hours was pace her flat and hyperventilate, rush to the toilet trying to throw up something other than bile-bitter emptiness. She'd been incapable of rationally assessing what she'd seen, the black-and-white facts had been too mammoth for her mind. So, of course she'd ignored Saul's calls. Of course she'd deleted his goodnight and good-morning and Thea sweetie, where ARE you messages. And of course she is rushing out of her flat, knowing he is on his way over.

Today, she feels even worse than yesterday; at least yesterday she'd had something to throw up and too much to think about. Today, she feels hollow and doomed and exhausted. There cannot be any explanation, any escape from what she'd seen. The bare facts are emblazoned, as harsh as a neon strip-light; but she can't close her eyes to them, she can't flinch away – they are imprinted on her mind's eye anyway. She feels wretched; beyond distraught. Horror, disbelief, anger and hurt collide cataclysmically. Saul had done something unbelievable but she has to believe it because she saw it with her own eyes. She finds herself alternately repulsed by him yet somehow scared of him too; she swings from yelling out loud that she never wants to see him again, to sobbing silently at the terrifying notion of a future without him.

He isn't who I thought he was. He is someone else. My Saul is gone. Who is this other Saul? Who is this person? A man who does terrible things.

Yesterday Thea reeled from the shock. However, the surges of adrenalin, the unremitting need to throw up, offered a bizarre respite, a temporary distraction, from deciphering the facts and admitting to the meaning. Today, she is consumed by the deceit, mangled by the hideousness of it all. Reality looms large and there is no escape from the truth.

Saul – do that?
Yes.
Him – with them?
Yes.

How dare he claim love and affection for me while paying for sex elsewhere. You cannot do the one and also the other. It is ethically impossible. It is morally reprehensible. Either love has lost its meaning or he never loved me in the first place. You simply cannot have sex with prostitutes and love your partner. And that's a fact. And the fact is that yesterday, at lunchtime, when I fancied a sandwich, Saul fancied a fuck.

Thea stumbles out from her flat. She shivers spasmodically despite the day being even more beautiful than yesterday. With shoulders hunched, she walks clutching her hollow, aching stomach. Her face is ashen, she's wearing slippers and an agitated expression and people stare as if they know what has befallen her, as if she is indelibly branded, stigmatized. Poor wretch – she's just found out her boyfriend uses hookers. Look at the state of her, staggering down Topsfield Parade – she's walking in the road! Is she mad? Is she drunk? Is she ill? No, she's discovered her boyfriend pays for sex. God, how awful.

'Alice?'

'Thea,' Alice answers immediately, 'are you OK? What's going on? I'm on my way, I'm in a cab, in Dartmouth Park – but the traffic is a nightmare. Is Saul there yet?'

'But Alice – I don't want to see Saul.'

Alice is stunned into silence. The thought 'not in a million years did I consider that' scorches her. What has he done, the bastard? She'll kill him. 'Where are you?'

'Outside.'

'Outside where?'

'Outside down a side street.'

'Are you still in Crouch End? Walk to one end of the street and tell me the name. Don't hang up.'

The taxi costs a fortune. The driver doesn't know Crouch End so he's fine with Alice rifling through his A–Z and directing him.

'Left – leftleftleft!' Alice barks. 'There! There she is. Slow down. Just stop, will you? Just stop and wait a sec – well, put your bloody hazard lights on, then. I'm coming back.'

Thea is pacing ten yards one way, then ten yards the other. She looks up at the sound of Alice's footsteps and stands still.

'Come on,' Alice says with calm kindness, her arm around Thea's shoulder, as if assisting a little old lady or a very small child across the road, 'I'm here.'

It was a little like knowing exactly what to do in an emergency. Outside of a dire situation, one fears one will lose the presence of mind to think straight, act on intelligence and do the right thing. However, when such circumstances arise, suddenly one reacts sagaciously and efficiently. And so it was with Alice.

'Alice, is Saul writing something on prostitutes? Are you publishing something in *Adam* about buying sex?'

'No.'

'I saw him go into a brothel yesterday, Alice. I waited for him to come out again. He did.'

Alice knew instinctively not to let the shock show. She knew not to rubbish what Thea claimed, neither to attack or defend Saul just yet, nor to raise or dash Thea's hopes. The recovery position she needed to put Thea in was to calm her down, make her feel safe and listen without prejudice and with minimal comment. Just then, it didn't matter whether Saul had or hadn't, whether he was a bastard deserving castration or a maligned man, whether Thea should go to an STD clinic, whether Thea should confront Saul, whether or not their relationship could survive this. Instead, there were practical measures to be taken which were far more pressing. Alice knew Thea had to eat, needed to sleep, must not be on her own and that Saul had to be fobbed off, temporarily at least. If Alice phoned him on Thea's behalf, he'd know there was a crisis and he would afford them no peace.

'Do you see?' Alice asked Thea, whom she'd taken back to Hampstead, made a hot-water bottle for and made drink flat Coca-Cola. 'It makes sense. You need to call him. And quickly.'

Thea looked at her phone for some time. And then she dialled because Alice kept telling her to.

'Hiya!' she acted for all her worth, contriving to sound as

breezy as anything, glancing at Alice for bolstering, hating his stupid lovely voice.

'Thea, thank Christ!' Saul exclaimed. 'Jesus, where have you been?'

'I lost my phone yesterday,' Thea claimed convincingly, 'when I was shopping. And I went to collect it and decided to take the day off.'

'But no one knew where you were!' Saul protested.

'But I phoned work,' Thea lied, 'and left a message on the machine.'

'I couldn't reach you,' Saul said softly, 'I was worried.'

And all those times I couldn't reach you, Saul? Were you really in meetings and up against deadlines? Or are mobiles not allowed in brothels? Perhaps they interfere with the equipment? Put you off your pace?

'I even went over to yours,' Saul was saying. 'I tell you, if you're selling it in three weeks' time, you ought to start having a sort-through. It was a pigsty, young lady.'

Oh, God. My flat goes in three weeks.

Thea had gone cold and shuddered violently at the realization. Alice draped her luxurious shahtoosh around Thea's shoulders.

'Are you coming to mine tonight?' Saul carried on.

'I'm tired,' Thea said truthfully, 'and I do have lots of sorting out to do.'

'I'll phone you later,' Saul said with such warmth in his voice Thea found it difficult not to believe that he really loved her.

At ten o'clock, half an hour after Mark had arrived home and, on raised eyebrow from Alice, had greeted Thea as if her presence was the most normal and expected thing, Thea phoned Saul and said she'd be over shortly.

'Do you think that's wise?' Alice asked her, worried by

the distracted glaze to her eyes. She'd rather Thea had another light snack, an aromatherapy bath and an early night as planned.

'I just need to see him,' Thea said. She wasn't going to confide to Alice that actually she'd suddenly been subsumed by an urgent fear that if Saul was alone he might pop out for a quick cash shag. Was that what he did? Those occasions when they stayed in their respective flats, when she phoned late to say goodnight and he explained he was just out buying biscuits or somesuch from the corner shop?

'Tread carefully,' Alice warned her caringly. 'You're fragile – I wouldn't say anything tonight. You really need to sleep. Would you like a valium?' Thea shook her head. 'We'll work this out, Thea,' Alice told her, 'we'll figure out what to do.'

Alice wasn't in the mood for a furtive text session with Paul. She needed to keep her phone open for Thea. In fact, for the first time, she resented Paul's messages arriving and left them unread. Mark had gone to bed early, with the diaries of Winston Churchill. Alice felt traumatized. How could Saul have done this to Thea? How could it be that Saul was that kind of man? Normal, nice blokes don't do that. Whoever heard of such a thing? And anyway, Saul has Thea, for Christ's sake – could he really abuse her so? Alice felt shaken. And the one person who could soothe her was the one upstairs reading Winston Churchill. Thank God for Mark. Thank God Mark was Mark, straight and steady and there for her. She cuddled up against him, sinking fast into the safety net he provided.

'Is Thea OK?' Mark asked, using his finger for a bookmark in case Alice wanted to talk or there again didn't. 'She looked a fright.'

Alice sighed, grateful for Mark's intuitive care but burdened at the secret she had to guard. 'She'll be fine,' Alice said. She let Mark return to his book for a while. 'Mark?'

'Yes?' he said, his finger bookmark at the ready.

'Nothing.'

'Are you OK, Alice?' he asked, closing the book and laying it down. 'You look a little out of sorts.'

'I feel a little low,' Alice confided in a whisper, the threat of tears a flint-edged pebble catching her voice.

Mark switched off the light and took her in his arms. 'It's OK,' he said, 'there there. Get some sleep. Everything passes.'

It wasn't Mark's simplistic optimism that raised a small smile from Alice, it was that he knew precisely what to do for her just then. He knew not to probe, not to reason. He just had to hold her close and soothingly and so he did just that. It was just right. And she loved him for it. And for the first time she felt searing guilt at her own transgression and profound regret.

To Thea, it seemed glaringly bizarre that Saul should carry on as if nothing had happened. In his eyes, however, nothing *had* happened. Why wouldn't he want to chat about the new place? Why shouldn't he twirl her in his arms and place celebratory kisses on her face? Naturally, he'd want to express the anxiety her disappearance had caused him. And of course he was eager to discuss mortgage minutiae. Of course he was going to ask her if she was all right. Of course he was going to comment that she looked pale and tired and of course he'd automatically place his palm tenderly on her forehead to assess her temperature. And of course Thea wanted to scream you evil deviant sod what the fuck do you think you are doing screwing hookers when you have me?

But she didn't. Not because Alice had told her to bite it back but because suddenly she found herself obsessed with a perverse mission of sorts. When they went to bed, she instigated sex: athletic, urgent, ravenous sex. She had a point, not love, to make. She had to feel him overcome with hunger for her. She needed to sense that his passion for her could send him to the verge of frenzy. So she writhed and gasped and twisted herself in mock abandon. She faked the pleasure of every thrust and grind. She let her voice lie most convincingly. What she sought was to analyse Saul's every move and groan. She needed to assess his response. Was he loving it? Did fucking her absorb and sate him utterly? She scrutinized his every hump and groan, evaluated the length and intensity of his climax and studied his breathing pattern and facial expressions throughout.

There was absolutely no doubt about it, she drove the man wild. Why the hell, then, was he paying for sex elsewhere?

'Christ, that was good,' Saul declared, post-coital triumph softening into affectionate gratitude. He rolled towards Thea, his hand gently cupping her breast while he kissed the tip of her nose.

And do you say that to all the women? Thea wondered, turning away from him, gulping against the swell of nausea.

'That'll certainly put me to sleep with a smile on my face,' Saul chuckled, switching off the light, spooning against her and nuzzling the nape of her neck.

It all felt dirty. As if everything needed a good scrub and a boil wash. Saul's sheets. Saul's bathroom. Saul's crockery. Thea's body.

'I have Pilates three times this week,' she announced after a lengthy, scalding-hot shower the next morning. Actually she had only the one class booked. Saul nodded as he tucked into two croissants on account of Thea claiming no appetite. 'And Alice and I are going to the cinema tonight.'

No, we're not – but Alice'll cover for me.

'Busy bee!' Saul said affectionately. 'You'd better start packing too.'

Oh, God. My flat. I have just over a fortnight.

'Yes,' Thea agreed, 'lots to sort out.'

'But we're off to my parents this weekend, remember?'

'This weekend? Oh. Oh, God. I forgot.'

I did forget. It's true.

'Yes – but it isn't a problem, is it? They're looking forward to seeing you again.'

'It's just that I promised Alice I'd—'

'Oh.'

'Sorry.'

'Don't worry. We'll go another time.'

'But you'll still go? You must, Saul – they'll be so disappointed.'

'Yes – I'll go. See if you can change whatever it is with Alice?'

'I'll try.'

No, I won't.

Thea couldn't leave Saul's flat fast enough, inventing an early booking at the Being Well. Yet, by the time she arrived at work, she sat alone in her room at the top and felt like running all the way back to Saul's. An hour later, she felt intense hatred. By lunchtime she was so confused that she wondered whether she'd imagined it all. During the afternoon, all doubt had been blasted away by pure anger. By teatime she was exhausted. When Saul phoned her, his voice made her shudder. She couldn't possibly countenance seeing him at all while her emotions were so varied and raw. She feigned flu and managed to avoid him for five days.

The Oldest Trade

I never noticed before. I never noticed, but suddenly I see that the world is full of prostitutes. Or is it that I'm becoming obsessed? Only a month ago the world seemed a very nuptial place – everywhere I looked I saw brides and weddings and everything pointed to love and romance. De Beers' adverts on buses. The local church festooned with flowers. Honeymoon special in the 'Escape' section of the Observer. Now my world is rife with the world's oldest trade. I've just been to my local newsagent's. I never before stopped to read those hand-written cards in the window. I couldn't believe it – an alarming number of them offer 'exotic massage' or 'adult fun' or 'toys and role play'. One advertised 'dominatrix. Nice flat.' What does Mr Patel think he's doing, condoning all of this? And the newspaper I've just bought has three different scandals involving hookers – a politician caught kerb crawling, a police raid on a vice ring in suburbia and a respected actor caught with an escort and Class A drugs in a Leeds hotel. If I'd bought a tabloid, I bet there'd be even more stories.

Have you ever noticed how every local high street has a dodgy massage/sauna establishment? But have you ever seen *anyone actually go in or come out? You should see the phone box near work, it's awash with cards advertising the services of Asian Nymph, Busty Blonde, Thai Princess, Fantasia Twins and scores of other unlikely-named sex workers. Who uses phone boxes nowadays anyway? Doesn't everyone have a mobile? Are they there only as a pinboard for pimps? I noticed that two of the cards have the same photo but with different names and phone numbers. As if, in the end, all the punter requires is a nice, accommodating vagina: surface details are interchangeable or irrelevant. Perhaps it simply doesn't matter what she looks like.*

Are they prettier than me?

Are they better in bed than I am?

How much does it cost?

How much does Saul pay?

How much money has he spent, over the years?

I hate him I hate him but how then can I miss him? I haven't seen him for a week. I'm running out of excuses. I've done the imagined flu. Now I'm fobbing him off with make-believe Pilates classes and non-existent arrangements with Alice. I know I can't keep kidding myself that I'll think about it all later, that somehow I'll know what to do. I don't know what to do. I cannot believe this has happened. Maybe it didn't. Perhaps I was mistaken. There's probably a straightforward explanation. There has to be. Saul Mundy does not use prostitutes. It really is the most loathsome and ridiculous notion.

'Alice? Can you meet me for lunch? There's something we need to do.'

'Of course I can.'

It is one of the most bizarre marks of their friendship but also the truest stamp of their intimacy and loyalty that neither Alice nor Thea has thought to acknowledge that they're on speaking terms again. In fact, they've slipped right back into being the closest of friends. There have been no outright apologies, no calm or emotional workshopping of their massive falling-out. Thea is in the midst of a crisis – why wouldn't she turn to Alice for help? And why wouldn't Alice drop everything to be there? Apologize? Who should apologize to whom? Didn't you know that love means never having to say you're sorry?

Thea and Alice retraced her steps of a week ago, or were they Saul's steps, back down Berwick Street. They turned left and stopped outside Black Beauty's stable. There was the doorway, wide open; the shabby staircase leading up.

'Do you want me to go up?' Alice asked.

Thea looked at her as if she was crazy. 'And do what?'

'I don't know,' Alice shrugged. 'Suss it out? Talk to them? Ask them if they know Saul?'

'No!' Thea cried. 'No! I don't even know why I need to be here.'

They crossed the street and loitered. The perspex shop was once again closed for an hour. 'Need any perspex?' Alice asked Thea, while they lingered, as if she was talking about toothpaste or postage stamps. Thea laughed nervously though a frown was stitched to her face. They watched and waited. No one went in or came out of the building.

'Do they have days off, do you think?' Alice pondered.

'What are we doing here?' Thea asked Alice.

'I don't know,' Alice admitted. 'If we loiter much longer, they might think we want a job.'

Thea tittered bravely but then a man went in and wiped her smile away.

'Christ,' Alice hissed, 'he could have been our fathers – did you see him? All suited and dapper and – *normal*?'

'I think I want to go now,' Thea pleaded, walking a few yards this way and then that, 'I don't know what to do.' She started walking away. 'I don't want to wait for him to re-appear. I don't want to time him. I don't want to stand here while he's paying – and having – sex right now, yards from where we are.'

Alice linked arms with her and they walked briskly away. She sat Thea down in a café and allowed her as much silence and middle-distance gazing as she needed. Finally, Thea looked up and mouthed, 'I don't know what to do, Alice. I don't know what to do about anything. What do I do with all my plans?'

'Do you love him?'

'Yes.'

'Is it enough?'

'I don't think so.'

'Had you any other doubts, any at all, before you uncovered all this?'

'None whatsoever.'

Alice shook her head and shrugged. 'I know, without asking him or you, that this man loves you absolutely.'

'But he goes to prostitutes!' Thea protested, suddenly objecting to Saul having anything in his defence at all.

'We don't know that,' Alice said, hoping she sounded more convinced than she felt, 'not for sure.'

'I saw him go in! I saw him come out!' Thea declared. 'I don't think Black Beauty runs the Anna Sewell fan club. I don't think "Models! top" sell Plasticine or Hornby toy railways.' Thea was hunched, rocking with the pain of it all. 'I want to run away.'

Alice felt powerless as she tried to comfort her. 'If you run from pain, it will follow you – but if you turn towards it, face it head on, it can only reach halfway,' Alice soothed.

'But that's like saying a problem shared is a problem solved and it's not, Alice, it's not,' Thea sobbed tearlessly. 'I've shared with you that Saul pays for sex, fucks hookers, visits prostitutes, call it what you will and what have I solved? My anguish isn't lessening, it's increasing.'

Alice sucked at her bottom lip thoughtfully. 'Perhaps he doesn't have sex with them, Thea. Maybe he has a perversion he's embarrassed about – maybe he likes to dress as a baby or a nun, perhaps he likes to look but not touch. Maybe he likes to be spanked or spat at or pissed on or God knows what.'

'He has *me*!' Thea bellowed. 'Let him spank me, if that's what he wants. I'll wee on him, if that turns him on. If he satisfies my every desire, why can't I satisfy his?'

Alice paused again. 'I'll do the devil's advocate thing, OK?' She waited for Thea's reluctant shrug before continuing. 'We don't know the specifics but what we do know is that it's Saul's secret. Don't we? Isn't it? A secret he'd categorically hate you to discover. You chanced upon his most private whim, however deviant we decree it. You weren't meant to know. He'd be mortified.'

'No!' Thea all but barked. 'No Alice *no*. Christ, sometimes I pick my nose and eat it, sometimes I waft the duvet and indulge in the stench of my farts, sometimes I fantasize about gang-bangs – those are the secrets of *mine* that I'd hate Saul to discover. Come *on*. No! No correlation.'

'At our age, we all have history,' Alice tried a different tack.

'This isn't history!' Thea objected. 'A week ago is *not* history!'

'The thing I'm sure about,' said Alice, trying to sound balanced and credible, 'is that he's not doing this to hurt you. OK? Can you hear that? Saul wouldn't do anything to hurt you. You *are* the love of his life and I think that you *do* know that. Whatever he's doing, whatever he pays for, it *is* a weird, upsetting, dark predilection – but on paper he's a wonderful boyfriend. You've never doubted him, you've never loved or been loved so deeply, so entirely. So, can you live with it?'

'Turn a blind eye?' Thea was staggered. 'Ignore the fact that the man I honour with my sexual fidelity fucks whores in his lunch hour?' Alice looked down at the table. 'What would you do, Alice,' Thea asked her levelly, just then thinking that Saul wasn't so much dark as the devil incarnate, 'if this was you? If you found out that Mark pays for sex?'

They looked at each other and tears sprang to both sets of eyes. They both knew that Mark simply wouldn't.

'I hate him, I hate him, I hate him,' Thea sobbed.

'The thing is,' Alice said carefully, 'I think you really want to hate him but I don't think you ever can.'

'I never want to see him again.'

'The thing is,' said Alice, 'at some point you're simply going to have to.'

Thea's Two O'Clock

'Hullo, babes.' Peter Glass was waiting in reception, halfway through the *Evening Standard* when Thea arrived back late from her lunch with Alice. Thea was not in the mood to be called babes. Just then she hated the male species without exception.

'How are you, Peter?' Thea asked perfunctorily, as she led the way to her room.

Do you pay for sex, Peter Glass? Is it a toss-up between one kind of massage and another? Did I win or lose today, hey?

'I'm the usual, babes. You know, stressed, overworked,' he laughed. 'It's my sodding lower back today, Thea. The pain is going down my leg – I'm hobbling, it hurts to drive even the Beemer.'

'OK,' Thea said, skimming through her notes on his last visit, 'down to your boxer shorts and onto the bed, please.' In the calm of her room, with something to absorb her, she was soon grateful to Peter for bringing her his aches and pains. For an hour she could take her mind off what irked her and concentrate instead on alleviating someone else's discomfort. It was something she knew how to do. Placing her hands on Peter's back, Thea began to rock his pelvis rhythmically to and fro.

'How are you, babes?' Peter asked, his voice suddenly softer as his body began to unwind under Thea's guidance. 'How's it going? All signed and sealed on the new place? Have you exchanged on yours?'

Thea stopped rocking and for the first time in her career, entirely took her hands away from a client's body mid-massage. Peter felt the chill and isolation and lifted his head, twisting round to look at her. She looked very puzzled. 'Are you all right?' he asked.

'Yes,' she said, though she didn't look it. 'Peter, is it possible for the vendor to unexchange a contract?'

'Revoke?' he balked as if the crime was so heinous as to be virtually unheard of. Thea shrugged. 'Fucking hell, Thea,' he said, returning his head to the hole in the massage bed, 'you'll be sued to within a pound of their entire deposit – they just changed the law to prevent misdemeanours like that.'

'I thought so,' Thea said with forced jollity.

'Cold feet?' Peter asked.

'Nah,' Thea faked her nonchalance, 'I was just wondering.'

She said no more. She rubbed some more ointment between her palms and effleuraged Peter's back with long, smooth strokes. When he wasn't groaning in appreciation and sighing with relief, he was filling her in on the details of his life, professional and personal. He'd pranged the Beemer, he'd chucked the girlfriend, bedded her best mate to make her jealous but since started dating a teacher.

'Not my usual type, Thea,' he marvelled, 'she's a bit older than me and not what I'd call a "stunner". But she's a great girl and she makes me laugh out loud.'

Thea hooked her fingers around the lateral fibres of Peter's latissimus dorsi, lifting and pulling medially. It silenced him

290

for a while and then he started a rant against a rival estate agent. She set about some deep tissue work where he didn't realize he needed it and for the time being, she managed to massage away the stress his adversaries had heaped around his neck and shoulders.

He has a good physique.
  Not really my type.
  But objectively, he's in good shape.
  But I wouldn't say he does it for me.

Thea trails her fingertips lightly up and down Peter's spine. Up and down. And then down some more. Down until she's reached the dimples above his buttocks. Just relax. Just relax. She leaves one hand there and takes her other to his right leg. She strokes up his hamstring and then down. And again. Then, with both hands she starts to massage his legs lightly. Up and down and up some more. She slides her hands around and travels along Peter's inner thighs. And up and down her hands go. This is not massage. This is not ambiguity. This is caressing. She feels nothing. It's easy to trace the hemline of his boxer shorts suggestively with her fingertips.

Peter has gone from being deeply relaxed and utterly motionless to springing up from the table, his face striated with embarrassment. For the first time in his life, he's at a loss for what to say. So he scrabbles into his clothes instead and starts wittering on about Christ is that the time, dear God he has clients waiting.

'I'd better go – thanks for the, er. I feel fine.'

Thea's Four O'Clock

Thea had intended to cancel Gabriel Sewell. She wanted to finish early; she'd had a dreadful headache since Peter's session and it could be a valid excuse not to see Saul for yet another night, to cancel Pilates and just go home, go home and curl up and not do any packing. But her afternoon had been back to back with other people's backache and, at five to four, she went downstairs and found Mr Sewell already there, expressionless as usual.

'Come on, Mr Sewell,' she said, with negligible charm or enthusiasm. He followed her up. 'How have you been?' she asked him cursorily, while helping herself to a long drink of mineral water.

'Not too bad, actually,' Gabriel Sewell replied, thinking he'd like a glass of water too, 'still blocked to the right. But the pain is substantially better.'

For the first time in her career, Thea wasn't remotely interested in her client despite his physical improvement being a direct credit to her. 'Look to the left,' she told him, 'and to the right. And to the left again, please. And to the right once more.'

'It's no longer what I'd term *pain*,' Gabriel defined, 'it's more *discomfort*.'

*Well, if it's only discomfort, Mr Sewell, I wish you'd can-
celled your appointment and waited another week.*

'Down to your underwear and onto your stomach, please,'
Thea said with scant interest. Perhaps she'd just give him
thirty minutes and charge him half the fee.

Thea commenced a pretty perfunctory massage, like a
musician practising scales or a showjumper taking his top
horse for a hack around the block. Something to keep it all
ticking over. Her mind drifted and she found herself wondering whether any of the girls in massage parlours were
actually qualified masseuses. And if so, which skill did they
consider their forte? Did they look in the vacancies section
of the Job Centre or local paper under 'masseuse' or 'sex
worker'? She wondered whether they started off with a cur-
sory shoulder rub to somehow legitimize what came next.
Saul always claimed he didn't really rate massage. Is that
because he'd never had a good one? Or did he just tell the
girls to forget the neck rub and go straight to his dick?

Thea looks down at Mr Sewell. He has a nice back, smooth
and slightly freckled over the shoulders. It tapers becomingly
to his waist and his legs are muscular and with just the right
spread of hairs to be attractively masculine rather than unap-
petizingly hirsute. Turning deaf ears to the small voice
warning her that she's mad, that this isn't going to help, that
this is a very bad idea and fundamentally the wrong thing
to do, Thea trails her fingertips down Gabriel's spine, just
as she had on Peter. And then her hands start to caress his
legs, interspersing strong strokes to the hamstrings with a
feathered caress of the inner thighs. But at the point where
Peter had objected and bolted away and left Thea feeling
wretched, Gabriel spreads his legs slightly and Thea finds
the signal a horrible but undeniable thrill.

Where else, Mr Sewell, she says silently to herself, *what
else can I do for you today?* She is fingering the seam of his

jockey pants blatantly. 'Turn over,' she murmurs. God, this is easy.

Mr Sewell's erection is impressive. In fact, it is so impressive that the very sight of it simultaneously excites but appals Thea. The shape of it leers up behind his pants. As bemused as Peter had been, Gabriel is now lying there, proudly tumescent. He is obviously, and quite literally, up for it. He is rock hard and eager and Thea can see his cock twitching expectantly, skewed slightly by the constraint of his underwear. She doesn't know whether to be shocked or titillated that this man, right here, would fuck her right now. He'd be quite happy to pay, there's no doubt about it.

'But I don't even particularly like you,' Thea thinks to herself as she looks down on his expectant body, 'you're not my type at all. You're surly and non-communicative and cold.'

'Miss Luckmore?'

Thea is horrified to see that while she's been deep in thought gazing at his penis, he's been staring at her intently.

'Miss Luckmore,' he repeats, 'is it à la carte – or can I order off menu? What, may I ask, are the specials today?'

Thea is catapulted from her safety zone into dangerous territory. She doesn't like it. Quick. Think of something. Feign innocence. Ignorance. 'I could do you an Indian head massage?' she suggests.

Gabriel smirks, his hand now lolling arrogantly over the mound of his cock. 'I assume that involves giving me head, then?'

'Pardon?' Thea flusters.

Gabriel snaps back to his more usual curt self. 'Look, are you up for it or what?'

Thea wants to cry. She feels mucky. 'I don't date clients,' she mutters. 'The ethics of my job discourage it. Sorry.'

'I wasn't talking about a date,' Gabriel says, 'just a blow-

job or something. Whatever. Never mind. I'll try the head
massage. Come on.'

*I'm going mad. I'm not thinking straight. I'm losing my grip.
I need to think but I can't. It's like I won't let myself. I have
to decide what to do but I'm incapable of making decisions
because I can't think about them. I have less than two weeks
before I move out. But how can I think of packing when I
don't know where home is any more? I've suddenly acquired
so much baggage. I can't move under the weight of it all.
Maybe I'll just shove the lot into storage and run away.*

Thea and Sally's Six O'Clock

Thea didn't cancel her Pilates class that evening though her head throbbed and she was utterly exhausted from her unbelievable day. However, she knew she was best off devoting an hour to shutting out all that tormented her; indulging in an hour tuning into her own body; centring herself, focusing on breathing, concentrating on all she really was – a skeleton swathed in muscles, joints and ligaments, assembled intricately but logically. She wouldn't be able to think about Peter or Gabriel and what had almost happened, she could forget all about Saul and what had happened. Respite, even for just an hour, was what she craved.

Alice wasn't at Pilates though she'd confirmed their session over lunch. Ultimately, Thea was slightly relieved – she actually didn't want to receive Alice's kindly glances and supportive squeezes and concerned whispers for her welfare. Thea didn't want to workshop her problems and woes over chips and wine after the class. She certainly didn't want to reveal to Alice her bizarre behaviour that afternoon. Thea just wanted to think about her body, about inhaling and exhaling, about maintaining neutral. It was nice, though, to see Sally, and Thea eagerly accepted an invitation to a light supper at the Stonehills'. It would be good to be in Sally's company, she theorized, to have no reason or recourse to talk about 'it'. It would be constructive to simply chat, to natter on topics other than how prostitution and her future seemed inextricably bound. Sally's invite was also a good reason not to go home and have to think about packing and it provided a bona-fide excuse not to see Saul for another night at least. Ultimately, Thea rationalized that to be surrounded by the Stonehills' perfect domesticity would be comforting and affirming.

In Highgate, Sally could harp on all she liked about sleepless nights, the sorry state of her sex life, the demise of her social life and language skills, and the destruction of her clothes by baby puke. However, for Thea, the scent pervading the Stonehill house was uplifting and restorative. Drying laundry. Baby shampoo. Flowers from husband to wife. Home pride. Everything smelt so warm and clean and cosy and complete and grown up. It was a fragrance Thea acknowledged she had always wanted in her life. Just then, she wished she could bottle it. Just in case.

Don't let Sally see me sad. Stop it, Thea, get a grip.

'I wonder where Alice was today?' Sally said, passing Thea tomatoes to slice while she spread oven chips on a baking tray.

Thea shrugged. 'She said she was coming when I saw her at lunch.'

'Have you two buried the hatchet, kissed and made up then?' Sally probed.

'God, yes,' Thea said, busying herself with tearing basil into slivers.

'You're like an old married couple, you two,' Sally laughed, trying to shave parmesan with a potato peeler. 'Talking of marriage, how's Saul? Richard's playing squash with him tonight. He'll be back home soon – he'll give you a lift home, if you like. Providing he managed to stick to just the one post-match pint, of course.'

The door-to-door distance from the Stonehills' house in Highgate to Thea's flat in Crouch End was less than a mile and a half. Just long enough, Richard would have thought, for a quick chat about how the purchase of the new flat was progressing.

'Can I ask you something, Richard?'

'Sure,' he said, presuming his professional capacity as an architect was required.

'Have you ever paid for it?' Thea asked him outright.

'Me?' Richard asked. 'No – we tend to use each other in our company.'

Thea's mind-set was so rigid that momentarily she didn't realize Richard had not grasped her question and she fleetingly imagined a bacchanalian orgy of architects. 'No,' she corrected, 'not architect stuff. Sex. Have you ever paid for sex?'

Richard stared in amazement, wondering if he'd just heard right. Fortuitously, the traffic lights between Archway Road and Shepherd's Hill turned red. Thea repeated the question. 'No,' he replied decisively, 'I haven't. But I do know plenty of blokes who have.'

'Who *have*?' Thea dissected his answer. 'Or who *do*?'

'Christ, Thea!' Richard laughed with a fleeting frown. 'What's this all about?'

'A client of mine,' Thea moulded the truth credibly with cleverly employed ambiguity, 'had the wrong idea about me.'

This seemed plausible to Richard so he continued. 'I know blokes who have paid for it just the once, Thea, but I also know guys who use prostitutes regularly,' he said. 'You'd be surprised.'

'Why?' Thea asked.

'Why do they do it, or why would you be surprised?'

Richard countered. Thea, though, just stared at him, simultaneously dreading details but desiring to know more. 'You'd be surprised how many blokes do. Professional guys like me, really,' Richard elaborated, 'with all the same privileges – a good wage, a gorgeous wife, a fabulous home, great kids.'

'Why?' Thea asked again.

'I suppose,' Richard considered, 'simply because they can. It's a "bloke thing", isn't it?'

'Is it?' Thea asked, forlornly.

'It's bizarre and contradictory,' Richard mused, 'but a man's sex drive is infinitely complex by virtue of the fact that it's so primal and base.'

'Virtue?' Thea balked. 'Vice – *virtuous*?'

'I mean – and this is in strictest confidence – there's a bloke in the office, my age, my position. He has a charmed life – great marriage to a gorgeous, fun woman. Anyway, occasionally he fancies a shag in the way I might fancy a sandwich. Morality and risk don't cross his mind. It's a physical requirement. He finds himself hungry and he nips out of the office and satisfies it.'

'Say his wife finds out?' Thea posed, hating this colleague of Richard's intensely.

'She never will,' Richard shrugged, 'unless she puts a private detective on him. But she never would because their relationship is great – you could say, guys who use prostitutes are committing the slightest and most negligible form of infidelity because emotional betrayal doesn't come into it.'

'But say she *did* find out,' Thea pressed, 'this chap's gorgeous fun wife?'

Richard was adamant. 'She wouldn't – you have no idea how easy and discreet it is.'

'Then how do you know he does it,' Thea countered, 'if it's so easy and discreet?'

The lights turned green. Richard drove across Archway

Road and pulled in along Shepherd's Hill, by the library, under the gentle orange glow of a waning street lamp.

'This might sound shocking,' he said, 'but one afternoon he basically offered me a recommendation.'

'What?' Thea exclaimed.

'He recommended the services of this new girl he'd just seen.'

'For fuck's sake!' Thea objected, gripped by a violent loathing for this colleague. 'What – like telling you Pret a Manger have a great new sandwich you should try?'

Richard laughed. 'Exactly like that,' he said, 'but in my case, it was like telling this chap thanks, but I don't eat red meat.'

'Fucking bastard!' Thea spat. Richard had never heard her swear, let alone imagined she could be anything other than sweet, temperate Thea.

'This colleague of mine is a really nice bloke,' Richard felt compelled to defend him. He drove on. 'You'd like him. That's the irony.'

'Promise me it's not you?' Thea said with steel in her voice and thunder in her eyes.

Richard glanced at her before indicating right and dipping down the long sweep of Stanhope Road. 'Christ, *of course* it's not me,' he said, obviously offended, 'it's never been me. It's simply *not* me – I just don't fancy it. Not during periods when I've been single. Not after nights out with the lads. Not when I've been far away from home.'

'Promise me,' Thea warned him.

'Thea!' Richard protested, regarding her quizzically. 'What's your problem?'

'It was unbelievably upsetting,' she declared, leaving the car, not checking the passenger door was shut properly, forgetting to thank Richard for the ride.

Thea savours a Lewis Carroll Moment in her hallway, encircled by closed doors. She can't decide where she wants to be, so she sits down where she is, for a long while, until she's quite calmed down. She stays where she is, takes her mobile phone and thinks about calling Alice to tell her what Richard has said. It's strange, what she heard from Richard is ultimately more illuminating than it is shocking. And though the details are deplorable, fundamentally it has been helpful.

I almost feel I now have reasons to forgive Saul; the information by which I can understand him a little better. Facts that should lessen the revulsion and shock of it all. Plausible explanations that could appease my turmoil. Perhaps I should be relieved, perhaps I should try and philosophize that actually it has nothing to do with me – he's just being a bloke. Maybe I should believe that his emotional fidelity to me is sacred to him. That everything really can be quite all right.

'But if Richard Stonehill can choose *not* to use hookers,' Thea shouts, 'why can't Saul?'

Ryanair's 10.10 a.m.

At Carcassonne, all Paul Brusseque knows, as he boards a Ryanair flight he's managed to find the fare for, is that there's this hot chick in England who's occupied his thoughts most of the time. Yeah, so she's married, but so what – from what he can deduce from the little information she's given him about husband and home, he reckons it must be on the rocks. Or else wide open. Something like that. Whatever. If she's up for some no-strings action, he isn't going to get his morals in a knot about it.

Tix. She had said something about sending him tix 2 uk. But she's a tease, this Alice Heggarty, a playful, tease of a flirt. Her text sex has tantalized him to distraction, to desiring the real thing enough to go for broke and board a plane for it. So he's her bit on the side, her bit of rough, her toyboy, her big boy, her fantasy incarnate. So what. It's a damn sight better than being a boring old fart of a husband who most likely can't satisfy her or probably cheats on her the whole time anyway. Is he in love with her? The husband? He'd be a crazy fucker not to be. Is Paul in love with her? Or is he just crazy about fucking her? Crazy enough to scrounge two days' leave and scrape together an air fare to surprise her. Sit back and enjoy the flight. But it's cool to go with the flow. It would be boring to always let your head rule your heart.

'Much better to think with your dick,' Paul laughs to himself.

Paul arrives at Stansted and wonders which way London is. And where he can change his euros. And when he should contact Alice. And how – text, telephone or just turn up? And where is he going to stay?

Alice's phone made her jump. She thought she'd put it onto silent mode. Her instinct was to hide the document she was reading on her computer. Silly, really, because the caller wouldn't know what was up on screen. In fact, even someone looking over Alice's shoulder would merely note the *Guardian* website and an archive article on British sex workers. Alice doing research. Inspired by her trip to Soho with Thea over lunch. Very up *Adam*'s street, after all.

However, Alice's phone ringing through a message surprised her. Paul. She might've known. He texted her around this time most days. It was strange but in the light of Thea's situation, Alice's pleasure in her extramarital dalliance had dulled a little. Paul's texts were still an ego boost and her replies remained fruity, but it was as if it was all now so fanciful as to be virtually harmless. It was a virtual affair, after all, because she hadn't actually seen or even spoken to him for a good three weeks. Last month, in fact. For Alice, the texts provided light relief from the demands of the day, an ego boost at opportune moments and a little light sauce into the blandness of her home life. Having a secret was still fun; quite safe fun, actually. It was all words and no action and where's the harm in that?

There is an enduring irony that actually there's a time and a place for spontaneity and if they are out of sync, the impact and attraction are severely compromised. Had Paul sprung his surprise visit the previous week, she would have fizzed with the outrageous arrogance of it. She'd have played hooky from work or she'd have smuggled him up to her office or she'd have lied to Mark and invented an industry drinks party that would take up all evening. But Paul's text arrived an hour after Alice had returned to her office from her trip to Soho with Thea. His text bleeped through just as Alice was trawling articles on the Internet, absorbing the facts and figures of the socio-economics of prostitution. Over 50 per cent of men have paid for sex; 50 per cent of those pay for it regularly. Of those, 75 per cent are ABC1 men, 30–60. *Adam*'s circulation was ABC1 men, 30–50. Alice calculated that the majority of *Adam*'s readers had paid for sex, and a fair proportion use prostitutes often. And then she considered her colleagues and wondered who had and who does and who wouldn't. And she couldn't decide; she just couldn't decide. But the statistics indicated that a percentage had to be punters. She wondered whether to impart this information to Thea. Would it help to know that Saul was not a deviant? That he wasn't acting alone? That he wasn't even in much of a minority? Or would it actually be of little comfort and no constructive use at all?

fancy a fuck?

Paul's message raised a short smile until Alice wondered if he'd ever paid for it.

where r u?

She'd reply later. For now, she put her phone onto silent mode. She bookmarked the webpage, logged off the Internet and turned her attention to spreadsheets and her division's budgets. Twenty minutes later she checked her phone.

Oh Paul, haven't you anything better to do today than bombard me with texts? Go and climb Mont Saint Victoire, or something.

nice weather!

Alice glanced out of the window. It was a nice day.

go climb a mountain / have a wank! Alice texted back. me v busy xxx

Her phone rang. 'Alice Heggarty,' she answered, her eyes fixed on a spreadsheet.

'And just how *busy* is "busy"?' Paul was asking.

'Listen, you!' Alice chided. 'I've a job to do!'

'How about a blow-job?' Paul riposted predictably.

'Go and have a *wank* – go and climb a *mountain*! Bugger off.'

'Well, there are no mountains in London,' Paul mused, 'and Leicester Square is not the place for a wank.'

Alice was struck silent. Paul was chuckling. Paul was *here*? There in Leicester Square? How could that be? She hadn't sent him tickets. She hadn't sent for him full stop. It never crossed her mind that he'd come unless she called. In an instant, she had to assess that affairs are not about control at all, but a teeter on the knife edge of chaos.

Paul loved every second of Alice's silence – he envisaged her shocked and delighted, rapidly rearranging all her afternoon meetings and planning the fastest route to him. He wasn't sure where Liverpool Street was in relation to Leicester Square.

'You're *here*?' Alice managed to exclaim at last.

'Yup,' Paul proclaimed.

'But when?' Alice asked. 'And how long for? And why didn't you say? I'd've sent tickets.'

'I wanted to surprise you,' Paul said.

Alice scanned her diary. She had very little on that afternoon and only momentarily did she wonder whether this was a godsend or not. She had no deadlines to oversee, no one to let down and thus no lies to tell – no excuse, really, not to take the afternoon off. Rapidly, she reasoned that the fact that the path to proscribed passion was today paved her way with no obstacles whatsoever was a Sign. It was Fate giving her the nod to go forth and fornicate. She felt almost protected. Surely if it was wrong, it wouldn't be so easy.

Where, when, how?

Crouch End?

Today was absolutely not the day to ask Thea to assist Alice's adulterous proclivities.

'Take the Northern Line to Camden Town and meet me in the shoe shop opposite the Tube in twenty,' Alice whispered covertly, leaping back into her role as adulteress.

Paul hadn't a clue what she meant. 'Is the Tube in Twenty a store too?'

Alice was a little irritated. 'Stupid! The *Tube* – the underground station – in twenty *minutes*.'

'Oh – OK! Cool.'

He'd annoyed her and the thrill of what was meant to be furtive had been diluted and that made her cross.

Is it a Sign pointing the other way, then? A dead-end street with an unmissable No Entry sign? As she packed her handbag, she decided to leave all sobering thoughts and responsibility behind in her office.

It's a quiet day, it's a lovely day, no one will know, why deny myself pure physical pleasure?

Alice was slightly irked to arrive at the shoe shop before Paul. She'd wanted to sashay in with a toss of her hair and beckon him over with the magnetism of her raised eyebrow alone. Instead, she found herself browsing shoes she'd never wear, glancing at her watch and wondering if the shop had done research into whether blaring hip-hop actually increased sales.

Paul was fifteen minutes late. 'Sorry, baby – that Northern Line is mental! I went too far up and had to jump off at Tough Nell's Something.'

'Tufnell Park,' Alice corrected. 'Hullo.'

'Hiya. Cool trainers,' Paul remarked, picking up a pair. 'How much is £70?'

'Well, let's see,' Alice said coolly, 'I reckon it's about seventy pounds.'

Paul laughed. 'I mean in euros,' he apologized.

'Are you seriously going to buy them?' Alice asked, glancing at her watch. She wasn't in a rush but she was bored of the shop.

Paul had a good look at the trainers. They were funky. But £70 was probably expensive. 'Nah,' he said, putting them back and giving Alice a squeeze. 'You look fab.'

'Come on,' said Alice though she wasn't quite sure where they were going.

They meandered into Inverness Street and walked slowly by the fruit and vegetable stalls. 'What do you want to do?' Alice asked Paul, assuming he didn't really want to buy apples or carrots.

He raised his eyebrow lasciviously and Alice smirked back. 'But let's get something to eat first,' Paul countered prosaically, 'I'm hungry.'

Alice watched him wolf down spaghetti bolognese and diverted her gaze as he chatted with his mouth full. She paid before he could order dessert. She wanted to cut to the sex. Paul Brusseque wasn't meant to be about friendly chit-chat and perusing trendy trainers. He wasn't meant to be a somewhat naive tourist in London. He wasn't meant to turn up late or be bamboozled by the London Underground system and the Euro–Sterling exchange rate. He was only meant to be about raw sex. He should grunt, not chat. He should be naked and manly – not fixated by trendy footwear. Ultimately, he should be her lover; rampant and masculine – not a cheery friend.

Had they been in the West End, she might have been tempted to blow a fortune on a hip hotel room for the afternoon. But they were in Camden Town with not a boutique hotel in sight, let alone walking distance. 'We'll go to mine, it's just up the road,' Alice told him, hailing a cab by whistling through her fingers, which charmed Paul no end. So he told her how cool he thought she was. And kept asking her to whistle like that again. And Alice wished he'd just be quiet. His sex appeal was ebbing away and she was desperate to fuck him before it disappeared entirely.

Come back, Paul, back to how I remember you.

But Alice, this *is* Paul. You want Paul as you've imagined him, as you've reinvented him since your trip to France. After all, a fleeting dalliance deepened by the economy of text messaging leaves plenty of room for fanciful embellishment.

By Belsize Park, to prevent Paul wittering on, Alice started kissing him. He was, after all, still extremely kissable on the surface. She closed her eyes to the familiarity of Haverstock Hill and transported herself back to Les Baux. Back to Clapham. The times and places where Paul had kissed her before. He tasted the same and his expert oscillation turned her on again, much to her relief.

In silence, she paid the taxi and led the way up the steps to her house. She didn't want to note Paul's reaction. No doubt he'd be gobsmacked by the beauty of her home and she didn't want to see the effect on him, didn't want to invite questions, didn't want to think about betraying her husband under his own roof.

'Christ, Alice,' he marvelled in a hush. She plugged his mouth with her tongue while closing the front door with a kick.

'Hullo, Mrs Sinclair.'

Oh, fucking hell.

Wednesday. The cleaner came on Wednesday afternoons.

'Hullo, Carmen,' Alice said to the robust Brazilian lady, relieved to detect that Carmen hadn't witnessed her snogging Paul, 'how are you?'

'Very good, Mrs Sinclair, thank you! I am doing ironing now – the house is very clean.'

'Thank you, Carmen.' Introduce Paul. Think of something. 'This is Paulo – he has come to look at the, at the –' *At the what, for heaven's sake? He's come to look at my tits, Carmen. I wanted him to screw me on the freshly laid linen on my bed, Carmen.* '– at the main bathroom.'

'You change your bathroom, Mrs Sinclair?' Carmen looked horrified. 'But it is very beautiful bathroom. Very new. Very clean.'

'Pressure,' Alice said, 'he's come to check the pressure. This way, Paulo. Follow me.'

Alice took Paul into the bathroom. She thought about pressure and allowed herself an exasperated glance in the mirror. Actually, the water pressure was wonderful, thanks to Mark's insistence on hi-tech pumping. 'Paulo,' Alice said loudly just in case Carmen could hear or was remotely interested, 'this is what I mean.' She ran the bath taps and the water gushed impressively and conspiratorially loudly. Alice turned to Paul and placed her finger over his lips. She unzipped his jeans whilst unbuttoning her blouse. She wanted to fuck and go. She wanted to have sex with him and then she wanted him to go. He fondled her breasts and took his mouth to them greedily while she enmeshed her fingers in his hair and regarded their clinch reflected in the mirror. They looked good. It was a sexy sight. She pulled his face up to hers and they tongued voraciously. Slowly, she knelt and eased down his jeans, pulled down his boxer shorts and took her mouth immediately to his glorious hard-on. She almost gagged. He'd had a long journey. He'd raced around central London. He needed a shower, ideally. A wash at the very least. But there wasn't the time for that. All Alice wanted was fast, urgent sex. 'Do you see what I mean, Paulo?' she suddenly called, for Carmen's benefit.

'Yes!' Paul called out, as Alice sucked his cock and caressed his balls.

Paul pulled Alice up, positioned so she could grab hold of the sink, facing into the mirror. He bent her over slightly, yanked down her knickers and penetrated her. She watched herself being humped, watched his face contorted with intense pleasure. This was precisely what she wanted – to be desired sexually to such a degree that the act itself was greedy, carnal, basic and verging on rough. She observed Paul – his teeth clenched, his eyes screwed shut. He pumped and thrust and came explosively.

'Did you come, baby?' he asked. Alice thought about climaxes and anti-climaxes and decided not to answer directly. She put her finger over her lips and mouthed 'hush' as she switched off the taps. Silence. As she watched Paul pull up his trousers, she felt his semen dribble out of her. They hadn't used a condom. How could she have been so stupid and reckless? What on earth was she thinking? What the fuck was she playing at? Alice detested herself.

'What shall we do now?' Paul asked, thinking along the lines of Bucking-Ham Palace, perhaps. Or Carnaby Street.

'I need to make some work calls,' Alice replied.

'You wouldn't know anyone whose floor I can crash on?' Paul asked. Alice looked confused. 'Clapham's not available – my mate's away and I forgot to ask him for keys.'

'Sorry,' Alice said, 'I don't think I can help.'

'Your mate up in that Crouch place?'

'No! I mean, she's moving soon – so we can't ask her.'

Paul looked at Alice. Alice looked back at him. 'Two nights, right? I'll book you a hotel.'

'Alice, I'm broke.'

'I'll pay for it.'

*   *   *

Should I go to an STD clinic?

Should I take the morning-after pill?

I desperately need Thea, but no way can I burden her with this. Not only will it upset her but there's far more on her plate at the moment than I could stomach. I wanted my cake but now I'll just have to choke on it. I'll just have to suffer feeling wretched all on my own and accept it as my comeuppance.

Alice doesn't doubt that a slap of humiliation would be cathartic, so she goes to the chemist and forces herself to maintain eye contact as she asks for emergency contraception. She knows that a dose of guilt would be medicinal too. She is subsumed by it when Mark comes strolling home a couple of hours later, with his customary cheery kiss, a lovely bottle of wine and the fresh ingredients for his home-made pesto. She isn't hungry. Her remorse and self-loathing have filled her up.

It is only when she's trying to wash away her shame in a scalding hot bath later that evening that she realizes she forgot all about her Pilates class. She won't get a refund now. It means that lousy, pathetic shag with Paul cost her £45. Plus his hotel bill. Actually, the price she is paying is far higher and she's acutely aware of it. She's taking a bath in the guest bathroom because she just can't face going back into hers. And she's told Mark she's going to sleep in the spare room, fabricating a dose of Thea's phony flu as the reason though in truth she feels she does not deserve to sleep with him in their marital bed. She ought to give Thea a quick call to check she's OK. But Thea's mobile is off because she's currently engrossed in her conversation with Richard Stonehill.

Oh, Thea. Oh, Thea. How can we be in such a mess when we're only in our early thirties and our lives until recently were really so charmed? How did everything plummet from our control so quickly? The major difference is that you're the victim in your situation and I'm the perpetrator in mine. You deserve only salvation and happiness – but privately I just can't see how you'll find this. Look at me with my faithful, adoring husband. What the hell was I doing? Please God don't let my comeuppance depend on Mark finding out. Please God, just don't let Mark find out – it will slaughter him. I don't want Mark to hurt. I never did it to hurt Mark. Please save him from pain. Please God, don't let Mark ever find out what I've done – I promise I'll never do it again. Please God, save Mark the torment – I swear it won't be me getting away with it; my shame and regret will ensure it. Honestly.

But do you know what? I don't actually believe in God. I'm scared.

I feel sick.

Oh, Thea, I so need to talk all this through with you. But I can't, I can't. You have an unfathomable amount to cope with. My isolation and my remorse must somehow carry me through and teach me to live and love better than I have been.

Saul's Three O'Clock

```
can i c u?

  no - pls undstnd

  fuck u! come on! i go 2nite . . .

  no Paul - not poss. pls, pls undstnd

  i came all this way 4 u . . .

  i didn't ask u 2

  oh no?

  cant - sorry. Ax ps: no more txts etc PLEASE
```

Etc.? Paul reads reams into the word on his phone. Was Alice referring to sex as an 'etc.'? Arrogant bitch. Paul decided it would be easier to simply hate her than to object, plead or protest. He didn't want to feel his trip was wasted. The fact that he'd ended up paying for his plane ticket slightly irked him – but ordering excessively from the room-service menu and raiding the mini-bar onto Alice's tab at the hotel gave him some satisfaction. There was more to London than Alice bloody Heggarty or St Clair or whoever she was. He'd damn well go to Buckingham Palace and Carnaby Street. He'd put Alice down to experience; after all, he liked plenty of it in his life; it was his chosen mode of living. Toyboy, sex tool, rich bitch's bit on the side? Fine. Whatever. Been there, done that. Tick that one off the list now.

*   *   *

Saul was looking forward to his three-o'clock meeting with Alice. He loved brainstorming ideas so he prepared well and arrived at the offices early.

'Hiya,' he greeted her, kissing her twice.

'Saul,' Alice responded cordially, offering her cheeks but not kisses. She was tired and she felt on edge. She wanted Paul Brusseque out of the country. She wanted to want her life back yet despite making the decision to cut the contact with Paul, she didn't feel like returning to Mark's warm, simple embrace. And the emotion, or lack of it, bewildered and depressed her. And now she was confronted with the dissolute Saul Mundy.

'Coffee?' she offered, swiftly deciding to fully immerse herself into Alice Heggarty, publisher extraordinaire, and keep her alter egos of cuckolding wife and best friend's keeper firmly out of office hours.

'Thanks,' said Saul. 'How are things?'

'Fine,' Alice declared, trying not to balk at the question or look remotely guilty, 'and you?'

'There's a delay on the purchase of the new place,' Saul bemoaned. 'I daren't tell Thea – she appears to be so overwhelmed by her flat sale next week. I've hardly spoken to her, let alone seen her – have you? Every time I phone she says she's too busy sorting her life out to chat. It's only packing – but Christ, is it taking all her time. She won't let me go over because she says it's all a mess – yet she claims she can't afford

314

the time to stay at mine!' Saul laughed while Alice thought he should have read into Thea's chosen phrases. 'She's a daft thing!' he said affectionately. 'When did you see her last? Pilates?'

'No. Not since the weekend. I had to cancel my class the other day,' Alice said, suddenly keen to swerve away from the subject. She tapped her desk. 'Let's get cracking,' she said. 'How's *Adam*?'

'How about *From Apple to Blackberry – technology gets fruity* – and not just because I'm hoping for a freebie,' Saul smiled.

'I like it,' Alice said, making notes. 'I met Nick Hornby's agent – but rather than a straight interview, I want to pitch for a piece on his experience as parent to an autistic child. I've suggested offering an increased fee as a donation to his TreeHouse Trust charity.'

Saul nodded thoughtfully. 'I was musing over a Fatherhood issue – writers, celebs, Joe Public.'

'I like it!' Alice enthused.

'Iconic father/child relationships,' Saul rolled on, 'from Homer and Bart Simpson, to George Bush Senior and George Dubya, Ringo Starr and Zac Starkey, Prince Charles and Wills, Beckham and Brooklyn.'

'And what about daughters!' Alice protested, raising an eyebrow to challenge Saul.

'Paul and Stella McCartney,' Saul laughed, 'Terry and Gaby Yorath, Jimmy and Lisa Tarbuck, Nigel and Nigella Lawson, Mick and Jade and Lizzie Jagger.'

'Homer and Lisa Simpson,' Alice laughed. 'We could integrate the Nick Hornby idea into such an issue. Good. What next?'

'I love the title *Ripper Ripped Off* for an investigative piece on copycat crimes,' Saul suggested.

'I suppose that would necessitate suitably grisly pics, then?' Alice said hopefully.

'Unquestionably. And how about *Adult Adolescents*?' Saul suggested, 'thinking about that whole resurgence in BMX bikes and skateboards and the Beastie Boys who I reckon are probably older than me. Buy a bike and recapture your youth, kind of thing.'

'Good,' Alice mused, 'good.'

She and Saul sat in affable silence, broken only by the occasional pensive murmur or thoughtful sucking of pens when inspiration alighted. Alice was trying to process a train of thought concerning a great title, *Back from the Brink*, because she'd heard an inspiring interview with a mountaineer who'd lost his limbs to frostbite but lived to climb another peak. Suddenly her mind's eye beamed up Paul, in his hiking boots, his muscled bronzed legs. She felt taunted and glanced away from the unwelcome intrusion to find her gaze, previously non-focused into the middle distance, fixed on her shelf. The framed first cover of *Adam*. Her award for Launch of the Year – that gravity-defying jag of perspex swooping into the wooden base. Without warning, she was bombarded with the perspex shop connection, next door to that Black Beauty and those Models! top. And out of nowhere, as clear as if he was speaking right then, she recalled verbatim Saul's comments at that very awards night almost two years ago. He'd proclaimed he liked to dip his finger into a 'fair few pies'. He'd said dollars couldn't buy his desire for diversity – well, yes, they obviously could, albeit not in dollars but his pounds sterling bought him pounds of flesh. And though, in hindsight, Alice could find double meaning in the comments he'd made about his career, there was one thing he'd said which leapt from her memory and assaulted her.

He said how much he loved Thea. He said – and it didn't even strike me at the time – that he was faithful to her 'in my mind and in my heart'. Why didn't he say 'body and

soul'? Why did he even have to qualify fidelity? He speci-
fied his suspect mind, his half a heart while being careful to
make no mention of the physical.

She blinked and halted a shudder as she slowly looked at
Saul, sitting opposite her, tapping a Biro irritatingly against
his lower teeth while he mused over more ideas for the magazine.

'*Paying For It*,' she announced calmly, her level stare
belying her racing heart.

Saul was still formulating '*That's Not What I Call Music
– our inevitable decline into our parents*' and thus failed to
grasp Alice's insinuation. '*Paying For It*,' Saul repeated, as
if she had alluded to first-class air travel or NHS prescrip-
tions.

'*Cash for Sex*,' Alice continued. She scrutinized Saul for
a reaction but there did not seem to be much of one as yet,
he was just looking at her intently. Keep the eye contact,
Alice. Keep the pressure. '*Hooked on Hookers*,' she tried.
Maintain the momentum. '*Jades and their Johns*.' Saul was
nodding slowly. Did she have him? She wasn't sure.
'*Prostitutes and their Punters*.' She thought she could detect
a slight falter to his nodding. '*Paying For It*,' she said again.
Time to raise her eyebrow and then glower. Saul was now
taking undue interest in his pen; putting his finger on the
ball point. Had she struck a heart chord? Time to go for the
jugular. This is for you, Thea. '*A Shag or A Sandwich? Buying
sex in your lunch hour*.' Alice paused to maximize the dramatic impact of her volley. 'What do you think, Saul?' She
let her question hang, the steel in her voice slicing through.
'This one is right up your street, isn't it? Right up your Soho
side street.'

Slowly, Saul looked at Alice. She was shocked. There was
no glimmer of guilt. No jump to self-defence. No arrogant
denial which she could then batter back. No blithering wreck

for her to chastise to the hilt. No tears of remorse she could refuse to mop up. Saul simply looked horrifically ashen; far worse than if he'd seen a ghost – more as though he'd foreseen his own death and it was imminent. '*You* could write this one, Saul, couldn't you?' she continued spikily. '*I have a stunning, gorgeous girlfriend but I pay for sex on the side.* Put it on expenses! I'll go to petty cash right now! Or do you have an account, Saul?'

'Alice,' Saul said, but without protest, more just to request she be quiet.

They sat in the loudest silence; time ticked excruciatingly slowly, reality suspended in a caught moment, their thoughts rocketing far too fast to harness. Nothing could be done. Time couldn't be turned back; neither words nor actions could be taken back.

'She knows,' Alice said quietly, at length.

Saul whipped his head away from the unequivocal meaning of the sentence and stared at Alice's door while unseen tears lacerated his throat like thorns.

'She saw you,' Alice declared hoarsely, her ultimate shot striking the very heart of Saul.

The toxic silence continued to fill Alice's office like an asphyxiating fog. Alice wanted to fire a million questions. Why, you bastard? What were you thinking? How could you? Why on earth would you? How often do you? What's it like? How does it differ? How much do you pay? How much have you spent? When was the last time? Will there be a next time? Why would you want to when you have a girl like Thea? However, Alice's voice was hampered from materializing by her surprise that Saul should dare to look so broken. Her onslaught was somewhat dependent on the assumption that Saul would jump to his defensive, or accuse her of lying, or lie that Thea was mistaken or that they had

318

no proof. Over the last few days, in imagined confrontations, she'd prepared for these responses and had perfected her final self-righteous lunge. Instead, she was confronted by a Saul who was speechless, defenceless and in imminent need of tissues.

Please God, don't let me actually have to comfort the bastard.

'How do you know?' Saul asked quietly. 'How do you know that she knows?'

'She's my best friend,' Alice said through clenched teeth.

'What am I going to do?' Saul said with little hope and negligible energy. He was suddenly devastated to realize that Thea hadn't had flu last week, she probably hadn't been at all those Pilates classes nor had she cancelled the trip to his parents because of a commitment to Alice. The simple truth was that she obviously didn't want to see him, she was actively avoiding him. The rejection was shocking. 'What do you think I can do?' he asked Alice because he had no idea and he desperately sought guidance from the person closest to Thea. Alice shrugged and narrowed her eyes with hostility. Why should she do any thinking on his part – a problem shared was a problem halved and he did not deserve to have his load lessened at all.

'For fuck's sake,' Alice declared, 'you have Thea. Why on earth would you want to even think about jeopardizing that, let alone go forth and fuck and fuck it up irrevocably?'

Saul's frown furrowed deep behind his eyes. 'I never, ever wanted to jeopardize my relationship with Thea nor hurt her in any way,' he declared quietly and with such passion Alice found she could have quite easily believed him.

'Oh, come on,' she rubbished, 'you have *no* excuse.'

'I have no excuse,' Saul agreed, 'you're right. My only defence is an explanation – and that is: I'm a bloke. I guarantee I'm not a deviant, I'm not a bastard – I just do what a hell of a lot of other blokes do. I have the most beautiful girlfriend whom I love deeply and want to share my life with but I also – occasionally – pay for sex. It's just sex.'

Alice was hearing it from his own lips. He was confirming it. He was verifying it. He was admitting it. He was owning up, confessing. She wanted to throw something at him. She wanted to scream at him. She wanted to see him squirm with suffering and be paralysed with pain. She shouldn't let him just sit there and qualify that he was a bloke, *c'est la vie*.

'I couldn't love Thea more,' he was saying while Alice eyed her Rolodex and considered hurling it at him.

'How can you talk of love?' she spat.

'I am telling you, I love that girl more than I have any other – she is my soulmate,' Saul countered emphatically. 'I love her as much as I can – which is more than I thought I could. I adore her. She has never doubted it. And nor have you.'

'Why are you pathologically unfaithful to her, then?' Alice lunged.

'I don't see it that way. It's just sex. It's nothing,' said Saul. 'Unfaithful suggests wilful cruelty and devious disloyalty.'

'Oh, fuck off with your skewed theories,' Alice hurled. A sickening silence throttled them again.

'You know what, Alice, you're right,' Saul said at length. 'You're right – it would make a fascinating article. And maybe I will do it for you, do it for *Adam*, my swansong if you like. You needn't even pay me – donate my fee to Nick Hornby's charity. But I'm warning you I can't write a self-flagellating parable of shame. I could, however, pen you a doctorate on how it is that men can divorce sex from emotion perfectly and yet still desire and believe in love and fidelity totally.'

'Saul!' Alice protested, outraged that he should have a plausible explanation and dispassionately astute grasp of the situation.

'Once in a while I pay for sex, Alice,' Saul said quietly. 'It's hardly a habit and it's not a problem. Nothing illegal, nothing violent. A straightforward quick shag. I don't do it because of Thea – our sex life is fabulous. I don't do it for some macho power drive. I'm not a misogynist and I'm not a sex maniac and I'm not stressed. I don't do it for any reason other than I can.'

'You *can't*,' Alice objected with a screech, 'you *can't* – not when you have Thea.'

'But I *can*. I can make the distinction. I can make the tenderest love to Thea, have passionate and kinky sex with her but very occasionally, if she's not around, if I feel horny or bored and I can't be bothered to wank, I think, I know, I'll go and get £80 out of the cash point and buy a quick fuck.'

'You're a reprehensible con man!' Alice shouted. 'You're a totally selfish, stupid, fucked-up loser.'

'I am going to lose the most precious thing I ever had,' Saul confirmed.

'You bastard!' Alice hissed. 'Who *are* you? Nice guys *don't* – OK? They don't do that!'

'Want a bet?' Saul objected fiercely. 'Do a poll amongst all the men you know. Go on. I dare you.'

'Fuck you – don't you dare try to justify or dilute it.' Alice had leapt to her feet. 'It's ridiculous, deplorable, unnecessary behaviour for a man with such a charmed life as you.'

'Alice, I have nothing to say in my defence. But for the record, I never meant to hurt Thea. For the record, there was absolutely no emotional betrayal. My only searing regret is that Thea knows. I don't know how I'll cope with her hurt. And the ramifications. Christ, Alice, I don't know if Thea and I can possibly survive this. I stand to lose the love of my life.'

Alice looked at Saul. There was no solution. There was no point yelling at him. There could be no happy ending.

His own acute awareness of Thea's intolerable pain was his own terrible suffering. She could see that, it was written all over his pain-lashed face. No amount of further scolding from Alice could improve a dire situation or make him feel worse. His destiny was that he would lose Thea.

'I have to go,' Saul said, his voice hollow and choked.

'What are you going to do?' Alice asked sadly.

He shrugged. 'I don't know,' he said. 'Allow Thea to call the shots. I have to leave it to her. I don't know – perhaps I should tell her I know that she knows. Do I try to fight for her? Do I try and justify? I don't know. Christ, I don't fucking know.' He stood up and turned to leave.

'Saul, you understand that I can't work with you directly,' Alice said quietly. 'I'm sorry. It's over.'

'I appreciate that,' said Saul as he reached for the door handle. 'I understand. I'll miss *Adam*. I'll miss you, Alice. I can't think about this right now. I'm losing Thea. I have to go. What am I going to do? What can be done? Goodbye, Alice. Goodbye.'

And Saul leaves and Alice feels exhausted. But the underlying emotion worming through her conscience and burdening her soul is Shame. Saul has no shame because he honestly considers he has done no wrong – though he acknowledges it has unwittingly caused his most loved one unfathomable pain. But Alice feels shame like a punch to the stomach. She is winded by it. She can't breathe. She is acutely aware that being so viciously moralistic and heavy-handedly sanctimonious with Saul has an ulterior motive in addition to defending Thea's honour and dignity – it appeases her own guilt. It is as if privately she had placed herself and Saul on a scale of deplorable sins and ensured that, out in the open, Saul lost. His vice is worse. He can go to hell. Alice had accused Saul of 'ridiculous, deplorable, unnecessary behaviour' for someone with such a charmed life. Deep down, she knows she should level the indictment in all its savagery at herself. What was it that he had said? He claimed infidelity was wilful cruelty and devious disloyalty. That it was a crime he was not guilty of. But she was.

Saul had never hurt Thea. If Thea hadn't witnessed him with Black Beauty or Models! top, she'd still be floating in her romantic waft of interior-decorating schemes and dreams of domesticity. Saul's hookers, whoever they were, had never had the wrong idea from him nor wanted anything more than his money. A simple cash transaction. Thanks. Have a nice day. And you. But Paul Brusseque had spent his meagre wages flying himself over to London to be with her. Did Saul send his prostitutes outrageous text messages? Of course he didn't. Did he ever make Thea suffer by cold-shouldering her so he could think of them? Never. Alice feels profoundly ashamed at the hurt and insult she's inflicted on Mark over the months. She goes to the shelf and places the framed first cover of *Adam* face down, and turns her award around.

I have behaved far worse than Saul – my actions have directly caused unhappiness and anxiety. Mark has had to bear the brunt of my impatience, my selfishness and my unrealistic expectations of long-term love. I've used and led on Paul Brusseque and behaved badly to him too.

Alice rests her throbbing head against the window pane. Her office is high up. It's a long way down. There's a long way to go.

Who was it who said something about it's not who you love it's how?

She hums a tune and knows it to be 'Love the One You're With'. Apposite indeed – but she's thinking of another quote, even more pertinent. Slowly, it dawns on her. It is not a lyric or film quotation – it is from an article she'd published. Christ – wasn't it in *Lush* years ago? She vaguely recalls she and Thea perusing the article while eating soup. She'd just split up from Bill, hadn't she? When was that – four years ago? Almost. Alice goes to the *Lush* offices two floors below and rifles through their archives.

From Heartbreak to Happy-Ever-After – 7 Steps to Take You There.

'Number 5: *It's Not Who You Love It's How You Love,*' she reads under her breath, in no mood to pronounce the excessive exclamation marks. 'Number 6,' she continues, '*Change What's on Your Wish List.*' Genius. Who wrote it? She recognizes the name – a staff writer long since lured away to *Red* magazine. However, Alice has always believed that her magazines' ethics are directly her responsibility. 'As publisher, I should practise what I've preached.'

Peter's 4.26 p.m.

'Souki, can you take my four o'clock, please?'

'Are you OK? You look dreadful, Thea.'

'I have to get some fresh air. I don't feel so good. Can you?'

'Well – OK. It's the ballerina, isn't it? Sure. You go. Oh, by the way, Saul phoned – *again*. You haven't fallen out, have you?'

'I'm just stressed about selling my flat.' Thea bent the truth while wanting to yell why the hell does everyone see us as this golden couple – it's a sham!

Thea walked quickly down Paddington Street, jaywalked over Baker Street and practically jogged along Crawford Street. She knew exactly where she was heading though she'd never been before, had no appointment and would be wholly unexpected. She'd taken the address from the files at work and had double-checked it on her pocket A–Z. Turn left. Straight on. Dog-leg right. It's here somewhere. But there's a few of them along this street and it's difficult to tell the numbers on these buildings. There! That's it. Here.

Thea burst into the offices of Henderson-Goode.

'I need to see Peter Glass!' she declared.

'Do you have an appointment?' said an enormous vase stuffed with overpoweringly scented lilies which Thea presumed was some high-tech gimmick until she spied a tiny woman with too much make-up sitting at the desk behind.

'No,' Thea said, 'just tell him Thea Luckmore is here.'

'What's it in connection with?' the painted pygmy enquired.

'Stuff!' Thea said, levelling what she hoped was a menacing 'I'm bigger than you – do it!' expression.

When Peter appeared Thea was taken aback. He seemed half his usual height and, as he walked towards her, it was without his usual swagger. In fact, amongst the other sharp-suited agents in the hyper-plush office, Peter seemed to lose some of his brash-bold expansiveness he brandished around the Being Well.

'Thea?' he asked, looking rather alarmed.

'I need to talk to you!' Thea tried to whisper though her breathlessness and agitation turned it into a hoarse hiss.

'Come over to my desk,' he said genially, but Thea eyed the open-plan office suspiciously and shook her head decisively. 'Come on, let's go outside for a mo',' said Peter, catching the receptionist's eye and splaying his fingers to signify five minutes. He guided Thea with his hand at her elbow, as if she was a loopy but harmless elderly relative.

'Come on, babes – the Beemer is as good a place as any for a chat.'

With a key that looked nothing like a traditional car key, he bleeped the car into life and opened a door for Thea. By the time he had walked around to the driver's door and slid into his place, Thea was banging her head on the dashboard, sobbing uncontrollably. 'Babes, babes!' Peter tried to comfort. 'Easy, easy. Come on now, babes – you'll set the air bag off in a minute.'

'I'm not a prostitute. I need somewhere to live. I'm single. I'm homeless.'

Peter wasn't sure which of the four revelations he should tackle first, nor really why it was to him that Thea had come. 'Slow down, darling, take a deep breath. Shit, I haven't a tissue. Hold on.' He sprang out of his seat and went round to the boot, returning with a butter-soft, relatively clean chamois leather. 'Here you go, you can use this.'

Thea blew her nose gratefully. He offered her a piece of mentholated chewing gum, popping two tabs into his mouth when she declined. He chewed thoughtfully and tapped her knee while her sobbing subsided into sporadic shudders and erratic gasps.

'Please could you help me,' she asked softly. 'I sell my house in just over a week but I have nowhere to live.'

'What about the ritzy-glitz apartment with your fella?' Peter asked carefully.

Thea looked at him, wide-eyed and fragile. 'I found out something a couple of weeks ago,' she whispered, 'that as well as professing to love me and proclaiming I could trust him, he uses prostitutes too.'

'Christ, babes, that's not good timing, not good timing at all.' Peter assessed how ghastly the situation must be for Thea and in an instant he understood both her recent, bizarre behaviour during his session and also her probing the ramifications of breaking an exchange of contracts. But just then, he had no answers and was for once stunned into silence. It was such an eerie sound for Thea that she felt compelled to continue. 'Look, I'm horrified I gave you the wrong idea the other week at the Being Well,' she confessed. 'I was in such a muddle – I don't know. My mind was wandering and I guess my fingers followed. I wasn't thinking straight.'

Peter tapped her knee soothingly while telling himself not to be such a prat for being momentarily offended that Thea didn't want to have sex with him at all. 'Nothing happened at the Being Well, darling,' he assured her with soothing equanimity. It was true. Nothing had happened. 'What a wanker!' Peter said with derision. 'I mean me – not your bloke. Your bloke is a wanker too. Actually, I'd say he was more of a prat. Poor old babes; there you were, stressed and in shock and therefore coming on to me in your sudden madness – but there was me turning you down! In your hour of need! I'm so sorry, sugar.' Thea wasn't sure what to make of Peter's take on the situation, his confession. It was as if he was apologizing for not having undertaken a charitable act. His expression softened and he squeezed her arm. 'I'm joking. I'm being an arse. I'm not much of a comedian, am I? I was trying to make you laugh. Thea, forget what happened – in the circumstances, I can quite understand you suddenly going full-on doolally.' Thea nodded. 'But you mustn't take it personally that I declined. I mean, look on it this way – I see you as this beautiful, classy bird way out of my league! You're priceless, babes, priceless. Not that I thought you were a real tart anyway. God, no.'

Thea smiled meekly. Peter was trying so hard to be comforting, to say nice things to pep her up, that it was irrelevant his chosen words were in such a sweet muddle. It was comforting to be sitting there, in the neutral but safe territory of his Beemer, all cream leather and overpoweringly air-freshenered; with Peter himself, gold signet ring, slicked hair and wide-boy accent at odds with his decent, endearingly artless character.

'Anyway, down to business,' he said. 'We need to find you a place to unpack, don't we? When do you complete? Next *week*? Well, you've struck gold, babes. I'm the daddy when it comes to short lets and fast service. No shit. I've got contacts all over this city – the best. Name your postcode, say your price and leave the rest to me. You'll have keys before you can say please.'

The fact that her load had been immediately lightened enabled Thea to slow down and walk calmly back to the Being Well. She'd be in good time for her six o'clock, time enough to go to the newsagent's and buy *Heat* and a chocolate bar – neither of which she'd fancied of late. Trying to choose between an Aero and a Biscuit & Raisin Yorkie, she spied a roll of Refreshers. But rather than make her want to cry, the sight of them made her seethe. She felt relieved.

Anger is good. Anger feels empowering. I can act on anger. Sadness and tears are destructive – I can only be shrunk by them.

She left the shop with a triumphant toss to her head. The smile, however, was wiped clean away when she came face to face with Kiki.

'Hullo,' Kiki said shyly, scurrying past, as she had done so many times on this street. Thea was rooted to the spot while Kiki walked onwards to the massage parlour. Despite the sky-blue day, out of nowhere fat raindrops suddenly fell, spreading in globs on the warm pavement like ink on grey blotting paper. From the depths of Thea's subconscious, memories of the Shipping Forecast exhibition sprang to the fore.

Bitch! She was there. That whore said hullo to Saul and then she saw me and scurried off. Fucking cow.

'Oi!' Thea pivoted and yelled after Kiki just as she disappeared into her place of work. 'Oi – come back here!' Thea shouted though her target had gone. Without a second thought, Thea marched her way after her. She didn't look twice at the door, she didn't stop to consider if she had to press a bell, let alone have an appointment. She pushed; it opened; she was in. It was like a takeaway restaurant where you can't see the kitchen but you can sense what's cooking.

Only it was very quiet. The subdued lighting, dark-red walls and screened windows contributed to an atmosphere of perpetual twilight. The air was overwhelmingly perfumed by cheaply produced, synthetically scented oil. Behind a bland office desk unconvincingly veneered as mahogany, sat a nondescript middle-aged woman dressed conservatively in a black polo neck. She was obviously startled by the sight of Thea. Not their usual walk-in – but not unheard of, either. All types catered for, and the like. She might even be after a job.

'Where is she?' Thea barked. 'That one?'

'I'm sorry, love?' the receptionist replied.

'The one that just came in!' Thea said, hands on her hips. 'Short one – oriental.'

'Kiki?'

'I don't know – the one who came in two seconds before me!'

'Yeah – that'll be Kiki. But Kiki doesn't do – well, you'd be wanting Miss Lula.'

When Thea grasped the receptionist's allusion, she suddenly felt her stomach twist and her inner voice scream what the hell am I doing in here. 'I need to see Kiki,' Thea said in a calm and measured voice. 'I need to talk to her.'

The receptionist shrugged. 'Who are you?'

Christ. I don't have time for this. I am the girlfriend of a man who may well have paid her for sex.

'Kiki!' Thea hollered in the vague direction of whatever was behind the stud wall demarcating the reception area. 'Kiki!' As footsteps could be heard descending a staircase, Thea and the receptionist stared at each other, mirroring expressions of agitated bewilderment while they anticipated the imminent entrance of a girl, hopefully Kiki.

It was. 'Yes?' she said, looking first to the receptionist and then, visibly confused, to Thea. 'Hullo?'

'Kiki?' Thea asked, her eyes darting with adrenalin and unease.

'Yes, I am Kiki?'

What was Thea meant to say now? She had no idea. She wanted to insult the girl, challenge her, shame her, shove her, make a citizen's arrest. Actually, Thea felt supremely anxious, as though she was being sucked into the vortex of a nightmare. She wanted to run out. But Kiki was standing in the way.

'You need me for something?' Kiki asked in shy, broken English; her face under the make-up legibly sweet and way too young. You dirty old fucker, Saul.

'You!' Thea started, pointing at her and wagging her finger in warning simultaneously. 'You! You!' Kiki didn't understand. Nor did the receptionist. But neither could afford for a punter to enter into this fray. They'd turn and take their money elsewhere.

'Lady,' the receptionist said, 'I think you'd better leave now.'

'But he was *mine* – and I loved him so.' Forsaking the velveteen-covered bench, the pile flat and sheened from where punters sat and waited, Thea crumbled dramatically to the floor, sobbing. The receptionist's priority was to get the girl out of reception, out of the house, preferably. Kiki's instinct was to crouch beside the weeping wreck and place a gentle hand on her shoulder.

'I take her,' Kiki told the receptionist. 'You give work to Lula or Mitzi, yes? I take her for ten minutes, yes? Come, lady, please you come.'

Thea was so tired with it all, she didn't bat an eyelid at being led by the hand deep into the brothel by a young prostitute she presumed her ex-boyfriend to have patronized.

Kiki took Thea right to the top, to a room not dissimilar in size or outlook to the one Thea gave her own massages from. Both had a bed. Both had a sink. But Thea's therapy table wasn't a small double bed laid with a pink sateen coverlet and matching pillows. Thea had a pump bottle of Carex handwash by her sink, not a large tube of lube. This room had a shelf with towels too, but in place of Thea's lotions and potions, was a rather paltry selection of dildos. Curtains, discordantly floral, lined heavily with blackout material, were drawn closed. The room was shadily lit by a single, central light bulb with a cheap lampshade and a fringed gypsy shawl draped over it.

'Please – you sit,' Kiki invited, placing herself demurely on the edge of the bed. Her soft voice, neat petiteness and incongruous politeness reminded Thea of the oriental air hostesses on TV adverts for their airlines. 'You would like water?' Kiki offered. Thea shook her head. 'You feeling better?' Thea shook her head forlornly.

Slowly she raised her eyes to meet Kiki's. 'Have you?' Thea whispered. 'Did he? My? With you?' Kiki's brow furrowed; Thea wondered if she had compromised the girl's integrity; client confidentiality. Actually, Kiki was trying to recall what this lady's man looked like. 'We broke up,' Thea continued. 'I need to put phantoms from my mind – OK? I need to know. Did he? Here?' Kiki didn't appear to recall Saul. 'Do you remember you saw me and him at a photography exhibition?' Thea prompted. 'And perhaps you've seen him along this street?' Still Kiki looked blank. With a sigh, Thea took the photograph of Saul from her wallet and without looking at it, passed it to Kiki.

Kiki concentrated hard and then she nodded and smiled. 'Never with me,' Kiki was pleased to confirm. 'Before here I work somewhere else – I think this man came there. But never with me.' Kiki watched Thea slump. She wondered how to explain in her poor English to this broken, sad lady that she shouldn't doubt the man's love for her. How could she put it to her that men like him were nothing special to any of the girls. And nor would any of the girls be remotely special to him. It was like paying in money at a bank – but he received a flesh receipt, not a paper one. A simple, invariably swift transaction. Kiki knew she'd be hard pressed to explain eloquently and she couldn't expect the lady to understand anyway.

'How many times?' Thea whispered.

Kiki shrugged. She didn't actually know the answer but thought the lady would want to hear 'Once? Twice?' so that's what she told her. 'But you work same street here,' Kiki confirmed, 'that is more why I know him.'

'What did he want?' Thea asked.

Kiki looked embarrassed. 'I don't know,' she answered honestly.

'How much? Don't answer,' Thea said hurriedly, 'I don't want to know. It's enough that I know for a fact that he has.' She put her hands over her ears and rocked as she wept.

Kiki sat herself close next to Thea and gently pulled her hands away, placing them in her lap with hers covering them. Thea considered how pretty Kiki's fingers were. 'I come from the forest,' Kiki began, 'and in the forest we say that true love is one soul in two bodies and that whole love allows the bodies to go this way and that way but the soul always remains. Men they need to—' Kiki stopped. She clenched her fist and then flicked her fingers to signify what she meant. 'They just do.' She shrugged. 'I am sorry for you. It is most hard to understand.'

'Do you like them?' Thea asked her. 'Your clients?'

'They are fine – I am careful. This place is good, the girls are good girls. Clean. I am lucky. Many girls like me not lucky, in danger.'

'Do you hate men?' Thea probed.

Kiki smiled and shook her head. 'No – I don't hate men!'

'Do you pity them?' Kiki didn't seem to understand. 'Do

you feel used?' Kiki looked a little taken aback. 'Are you really into sex?'

Kiki laughed and shook her head. 'The feeling of sex is nothing special to me. This job is easy. I never feel it in here,' she says, tapping her heart, 'I never feel it in here,' she continues, tapping at her temples. 'I come from simple family in the forest,' she qualified, 'I can send them much money. They are proud of me.'

'Where is the forest?' Thea asked. 'Do they know what you do?' Kiki's fleetingly downcast look answered her. 'But don't you want a husband? A boyfriend?'

'Oh, I have a boyfriend!' Kiki glowed.

Thea looked horrified. 'But does he know what you *do*?'

'Yes, he knows. He knows this is just my job and all the love I have I give to him.' She regarded Thea. 'We are one soul in two bodies and our love is whole. I go to work and so does he.'

'What does he do?' Thea asked, half expecting Kiki to say 'pimp'.

'He owns two shops for sports shoes,' said Kiki, 'in Ealing.'

'But,' Thea sighed heavily.

'Lady – you are beautiful and clever and with special gifts,' Kiki said softly. 'Maybe my world seems dark to you? It frightens your soul? It is not so. Mostly it is boring! And mostly the men are just bored. Perhaps a little lonely.' Kiki laughed shyly. 'You want to watch? You can watch – I don't mind. You will see it is not – *exotique*! Sex this way is just very boring.'

Thea was bizarrely touched but she shook her head to decline. She'd seen and heard enough. 'You are beautiful too,' she told Kiki, and she meant it. 'And you are very kind. I'm sorry for shouting. I am just hurting so much. My world has imploded. Perhaps the truth is that I am weaker than you because I just can't grant Saul the freedom to be himself. I want him to read a book or something when he's bored.' Thea spoke too fast, too eloquently for Kiki but she could understand her sentiment implicitly.

Thea's gaze fell on an old travel alarm clock placed surreptitiously in the corner on the floor. 'Oh Christ, I'm going to be late for my five o'clock,' she exclaimed. 'And you will be too,' Thea regarded Kiki with a brave smile.

'I take you out private way,' Kiki said. Before they left the room, Kiki turned to Thea. 'Please, you will remember one soul in two bodies? Men are not bad – they are just being men.'

'Thank you,' said Thea, touched, utterly exhausted and still unconvinced.

The rain had stopped. The daylight was dazzling. Thea squinted as if she'd been in the dark for a long time. One more client and then she could go home and resume packing. There were two messages on her phone.

    hi hon. shall i swing by 2nite - help u
    pack? missing u, v v much Sxxx

    fancy supper chez me? wine + dvd? Axxxxxxxx-
    xxxxxx

She phoned Alice to say she'd be round at eight.

She sent a text to Saul as she rushed back to the Being Well. not 2nite - flat chaos Tx

His reply buzzed through just before she entered her room to commence the session.

    but me going 2 b'ham & glsgw 2moro x2 nites
    for EMAP focus groups . . . Sxxx

Thank God for that, thought Thea.

Alice, Thea, Mark and Saul

'Mark, can you set up the DVD for Thea and me?' Alice called from the bathroom. 'She's coming over while you're at that golf thing. I'm having a Jo Malone luxuriate in the bath – the Tube was mobbed today.'

'No problem,' Mark replied from the bedroom, changing out of his suit into something more appropriate for a golf expo at the Business Design Centre in Islington. Saul had sent him press tickets. 'Is she OK, our Thea?'

'She's bored of packing,' Alice said. 'Mark – we might need to put her up here with us for a while?'

'Is she OK?' Mark asked again, his concern genuine. 'Has something happened with Saul?' Alice said fine, fine hurriedly. Mark was well aware how Thea and Alice had always been thick as thieves together – momentous events befalling one or the other to be dealt with together in exclusion of the world around them. He both admired and gently envied the self-sufficiency the two of them gained from their friendship. When they'd fallen out a couple of months ago, Alice had seemed so displaced, so at a loss, so narky. He still wasn't any clearer on the cause of their impasse nor did he expect Alice even to sketch Thea's current predicament. Mark considered how, on a scale of intimacy, there was a gulf between men and their close mates and women and their best friends. He could acknowledge that Alice possibly needed Thea in her life more than she did him. But it was easy for him to feel gratitude rather than resentment. Thea was Alice's great leveller; Thea was the one person who could chastise his wife; Thea was Alice's enduring ally and, Mark knew, an important fan of his. He knew only Thea could chide Alice for her impatience and calm her hot-headedness, that Thea could scold her when she was being churlish; he'd heard her admonish Alice for sulking with him and he knew that Thea reasoned with Alice on his behalf when it came to the pressures and commitments of his job. Good old Thea – he hoped she was all right.

A buzzing caught his attention; it came from under his discarded work shirt, placed for the moment on the floor until he could transfer it to the laundry basket once Alice vacated the bathroom. Under his shirt he found her phone. He picked it up. Message, it flashed. Paul B, it said. Read now? it asked.

Paul B?

Yes, pressed Mark.

ur a bitch - but gr8 tits

It took a while for Mark to actually translate the message, being unaccustomed to the abbreviations of text messaging. He was shocked and indignant. Poor Alice being bombarded by filth – like those obscene pop-ups that occasionally assaulted their home computer screen, worming their way onto some seemingly innocuous website or other. He was sure there must be a way to block them from mobile phones. He was about to call through to Alice about it when he stopped and sat down heavily.

Message Paul B Read now?

It wasn't unsolicited.

It couldn't be.

For the phone to recognize Paul B, Alice needed to have inputted his details. Paul B, whoever he was, was known to her and her tits were known to him. Mark felt less insulted that this Paul B thought his wife was a bitch than he felt mortified that this man was commenting on her breasts. How the hell would he know? Alice was saying something.

'What?' Mark asked, distractedly, his eyes fixed on the screen of Alice's phone.

'I said, don't hang on for me – I'm sloshing on an intensive pro-vitamin hair-restoration mask and it needs to stay on for ten minutes, then have three rinses.'

Ten minutes and three rinses. How long did a rinse take? Multiply by three.

Mark's dilemma lasted seconds. Spy and perhaps suffer? Or ignore and forever wonder? Ten minutes plus triple rinsing was time enough but there wasn't a moment to lose. He scrolled through to the envelope icon. His thumb hovered. Stop singing, Alice. I can't read your text messages with that racket going on.

`fancy a fuck?`

Another.

`u know u want it`

Another.

`can i c u?`

Another.

`fuck u! come on! i go 2nite . . .`

Gutted, winded and blown apart, Mark was crippled by a searing pain in his stomach. He wanted to ask himself what it all meant but he knew not even he could be naive enough to expect an innocent explanation. No matter how much he loved Alice, no matter how much he'd love to give her the benefit of his confounded doubt, the meaning of it all was clear as muck. He couldn't even read between the lines – the nature of text messaging presenting stark facts in black and white. There wasn't the space for purple prose, just a tiny screen filled with `fancy a fuck?`

My wife.

My wife is having an affair.

My wife has been sleeping with someone else.

Who is Paul B?

How dare he call them 'tits'.

Mark was devastated. Over and above the scorch of pain and the nausea of disbelief was the horror of feeling a total fool – the quintessential cuckold of a piss-taking young wife conducting her affairs via the puerile medium of text messaging.

I could never be a Paul B. I'm too old-fashioned. Too stupidly gallant and respectful. Those are the qualities I thought she loved most about me. It appears they mean the least. What an idiot. And one thing I have to ask myself – which plunges the final twist to the dagger thrust – is why has she kept not one of my messages?

He could hear Alice rinsing out the special hair treatment for the second time.

Foolish girl – does she not realize I'd love her were she to wash her hair with Fairy Liquid? Or is it foolish me for even deigning to think she maintains her beauty and sets her standards for me, rather than Paul B? Standards? What sodding standards?

He could hear Alice releasing the bath water.

And I haven't even read the messages she sends.

Mark knew Alice was seconds from appearing. She was the last person he wanted to see. Quickly, he put the phone back on the floor, under his scrunched shirt.

No doubt it'll stay there. Alice is blind to dirty washing.

It's always me tidying away. When has she ever cleared up after the mess she makes?

* * *

'Mark set up the DVD for us,' Alice told Thea who'd arrived just as Alice finished a lengthy, meticulous blow-dry.

'Your hair looks amazing,' Thea remarked, holding up swathes of it as if admiring skeins of silk.

'I used some new product we were sent to trial,' Alice said. 'I pinched one for you too. Hang on. Here you go. Now, white or red wine? Look! Mark's even left out the corkscrew so we don't have to go on our usual hunt.'

'Good old Mark,' Thea said fondly, opting for Sancerre and reaching for glasses while Alice uncorked the bottle. 'How are things? How are things with Mark?'

'It's all going to be fine,' Alice evangelized though she busied herself with opening Kettle Chips to hide the slash of guilt, the scorch of pain traversing her face. 'It's going OK, Thea. Things are better – I feel much more balanced.'

'Good for you,' said Thea, 'good for you, Alice – I'm fucked.'

Alice hugged her sympathetically. 'What are you going to do?' she whispered, holding her tightly. 'Are you any closer knowing?'

'No. I don't know. But I could move into rented accommodation for a while,' Thea said, her flat intonation suggesting she'd learnt the sentence by rote to quote while inwardly she had yet to figure out the manifold ramifications behind it.

'Where? How?' Alice asked, wondering whether Thea would be better off moving in with her for a while.

'One of my clients is an estate agent,' Thea said. 'I asked him earlier today to help. He's found me a place in a mansion block in Highgate already. I'm going to see it tomorrow.

It's not available for another couple of weeks though. Can I perhaps stay here in the interim?'

'Of course you can,' Alice said, 'but Saul?' Had Thea come to her ultimate decision? Already? Unaided? 'I mean – have you told him? About rented accommodation at the very least? Have you spoken to him, have you talked at all?'

Thea's gaze dropped, her brow creased and she bit her lip. 'Haven't told him yet,' she mumbled. 'Actually, I haven't seen him for days. I keep fobbing him off. I keep putting it off. I don't know what to do.'

Alice wondered whether now was the time to tell Thea that Saul now knew that she knew. No. It wasn't a good idea. 'But –?'

'What am I going to do?' Thea forces a whisper crackled by the imminence of tears. 'Everything was sorted and now it's all a mess. And now it's gone. All gone. My immediate future, my long-term future. I'm scared.'

Alice racks her brains for something wise to say. Thea beats her to it.

'Even if I manage to forgive, even if I get my head round the theory that men can totally divorce sex and emotion, even if I truly believe that I am absolutely the love of his life – I will never, *never* be rid of this suspicion and hurt,' Thea says, 'and my own principles that hold it's *wrong*. It's not *nice*. Good guys *don't*.' She pauses and she and Alice scour each other's faces, their expressions mirroring turmoil.

Alice watches Thea's face crease with despair. And suddenly she is looking at Thea aged fourteen years old. Almost twenty years later, her eyes are filled with the same dreadful fear, exquisite sorrow and terrible bewilderment as they had been when her father had left home. It makes Alice shudder and be thankful not to be Thea. Just as she had been at the age of fourteen. Just as she had been grateful that her father was nothing like Thea's. At fourteen, she'd rushed home from

341

school and flung herself in his arms, held him tight, felt so lucky that she had him for her father. And now, aged thirty-three, Alice desperately wants Mark to be home soon from the golf show, so she can hold him and rejoice that he is nothing like Saul.

Alice thought it might well be a good idea to inform Thea that Saul knew she knew – it might just facilitate Thea to come to a conclusion. 'Saul was in for a meeting yesterday,' she began.

'I went to a brothel today,' Thea butted in because it was actually far easier to discuss than her relationship.

Alice was suddenly incapable of any sound, let alone speech itself. All she could manage was a silent, gaping jaw-drop of prodigious proportions. Thea couldn't help but giggle at her dumbstruck expression. It was perhaps the first time she'd been the one to shock the other into silence. In fact, it was probably the first time she'd actually done anything categorically shocking. Alice took a gulp of wine. 'Where? Thea!' she managed to gasp. 'What the *fuck* were you doing there? Thea!'

'I went to confront the enemy,' Thea said, 'so I went to that brothel just near the Being Well. I needed to face my fear. *I destroy my enemy when I make him my friend.*'

'Who?'

'Abraham Lincoln.'

'What are you on about, Thea – you're inspired by the founding father of the United States to take yourself into a brothel in Marylebone and befriend the prozzies? Are you *crazy*?' Alice was desperate for details yet wondered what on earth she was about to hear.

Thea looked a little sheepish. 'Not crazy – I just needed proof that this never had anything to do with me.'

'And?'

'It was the best thing to have done,' Thea proclaimed. 'It

was horrendous and surreal but in retrospect, I have a sense of peace now.'

'Jesus, Thea!' Alice couldn't disguise the admiration in her voice though she worried it was inappropriate. 'Why didn't you tell me! Why didn't you phone! What was it *like*?'

Suddenly, Thea looked back on her visit as a veritable expedition, an adventure. She'd been in a brothel, for heaven's sake! She'd sat on a bed and held hands with a hooker! Surely she was the only person she knew to have done anything like that. Apart from Saul, of course. And perhaps half the men she knew, if statistics were true. 'I've seen a couple of the girls around,' she told Alice, 'you know, buying chocolate, posting letters – just like me.' She didn't want to tell Alice about the Shipping Forecast, about Kiki greeting Saul. She didn't want to force herself to see how blind love had clouded her view of reality for so long.

'Christ!' Alice marvelled. Sod watching *Ocean's Eleven* on DVD as planned.

'Today, I caught sight of one of them and I don't know, I just went a little mad,' Thea admitted sadly. 'I wanted to insult her. I wanted to hate her, I wanted to blame her, I wanted it all to be her fault. But I couldn't and I didn't – because it isn't. Now I see how she doesn't go out soliciting men. Their predilection is not her fault, not her responsibility, not of her creation.'

'Who *is* she?' Alice gasped, wanting to forsake the academics in favour of specifics. 'What's she like? How old? What's her name? What does she look like? What did you *ask* her? What did she *tell* you? Oh my God, did you see any of the clients?'

'She's young – I didn't ask how young because I didn't expect her to answer truthfully,' Thea said. 'She's called Kiki but I don't expect that's her real name. She says she's from a forest.'

'A *forest*?' Alice exclaimed, imagining Little Red Riding Hood in a crotchless basque under her scarlet cape.

'That's what she told me – that her family still live in the forest and she assists them financially. Her take is that a man's sexual needs are distinct from his emotional allegiance and need never impinge on his commitment as a husband.'

'Right,' Alice said, thinking that's as may be but I couldn't cope with it.

'I asked her if she was a sex maniac,' Thea said.

'You didn't!'

'I asked her if she hated men.'

'You didn't!'

'I asked her if she hated women.'

'You didn't!'

'She held my hand.'

'She didn't!'

'I asked her if she enjoyed her work.'

'Does she? What did she say?'

After a week or so of comforting her friend, sharing her pain, letting her cry but feeling powerless to really help, Alice rejoiced in the apparent return of Thea's initiative and strength. After a fortnight of not really knowing how to advise Thea, of being unable to hearten or soothe her, it transpired that the answer lay in a tour of a brothel.

'The strangest thing is that actually I liked her,' Thea concluded, half an hour later. 'She's sweet and kind. She's nothing like the stereotype.'

'God, you're gracious,' Alice marvelled.

'You know, they used to call prostitutes "erring sisters". And actually, I did feel a sense of kinship – I don't know – collusion? She's *not* my enemy, she's a girl,' Thea shrugged, 'doing a job there's a demand for.'

'God, I think you're brave and amazing,' Alice said with great tenderness and pride. 'I wonder where this forest is?'

'I don't know,' Thea said. 'She's oriental so I suppose it's in Thailand or somewhere.'

Alice nodded. Then she stared at Thea. Though she sucked in her lips, she was helpless to prevent an almighty snort of laughter. She bit her bottom lip hard but she knew she was moments away from an uncontrollable fit of giggles.

'What?' Thea asked, confusion making her eyebrows stutter.

'Thea,' Alice squeaked, 'the *forest*?'

'Yes?'

'Do you think she might have been saying "Far East"?'

Thea frowned. Then she groaned. Then she covered her face with her hands while Alice pronounced 'forest' again and again in a mish-mash Malaysian accent. Soon enough, Thea tried it. Far East. Far East, of course!

'Oh God,' Thea didn't know whether to laugh or cringe, 'oh God. What a day. I'm going mad.'

* * *

'Oh God, what a day,' Mark said to himself as he walked around the golf expo aimlessly and with no interest. It seemed the most sensible place to go, in the circumstances. He didn't want to pace around and around the block. He wasn't in the habit of sitting by himself in bars, let alone drowning his sorrows. So he meandered through the stalls and stands with Paul B's text messages leaping out at him wherever he looked. 'There must be some mistake,' he repeated as a whispered chant, 'there must be an explanation.'

Alice wouldn't do that to me. Alice wouldn't do that to me. Alice wouldn't do that to me.

'Mark! Hullo, mate.'

Mark looked up and saw Saul. 'Saul,' Mark shook his hand, 'I didn't realize you were coming. Were we meant to meet?'

'I only decided at the last minute,' Saul assured him. 'I

had nothing else planned. And it's sort of en route to Thea's – I'm going to pop by later and see if I can help with the packing.'

'Oh, sure,' said Mark, 'she's at ours, having a chick-flick comfort-food evening with Alice.'

While Saul was struck by the fact that Thea had lied to him about how she was spending her evening, Mark suddenly wondered if Thea knew Paul B. And if Thea knew, then did Saul too?

'Seen anything you fancy?' Saul asked.

'Fancy?' Mark barked with a deep frown.

Saul regarded him quizzically. 'New balls?'

'New balls?' Mark snorted with derision. He pinched the bridge of his nose and rubbed the corners of his eyes.

'Are you OK, Mark?' Saul asked. 'Are you all right?'

'Fuck knows,' Mark replied hoarsely. Saul reeled from the response. He'd never heard Mark swear, he'd never known him to be anything but composed and always all right. He was thoroughly taken aback.

'Come on, buddy,' Saul said with a hand on Mark's neck, 'let's get a drink.'

Saul didn't think spirits were Mark's thing yet he watched as he downed two neat vodkas in as many gulps. 'I think Alice is having an affair,' Mark announced, his voice rasping from the scorch of alcohol.

Saul was startled. '*Alice*?'

'You see her,' Mark said, 'what do you think?'

'She's never given me any reason to think she's having an affair,' Saul declared. She hadn't. Nor had Thea.

'Look, I don't want you to feel compromised,' Mark said, 'but has Thea mentioned *anything* to you?'

'Not a sausage,' said Saul, attempting to discredit Mark's suspicion by making light of it. 'And she tells me everything.'

Does she, Saul? Are you sure about that?

Mark sunk his head into his hands. 'I don't know,' he said, 'I don't know.'

'What *do* you know, exactly?' Saul probed.

'She can be pretty moody,' Mark said.

'Yes, but all women can be,' Saul pointed out. 'Alice is naturally slightly highly strung,' Saul countered. 'The fact that she's spirited makes her attractive.'

'She can be a flirt,' Mark stated. 'I've known her for years, remember.'

'There's flirting,' Saul reasoned, 'and there's putting your money where your mouth is.'

There speaks an expert. Except you don't flirt, do you, Saul, you don't really have to. Your girls are a sure thing. We know where you put your money and we don't really want to know where you put your mouth.

'I swear to you, Mark,' Saul said, placing both hands flat on the table for emphasis, 'I've never seen even a *hint* of anything untoward – and I've been around her at work *and* play, remember.'

Mark nodded but Saul could see he remained unconvinced. 'I found something,' Mark said darkly. 'Her phone. I found a text message from someone called Paul B.' Saul could only listen – the image of Mark covertly burglarizing his wife's telephone was so atypical as to be frankly disturbing. 'Who's Paul B?'

'Paul B?' Saul thought hard. 'Honestly, Mark, I have no idea. There's no Paul B on the mags that I know. I've never heard Thea mention such a person. Look, can I ask what the message said?'

'Oh, you know,' said Mark with cutting lightness, 'the usual – fancy a fuck, great tits, when can I see you.'

Saul was stunned. And a private part of him wanted to phone Alice immediately and accuse her of hypocrisy of the highest degree, declare her misdemeanour a crime far worse than his.

'What drove you to read them?' Saul asked. 'Have you been going through a bad patch?'

'Not really. I mean, I'm used to her blowing hot and cold – she always has done and I've loved her for years. As you say, she can fly off the handle and she can be moody. It was a bit rocky a few months ago but actually, recently, it's been quite nice and even.'

'I'm sure there's an innocent explanation,' said Saul, though he wasn't so sure and was keen to know more.

'I mean, we've been through much stickier periods – when I've been abroad a lot or working crazy hours,' Mark continued, 'but I've cut down a lot on the travelling – and I'm delegating more now I have a wider team.'

'I'm sure it's not what you think,' Saul said, because though he'd now quite like to doubt Alice, he liked Mark and felt he didn't deserve this angst, however unfounded.

'Do I turn a blind eye?' Mark said, asking himself more than Saul. 'Even if evidence to the contrary is staring me in the face?'

'You know what,' said Saul, 'it's far easier to flirt in emails and texts than face to face. Maybe it's some bloke at the printers or in distribution that Alice keeps sweet. I'm sure it's harmless.'

'How do I find out?'

Saul was stuck. 'I don't think you should go looking for answers unless you can ask the questions directly,' he said after much thought. 'Can you ask her to her face? Will her trust be undermined that you've been searching through her things?'

'I don't know,' Mark shook his head, 'I just don't know what to think or what to do.'

'Listen,' Saul said, 'it's not as if the messages said "great fuck" or "thanks for showing me your boobs". There's no *real* evidence, Mark. You work with numbers, Alice works with words. I assure you our industry is full of boozing, flirting reprobates – and that's the blokes!'

'And my industry is full of strait-laced boring fucks like me,' Mark declared morosely.

If we were girls, Saul thought to himself, *we'd be giving each other a hug at this point. If this was Thea and Alice, they'd be holding hands, their heads together, physically backing up the emotional support.*

Suddenly, Saul thought how much he loved witnessing Thea and Alice's friendship, the intensity of their relationship even when they bickered or, as recently, fell out. Was this Paul B the reason why they fell out? Possibly. Saul thought of Thea's proud-held standards on fidelity and loyalty and what love meant and required. He felt hollow and desolate. He was going to lose her.

'I'd better go,' said Mark. 'Thanks for the drink – and the, you know.'

'Any time, mate, any time,' Saul said earnestly. 'How about one for the road?' He didn't want Mark to go. Mark's quandary was a distraction from his own predicament. Mark, however, declined. 'Listen – don't delve,' Saul advised. 'It won't get you anywhere but the wrong end of the stick.'

Mark nodded and left.

When he returns, Mark finds Alice and Thea snuggled up on the sofa, wineglasses drained and a monster-sized packet of Kettle Chips empty.

'Hullo!' Alice greets him with an expansive smile though Thea seems almost too exhausted to even look up.

'Hiya,' he says.

'Have you had a nice evening?' Alice asks. 'Were there some gloriously naff golfing trousers to buy?'

'Plenty,' Mark says, 'but none in my size.' Alice laughs. Mark analyses it and deduces it to be genuine. It makes him feel confused. 'I'm going to turn in,' he tells them because he wants to see if Alice's phone is still lying under his shirt just up the stairs.

'Thea's going to crash in the spare room tonight,' Alice calls after him.

His shirt is where he left it. Alice's phone is where he'd put it. Keeping an ear on the sounds of life downstairs, Mark takes the phone and scrolls to the envelope icon. He selects her Inbox again and rereads the messages. Perhaps Saul is right – there's nothing that unequivocally confirms anything has actually happened. He scrolls to Sent Items, his heart thudding so loudly it almost drowns out the sound of Alice and Thea chatting. His thumb hovers. This is not right. This is like sneaking a read of a diary. This is not the thing to do. But to Mark it seems like his only option. He has to. And he makes a pact with himself that he must deal with what he might find. He presses the Select button and Alice's sent messages flash up. Thea Thea Mark Thea Mark Thea Paul B Paul B Thea. He can't open them fast enough, his hands are shaking.

`no Paul - not poss. pls, pls undstnd`

Another.

`cant - sorry. Ax ps: no more txts etc PLEASE`

He scrolls back to Paul's messages and from the times and dates of these he can equate Alice's answers. He asked to see her. She said she can't. She's asked him not to contact her – even by text. She's adamant – see, `PLEASE` is in upper case. There are five from him but only two from her. He was the instigator. Both her replies are rejections. There is no reply to his fancy-a-fuck message, no response to his compliments of her breasts.

She hasn't dignified his advances with replies!

Mark is so relieved he could almost cry. And once he's

read Paul's messages and Alice's a final time, he feels desperately guilty.

What was I thinking? How could I! I'm married to the most beautiful woman on earth – of course men will be falling in love with her, left, right and centre. Of course they're going to try it on. But see – she's my wife, her home and her heart are with me. I can't believe I pillaged her privacy. I can't believe I doubted her. What was I thinking?

*   *   *

Saul has sent Thea a text message to say he's been at some golf thing in Islington and he might as well take a bit of a detour and just pop by for five minutes. He is desperate to see her, even if it all comes out. He misses her terribly and is so anguished by the pain she must be feeling that he needs to hold her despite being the unwitting perpetrator. He must be capable of making things better, he must be able to make amends – surely? He wants to hold her even if she hits him. He's willing to proclaim the purity of his love for her even if she hurls hatred back at him and finishes the relationship there and then.

But he's walking down her street, checking his phone and she still hasn't responded. She must be back from Alice's by now. She must have loads to do. He so wants to see her. He rings the bell, knocks and then uses his set of keys to enter. He's always done so. Thea's always been at ease with it. Always welcomed him with a kiss, chatter and the flick of the kettle button. But she's not here. He can't even see the kettle. Just boxes and crates and piles of belongings. It's crowded and messy but it's stark and impersonal. Thea really isn't here. She's packed her life up. She's moving on.

Cold Feet

What do we want most? Alice to be punished though she's already walking with conviction along the road to her marriage's salvation? Shall we have Mark remain content, safely just beyond the reach of hard facts? Do we want Saul to suffer – to atone, to learn, but be damned? Do we think that Thea might be able to put it into some perspective of sorts, better still could she put it into a box labelled The Past and discard it? Is it possible that she could accept, understand, forgive and move forward positively into their long-planned and potentially sparkling joint future? Or are we rooting for Thea to deliver the ultimate scathing soliloquy as she dumps him? Do we want her to destroy him? Do we feel Saul deserves that? Do we want to see Saul foundering in the gutter, weeping and broken, while Thea waltzes away triumphant but with dignity? What is appropriate comeuppance for Saul – and what reward would be appropriate for Thea? Should Saul be allowed to confront Alice and declare a pot-kettle-black situation? Is it deluded to hope for happy-ever-afters all round? Is it right that Alice could get away with it? Are we ready to consider that Saul and Thea might need to have futures without one another?

*

Thea has already phoned the Being Well to see if her nine-
or ten-o'clock slots have been filled since last night. Souki
confirms they're still empty.

'I'll be in later, then,' says Thea. 'I have things to finish.'

She's already phoned Saul to say the words he's been
dreading but anticipating.

'Saul? It's me. Are you back now? From Glasgow? Good.
Are you busy? Oh. But I need to see you. We need to talk.'

She phoned from the bus as it approached Tufnell Park.
Saul estimates she'll arrive in twenty minutes. He paces his
flat, he's choked. The wait is unbearable though he dreads
her arrival. What will you do, Saul?

She's the love of my life.

Will you fight for her?

I wish I could.

Why don't you?

*No. I can't. She knows. Don't you see? She knows but
she doesn't know that I know that she knows.*

Do you not believe you can somehow get round that?

*If she ever knows that I know that she knows, her self-
respect will be compromised. The subject will be open for
discussion and dissection and what good would that do? No
amount of debate can repair us or soothe her. So I've decided
it would be best if she never knows that I know that she
knows.*

So that's it? You'll let her end the best two and a half
years of your life? Strike out that match made in heaven?
Are you sure you're not just being a coward – justifying what
can be seen as an avoidance of confrontation?

*You don't understand. I know that girl. I know that her
trust in me has gone. I don't want to be only half loved.
And I know she won't settle for half her dream.*

Here she is, Saul. Can you hear her coming up the stairs?

Please use your keys. Please let this still be your home.

The doorbell rings out. Reluctant but resigned, Saul goes to answer it.

'Hiya,' he says, his heart rejoicing at the very sight of her, despite the thud of imminent futility throbbing in his head.

'Hullo,' Thea says. She doesn't want to look at him. It's too painful. He was her dream come true but she was plunged into a nightmare and it's time to make sure she's wide awake. She stands awkwardly, as if she has an infernal itch at the back of her knee, a stiff neck, slight paralysis of the face. It makes Saul feel discomfited but impotent: if he makes it easier for her she'll know he knows she knows and yet he's convinced that ultimately that will be worse for her. Though Saul would be pleased to fall on his sword right now to save her the agony of what she needs to do, he can't help her. The balance of her future, the ease of her upturn, is what matters to him most.

'Babe,' he says quietly, hoping he's managed to etch a look of concern over the expression of dread he's keen to conceal. 'What's up?'

Thea shakes her head and regards her toes. 'I can't,' she croaks, 'I have cold feet.'

Should I ask her why? I would, wouldn't I – if I didn't know that she knows.

'Why?' Saul whispers, taking her hand. 'I can warm them up – your cold feet.' Thea keeps staring at her toes, peeping prettily through sandals. She's been incapable of planning what to say. 'Thea, please,' Saul pleads, 'don't.'

Fuck it. I don't care now what she finds out. I just need to keep her. I must. She has to keep me.

'Saul,' Thea whispers, 'something's not right.' She glances up at him and looks away. 'It's better this way – before things get messy with mortgages and stuff. It's just not right.' The silence that ensues is so loaded it's deafening and time stands still, choked by the fog of neither person knowing what to do or say next.

'You know, Thea – nothing you can do could make me love you less?' Saul declares, gripping her arms to pull her close. 'Do you want some space? Some time out? Take what you need, sweetie. Anything. And I promise you I'll back off – but I'm telling you, I won't stop loving you.' He steps towards her and gently touches her chin.

Tell me it never happened, Saul. Tell me I'm mistaken. Promise me you've been faithful to me. Promise me you're an ordinary, good boy. Say it out loud and I'll believe you because I believe you'd never lie to me so if I ask you, you'll tell me the truth.

But Thea knows what the truth is so she encircles his wrists to keep him at bay – it would be too easy to melt into his arms and then too difficult to extract herself again. 'I'm not as tolerant as you,' she explains. 'I can't love you unconditionally.'

'Have I ever given you reason to doubt the sanctity and totality of my love for you?' Saul asks her hoarsely. 'Have I ever given you *direct* reason?' Saul emphasizes. He needs to be pedantic and semantic because otherwise he knows she can say to herself yes yes yes you have you whoremonger.

Let her go, Saul.

'Saul, please,' Thea starts to cry.

Please Saul, let her go.

'I don't love you enough,' Thea sobs, 'I don't love you in the way you love me. I don't love you enough to allow you your entire personality.'

Saul, you have to let her go.

'Will you change your mind?' Saul asks. 'Ever?' He pulls Thea towards him and she yields into his embrace. He is not going to let her go. 'Please, Thea. Just take time out – as much as you need. I'll wait. You can't let Us go.' She buries her face in his chest and he kisses the top of her head. He's always loved kissing the top of her head. He's always marvelled at the way they fit. Snug. They're just right. They're just so right. But it's all gone horribly wrong. 'I'll wait,' Saul repeats.

'Don't!' Thea cries.

'You come to love not by finding a perfect person but by seeing an imperfect person perfectly,' Saul proclaims. Thea raises a tear-stained face to him. 'It's a quote,' he admits with a humble grin, 'I found on the Internet.'

How very Saul, Thea thinks.

Once upon a time it would have made me love you even more.

'I can't go through with this,' Thea says, 'I can't.'

'Please, please don't do this, Thea,' Saul begs. 'Whatever has happened, I can fix. Whatever's happened, we can get through.'

Thea shakes her head.

'Talk to me,' Saul implores. He's ready for anything. He's fighting for his life. 'Thea, think about it – your flat sale, all that stress. You sell in three days' time. We're days from exchanging. You can draw a line under whatever it is. Let's just go for it. Start our life.'

'I don't want to live there,' Thea says. Looking alarmed, as if she'd forgotten all about the place of their dreams being at their fingertips.

'OK,' Saul says, 'it doesn't matter. We'll let it go. We'll buy somewhere else. It doesn't matter where. We just have to stay together. Don't let Us go.'

'Let me go,' Thea pleads sorrowfully, imploring him, seeing eye to eye. He looks six years old, with his blotched cheeks, twitching lips and eyes springing with tears. The last time she saw Saul cry was at Juliette Stonehill's baby blessing. He looked so happy then, when he was crying. He looks devastated just now. Really wrecked. Thea shakes her head. And Saul shakes his.

WHAT CAN I DO?

You can let me go.

Saul lets her slip from his hands. He has to. He has no choice. He has no control over this decision.

*　*　*

Tomorrow, Thea will move in with Alice and Mark for a fortnight or so until the nice rented flat in a mansion block in Highgate Village found by Peter Glass becomes available. Yesterday, she walked away from Saul. Tonight, she is sitting in the middle of her landing, appreciating a final moment or two of Lewis Carroll Living. Actually, there's no room to sit in the living room anyway, it's piled high with packing boxes. Sitting there, on the landing, with the doors closed in a teasing whirl around her, she spies a bent nail lying on the floor. She looks up at the wall and deduces that this nail is the one that held up her framed autographed photograph of David Bowie. She picks up the nail and fiddles with it absent-mindedly, her mind ricocheting from one monumental issue to the next yet unable to alight constructively on any. It's too strange to think philosophically that her flat is sold, it's no longer her home, bye-bye. It's too soon to consider she'll need to tick the 'single' box when filling in forms. It's too raw to realize she has no soulmate called Saul, no soulmate full stop, no more soulmate. It's not possible to think straight at all, really.

Time for bed. It's late and tomorrow will be tiring and trying. But she wants just to sit here a while longer. It's nice and quiet – and anyway, every decision she makes – even to stand from sitting – necessitates untold energy.

The pain weighs heavy. Crying hurts. The pain under-scores everything she does. It's the punctuation mark at the end of every thought. It catches in her throat and alters the timbre of her voice. It stumbles her walk and has decimated her posture. It prevents her digesting her food. It inhibits her hearing the loving support of Alice, of Sally, of Souki, though she attempts to listen. It is the bed of nails on which she tries but fails to sleep. It hurts, it hurts. It hurts all the time.

Thea looks at the nail, bent and discarded. With a calm, considered intake of breath, she scores along her roping scar with the nail. She doesn't need to puncture deep enough to draw blood; a simple, long, sharp scratch through the sen-sitive and fragile keloid surface is sufficient agony. The immediacy and the shock and the uncompromising reality of pure physical pain somehow provides instant respite from the agonizing twist of emotional anguish.

Avon Calling

Thea regarded her two holdalls which contained everything she'd possibly need for the moment. She now thought she probably could have been far more ruthless when packing up her flat. The local charity shops hadn't done very well by her at all yet the storage company was making a fortune out of her. Each bag was heavy, yet when lifted one in each hand, the weight evened out and dispersed a little. There was a sense of symmetry, a feeling of balance. Anyway, she wasn't walking far, just downstairs to the waiting taxi.

Thea had said goodbye to her flat so many times over the last few weeks that when the time came she found it quite easy to simply lock up and leave. There was just time for a backward glance and surreptitious little wave as the cab headed off. Thea had two sets of keys in her hand, one to be relinquished at the local estate agent for the new owner of the Little Bit of Lewis Carroll Living, the other set to let her into her temporary home with the Sinclairs in Hampstead.

'Love, I'm going to have to put the meter back on in a minute,' the taxi driver cautioned as Thea sat still and continued to stare at Alice's house. Suddenly, she was feeling peculiarly light-headed and refreshingly unburdened. Her belongings were in storage, she was rid of her mortgage and had been given time off work on compassionate grounds with the Being Well's blessing. There wasn't much to do at all really. Apart from watch daytime television on Alice's vast plasma until she came home from work. Or, God forbid, mope.

'Actually,' Thea said, as a thought seeded itself, 'drive on, please.'

'You pay for this journey first, young lady,' the cabbie retorted gruffly, 'and then I'll drive you wherever you want.'

'Fine,' said Thea, refusing to round the fare up to the nearest pound, let alone add on a tip.

'You women,' the cabbie muttered with intentional audibility, 'you can never make your bleeding minds up.'

'Oh yes I can,' Thea muttered back, certain that she didn't want to watch daytime television and definite that she didn't want to mope. 'Drive on.' She texted Alice to tell her of her change of plan and then she switched her phone off before Alice could call her to workshop it.

'Are you going somewhere nice for the weekend, dear? They say the weather is to be very good. I'm going to stay with my son for a week – see my grandchildren.'

Thea turned from gazing out of the train window to regard a neat elderly lady, who must have boarded the train at Reading, sitting opposite her and keen to make conversation. Thea accepted a digestive biscuit and settled herself in for light chat about this and that as Great Western rail continued to carry her away.

'I'm going to see my mum,' she told the lady. 'I haven't seen her since Christmas, it's a surprise visit.'

Gloria Luckmore didn't much like surprises. She liked arrangements and she liked them well in advance. She liked to be able to balance the kitchen calendar with her pocket diary and she did not like having to cross things out. Gloria did not like mess. She would always pencil something in, in the first instance, then carefully rub it out and rewrite it in black ink once it had been confirmed. She considered impromptu to be the bane of modern living. She deemed the concept of popping in or just dropping by to be insulting – something a person decided to do at the last moment because they had nothing better to do. Despite her stringent parameters for socializing, Gloria Luckmore's calendar and pocket diary were actually extensively crocheted in black ink. However, she never organized anything for six p.m. She had a permanent arrangement with herself for that slot – the meticulous ritual of a gin and tonic sipped listening to the Radio 4 news whilst looking out of the sitting-room French doors to the garden. Thus, she felt sheer indignation that her doorbell should compete with the Greenwich Mean Time pips. Defiant, she sipped her drink and listened hard to the headlines, blocking out another round of ringing. What Gloria loved about Radio 4 was the dignified pace of announcement which bestowed equal dramatic impact to each news headline. Nothing could possibly be so important as to interrupt it. Whoever wanted her at her front door would jolly well have to wait. She sipped and listened and ignored the rapping of her letter-box.

'Mum?'

The voice drifted through the hallway and suddenly filled the living room, interrupting the radio voices and rendering Gloria's G & T temporarily undrinkable.

'Thea?'

Gloria went to her front door, slightly alarmed. She didn't need to consult her calendar or her diary. She knew her timetable by heart and a visit by Thea hadn't even been suggested, let alone arranged. Why was her daughter outside at six p.m. without warning, request or invitation?

'Hullo, Mum.'

With two large holdalls.

'I was going to ring but –'

And significant weight loss.

'I need somewhere –'

And a dullness to her eyes, dark shadows surrounding them, alluding to much crying and little sleep.

'I broke up with Saul.'

'Come in.'

'My flat was sold today.'

'Come on in.'

'I've been given time off work.'

'In, darling, in.'

It wasn't as if Thea had nowhere to go – Alice and Mark had been looking forward to laying their home and their friendship at her disposal for the couple of weeks before the rented flat was available. It wasn't as if Thea had bolted back to her childhood home to snuggle down in her old bedroom, to be surrounded by furling posters of David Bowie left in situ over the years, shelves brimming with the friendly familiar faces of dusty soft toys, dressing-table drawers revealing a treasure trove of forgotten trinkets, boxes under the bed containing teenage diaries and years of letters. Thea had never actually lived in this house – her mother had moved here from London once Thea had left home for university. So it wasn't the reassurance of nostalgia that Thea craved. It wasn't even as if Gloria was her enduring confidante – as fond of each other as mother and daughter were, they were actually pretty self-sufficient and private. However, as Thea unpacked in the small spare room, she felt pleased to be there. It was nice to look at the old framed photographs – when she still had a ponytail, her brother long before he grew his terrible beard. This wasn't running away, this wasn't hiding in the past, this was instigating some space from London, putting necessary distance in time and miles between what was and what soon would be. This was a prudent thing to do. However long she decided to stay, Wiltshire would provide a sensible hiatus. A breather between the chapters of her life.

'Now darling, my day is chock-a-block,' Gloria said apologetically the next morning over a breakfast of triangles of toast queuing politely in a toast-rack and leaf tea brewed correctly in a china teapot. With a twitch of the lip and a light hum, Gloria consulted her pocket diary as if to see whether she could possibly slot her daughter in somewhere between her ladies' guild meeting at quarter to eleven, lunch with Sandra Langley at twelve o'clock and her voluntary work at the Leonard Cheshire home from two till four.

'I'm fine, Mum,' Thea assured her, 'I just need a bit of a rest. I'm fine pottering around by myself.'

'Go for a nice walk,' Gloria suggested. 'I'll be back at four fifteen. I'm playing cards this evening but I don't need to leave until quarter to seven.'

'I'll go for a nice walk,' Thea confirmed, really quite relieved that time would be her own, that she need answer to no one but herself, that it wasn't her mother's style to ask questions in the first place anyway. Gloria's concern was registered as an anxious glance at her daughter. They smiled at each other quickly and then Gloria was on her way.

The village of Wootton Bourne, positioned on the Wiltshire–Avon border, resembled a ribcage: the remaining buildings of the original three-hundred-year-old hamlet forming a spine, the newer buildings branching off in a hug of ribs to either side. The village green, bisected by the main street, was the lungs, the duck pond the heart, the war memorial the sternum, the bourne a small stream like an artery or vein (depending on which direction of approach) running along one side then under the road and out of, or into, the village. The lifeblood flowed from the inhabitants' love of their village and keen sense of duty to its appearance. The communal verges were now, in June, on the cusp of their floral magnificence. There was no village pub, no shop at Wootton Bourne. There was one post-box with a daily collection – a bright red rectangle flush against Mr Kington's wall. Wootton St Mark, the sister village only a stroll away but over the bypass and consequently rarely walked to, had a picturesque church, a pub and a small shop.

Other than residents, no one really needed or much wanted to travel through Wootton Bourne. It had no brown leisure signs heralding it, and maps showed no pub, no shop, no pottery, nothing. Thus, with scant traffic, there was no need for pavement or even footpath. The tarmac simply petered out into the lovingly maintained verges and the villagers were pretty much left alone. The precious pace of life they attained was deeply valued and painstakingly protected and Wootton Bourne had the air of a private manor.

Whatever their age or style, all the buildings were constructed from Bath stone: the detached eighteenth- and nineteenth-century cottages, the one small run of terraced housing sitting impishly like Victorian children on a grassy bank, the Georgian farmhouse, the Edwardian school house, the sixties squat boxes, the modernist barn conversion. Initially, Thea had been disappointed that, in a county of postcard perfect cottages and in a village of classic and varied vernacular architecture, Gloria had bought herself a modern house, set along a lower rib of the village. Actually, though, it suited her needs perfectly and the mellow tones and subtle hues of the masonry gave a tangible softness and pleasing warmth to an otherwise plain design. The rectangular garden was flanked on three sides by easily maintainable borders, on the fourth by a square of patio accessed from the sitting-room French windows. Gloria could tinker with her perennials and evergreens without stressing her back and it didn't take much effort to manage a pleasing display perfect for gazing at while having one's G & T at six each evening.

Everyone knew everyone in Wootton Bourne but no one had the slightest desire to know anyone else's business. There wasn't a village busybody, there was no grapevine, no gossip-mongering, no rival cliques. If there was a local cad or village trollop or resident bankrupt or community bisexual, it was of no interest. This wasn't village life as most city dwellers imagined it according to the standards misleadingly set by *The Archers* or *Heartbeat* or *Balamory* or *Midsomer Murders*, this was village life precisely as the inhabitants of Wootton Bourne wanted it. It was refreshingly, fundamentally, dull. It was the environment Thea needed and, as she meandered around the lanes until peckish for lunch, she congratulated herself on her sensible decision to stay awhile.

After Thea's initial doorstep revelations, nothing more had been said on the subjects and Gloria wasn't quite sure how to go about counselling her daughter who was so guarded. Gloria's schedule, the routes of Thea's daily walk, what to eat morning, noon and evening and the occasional shopping list was ample discussion.

'I've been wondering, darling – where's your car?'

'Back in Crouch End.'

'Is it running all right? Why did you decide not to drive?'

'It's fine. I didn't drive because I didn't know I was going to come here until I was sitting in a cab outside Alice's. And I hadn't taken my car there because it's Residents' Parking or two-hour limits in Pay and Display.'

'Fancy having to pay for the privilege of parking outside your own house.'

'Ridiculous, isn't it, 20p for five minutes.'

'Good God. Well, you can drive my little Micra if you like.'

'Thanks, Mum. Would you like me to pop into Chippenham to pick up a few things for supper?'

'Yes, darling, why don't you do that.'

It was only speaking to Alice a couple of days into her stay that Thea realized just what a tonic a dose of this particular village was just then. Alice of course wanted to know how Thea was, what she'd been thinking about, whether she'd heard from Saul, how long she thought she'd stay, if she was feeling low or feeling any panic or anger or regret.

'We're running an article in *Lush*, you see,' Alice said, 'called "*Five Minutes to the No Entry Sign*". It makes a lot of sense – when you're suffering a trauma, as you are, you should allow yourself five minutes twice a day to thoroughly immerse yourself in all manner of related angst but then you have to envisage a No Entry sign over the subject at all times in between.'

The surprising thing was that during her first few days, Thea had hardly touched upon thoughts of Saul. She'd been too preoccupied walking down this lane and over that field, appreciating that hedgerow or this brook, to navel gaze at her past or flinch from her future. She hadn't tripped at all. But she didn't want to workshop the fact with Alice, who would no doubt worry she was in denial and have another article to quote on the matter. So Thea murmured appreciatively but non-committally and reminded Alice it was her mother's phone and she ought to keep it short.

'But are you OK, Thea?' Alice pressed. 'Because I could always come and see you this weekend.'

'I'm fine, Alice,' Thea said.

'Well, just phone if you stumble, or text if you have a signal,' Alice implored her. 'Say hi to your ma.'

'Will do – she sends her regards. Love to Mark.'

'Bye, sweetie – I'll call again soon.'

'Thanks Alice, thanks.'

It wasn't that the novelty started to wear off, it was that as Wootton Bourne became more and more familiar, there were fewer new details to note and absorb which meant thoughts in abeyance now had the space to resurface. 'Look! Kestrel!' she would hear Saul announce at the split-second she spied the bird. And then she'd go off on a tangent wondering if there were any parakeets in Wiltshire because Saul had told her there were ten thousand in Richmond Park and a fair few on Hampstead Heath. And suddenly she'd profoundly mourn the fact that they'd never seen them on Hampstead Heath and they'd never made a trip to Richmond. And now they never would. And if she positioned her hand in a certain way whilst walking, she could conjure the feel of Saul's hand holding hers. And if she tucked the single duvet against her back, she could convince herself of Saul's presence as she drifted off to sleep. But such imagining had a precise and limited time constraint. The loneliness at admitting that actually you were walking all by yourself, or waking alone in a single bed, was extreme. Thea became frustrated that she should suddenly be craving so intensely the presence of the person she thought she never wanted to see again. It was bizarre to not know where he was or what he was doing at that precise moment but to know for a fact that they were living in tandem. Parallel lives for Saul and Thea? No happy ever after? That can't be right. No entwining? No two equals one? No. Two distinct bodies, two separate souls, two unconnected lives to be getting on with.

I miss you, Saul, Thea could admit out loud in the discreet privacy of a solitary beech clump, weeping into the shoulders of the trees. She knew it wasn't so much cathartic as dangerously isolating to choose to cry where no one could hear. She tried to think of Alice's No Entry signs as she walked vigorously along the Ridgeway by herself. It was comforting to be striding along this ancient right of way, negotiating its chalky furrows kidding herself with excessive interest in the country's ancient history. If she kept walking and watching and observing and humming she couldn't dwell on the fact that she and Saul had never walked the Ridgeway together. Yet she found herself positioning the fingers of her right hand in such a way as to clearly imagine Saul's fingers interwoven with hers. His voice so vivid. His presence so tangible. He's here. Next to me. Look, Saul – kestrel!

I'm alone.
I'm on my own.
I'm in the middle of nowhere.
I don't know where I'm going.
Oh Saul, oh Saul. What happened to us?

Gloria was concerned to see that, despite her daughter's hearty tramping of the surrounding countryside, Thea's complexion was palling visibly. Gloria could tell that it wasn't blisters or aching limbs which caused Thea to walk so slowly towards the house after four hours on the Ridgeway, it was the weight of angst that her daughter was shouldering. It pained her to realize that Thea was trying to conceal her torment; it shamed her to admit that by acting jolly and keeping conversation light herself meant she could veer away from saying but darling tell me what happened with Saul that you should look so fragile and have nowhere to live for a fortnight. The amiable chitter-chatter of fortnightly phone calls and thrice-yearly visits was the blueprint for their relationship and Gloria didn't want to jeopardize that. Even if she did probe, her daughter most probably wouldn't confide anyway.

'Are you all right, Thea? You look a little peaky.'

'It's probably just a cold or something.'

'Sit yourself down and I'll bring you a nice cup of tea. We've been invited to the Craig-Stewarts' tonight. Drinks and nibbles. I've said yes. Won't that be nice?'

'Lovely.' Thea continued to feel it her duty to keep her grief and confusion concealed until she had the house to herself and she could slump to the floor in her mother's spare room, hurl her forehead against her knees and cry her heart out.

The Craig-Stewarts' drinks and nibbles evenings were eagerly attended by their wide social circle. Nibbles was an understatement. Nibbles was a risibly modest term for the lavish finger buffet laid on. Their lovely manor house was on the periphery of the idyllic National Trust village of Lacock. The level of chatter in beautifully rounded vowels complemented perfectly the stately yet comfortable furnishings. The Craig-Stewarts themselves were gracious, effortless hosts bestowing genuine interest and generous cheer on all their guests. It wasn't that they wanted to put on an impressive spread, they simply wanted their house to be populated with their friends, and the sumptuous food and flowing drinks were far more a symbol of their gratitude than a mark of their prosperity.

Thea fixed a smile to her face and tried to make it seem that her non-existent appetite was being sated by a single filo tartlet. Every time Mrs Craig-Stewart wafted past, Thea would busily nibble and sip and grin. She wished she hadn't come. These lovely, kind, happy souls. She was the youngest there by at least twenty years. *When I grow up, I want to be Mrs Craig-Stewart.* To be surrounded by such gaiety, such exemplary domesticity, the furnishings of such a happy and long marriage, were discordant to someone with a heart as lacerated as Thea's. She tried not to be spoken to, taking great interest instead in the affable assembly of benevolent ancestors whose portraits lined the walls, and the framed photos of flatcoat retrievers, springer spaniels and good horses convening on the occasional tables, mantelpieces and window sills.

'She was a poppet, was our Maisie, an absolute poppet,' Mrs Craig-Stewart was saying, suddenly at Thea's side and gazing tearily at a photo of a dog. 'Now Chip here, he was a thug! Huge character but what a yob! Do you like dogs? And horses? Let me show you something, let me show you the photograph of Max and Poppy.' Politely, Thea allowed herself to be led by the elbow to another table of photographs, preparing herself to coo at a photo of two labs or thoroughbreds. Instead, she was shown the wedding photograph of Poppy Craig-Stewart. Last summer. Three years younger than Thea. Gazing adoringly at her brand new dashing husband. What a gorgeous dress. What a beautiful couple. What a wonderful day. What a perfect match. She wished she was Poppy Craig-Stewart. Though Thea genuinely wanted to congratulate Mrs Craig-Stewart and tell her how stunning her daughter looked, how handsome her son-in-law, she found herself gripping hold of her hostess and hollering out uncontrolled sobs.

'What am I going to do what am I going to do what am I going to do?' Thea wept. Momentarily, Mrs Craig-Stewart didn't know what she was going to do either.

'I'm going to find your mother, that's what I'm going to do,' she assured Thea soothingly, relaying the strategy to her husband by a subtly coded raised eyebrow.

'Thea, gracious,' said Gloria, just as alarmed by the spectacle as by her daughter's distress, 'goodness. Thea. Oh, dear me.'

'What am I going to do, Mum?' Thea hyperventilated.

'I'm going to take you home,' Gloria said decisively,

glancing apologetically at the kind concern of her social set.

The fifteen-minute car journey allowed Thea's weeping to abate but left her so exhausted that she just about made it upstairs to bed unaided. When Gloria came in with a cup of hot chocolate, she found her daughter fast asleep. She drank the hot chocolate herself, feeling a touch guilty that she should be relieved not to have to counsel her daughter just then.

'Are you OK, darling?' Gloria asked over breakfast the next morning.

'Fine, thanks, Mum,' Thea replied.

'The fish-and-chip van goes to Wootton St Michael this evening,' Gloria announced, 'if you fancy it?'

'Maybe,' said Thea.

'Gosh, I must crack on – another chock-a-block day! See you later, darling. I'll be popping back mid-afternoon, then back for G & T by six.'

'Bye, Mum,' said Thea. When her mother left, Thea wondered if she had the energy to drag herself from kitchen table to sofa for a dose of inane morning television. It appeared she didn't. She'd just have to stay put and concentrate on finding tessellations in the rattan table mats instead.

Gloria tootled along the lanes making a large effort to praise out loud the beauty of the day and the glorious landscape. Off she went to the library, to pick up and then deliver books ordered by the ancient but still formidable Mrs Frederick. That done, she headed to her friend Elizabeth's for morning coffee.

'Is your daughter all right?' Elizabeth asked. 'Poor duck.'

'Oh, she's fine this morning,' Gloria assured her. 'A good night's sleep.'

Next, Gloria headed to Margaret's. They were to have a long-planned meeting about the hanging-basket design for the summer fair at the school where they were governors. She needed to collect Sylvia en route and fill up with petrol. Gloria was motoring along, humming to Classic FM, when she found herself pulling abruptly into a lay-by. It wasn't actually a lay-by at all, it was the pitted sweep before the rutted entrance to a farmer's gate. But it served the purpose for Gloria to swerve and stall her car while her mind racketed and Beethoven's *Pastoral* soared out. She didn't have to think long about what to do. She started her car and hared off the opposite way, without a backward glance in the direction of Sylvia's house, without a second thought for arrangements made and committed in black ink.

'Thea?' Gloria says, shutting the front door quietly. 'Darling?'

Her daughter is still sitting at the kitchen table, pronging a fork into the spaces of the rattan table mat.

'Thea?' Gloria sits down and shuffles her chair close to her daughter. 'Darling?'

She places her hand on her daughter's and just as Thea absent-mindedly wonders how many seconds it now takes for an age-revealing pinch of skin to flatten on the back of her mother's hand, she finds that tears are falling without warning.

'Oh, poor darling,' Gloria whispers, 'you poor old thing.'

'What am I going to do?' Thea croaks.

'I don't know,' Gloria admits because she doesn't know what's been going on anyway.

'Love isn't meant to go wrong,' Thea objects, 'not when it's true love.'

Gloria sighs. 'That's what one would think,' she says, 'but believe me, however good we think we are at being in love, the rules are not of our making and are thus beyond our control.'

'He was unfaithful to me,' Thea whispers. 'Saul.'

Gloria was immediately indignant that history should be repeating itself. 'Oh, Thea, he left you for another woman? When you were on the point of setting up home together? That's beastly. Beastly.'

'No!' Thea objects. 'I've left him. I don't want him now.'

Gloria paused. 'But does he want you?'

Thea hasn't been asked that question before. She nods and shrugs.

'But do you still love him?'

Again, Thea shrugs but finds she can neither shake her head nor nod.

'But darling,' Gloria objects as if this is all a regrettable storm in a teacup, 'forgive him, have him back and forget it. For heaven's sake. Life's too short. Love's too precious. Goodness.'

'No!' Thea protests.

'But he hasn't left you for someone else,' Gloria states, 'and he still loves you and wants to be with you!'

'You don't understand,' Thea counters.

'Oh, yes, I do, my darling,' Gloria says in a hollow voice. 'Your father left me. He no longer loved me. He fell in love with someone else and nothing I could do could win him back. It was irrelevant how much love I still held for him – it was actually worth nothing. He didn't fool around and regret it, he wholeheartedly bestowed his love on another woman.'

'Are you saying that's worse than Saul fucking women behind my back?' Thea bites back from adding 'and he pays for it' because she deems that far more offensive than having uttered 'fucking' out loud in front of her mother. The truth is that Thea feels deep shame at Saul's transgression. Alice can be the only person she'll ever tell – and even then, she's left some details undisclosed. Why couldn't Saul just have had a simple affair? Such a crime was far more normal, far easier to deal with, surely?

Her mother, it appears, vehemently disagrees. 'I am saying precisely that. Men can do that whole physical sex thing – you have to realize that. *You* are still loved,' she declares in an uncompromising tone, warning Thea not to controvert the luck and fortune and love she was denied. 'Goodness, it wasn't so long ago that women knew to allow their men-folk visits to prostitutes!' Thea looks up sharply. Gloria brushes at the air dismissively. 'In France, those French men all have mistresses. And I really needn't comment on our Royal Family. Think about those colourful tribes in Africa – or those Mormen in America – they all have umpteen wives. Under the same roof!'

Suddenly, Thea loves her mother and her logical plural-ization of Mormon. And she really doesn't want to tell her all of it. Not just because she's ashamed of the raw truth; she also does not want to distress her mother unduly. If Gloria didn't need to know, then Thea didn't need to say it all out loud again.

'Darling,' Gloria butts in, 'if Saul was a stupid man but begs your forgiveness and lays his love, his apology, his com-mitment at your feet, please don't stamp on him or, worse, step over him. If what he did has absolutely no bearing on how he feels about you, I implore you to be philosophical about it all. It's such a waste otherwise.'

'But I can't forget,' Thea says.

'You can, with time – it's worth it,' Gloria insists. 'Do you not realize that you can't make someone love you? Do you not appreciate, therefore, how you are truly blessed? I loved your father but he didn't love me. It's far harder for me to cope with the knowledge that his heart, his soul, his intrinsic emotional pull, was to a woman other than me. How I wish he'd just had lots of silly sex elsewhere but come home to me with his emotional loyalty intact. Instead, the man I assumed I'd spend the rest of my life with, the father of my children, left me because he fell out of love with me and in love with someone else.'

'But my trust is gone,' Thea says, 'and so is my dream.'

'Well, if there's one person who can help you find them again,' Gloria says empathically, 'it's the man who loves you. You should not compromise your future happiness because of some sanctimonious adherence to unrealistic expectations of Romantic Love,' Gloria all but chides. 'Crikey, you're so vehemently moralistic you're almost a prude, darling.'

'But you don't understand,' Thea pleads.

'Oh, but I do,' her mother claims impatiently, while taking a Biro and scribbling fractiously through the failed arrangements so clearly written on her calendar. 'It's *you* who doesn't understand. How I wish your father had merely done a Saul. I wouldn't have been on my own for almost twenty bloody years.'

Gloria wasn't sure about going away that weekend but the trip to Bournemouth had been planned for months. It was only for two nights and Thea had mentioned Alice might come to stay. So Gloria left her daughter in charge of the Micra and the hanging baskets and set off with Lorna and Marion.

Though Alice was half expecting Thea to call and cancel the arrangement, she was pleasantly surprised, as she stepped into a cab for Paddington station, that she hadn't heard from her. However, her phone rang as the taxi lurched along the speed bumps in Maida Vale. It was Thea. Christ. Give her the benefit of the doubt.

'Alice?'

'Are you going to blow me out, Miss Luckmore?'

'Yes.'

'Thea, I'm in the bloody cab! I bought first-class tickets.'

'I'll pay you back.'

'It's not the point, silly. Why are you cancelling? It's not good to spend so much time on your own being maudlin. You promised your mum – you promised me.'

'I – it's just. Actually, if you want to know, I've phoned Saul. Alice? Hullo? Why? Because I need to see him. So he's coming.'

'Thea, hang on – excuse me, can you stop the cab please – Thea? Talk to me. What are you going to do? When did this all come about? Are you sure?'

'No, I'm not sure. But I need to see him.'

'Look, you phone me, OK? If it all goes pear-shaped. First-class rail tickets have no restrictions.'

'OK. I'm sorry, Alice, for being so flaky. I'm sorry about the taxi. It just suddenly seemed the right thing to do.'

'Don't worry about it,' Alice said, wondering if she should take the train anyway, hide around the corner in case she was needed.

Saul couldn't focus on anything; not his newspaper, the view from the window, his fellow passengers, his revolting coffee nor the myriad thoughts thundering around his head. It seemed adrenalin had replaced blood in his veins and it surged through his body causing him to feel unnervingly light-headed and hollow. All moisture was being rapidly perspired leaving him dehydrated and nauseous but too agitated to drink. He hadn't known where she was, this last week or so. He'd stopped texting. He'd relinquished hope and taken his flat off the market. When a call came through that morning showing a provincial number, he'd assumed it to be a freelancer.

'Saul Mundy speaking.'

'It's Thea.'

'Thea? Christ!'

'Saul, might we talk? Could you come to Avon?'

'Avon?'

'I've been at my mum's.'

'Your mum's?'

'She's away for the weekend.'

A weekend with Thea?

Saul wasn't sure whether he felt optimistic and excited, or apprehensive and pessimistic. He'd already been dumped so she could hardly be summonsing him to dump him again. Though he felt that it had to be positive that she was asking to see him, he didn't dare take it as given. He packed slowly, aiming for an early-evening train, to avoid the aggravation of rushing, the hassles of rush hour, the frustration of a full-price ticket. Perhaps she'd had enough space and thinking time to come to terms with everything. It might not be too late to resuscitate the purchase of the apartment. Justifying it as a purely practical measure, Saul packed the estate agent's particulars just before he left. He was looking forward to seeing Thea, just to look at her, to be with her; whatever the outcome.

When he reached Paddington and found himself a seat on the seven-fifteen train, he couldn't stop his heart from speeding up, though his head warned him to slow down. However, the further the train took him from London, the more apprehensive he became; stabs of caution and surges of pessimism mingling acidly with the adrenalin. Just let her talk. Just don't let her go a second time. Don't tell her you know she knows. Just head for the future and bypass the past. Powers of persuasion, the power of love. What on earth would he feel when he saw her? What would she say? What could he say? What was she expecting him to say?

When it came to it and they met outside Chippenham station, Saul could not take his eyes off Thea and Thea couldn't look at him at all. It was as if he wanted to soak up all the glorious details he'd been denied recently yet she could only flinch away from the personification of heartache that was staring her in the face. On the drive back to her mother's house, Saul didn't know whether to take Thea's lead and speak when spoken to, whether to fill the silences with ingenuous chatter, or try to thaw the situation with a pre-emptive outright declaration of love. However, it appeared not possible to be simply himself in such an unexpected, portentous situation. He found himself wittering at length about minutiae of articles he'd written and articles he'd read. He sounded like a bore and in spite of his jolly countenance, he felt depressed. He didn't know Avon. He'd only visited Thea's mother a couple of times. He could sense Fate lurking just out of view. From Thea's lack of expression, Saul had no idea whether his future was about to be blessed or cursed. It wasn't in his hands, that was for sure. He felt nervous – it was an emotion he was not familiar with.

'I've put you in here,' Thea said politely, showing him the spare room; guest towels folded neatly on the edge of the bed.

'Thanks,' he said. 'I'll just sort my stuff out then.'

'Would you like some supper?'

'It's a bit late,' Saul said. 'I haven't an appetite anyway.'

'A cup of tea?'

'Sure.' What was this? A B&B?

They drank their tea and avoided eye contact. They watched the ten o'clock news and didn't comment. They took undue interest in the weather forecast.

'Thea—'

'Saul, I'm tired. Let's just get some sleep tonight.'

'Sure. I understand.'

'Have you everything you need?'

What a fantastically loaded question but Saul knew Thea was too tired and wary for him to comment. 'I'm fine,' he said, 'see you in the morning. Sweet dreams, hey.' They went to their separate beds and slept fitfully. The tangibility of their physical proximity was exasperating – how easy would it be to creep from one room to the other, from solitariness to togetherness? How tragic that, currently, the chasm between them meant that such a passage was impassable.

'How did you sleep?' Thea asked, feeling a little shy of Saul the next morning.

'Not well,' Saul admitted wearily, half tempted to cut straight to the point and prevent this ambivalence being prolonged. He wasn't good at waiting, at feeling nervous, at not having control.

'Shall we go for a walk, then?' Thea said. 'We can go along the Ridgeway.'

'Sure,' said Saul, 'whatever.'

Thea wanted Saul to take the initiative and hold her hand. But today he seemed more distant, somewhat guarded, so she contrived to bump into him once or twice, to have her arm brush his accidentally-on-purpose, to position her hand enticingly close. Though Saul of course wanted to hold Thea's hand, he'd rather it wasn't snatched away so it seemed safer not to in the first place. It was down to Thea but she couldn't quite do it either.

'Hear that?' Saul asked, suddenly animated.

'What?'

'Listen – there. That *mew! mew!* Plaintive calling. Where is it? There, Thea – look! Buzzard.' With Saul's arm outstretched over her shoulder and alongside her cheek to provide a direct angle of view, Thea saw the buzzard circling, now so close that the calligraphy of dark markings and fawny dapples on the underside of its wings were clearly visible. Are there any buzzards on Hampstead Heath, Saul, any in Richmond Park – is this our only chance to see one? Unable to resist, Thea gently cocked her head so she could rest her cheek against Saul's arm as she observed the bird. She could sense him gazing at her. If she didn't know what she knew, if she hadn't seen what she'd seen, this would all feel so perfect. Just then, she found she could pretend that it was; she found she could forget what had been. Lightly, Saul kissed her temple and she turned towards him, sinking fast into his enveloping embrace. She clung to him, her eyes closed, her face pressed into his chest. If she didn't pull away now, she knew she would never be able to. She needed to try to pull away without actually pushing him away. When she did, she saw the buzzard perched on a fence stake amazingly close. Look, Saul, look.

'*My heart in hiding/ Stirred for a bird*,' he said to her, '*the achieve of, the mastery of the thing!*'

'Don't tell me – you dug it off the Internet?' Thea found she could tease him.

'Gerard Manley Hopkins,' Saul objected. 'Funny what you remember from A-level English.'

They walked on, in awkward silence. Thea quietly engrossed in trying to recall quotes from her English A level. Saul wondering whether he was correctly reading her signals to hold her hand. He tried it. Initially, she didn't resist.

'Let's go to the Polly Tea Rooms in Marlborough,' Thea announced, now finding an itch on her shoulder which required both her hands, 'though it may be full of tourists.'

'We'll put on our best American accents then,' Saul said, taking her hand again as they walked back to the car.

When they arrived in Marlborough, they did just that. They passed the infernal wait for a table by saying things like 'Gee, honey, I sure am hungry' and 'How damn cute is this li'l ol' town?' Thea only just managed to keep giggles at bay. Saul was bolstered. It simultaneously heartened but alarmed Thea how easily, how quickly, she could merge back into the familiar and effortless dynamic with this man.

How Saul wanted to rush back to the house and take Thea to bed. He wasn't particularly horny – the oversized scones and gluts of clotted cream hampered that – rather he was flooded by a desire to display the veracity of his love through quiet intimacy. He just wanted to lie with her, allow his touch and his gaze to say it all. However, Thea's hands were beyond reach, fixed as they were at ten-to-two on her mother's steering wheel. Thea in the driving seat. Thea stalling. Thea putting the brakes on. It was only when they arrived back at Wootton Bourne that Saul realized that actually, he held the key.

'I think I'll just tidy up, do some hoovering.'
    'The house is immaculate, Thea.'
    'I must water Mum's hanging baskets.'
    'Not in direct sunlight – you'll scorch the plants.'
    'Well, in that case, I think I'll just have a quiet hour or so with the papers until the sun goes in.'
    'No, Thea, talk to me. Talk.'

Thea frowned and flinched and shook her head. She felt trapped. Tidy. Hoover. Water the garden. Read the papers. Quiet hour. Be quiet. She glanced at Saul, who was holding his hand out to her. She spun from him.
    'Thea – we can't let this go. It's too good – we must be able to find a way.' Saul was standing close behind her. 'Our lives were sorted – our future was all mapped out. It was brilliant.'
    'It was the best thing that ever happened to me,' Thea said hoarsely.
    'Well, don't let it go!' Saul exclaimed gently, as if to a simpleton.

'Easy for you to say!' Thea balked, rushing through the French windows into her mother's garden. Saul followed her. 'Fuck off and leave me alone, can't you!' she hissed.

'Excuse me, but it was you who invited me here,' Saul corrected. 'Why was that, Thea? Why summons me?' She couldn't answer and she didn't want to say I don't know. 'We can work through this,' Saul said, 'we must be able to. We were the strongest couple I know – we were the envy of so many. We had everything.'

'I loved you enough to spend the rest of my life with you,' Thea said sadly, 'and now I face a precarious time on my own. At the age of thirty-bloody-three. When I should be feeling settled and calm.' She took a petulant kick at her mother's Impatiens.

'For Christ's sake, Thea,' Saul said, 'you're answering all your questions and doubts. That's precisely what we are, that's precisely why we should try and sort it – we're now at an age where we don't have the luxury of our twenties, of all that over-wrought drama and game playing and emotional self-indulgence. Perhaps there isn't time to split up. Long, drawn-out conflicts are a waste of time. It's all semantics. Let's get on with life. Let's get through this. Let's sort it out. Let's get on with growing up and growing old.'

'I don't want to get old with you,' Thea stamped.

'Why not?' Saul asked. 'Why not, Thea? What have I done?'

His words hung in the air like laundry on a line. He'd asked her outright, he'd put himself on the line. He was hanging his dirty washing out in the open – possibly for her to tear down and hurl back at him. He was laying himself bare. It's your chance, Thea. Insult him, blame him, shame him, curse him, listen to him, forgive him.

'I never doubted it. I never doubted you,' she said flatly, 'but now I do and that's the end of the story. That's the close of our fairy tale. We didn't live happily ever after. The End.

Deal with it.'

'You sound horrible,' Saul frowned.

'*You're* the horrible one,' Thea shouted and she bolted through the house and out.

Traversing the ribs of Wootton Bourne, Thea initially stomped fast, muttering insults under her breath. Soon, her pace slowed and she reflected on what had been said. Saul was completely right. They were a brilliant couple, they were at an age where such a sound union should be valued, snapped up and for ever treasured. But she knew too that she wasn't hastily throwing it out like the tantrum she'd just had. Over the last few weeks, through Kiki, through Richard Stonehill, through Alice, through the rawness of her own desolation, through a naked need to face fact, Thea had gradually accepted that Saul's particular take on what was morally acceptable grossly conflicted with her own deeply revered ethics. She was satisfied that she'd come to terms with her own limitations as well as those she perceived to be Saul's. Ultimately, it was not so much the fact that she knew what Saul was capable of; it was that she finally knew what she was incapable of. Unconditional love.

I can't do it. I'm not that generous, that liberated, that laid back. I used to feel that being in love was enough, but now I know that it isn't. There actually needs to be more to love than love itself.

She knew unequivocally what she believed in and what she needed and she was adamant that, for her, moral compatibility was a fundamental requirement.

She looked behind her. There was no one there. She realized she'd been expecting him to follow. Had he packed up and left? Without them getting to the heart of the matter? She returned at a brisk pace.

*

'Everything changed,' Thea explains, coming in to find Saul sitting exhausted on the stairs. 'It wasn't right. I couldn't do it.'

'Then why the fuck drag me up from London?' Saul sighs. 'It wasn't to go bird-watching on the Ridgeway.'

Thea fidgets and shrugs and tries to look at him and can't.

'Do you realize this is the first time *ever* that you and I have actually had a full-blown fight?' Saul says. 'That's why all of this is so stupid.'

'I'm sorry, Saul,' Thea whispers, 'it's not you, it's me.'

'I know, Thea,' Saul announces in a hollow voice. He lets it hang. He could be simply acknowledging that yes he knows it's her, not him. But then he turns it into a noose by which he may well hang himself. 'I mean, I *know*, Thea, I know that you know.' He nods to himself. Thea's eyes flick over to his and are caught, like a startled doe in car headlights. 'I know that you know,' Saul says quietly, hating it that Thea looks so appalled, so terrified. 'I know that you saw me. All right?'

It is Saul's final bid. He is standing tall, his honesty a sword which, depending on Thea's reaction, he will either fall upon or brandish like Excalibur. Saul watches as she slowly hauls her gaze away from the middle distance, where it's been fixed for loaded minutes, back to him. He must meet it, he tells himself; he mustn't flinch from it.

When Thea finally looks at him, he is winded by the hurt and trauma which striate her face. When Thea finally looks at him, all she sees is Saul. Good old Saul. The same Saul. Her old Saul. And then she alights on the greatest, most tragic irony – that looking into the heart of undeniable truth really does mean that all hope is lost.

It is simply Saul himself standing before her. The unmistakable reality is out. She'd have to love him for who he is. But the reality is, she knows she can't. It's asking too much. It's demanding too substantial a compromise.

'I'm sorry, babe, I'm sorry. It must have half killed you,' Saul says, visibly racked by his awareness of her pain. 'It meant nothing – please, please believe me. It's just the stupid boy-bit in me.'

'I don't want a stupid boy,' Thea says quietly, 'I want a nice man.'

'I am a nice man,' Saul says with conviction.

'Nice men do not do that.'

Saul sighs. 'Look, we could discuss the psychology behind this – and the facts and statistics that clearly define just what nice men do,' he says evenly, 'but I don't think that's the point. The only point is if you feel there's an inkling of hope we can make our relationship work in the face of this. If I swear it won't happen again – and with or without you, I doubt it will – would you believe me? Can you trust me? Could you remember how you used to love me? Should we try going to Relate or some other counselling?'

'I don't want to *workshop* the fact that you pay for sex!' Thea protests in a whisper. 'I'm not prepared to hear your gory details just so you can assuage your guilt!'

'Thea, I know you're hurting,' Saul tells her, 'I know I caused it but I know I can be the antidote.'

'No, Saul – you can't,' Thea's voice fragments, 'as much as you'd like to be – and I'm sure your self-belief is honest and good in intent – but you can't make me feel better because you made me feel this wretched in the first place.'

'I didn't mean to,' Saul says firmly.

'Well, directly or indirectly you have,' Thea says levelly.

'But I love you, Thea,' Saul says. 'Surely such roots form a basis for survival, for growth?'

'Saul,' Thea says, 'that's what *you* want. You love me. You want us to work through this. You want to make me feel better, feel safe with you. You want us to live happily ever after. But I'm not that strong a person to forgive and forget. And I'm not like you – my morals are different.'

'That's where therapy might come in,' Saul suggests.

'Oh, shut up about sodding therapy,' Thea says. 'You read too many magazines. My heart is broken, my dreams are smashed, my trust is decimated and my hope is shattered. It's going to take more than an agony aunt or psycho-babble Superglue to fix it.'

'I devote my life to building you up again,' Saul declares.

'But Saul,' says Thea, though she knows it may well be the last word on the matter, the last thing she says to him, 'I don't love you enough to let you.' They stare at each other in horror. 'I'm sorry – the weakness is mine,' Thea admits, 'my love is not unconditional. I don't love you as much as you love me. We are not compatible. I'm a girl who's always believed in knights in shining armour, in fairy tales, in good old-fashioned fidelity, in swans mating for life, in lovey-dovey monogamy. *Amor Vincit Omnia.*' Thea paused. 'But I've come to see that actually love doesn't conquer all,' she says, 'not for me. Not now.'

They slump over each other in the hallway of Gloria Luckmore's pristine house, Saul and Thea. Like two boxers in the fifteenth round, bruised and bloodied, exhausted brains addled with the battering of their first, last, fight. Nobody won, both lost. They look a mess, they really do. You flinch from the sight of them. But given time, the scars will heal and gradually fade. Ask Thea about that.

Friends

'It's weird,' Alice remarked, handing Thea her olive stone because she couldn't see where else to put it, 'I know you don't own this place – but actually, it's much more *you* than your old flat.'

'It's funny,' Thea agreed, delicately spitting an olive stone into her hand, alongside Alice's, 'but I'd have to agree. I thought I'd miss the Gothick quirkiness; I thought I needed my little slice of Lewis Carroll Living; I thought I'd find the ordered layout here boring; but over the last couple of months I've actually grown to love it – it's bright but quiet. I like having the long hallway and the feeling of flow, a sense of space. There might be a flat two floors above coming up for sale – the same size as this but positioned on the other side – with an even better view.'

'Would you buy it?' Alice asked, popping another olive into her mouth and racing ahead with a thought that she and Mark could assist Thea financially.

'Maybe, if I can afford it,' Thea said, knowing she probably could because Mark and Alice would happily help.

'I'd buy you an olive bowl as a house-warming present!' Alice said, tipping another two stones into Thea's hand.

'Hold on, let me grab a saucer from the kitchen,' Thea said.

Alice followed her. 'Come for dinner on Saturday night!'

Thea wiped her herby, oily hands on her jeans and raised an eyebrow. 'Oh God, you're not going to try and set me up, are you?'

'I'm thinking of having all my hair chopped off,' said Alice, making a glaring attempt to change the subject.

'It's too soon, Alice,' Thea said quietly.

'I've been growing it for four years!' Alice objected.

'I'm not talking about your hair,' said Thea.

'I know,' Alice replied with quiet insistence, 'but perhaps I'm allowed to be your judge, Thea. It was ages ago – back in the spring. Now it's practically autumn.'

'It's not even September for another two days!' Thea objected. 'Next you'll be telling me you've been married for five years.'

'Well, I have, in a manner of speaking,' Alice retorted, having a grin at her own expense. 'It'll be three years this year, so I can indeed say the year after next I'll have been married five years.'

'Look, please,' Thea said, opening bread sticks and a tub of houmous, 'I just don't feel ready. And I don't want to analyse it any more. I'm not living in the past. I'm not mourning. I'm fine, now. I just don't fancy having to decide whether I fancy someone or not just yet. I'm not in the mood.'

'It's only Mark's cousin anyway,' Alice said. 'Harmless. Practically family.'

'The American one?' Thea asked.

'Yes,' said Alice, 'one of them.'

'Not the one at your wedding who then emailed me, by which time I was already with Saul?'

'No, a different cousin. Mark has about sixty-seven of them.' Alice paused. 'Have you heard from him, from Saul?'

After weeks when Saul had been Thea's only topic of conversation, there had followed the more recent weeks when his name hadn't been mentioned.

'No,' said Thea evenly, 'no.'

'When did you take off your ring?'

'After the last phone call. Four or five weeks ago.'

'What have you done with it?'

'I've put it in my odds-and-sods drawer.'

'Odd sod indeed.'

They munched on vine leaves thoughtfully. 'You'll be proud of me,' Thea said. 'I even bought the *Observer* today for the first time in ages and found I could skim through Barefaced Bloke's column with no need to read between the lines.'

'He still freelances for *Adam*,' Alice admitted, 'but I don't speak to him directly and I haven't seen him. He sends me his work as simple attachments.'

'A simple attachment was the pinnacle of my hopes and dreams,' Thea said, a sad glaze to her eyes suddenly dulling the ease of their afternoon. 'It's still bloody scary, Alice.'

'I know,' said Alice, giving Thea's leg a comforting squeeze, 'but someone or other said we don't have dreams unless we have the power to fulfil them.'

'Someone else said love is a grave mental illness,' Thea rejoined, 'Plato, I think.'

'Yes, but while you're waiting for the right man to come along, you can have plenty of fun with the wrong ones,' Alice said, 'according to Cher.'

'I'm not entirely sure that Cher and Plato equate on the philosophy stakes,' Thea remarked, 'and I'm not waiting for Mr Anyone, anyway.'

'Well, Woody Allen is arguably the Plato of our age and he says that love may well be the answer but sex raises some good questions while you're waiting for the answer.'

'Alice!' Thea chastised. 'Stop it with the American rent-a-quote, would you? I'm *not* looking for love and I'm *not* in need of sex and I'm not questioning anything – I'm just getting on with things.'

'So just come eat with us Saturday, huh?' said Alice. 'A girl's gotta eat.'

'Why are you talking in an American accent?'

'I don't know.'

'You have to promise me you're not match-making,' Thea warned her.

'Cross my heart, hope to die, bla bla,' said Alice, thinking a little white lie never hurt anyone. 'Come on, I'll help you clear the lunch stuff away. Then I'd better go and help Mark pack. Poor bloke having to fly to Hong Kong on August bank holiday. Oh well, at least he's only going for three nights this time.'

Thea awoke in the small hours with a start. She sat bolt upright in bed with her heart racing at the sense and suddenness of the idea that had woken her. She glanced at the clock. It was just gone four in the morning. She dressed. She rummaged in her odds-and-sods drawer and then she left her flat and drove to Hampstead. She sat outside Alice's house for a while, wondering how best to wake her. She wanted her P.I.C. but she needed her in good humour, not grumpy and shocked. If Thea rang the doorbell, or called her by phone, Alice might panic that something had happened to Mark who was currently en route to Hong Kong. For an hour she sat in her car, fingering the nap of the dark blue velvet box. She sent Alice a text.

`r u awake? txxxxxxxx`

No reply. She sent another.

`r u awake for a chat? Txxxxxxxxx`

No response. She sent another.

r u awake? am in my car outside your house
. . . txxxxx

Thea saw the curtains at Alice's bedroom window ripple. Then she saw one side flung back as bed-headed Alice peered out. Thea leapt from her car and waved. The curtains closed. Thea made her way to Alice's front door.

'Thea, it's fucking six o'clock!' Alice bleared. 'What's going on?'

'It's my ring,' Thea told her. 'I know what to do with it and I want to do it right now. With you. Get dressed.'

'Don't be stupid – I'm going back to bed. You go and shape your idea in the living room and I'll see you in a couple of hours. It's a bank bloody holiday – I don't have to get up at all.'

'No, Alice – no!' Thea said. '*Now*. Get dressed. It won't take long. You can have a lie-in later.'

'Oh, bloody hell,' Alice said, padding away stroppily to do as she was told.

Thea and Alice drive to Primrose Hill. It's deserted apart from a couple of insomniac dog-owners, or perhaps it's the dogs, taking each other for a walk.

'I can't believe you're making me do this,' Alice says though actually, now she's dressed and in the fresh air, she's alert and feeling quite affable.

At the top of Primrose Hill, in the dawn of August bank holiday Monday, Thea and Alice take a seat on one of the benches with a view. Alice gazes at the ghostly panorama of London. The design of the rubbish bins on Primrose Hill echo the shape of Canary Wharf. Everything seems a little unreal, distorted.

Thea opens the small, navy velvet box. She removes the ring and lays it in the palm of her hand, offering it to Alice to inspect. Alice takes it and looks it over thoroughly, reads the Yeats inscription silently. She puts it back in Thea's out-stretched hand.

'I didn't want to throw it away,' Thea says quietly, seemingly to the ring itself, 'because I don't want to rubbish what I had with Saul. I didn't want to bury it because that seems negative – vindictive, almost. But I don't want to keep it. I need to do the right thing by it. I just want to let it go – just let it all go.'

Thea stands and then, with a competent throw, launches the ring as high as she can. She turns away. She doesn't need to see where it lands, she's pleased that she's released it to a place, a time, sacred to when she and Saul were very very happy. Now she's spread their dreams under other people's feet. She hopes they'll tread softly. She faces Alice who has tears in her eyes.

'Ready?' Alice asks, linking arms with her.

'Yup,' says Thea, leading the way.

'The thing is, I do really want to love again,' Thea said a little later over a Starbucks latte and supposedly healthy muffin despite its monstrous proportions. 'I'm very good at it. But I don't want to *just yet* – do you see? I have to have faith in my own time frame. I've done the mourning and the grieving and the anger and the desolation. I had that frightening but thankfully brief period of denouncing all men as bastards and condemning love as ridiculous. Now I'm back on an even keel but I don't want to force my passage through.'

'I understand,' Alice assured her, 'I do, truly. I know I tease you for being soppy but actually I've always admired your tenacious pursuit of romance.' She dunked her croissant into her cappuccino. 'Though I have always warned you against setting fairy-tale standards for matters of love and eternity.'

'It's weird – because I've actually taken a leaf out of your book,' Thea confessed. 'I used to think that falling head over heels in love was the benchmark. But it wasn't head over heels, it was heart over head and actually, I like your idea that you should use your head so as not to lose your heart.'

'Love and marriage, or longevity, or whatever you want to call it, do go hand in hand,' Alice assured her, 'but perhaps it takes a certain type of love to succeed.'

'I'm not going out there armed with fixed criteria on what makes a Potentially Good Husband-Type!' Thea objected.

'I'm not saying you should,' Alice stressed, 'but don't hold it against a nice chap if you don't necessarily feel that elusive tingle of yours on day one.'

'I know. I agree. But I still think a shared belief in fidelity, in the value of companionship, the notion of pairing for life, is a good starting point.'

'Yes, but so is acknowledging practical issues,' Alice said, 'careers, money, long- and short-term goals. Respecting each other's lives independent of the union.'

'I do still love the idea of being in love,' Thea said.

'You wouldn't be you if you didn't,' Alice assured her warmly, 'but be prepared now for knights in shining armour to come in many guises,' she added knowingly. 'Some of them aren't conventionally dashing – they don't suddenly sweep you off your feet and whisk you away on a gallant white charger. I should know. Believe me.'

'You mean he might be wearing a suit and driving a nice Lexus,' Thea said, 'like Mark.'

'I do,' Alice agreed wholeheartedly.

'I guess you've always thought that there are rules for love,' Thea mused, 'while I've simply believed that love just rules OK.' The Starbucks in Belsize Park was starting to fill up but such is the quality of that branch's milk froth, Alice and Thea were still lingering over their first cups of coffee and had no intention of relinquishing their seats. 'Oh Alice,

393

bloody hell – of all our years, hasn't this one been the maddest for both of us?' Thea proclaimed wistfully.

Alice cast her gaze out the window and nodded. Mad was only one word for the year they'd had. She still wasn't sure it was plain madness that drove her to Paul. In retrospect she acknowledged that the affair itself was madness but perhaps what drove her was insecurity. Or her sex drive. Or her own unrealistic expectations of love and marriage due to impracticable emphasis on sex and lust.

'How are *you*?' Thea asked her quietly, having skim-read her thoughts. 'Have you heard from That Paul?'

'No, I haven't,' Alice answered truthfully. 'It's so weird how I went from deifying him like he was Love God Number One to being really quite irritated by him. I was so impressed by his visible masculinity, I was so swept away by the physical roller-coaster thrill, it was bizarre to discover so suddenly that I didn't really like him all that much. In fact, he got on my nerves.' She was just about to denounce his taste in trainers and mock his inability to navigate the London Underground system when she stopped. It shocked her to remember she never told Thea about Paul's impromptu final trip, though she'd spent her lifetime telling Thea everything; the mundane to the outrageous all in the most intimate detail. Yes, Thea was going through the vortex of suffering back then, but also Alice had known all along what she was doing was wrong and she was ashamed. She hadn't wanted to talk about it. She was doomed to have it as her guilty, gut-twist secret.

'You look a bit sad,' Thea said, 'a little distracted.'

'If I had an itch after two and a half years of marriage, what'll I feel like after seven?' Alice admitted sheepishly. 'Say I meet another Paul-type at some point,' she said, 'and I'm lured into another crazy shag fest.'

'But *you* did the luring, Alice, didn't you? If you're honest.'

'I did,' Alice confessed, 'but in a perverse way, that's the point and that's what unnerves me. Though I admit it was crazy and dangerous, it was fun too. Initially. I suppose I'd tucked that side of me – the flirt, the sexy minx – out of sight while I busied myself setting up home being a married woman. It's like the two can't coexist. But actually, it's a side of me that makes me sparkle. And that's what scares me. I must keep a lid on it for the sake of my marriage, but doesn't keeping it in check also sacrifice a little part of me? I don't know if that's a good thing.'

'I think it is a difficult thing – but I don't think it's a bad thing. Look on it as being abstemious and, by definition, as being good for the soul,' Thea said. 'You and Mark are such a *team* – more so now than ever I've known. If you hadn't challenged it when you did – and with thankfully no fallout – perhaps you wouldn't be as content as you are now. I'd hope that Brad Pitt himself could accost you and you'd turn him down without a glance or falter. I suppose you'll have to train yourself not to let the thought cross your mind; train yourself to find the inclination unappetizing.'

'I feel it's really insulting to Mark to say this,' Alice confided, 'but I can admit to you that the thought I'll never again have that rampant, urgent, animal sex makes me feel low. Isn't it wrong to cauterize one's passions? I *love* that sense of being ravished, being someone's fantasy incarnate, being fucked within an inch of my life.' Alice shrugged. 'Pure sex without the encumbrance of love is the most massive turn-on.'

She stopped abruptly. Simultaneously, she and Thea fell on the silent connection with Saul. Was it something to declare out loud? Was it something they could constructively discuss? No. It wasn't the same. Alice acknowledged how Mark didn't know about her fling into adultery whereas Thea knew way too much about Saul. And then Alice thought about how she and Mark had such a charmed life while Thea had been through hell. And the horrible knowledge that, if she'd been caught, Mark would have been as distraught as Thea. She wondered whether Thea ever wished she'd never come across Saul that ghastly day.

I suppose I'm wanting her to say yes, she wishes she hadn't. Ignorance being bliss, and all that. But actually, despite the anguish of it all – the loss, the trauma, the disbelief and the shock – I know Thea is relieved that she did. She's right to expect back the dedication and commitment she bestows. I was going to say 'you get what you pay for' but it seems a bit close to the bone though I suppose in some ways that is precisely what has happened to Saul. I suppose 'what you settle for is what you get' is more appropriate. And Thea shouldn't have settled for it. Nor should Mark have to either.

'I guess I have come to see it's not about getting away with it,' Alice declared, 'it's about not fucking it up in the first place.'

* * *

Saul was looking forward to seeing Ian. It had been quite some time since they'd descended on the Swallow for an evening of pints and sausages. Over recent months, Saul had generally eschewed offers of company and declined invitations to socialize, using deadlines as an accurate though not entire excuse. The only thinking time he wanted was that devoted to articles and columns – life without Thea was so sterile, he needed to fill it with creativity. Since Thea had left him, Saul had immersed himself in his work, diversifying on the way. In addition to his regular columns and freelance features, he took on work for other magazines and also landed himself a weekly slot on Robert Elms's radio show, bantering on London legends, scruffing down his accent to deliver all manner of anecdotes. Most gratifying was the publishing deal he'd landed to collate a charity anthology of men's magazines columnists.

It wasn't that work was fantastically stimulating, Saul just needed as much of it as possible to fill his time. As chuffed as he was about his radio slot, as proud as he was about the book deal, the satisfaction was tempered by having no Thea to share it with. No excited girlfriend jumping up and down, hugging him with congratulatory delight. Ian's interest, Richard's praise and his parents' pride didn't really amount to much in comparison. So Saul took on more commissions and touted for even more work to try and slake the void. If he didn't have time to notice he was on his own, he wouldn't have the time to feel lonely. So, when Ian phoned him on the off chance he was free that night, Saul didn't hesitate to suggest the Swallow.

'How about *Not the Top Shelf*?' Saul tried another possible title for the book.

'It would probably put off half the readers you're trying to attract,' said Ian.

'True,' said Saul, 'perhaps a shout-line like we'd use on a mag – something like *What a Bloke Wants*.'

'That sounds more like an article in *Cosmo*,' Ian said. 'Another pint?'

'Thanks.'

'I ordered food,' Ian announced when returning with two pints. He regarded his increased girth forlornly. 'Not that I need it. Call me Fat Bastard.'

'How about *Five-Bellies Ashford*,' Saul teased.

'It's being married, mate,' Ian rued with a not unhappy sigh. 'My wife is such a good cook it would be rude to refuse and she takes it personally if I leave a scrap.'

Saul laughed. 'How is Karen? When is the baby due? And shouldn't it be Karen eating for two, not you?'

'I'm eating for three, mate,' Ian bemoaned. 'She's either feeling sick or else she has indigestion – she tells everyone "Ian's certainly pulling his overweight in this pregnancy". She's funny, my wife. And God, pregnancy suits her. Her hormones have gone haywire – to my advantage, if you get my meaning!'

'When's the baby due?' Saul repeated. It was strange but since splitting with Thea he'd developed an interest in all topics nuptial or domestic. After squash with Richard, he really liked to hear about Sally, about Juliette, about the trials of sleepless nights, the stress of teething, the nightmare of flying with a baby, the all-consuming exhaustion of it all. It was affirming, not depressing, to hear of such things. For Saul, it was far more constructive than going on the rebound. Case histories of those he knew enabled him to hold on to his faith and believe that love could work.

'Valentine's Day, would you believe it – blimey, four months today exactly,' Ian was saying. 'How are things with you?'

'Busy,' said Saul.

'Seeing anyone?'

'Christ, no,' said Saul.

'What – just lots of no-strings sex, then?'

'Hardly,' said Saul, 'I'm so busy with work.'

'Have you – can I ask about Thea?' Ian asked. He'd be informing Karen that Saul looked wan, thinner, but he didn't think he'd make a point of it to Saul.

'We don't really speak now,' Saul told him, 'at her instigation.'

Ian contemplated his pint. 'It's a shame,' he said, 'I liked her. We all did.'

'You're not the only one,' Saul said glumly, looking at his pint and not fancying another sip. However, as a matter of habit, he raised the glass to his lips to mirror Ian.

'Perhaps if you give her a little space,' Ian suggested, not really knowing what else to say but knowing it was the sort of advice Karen would dispense.

'It's not that simple, believe me. Even now, four months on, my head says let her go but my heart says fight for her,' Saul said. 'How's work?'

'Manic,' Ian said, hardly realizing they'd changed the subject, let alone left the previous one hanging. 'They've made me a partner.'

'Congratulations.' Saul chinked Ian's glass and they drank a toast. The beer tasted fine now. And the sausages looked mouth-watering.

'Look,' said Ian, having wolfed down his portion, 'just tell me to fuck off if I'm speaking out of line, but I don't know if you remember Karen's friend Jo?'

'Jo?' Saul said with no recognition.

'We were trying to set you up with her at much the same time as you and Thea got together. Brunette. Quite busty. Attractive. Bubbly.'

'Vaguely,' Saul said. 'Has Karen got you match-making?'

'Not just Karen,' Ian said cautiously, 'we both reckon the two of you might have a laugh together. Nothing heavy – just some company. Sex, if you're lucky!'

Saul drained his pint. 'Maybe,' he said. 'I'm not in the mood, really, if I'm honest with you. Perhaps in a little while. I don't know. But not just now.'

'My round, mate,' said Ian, rising to go to the bar. 'Same again?'

*   *   *

It was the first time in a couple of months that Saul thrashed Richard with ease at squash. Richard was pleased to lose in such dramatic style, it could only mean that his friend's spirit was restored.

'Time for a swift half or five?' Saul asked.

'I'll just phone Sal,' said Richard.

'So, how's the family?' Saul asked, thinking there were few things as pleasurable as a long, thirst-quenching drink of lager when one had so earned it. He and Richard drank down half their pints in affable silence.

'Really well,' Richard replied with a friendly burp under his breath. 'Juliette is just adorable – I reckon she'll be walking by her first birthday.'

'How's Sally?' Saul asked.

'She's talking about going back to work part-time,' Richard said. 'She loves teaching – and I love it when she teaches because I don't bear the brunt of her bossiness.'

'I don't think of her as bossy,' Saul mused, 'not on the Alice Sinclair Scale of Bossiness.'

'She comes a close second, does Sal, I assure you,' Richard said, finishing his drink and heading to the bar to buy the next round. 'How's it going with you?' he asked Saul on his return. 'How's the book coming along?'

'Good, great,' said Saul, 'though I'm struggling for a title.'

'How about *Between the Sheets*?' Richard suggested.

'Bloody hell,' said Saul, 'that's not bad at all. Christ! Cheers! I'd got as far as *Do You Like My Column*?'

'Sounds gay to me,' said Richard.

'You're right,' Saul acquiesced.

'Is it all work and no play?' Richard asked. Saul shrugged. 'Makes for a dull boy,' Richard warned.

'Life *is* dull,' Saul admitted, 'unless I fill it with work. I spend my weekends writing articles on "The Whys and Wherefores of Wi-Fi" – and the like. Mind you, I'd rather do that than mope or get bladdered for the sake of it.'

'Do you hear from Thea?'

'No. Not now.'

'Do you miss her?'

'What do you think?'

'Sorry. I'm sorry. But what the fuck happened, mate?'

'Do you really want to know?' Saul regarded Richard levelly. 'I was seen. With my pants down. Literally.'

Richard was baffled. 'You were playing around?' It seemed inconceivable. 'On Thea?'

'No,' Saul declared, 'I wasn't. But I was paying around.'

Richard only gawped because suddenly he recalled that bizarre drive back to Thea's when she cross-examined him on the theories behind modern man and the oldest trade.

'You seem surprised,' Saul defined.

'I guess I am a little,' Richard admitted. It didn't seem right. It didn't seem right to tell Saul about his conversation with Thea. It didn't seem right at all.

'You don't?' Saul asked. 'Not your thing?'

'Nah,' Richard confirmed. 'Why pay for junk food when I have fillet steak at home?'

'Because sometimes you crave the plastic ease of a Big Mac,' Saul said, 'even if you end up questioning your purchase when it repeats on you, quite unpleasantly, afterwards.'

'I understand,' Richard shrugged, 'it's just never been my scene.'

'Thea would never, ever have understood,' Saul shrugged, 'and I can't blame her – she's a girl, I understand the impossibility of her getting her head around the theory. There was no chance. Her sense of betrayal was complete. She could never trust me again and I'd never be able to override the hurt and horror she feels.'

'And since?' Richard probed. 'Have you been bingeing on junk food?'

Saul laughed bitterly. 'Hardly. You could say I've become

something of a health-food freak. I haven't been near a woman since.'

'Are you ready to?'

'I don't know – probably,' Saul theorized, 'but I can't muster much enthusiasm.'

'You should,' Richard encouraged. 'I mean, in between junk food and home-cooked dinner, a nice wholesome snack might do you good.'

Sally was in bed when Richard returned. She was sitting up, engrossed in a book about taming toddlers.

'Hullo!' she said, as if she was pleasantly surprised to see him.

'All quiet?' Richard asked.

Sally nodded. She put down her book and held out her arms. Richard went over to her. 'One day,' Sally said coyly, 'when you've played squash, *don't* have a shower – come home with your sweaty pheromones and ravish me.'

'Strange request,' Richard mused, 'but one which I'll be happy to grant.'

'How was Saul? What is his news? Did he say anything?'

'He's fine. He's cool. He's still working like an obsessive.' Richard paused. 'He didn't really have any news.'

'Did he say *anything*?' Sally pressed. 'You know – about Thea, or something?'

Richard thought for a moment and was careful to make it look as though he was racking his brains. 'No,' he concluded, 'he didn't. You know us blokes, Sal – we don't talk on that heart-baring level you girls do.'

'But he's all right, is he? Is he seeing anyone?' Sally asked.

'No,' said Richard, 'but I did ask.' He kissed her shoulder. He felt uncomfortable about being economical with the whole truth. It felt odd not to tell his wife everything. But changing the subject in his head helped, and the sight of her silken skin, the glimpse of nipple half revealed by the bed linen was irresistible.

'I'd love to have sex,' Sally said apologetically, 'but I'm absolutely exhausted.' She snuggled close to Richard. 'Us mums seem to expend more energy at Tumble Tots than the tots.'

Richard liked hearing Sally refer to herself as a mum – as their marriage lengthened it had strengthened. He had so much more than he started with. He still had the cute girl-friend but he also had a beautiful wife, a great shag, a best friend and the mother of his child. Amazingly, they were the same woman.

'Night,' said Sally, half asleep already.

'Night, babe,' said Richard. He sat up in bed unable to read the new issue of *Adam* or the last chapter of the John Irving, both of which lay open on his lap. He had lied to Sally and he couldn't really lessen it by philosophizing whether he had truly *lied* or just pertinently withheld ele-ments of the truth. Why exactly had he not revealed his dis-covery of the true reason for Thea and Saul's split? To protect Sally? Yes, partly. She'd be really quite shocked to learn that Saul did *that* – she'd be distressed on Thea's behalf and she'd take against Saul. Richard was immensely fond of Thea too and, thinking back to that conversation in the car, he shud-dered at the level of torment that poor girl must have gone through. It occurred to Richard that Thea had not specific-ally divulged her discovery for a reason: she was keeping it secret precisely so that she didn't have to discuss it. He had to respect that. Finally, he thought of his mate, Saul. Poor bastard. God, how Richard sympathized. It may not be *his* thing – but he was actually at ease with the notion that for Saul, as for other men he knew, paying for sex was a mind-less bit of recreation. For Saul, though, it had now destroyed the dreams he'd so cherished, and Richard felt for him.

Maybe the main reason why Richard hadn't told Sally was respect for Saul. After all, Saul had confided in him. And actually, Richard held fidelity to a friend to have equal gravitas, commensurate inviolability, to that with which he honoured his wife. Funny thing, fidelity.

* * *

'Can I do something sneaky?' Alice asked Mark in a beguiling voice, phoning him from her office on a late November afternoon.

'Oh God, what have you done?' Mark said, hoping Alice hadn't done something so sneaky as to take too long to divulge. He had a meeting starting in five minutes and through the clear logo on the frosted-glass door of his office, he could see his secretary to-ing and fro-ing with plates of biscuits and jugs of tea and coffee.

'Nothing yet,' Alice remonstrated, 'but I was thinking about booking a table for six on Saturday night,' she told him.

'Saturday night?' Mark questioned.

'Yes,' said Alice, 'I thought I'd phone Janine and Laurence.'

'*Janine and Laurence*? But I thought you found them dull,' Mark protested, 'after they organized that murder-mystery dinner that went a bit wrong?'

'That's the point!' Alice revealed excitedly. 'I thought I'd invite them *and* Thea! But I've told Thea that *you* organized it and she has to come to give me moral support.'

'Darling, apart from the fact that you've given me the role of Big Bad Wolf, why on earth do you want to spend our third wedding anniversary forcing your best friend to socialize with a couple you don't much care for?' Mark despaired. 'Anyway, I have a reservation at Claridges, you daft girl – you're not going to have me cancel it, are you?'

'Yes, cancel Claridges,' Alice said, 'we can do Claridges

next year. Because you see, I was thinking you could invite Joel too! Sneaky old me!'

'Alice Sinclair!' Saul exclaimed. 'Joel is only over for a brief visit – I have a feeling he flies out at the crack of dawn on Sunday.'

'Oh, he travels Business Class,' Alice brushed, 'he can always change his flight. Please phone him, pretty please?'

'But more to the point, darling,' Mark said, 'I thought you'd approached Thea about meeting Joel when he was last over and she'd rejected the idea.'

'That was ages ago,' Alice told him. 'She's my best friend. I know her. And I know this is good timing.'

Mark sighed with happy exasperation at his wife. 'I have to go, Alice – I have a meeting.'

'OK!' Alice chirped. 'I'll see you later. Do you think I'm the sneakiest minx in the world?'

'Yes,' said Mark, 'I bloody do. You're like a maverick Jane Austen busybody.'

'But you love me anyway! See you later, darling.'

Funny thing, friendship, Mark thought as he made his way to the boardroom. In the past he'd felt excluded from Alice and Thea's intimacy. He'd also been privately envious of their bond. He had many friends himself but none with whom the tenets of friendship ran so deep. Over recent months, however, he'd been touched by the unstinting support Alice offered Thea and he'd been moved at Alice's private distress for her friend. He decreed it the mark of a good person when dedication to the deeds of friendship was obviously so paramount. He knew that Alice saw him as her best friend too. She'd told him so one morning over the Sunday papers. He felt greatly honoured by such a role.

However, it transpired that Thea had already organized a weekend in Wootton Bourne with her mother. And Janine and Laurence couldn't make it anyway. And Mark never did phone his cousin Joel. So Mr and Mrs Sinclair celebrated their third wedding anniversary in style at Claridges. Just the two of them.

The simple lack of her is more to me than others' presence

Edward Thomas

I've been thinking about fidelity. I've been thinking about love. I've seen Ian and Karen's friend Jo a few times. We have a laugh, we have good sex, she's interesting and attractive. I have to admit that it's a relief, refreshing even, that she's so different to Thea. However, sometimes I feel like I'm cheating on Jo by missing Thea still. And, conversely, occasionally I feel I'm betraying Thea by enjoying my time with Jo.

I do miss her, my Thea, my ex. I love saying her name. I hate saying 'ex'. When I least expect it, I get winded by a sudden pang. When I heard Lynne's terrier Molly had died, I was grief-stricken because I was transported back to that disastrous second date with Thea. And then on to thoughts of her scar. I felt bereft. I thought, did I kiss that scar enough? And I couldn't quite remember if it snaked this way or that. Ultimately, Lynne ended up comforting me even though her dog had just died. If I'm carrying tension in my shoulders I have to tell Jo: no, left a bit, up a bit, over a bit, deeper if you can while I remember how Thea knew instinctively what to do. I gave my Armani jacket away. I buy *Heat* magazine every week.

But it's not that I harbour even the most silent of secret hopes that Thea and I will be together. I don't because we won't. I'm OK about that. I understand. I've come to terms with it. I now believe that the love of one's life may not necessarily be the person one ends up with. And we have to work bloody hard not to make that fact a tragedy. It's no reason to be maudlin or unprincipled, it's no excuse to reject or downplay the potential of future relationships. I have come to acknowledge that the intensity of the love I had with Thea – that perfect blend of companionship, desire, affection – has become a yardstick. It's something to aspire to because I know it exists – after all, for a blissful two and a half years I was lucky enough to come by it.

I know I won't ever feel for Jo the way I feel for Thea but I suppose that doesn't mean that we can't have an enjoyable relationship. I know intrinsically that the love I felt for Thea can never be equalled. But it's not something I should continue to mourn. It's not something to bury. It's something to revere. It's a legacy. Being in love with Thea Luckmore has made me a better, more complete person. The experience enhanced my life.

And do I still pay for sex? I haven't since I split from Thea. But, if I'm honest, that's not because I'm a reformed character who's learnt his lesson. That would imply conscious misbehaviour. For me, such purchases were a simple and non-invasive way of sating a peculiar yet common hunger. Read my column in last month's *Esquire* – 'Love and Sex – hands up who can do the one without the other?'. I suppose it is one of my life's great ironies – I may be a hard-working bloke but I'm a lazy wanker. Literally. I still don't consider it a crime or a sin or genuine adultery. To me, emotional infidelity is heinous – the ultimate betrayal – and I can never be accused of that. Christ, that one time years ago I came close to feeling it, I felt a moral obligation to finish with Emma immediately. That's why I feel uncomfortable about really liking Jo but still missing Thea. I don't fuck Jo and imagine I'm making love to Thea. I don't compare Jo unfavourably with her. I don't see Jo so that I don't have to think about Thea. It's just I do still miss Thea, I really do. We were very much in love, we really were. It was beautiful. Perhaps I need to be patient. Perhaps next month I'll find that I think about Thea less than I do now.

Has Thea met someone? I don't know. I don't know how I'd feel about it – whether I'd want to punch the bastard or shake his hand and tell him to look after her. In fact, I can't actually think about her with another man. So I don't. I've decided not to and, being a bloke, I can do that. You should read my column in the *Observer* magazine this Sunday: 'Barefaced Bloke wonders whether his ability to compartmentalize is a skill or a weakness.'

Love is the triumph of imagination over intelligence

H. L. Mencken

I saw Kiki today. I mean, I saw her as a client – my client. Poor girl had ricked her ankle tripping on the kerb. Bloody Westminster council – I told her to write to them, I've told her I'll check the letter for her. Anyway, I didn't charge her for the treatment – I figured I owed her, minute for minute, for the time she gave me. She's a lovely woman. I don't feel sorry for her or sad, I don't feel threatened or repulsed, it's her career and she doesn't regard herself as a victim at all. I see now how my turning on her – and then turning to her – enabled me to let go of Saul. That day, she seemed to represent every prostitute in the world and I felt rage and hatred and fear. I really felt that, as a woman, she was letting us all down. Until I stopped and sat on her bed and let her hold my hand. Don't you see, as in all trade, the control is with the purchaser not the provider? The instinct is within the punter, it's not forced by the prostitute. Demand. Supply. It is absolutely not a case of chicken and egg. Man came first and Woman saw there was – quite literally – a hole in the market and, to put it crudely, a market for that hole.

Saul Mundy was the love of my life. I was deeply in love with him and it was a glorious state to be in. I was so looking forward to running headlong, hand in hand, into our future. And then I found out. And I cannot begin to describe the untold shock. He wasn't who I thought he was. Worse still, he didn't see love the way I see love. How can you look forward in the same direction if you don't see eye to eye? I know all the theories that it's a bloke thing to be able to keep sex and love apart. I know all the facts about how many men use sex workers. I know that it needn't mean that their wives don't satisfy them, or they have secret perversions, or they're lonely. They do so simply because they can. And they can do so with fundamentally no ramifications on their home life.

But do you know what, there are many men who *don't* pay for sex and, actually, I'd like one of those. The control is with the purchaser, remember, not the provider. I know Saul wanted to provide me with more than all the love I could ever need but actually, I'd rather invest in someone else. Saul was my long-held dream, my fantasy incarnate, who swept me off my feet, who made my spirit soar and my heart fly free. Ultimately, I suppose it was me who didn't love him enough. I couldn't allow him his entire personality. I couldn't love him unconditionally. He was just being himself but I didn't like him enough to let him.

I'm so glad that I experienced the level of love I attained with Saul. It gave me proof it exists. And I'm glad that I mourned Saul so deeply – thoroughly enough to visit a brothel in my quest to confront my fear and understand him. I'm so relieved that my belief in love remains unsullied. Actually, my belief in love has strengthened because it's deepened. It's had to. True love needs to be more than a feeling, more than that rush of phenylsomething. I must have Alice tell me how to pronounce it once and for all. I can see now that the success of love is dependent on the sum of its parts; on the presence of friendship and affection, understanding and tolerance, moral compatibility and practical support. Essential elements in balance.

I wonder whether Mr Mencken meant it derogatorily, that love is the triumph of imagination over intelligence? Wasn't he the man who said marriage is a wonderful institution 'but who would want to live in an institution'? How awful to be so cynical and so decided against love. Did he not read *Sense and Sensibility*? Did he never soar with another person? What is life worth if you don't believe in happy-ever-after? Is that deluded – or is such hope positive and affirming? I have come to see that the course of love might be a tough climb and we have to accept that it might lead us to pastures new rather than the fields carpeting our previous dreams. Life might be easier if we lost our need to find love – but I feel for those who shun the fantasy. The earth can't move for those who don't believe that love makes the world go round.

Love is that condition in which the happiness of another person is essential to your own

Robert Heinlein

I like to believe that if we're good in life, if our thoughts are honourable, our goals worthy, our deeds and dealings principled, then happy-ever-after is our reward.

Would you just look at me and what I have. A beautiful wife, a career which is well paid and stimulating, a large circle of good friends, a stunning home. It is a charmed life I lead. I am the envy of many. I feel truly blessed.

Twenty years ago, we did 'The Miller's Tale' at school for our A-level Chaucer. I vividly remember thinking silly carpenter, let that beautiful spirited Alyson run free. Can't you see she will indeed cuckold you if you repress her spirit and try to cage her like that. Don't deny her that feistiness. If you corral that filly you'll destroy her spirit, and she'll just stand there, beautiful but broken. A façade. She'll hardly love you for it.

Did my wife have an affair? She may have done. If I'm honest with myself, I'd have to admit that I had reason to suspect so. But the point is I don't know for sure. What I do know is we are very happy now. We were going through a bad patch back then – as I expect all marriages do. We were distant – very literally, in my case, with all that travelling for

413

work. She was stroppy and needy. I was too busy, too tired, too stressed to pay attention.

Was I turning a blind eye or was I just choosing wisely not to look? I admit I didn't try too hard to find out. Instead, I found it easier to look for evidence to the contrary. Because I'm an optimist. And what I do not know cannot hurt me. Where is the sense in panic when there is no real proof of transgression? I don't think that to hold on to an element of naivety is foolish; I think it's sometimes wise.

I love my wife and I admire her. Whatever she did or didn't do, she never made a fool out of me. She came through it all with her spirit intact and my love for her not damaged, her love for me rejuvenated. And she does love me. I know she does. She tells me often enough.

Love is often the fruit of marriage

J.-B. Molière

I laughed. I thought it was not just pretentious but also rather incongruous to see my local grocer using a quote by Molière to advertise exotic fruit baskets. But, as I walked back home with my ridiculously expensive Charentais melon and out-of-season cherries, I committed that Molière quote to memory and I refer to it often. It's become the blueprint for my marriage.

When I proposed to Mark, I suppose you could say I was on a reverse-rebound. God – that sounds like a shout line for an article in *Lush* – maybe I'll even suggest it at the meeting on Tuesday. What I mean is, rather than getting over my then-ex Bill by shagging around or serial dating to distraction, I grabbed the antithesis of every man I'd ever had because I realized I'd never found happiness with any of those men I'd fancied rotten. Call me self-centred and manipulative but I calculated that Mark would never leave me, never behave badly, that I'd never have to feel that gut-hurling insecurity again. So I decided that to marry him would be an excellent idea. I knew that he'd always held a torch for me. And it was precisely that. Mark was a beacon of light when I was stuck in a murky place. Deep down I know I was not actually 'in' love with him and for a long while I felt privately ashamed about that. Until I was at the grocer's and saw the Molière quote a couple of weeks ago. I can see now that I proposed to Mark because I knew that he was the one man I sensed I could love deeply.

Perhaps I was naive to think that love would flood me on our wedding night, or on our honeymoon, or on our first anniversary. For something to grow, roots are needed and for roots to establish, time, effort and care are needed. For a long time, I didn't bother to feed or water or protect it from storms and frost. I'm a lazy gardener, as Mark's mum Gail can attest. I now marvel at my fortune to have such a fine man as my husband. Mark Sinclair is kind and sensible and mannered and loving and principled and loyal and steadfast. He's my husband and my best friend and I'm a lucky girl. He is always consistent in his love for me. He allows me to be spirited, he tolerates all my temperamental, attention-seeking nonsense and when I say sorry he accepts without compromising his self-respect.

But I don't find him particularly sexy. For a horrible and dangerous period early in our marriage, I tried to equate not fancying Mark with being his fault. I thought if I didn't fancy Mark, how could I truly love him. And if I didn't fancy Mark, I blamed him for a core part of my personality he was failing to satisfy. So along came Paul in all his brawny glory and I thought that to succumb to pure physical attraction was my *right*. It wasn't. It was my greatest wrong.

Thank God Mark never found out because actually, I was treading a precarious tightrope by which I could so easily have hanged myself and, worse, Mark too. Thank God he never found out because I can't start to imagine his hurt. Thank God I saw that sex for the sake of it wasn't the answer.

I do sometimes miss that energizing sensation of animal magnetism. I do sometimes wonder if I'm OK with Mark not exhibiting wild desire for me. I do sometimes worry that if someone else did, would I be able to resist? Because I love being the centre of attention and I love the physical charge of sexual electricity. Will I crave it again? I don't know. The only thing I crave at the moment is Marmite on chocolate biscuits – but that's because I'm pregnant. Now I know what sex is all about – it's about making babies.

But say some swarthy, well-hung warrior came along, brandishing his lance and thrusting his dagger? Would I want to be swept off my feet? Actually, I feel confident that I'm stronger now and I have the weapons to fight it. I have the fortress that is my marriage. My home – my castle. My impending child – my future. My very perfect gentle knight – my husband. Stay inside, Mark, I'll pull up the drawbridge against intruders.

Christ, I sound like Thea.

Mr Alexander's Three O'Clock

Souki booked Mr Alexander in for a three o'clock with Thea. 'He's over on business,' she told her, 'and slept awkwardly on the plane. Apparently you were recommended by someone he knows.'

'Gabriel Sewell, probably,' Thea said. 'We seem to have a steady stream of clients connected with him.'

'Do you know, I always quite envied you Mr Sewell,' Souki laughed. 'I thought he was scrummy.'

'Well, if his back ever plays up again, I'll book him in with you for acupuncture,' Thea assured her. 'Good Lord! Peter Glass, you're *early*!'

'Hullo, babes,' Peter said, 'my neck is killing me. But I have to leave at two thirty – I'm about to do a major *major* deal on the most fuck-off-gorgeous apartment I've ever handled.'

'Peter,' Thea bemoaned as she climbed the stairs, 'you know I like having you for the full hour – you know you need it.'

'What I need is the commission from this sale, sweetheart,' Peter enthused. 'Then it'll be Maserati time.'

'Oh, right,' said Thea ingenuously, 'is the food good there?'

'It's a *car*, you dumb bird,' Peter said affectionately as he undressed, wincing in pain.

'I'm sorry I'm late,' Mr Alexander said, his American accent reminding Thea of an actor she couldn't quite recall. He was certainly handsome enough for Hollywood though it transpired he was a university lecturer and lived in New York.

'I had the most God-awful sleep,' Mr Alexander explained, while Thea put her notepad on her knee and wrote down *Mr Joel Alexander, 37*.

'That's the horror of long-haul economy seating,' Thea said, 'not that I've ever had the luxury of business class.'

'This *was* business class,' Mr Alexander shrugged, 'but I guess I fell asleep whilst reading and spent the whole flight slumped upright. What kind of dork doesn't take full advantage of fully reclining seat–beds?'

Thea laughed. 'How long are you over for?'

'A week,' he told her. 'I come over every now and then – lecturing.'

'What in?' Thea asked.

'A plane,' Mr Alexander replied, deadpan. Thea looked up from her notes and was greeted by his wry smile. 'Classics,' he told her.

'Oughtn't you to be grey-haired, stooped and wrinkly?' Thea remarked, thinking she might have swapped to Classics herself if the lecturer had looked anything like Mr Alexander.

'Botox, hair dye and marathon running,' Mr Alexander shrugged.

Again, Thea was momentarily taken aback and she found herself glancing suspiciously at his forehead and hairline.

Mr Alexander held up his hands in mock surrender. 'Hair is natural,' he assured her, 'as are any wrinkles, or lack of, that you see or don't.'

'And the marathon running?' Thea asked.

'That's true. I run three a year,' he told her. 'Next up is the London Marathon next spring.'

'Golly,' said Thea, slightly surprised by her choice of word and the sudden plumminess of her accent. Why was she going all English Rose? Was it to counterbalance his All-American Hunk? 'Isn't that a frightfully long way to fly for a jog around the block?'

'A *jog around the block*!' Mr Alexander laughed. 'Actually, I'll be living here by then, I'm taking a visiting post at Oxford.'

'Jolly good for you,' said Thea, hoping she sounded more Jane Austen than St Trinian. 'Righty-ho, let's have a look at you. Face the wall, please.'

Tall, broad-shouldered, athletic build. Very good musculature.

'And turn to the window.'

Good posture – all the way up and all the way down. Nice profile.

'And now turn to look at me.'

He really is handsome.

As Thea massaged Joel Alexander, she tried to temper her smile. She thought it was somewhat unprofessional – though of course he couldn't see her, lying face down as he was. However, she was smiling because when she'd asked him to turn to face her, the masseuse in her had taken a good long considered look at his body but the girl in her had felt a dormant fizz of attraction. And when she had told him she could alleviate the discomfort he felt because actually it was only a tightness in the thoracic, she'd smiled in triumph, he'd smiled in relief and then they'd smiled at each other for a second or two longer than was necessary. In the past, Alice had asked her if she fancied any of her clients. And Thea had primly rejected such an unethical suggestion. But here she was, thinking Christmas had come three weeks early. Santa had brought her a gorgeous surprise. And she hadn't even put him on her list.

'There you go,' Thea said quietly, placing her stilled palms on his back before lifting them away gently and covering him with a towel. 'Dress when you're ready. Take your time.'

'Thanks so much,' Mr Alexander said, sitting comfortably in one of her plastic chairs when she came back in. 'Thanks.'

'Hot and cold, if you can,' Thea advised, 'though I don't know how easy it is to lecture with a pack of cold peas strapped to your shoulder.'

Mr Alexander laughed. 'I don't need to be in Oxford until tomorrow – so I'll have room service bring me up frozen peas and a hot-water bottle. I'm sure they've had stranger requests.'

'Well, have a good trip,' Thea said. They stood and shook hands but loitered. 'And have a great Christmas,' she added.

'Yeah, you too,' he said.

'Oh, and good luck with the Marathon,' Thea added.

'You can always meet me at the finish line and give me a rub down,' Mr Alexander said, 'if you're free next spring.'

Thea blushed. Wasn't this flirting? Was there loaded meaning in the 'if you're free' bit? Was she meant to flirt back outright, or act all demure? What were the rules again? It seemed all she could do was blush like a teenager. And no doubt that was simply down to phenylethylamine.

'Or perhaps you'd just have a quick drink with me sometime later this week?' he said.

Oh stop blushing, you stupid girl! He's only a bloke. It's only a drink. For heaven's sake say yes, thank you, that would be nice.

'Yes, thank you, that would be nice.'

'Good,' said Joel, 'cool.'

'Oh, I forgot to ask,' Thea said, as they headed downstairs to reception, 'which of my clients do you know?'

'I'm sorry?' Joel said.

'Apparently you were referred by a client of mine?'

Joel looked at her. 'No, not a client. A friend of yours. Mark Sinclair. He's my cousin – actually, he's more than that, he's a very good friend of mine too.'

Acknowledgements

Special thanks to Bethia Hope-Rollins, Laura Curry and all at the Pilates Place in Crouch End. Also to Dan Rollins – masseur extraordinaire – and Brent Osborn Smith – genius osteopath – thank you for helping me (and my thoracic . . .). Many thanks to Dawn Gobourne at Haringey Library Services for making me her unofficial Writer in Residence – and providing all those cups of coffee. I'm indebted to my support network: the team at HarperCollins, especially my brilliant editor, Lynne Drew; my wonderful agent, Jonathan Lloyd, and my team at Curtis Brown Ltd; my copy-editor the ever-meticulous Mary Chamberlain, and the tireless and jolly Sophie Ransom at Midas PR. Discreet but sincere thanks to the prostitutes, their maids and their clients in Swindon, Peterborough and London who were willing to talk to me with such honesty, humour and good grace.